RICHER THAN ALL HIS TRIBE

RICHER THAN ALL HIS TRIBE

BY

NICHOLAS MONSARRAT

William Morrow & Company, Inc.
New York

Of one whose hand,
Like the base Indian, threw a pearl away
Richer than all his tribe . . .

Othello, near death

CONTENTS

THE ISLAND OF

PHARAMAUL

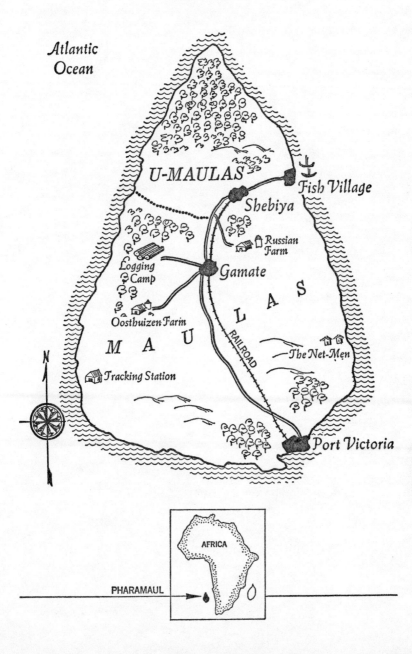

1: IT IS MY EARNEST HOPE THAT, GIVEN GOOD WILL ON BOTH SIDES

THE ROYAL PERSONAGE, a hesitant cousin not yet forged into the mould of greatness, cleared his throat, shuffled the pages of his speech, and began timidly:

"I *am* conscious—"

Then he stopped dead, as if he had made his point, and expected the audience to applaud it. He had lost track already, and there was still a very long way to go.

How awful if they did start clapping, thought David Bracken, the Chief Secretary and chief architect of this occasion; how awful if someone with a sense of humour, or someone with a grudge, started a slow round of applause, as though the phrase "I *am* conscious" had set all their minds at rest. . . . He looked at his feet, immaculate in their white buckskin boots; he felt the weight of the absurd cock's-feather headdress pressing down on his forehead. He looked at his wife, but Nicole, who had that sense of humour in abundance, was already biting her lip. He looked round him, waiting, as they were all waiting, for the ceremony— Independence Day in Pharamaul—to get under way.

The day of independence was hot, oppressive, and airless. The flags clung listlessly to their flagpoles, all the way round the cricket field, which was Port Victoria's only point of assembly for so huge a crowd. Shimmering heat rose from the cracked earth, stifling all movement, seeming to seal in the enormous silence on the concourse. In the grandstand, there was some shelter; on the dais which housed the "official party," the sun flailed down mercilessly.

It beat upon parasols, helmets, plumes, white duck uniforms, tight collars, raw necks, tortured female knees; it slowly cooked the Consular Corps in their roped-off section; it roasted the Royal Pharamaul Police Band—white-helmeted, white-tunicked, with

1

here and there a leopard skin for the bass drummers—as they rested from their labours after "Selections from *H.M.S. Pinafore.*"

Above them all hung a pale burnished sky with a single small aircraft (a fugitive? a late arrival?) droning across it like a drowsy bumblebee outside a windowpane. This was the only movement. The rest of Port Victoria, the rest of Pharamaul, was waiting, waiting for history.

The Royal Personage tried again, each syllable echoing back, like a shout of disagreement, from the Tannoy speakers strung all round the ground:

"I am conscious—that this is a momentous day for you—the people of Pharamaul."

They, the people of Pharamaul, the Maulas and the U-Maulas, had come from far and near for their momentous day. (*"Momentous!"* thought David Bracken irritably. What could the pompous word possibly mean, to a Maula from up-country? Why couldn't he just say "great"?) They had come from Port Victoria itself, with its reeking slums and waterfront hovels; from Gamate, the "native capital," where a hundred thousand Maulas lived in beehive huts, of clay and wattle, which had been designed a thousand years ago, and put up (some of them) only yesterday.

They had come from the near-jungle round Shebiya, the stronghold of the U-Maulas (literally, "not-Maulas") and from the now-sophisticated "Fish Village" on the northeast coast, where the fish-processing plant was working overtime, and they had shop-stewards who wore socks and shoes.

They had come from far and near, because they had all been called. Yet they had been called by different voices. Some had read the newspapers and heard the broadcasts; some had received gold-embossed invitations by command of Her Majesty the Queen. Some had been told by their chiefs to be present without fail on this important day; others had only heard rumours of the Great *Aboura*—the tribal meeting which, it was said, was to be different from all other tribal meetings, within the memory of the oldest old man.

Some had been summoned by that mysterious African telegraph which tells a man his son is dead before a police-runner can reach his hut.

Some had come in taxis, some in carts and ox-wagons; some astride donkeys, some carried by their grandchildren. Some had walked all the way—and "all the way" might mean three hundred miles of bush country and parched plain, winding track and yellow dust; a *trek* of three weary weeks, with the journey back still to be faced.

Their clothes often told where they came from, and told, also, much of the social history of Pharamaul. There were the young bloods of Port Victoria, in smartly draped coats and skintight trousers, their heads crowned by wide-brimmed Panamas. There were elderly Government clerks in their best silk suits, carrying umbrellas. There were country folk from Gamate in blankets and beehive straw hats, yellow and tattered; there were men in ancient army greatcoats, men in long-tailed shirts like nightgowns, men in rags. Up in Fish Village, they wore white boiler-suits stamped with the Government mark—and they were wearing them now, three hundred miles from home.

They were all here for their momentous day; half a nation, which had been on the move for hours or days or even weeks, now stood still where most of them had camped the night, and watched and listened. The men were crowded by the tens of thousands in the center of the field, while the women in their bright head-scarves kept to the outer ring, in accordance with the custom. There were acres of schoolchildren, safely corralled behind ropes, waving big and small Union Jacks—the new flag of Pharamaul was not yet in production. They had been chattering and jumping up and down before; now they were as still as bright-eyed mice.

A few of the spectators knew exactly what this was all about, and boasted their knowledge. This was Independence Day, and their country at last belonged to them, Maulas and U-Maulas alike, and was being handed over at this very moment. There on the platform, they said, was the Queen's cousin, come to make this gift—or, some claimed with a smirk, to surrender and go away. There was the Earl who was going to be Governor-General, and his wife, whose photograph in the *Times of Pharamaul* had made men roll their eyes and who (it was rumoured) was to be seen stark naked on the cover of some book which only rich white men could buy. Ow!

There was Mr. Bracken, Chief Secretary, who did all the work for Government, and was staying on. There was Major Crump, the police. He *would* be staying on! And there—but who needed to point him out?—was Dinamaula Maula, once Paramount Chief, now to be Prime Minister. He was the real man of the future, whichever way you looked at it.

But it was only the smart ones who knew all this, or even half of it. For the rest, the great majority of the crowd, it was Independence Day—but what the words meant, who could tell? A few older men, from the north, could have said only that there on the platform was a child of Queen Victoria, the great Queen who lived for ever, the mother of them all: a child who had come to give them royal greetings and wish them heavy rains.

The child of Queen Victoria was doing a little better now, though his hands were visibly shaking, and he floundered badly over the words "most auspicious occasion" and had to repeat them. Let him just get through it, thought David Bracken, still gazing at his boots, but willing the speaker onwards all the time. Let this thing go off all right—and everything else which was to come after. It was so important!

Bracken had worked more than a decade for this day, knowingly or unknowingly; he had served Pharamaul as District Officer, as Resident Commissioner, and now as Chief Secretary, for twelve years of heat and boredom and steady toil and setback and occasional, secret joy. He had been an eager, ignorant thirty-one, a "late entry" green as the grass of England, when he first started; now he was a furrowed, seasoned forty-three. It had all been worth it, a hundred times over, but it was such a big slice of a man's life. Let it not go to waste!

He glanced sideways down the row in which he sat, looking at some of the people who had also worked for this day, or must do so now. Closest to him, closest in all things, was Nicole, who had also borne the burden and the heat of their exile. Twelve years, two children, and a bone-dry climate had done their worst; she was still, at thirty-four, a patently attractive woman who had never failed him, either in love or in cool judgment. It was she, not he, who really deserved the medals and the small dividends of rank.

Next to her were Keith Crump and his wife: Crump, head of the Royal Pharamaul Police, a tough and hardened campaigner who had kept the same grip, and maintained the same fabric of the law, from the old days of revolt and bloodshed to this peaceful day of independence. Thank God he was staying on, for as long as he was wanted. Then there was a trio of tribal chiefs—one each from Gamate, Shebiya, and Fish Village: three calm, impas-

4

sive, expressionless men in ceremonial robes, who also maintained their law and who, when they spoke in the House of Assembly, did so with all the authority and pride of rulers.

It was a compromise, between ruling and representing, but it had worked well enough.

A cheerful young face could be sighted beyond them; it was the new Government House aide, Paul Jordan, who looked as young, impulsive, lighthearted, and keen as David Bracken himself had done, when he first arrived. He would soon learn. . . . That brought the roster down to the couple with whom they would all have to live for a very long time: the new Governor-General and his improbable wife.

The Earl of Urle's reputation had preceded him. He was a Labour peer who should really have been a romantic poet, like Lord Byron, or an erratic impresario like the Duke of Bedford: a jumpy, nervous, wildly enthusiastic young man who had gone into politics because his father had once snorted "Don't!" In the House of Lords he had espoused all the right causes: abolition of the death penalty, protection of sea-birds, drilling for offshore oil, national theater, proportional representation, consenting males.

Now, by one of those haphazard turns which drive historians mad, he was Pharamaul's first Governor-General; and beside him was his wife, who had already excited such widespread lust: a one-shot erotic poetess who had written a notorious narrative poem, banned in half a dozen countries, which read like a catalogue of her past lovers, complete with their achievement-ratings. It had been called "O Come! All Ye Faithful," and its jacket alone, on which was a nude photograph of the authoress quartered like an anatomical Ordnance Survey map, was a collector's item. She was now the First Lady of Pharamaul, entitled, among other things, to the curtseys of all lesser females.

She had been known as Bobo Tempest, up to the moment when matrimony struck. Now she was Barbara, Countess of Urle—and as much like a countess as "Beat me, Daddy, Eight to the bar!" was like Beethoven's Fifth. But there she was, and here she was, crossed legs, wall-to-wall bosom, and all. David Bracken looked away, as any good husband should. But there was going to be plenty of trouble with that one.

And was there going to be trouble with this one? . . . David Bracken was now looking directly at Prime Minister Dinamaula (it was going to be difficult to think of him as P.M., when he had

5

been "Chief" for so long). He had put on weight recently, David noted (and sucked in his own stomach at the same time); and his face at this moment had a kind of brooding heaviness very different from its normal cheerful cast. Of course, this was a great day for Dinamaula, a proud day, *the* day. . . . The fact that he was wearing his magnificent tribal robes, and the lionskin cap which was his badge of rank, seemed a subtle pointer to the idea that, when all the white man's nonsense was over, this would prove to be his ceremony, perhaps his alone.

The two of them had been enemies in the old days, when Dinamaula was sent into exile; they had been guarded neutrals when he was allowed to return as Chief; now they were friends, strong allies in this new endeavour. But who could say which would be the next word to use, as the map of Independent Pharamaul was unrolled?

At Dinamaula's side sat his wife, a big unsmiling country girl from Gamate: a shy or stupid girl who scarcely ever uttered a word, who had fallen far behind in all this new chapter of history: who was, David Bracken decided, the most difficult dinner guest ever likely to grace the board at Government House. There could be trouble there, too, unless she produced a family, and above all an heir.

While David's thoughts were still wandering, Nicole nudged him and whispered excitedly:

"I can see the children!"

He came to, quickly. "Where?"

"There. Just in line with the band-leader, or whatever he's called. By the flagstaff."

He searched among the sea of faces, the maze of green uniforms in the "School Enclosure" which she had indicated. Presently, with real pleasure, he caught sight of them—two small heads side by side, two rapt expressions, two accredited delegates from Miss Prinsep's Select Academy.

The faces round them were all white, though they were outnumbered by a myriad of black ones from the other schools of Port Victoria—the free Council Schools which, even after five years, were still the preserve of "native" children. That was something else which, before very long, was bound to change. . . . David smiled involuntarily. Timothy and Martha. It was easy to pick them out, now. Perhaps because they were a little taller and cleaner than the rest. . . .

"Aren't they sweet?" said Nicole fondly.

David Bracken retreated from this thought, as he always did. "They're two perfectly ordinary children, thank God."

"How can you say that!" She was almost clasping her hands. "I hope they're not getting too hot."

"It won't be much longer now."

He wished that this was true. But at least the contribution of the Royal Personage had limped to a halt, and now it was the turn of the Earl of Urle.

The new Governor-General made an unusual start, by clasping his hands above his head, in the manner of a winning boxer, as he acknowledged the applause. Then he began his speech, and his speech was terrible.

It became clear, immediately, that his lordship wanted to be loved, and in pursuit of this he overdid the flattery grossly. He seemed to be appealing over the heads of the "official" audience to the common people of Pharamaul; and neither side appreciated this in the least. He talked about "new emergent nations which must redress the stupid imbalance of the old." He congratulated them on throwing off the shackles of an outmoded social system. He assured them that colonialism was dead—"dead as slavery itself." He said: "I have come here, in all humility, to learn all I can from you." He proclaimed his ideal as "a land flowing with milk and honey," a mystifying phrase in a land where milk was notoriously unsafe, and honey only attracted ants.

A joking reference to Dinamaula's "little trip abroad, happily with a return ticket"—the five years' exile in England—set everyone within earshot squirming with embarrassment.

Dinamaula himself sat motionless under the weight of rubbish, letting the foolish words flow over him, ignoring this clown who had already muffed the swearing-in ceremony at Government House, and was now making a botch of his first public speech, the one which was meant to set the whole tone of the future. But he recognized the speech, from long experience, from patient platform participation in a hundred London protest rallies, anywhere between Trafalgar Square and the Albert Hall.

This was the authentic voice of the English left—unctuous, self-deprecating, confessional, writhing in spread-legs surrender: the voice of the Tailwaggers' Club: the voice which hailed every black man as an angel, because he was black.

It wasn't true, and the black man knew it best of all, even as he swallowed the soothing syrup and cashed the larded cheque.

Dinamaula would rather have had David Bracken's crisp authority any day of the week, dated and doomed though it had to be. . . . He heard, as if from far away, the Governor-General saying something about "the Chief Secretary staying on, as long as he can be of any help at all," and he thought: At last this idiot has said something sensible, and he brought the palms of his hands together in the sharp beginnings of applause, and glanced round him, so that everyone else was forced to join in.

Then he looked down the row, and smiled and nodded to David Bracken. . . . But now it was his own turn to speak.

As Dinamaula rose, the whole huge gathering came to life. Here was the man they had journeyed from near and far to see, and this was something they wanted to show him, beyond any doubt. The growl of greeting—"Ahsula! Rain!"—swelled into a deep-throated roar as their Chief stood and faced them; men began to stamp on the ground, raising a thick swirl of yellow dust, making the whole concourse tremble. In the center, the thousands of men beat upon the hot earth, and deafened the sky with their clamour, and raised their arms on high again and again, each arm and each up-thrust an oath of homage; on the outer fringe the women went U-lu-lu-lu-lu! on a high-pitched, hysterical note, screaming their wild adoration.

This was the true voice of Pharamaul, so far removed from the plumes and the parasols and the white man's speeches that the white men, and their womenfolk, could only look at each other in amazement, struck with the thought that they might be on the wrong stage in the wrong play. It was a moment of utter division, made sharper still as Dinamaula raised his arm for silence, and received it instantly, and said, in a controlled, carrying voice:

"Your Royal Highness—your Excellency—and *my people!*"

Rather naughty, that, thought David Bracken, and dropped his head as the clamour burst out again. It was really another version of the Governor-General's direct popular appeal, though a rather more attractive one. It could even seem dangerous, if one had a keen nose for trouble and took seriously the idea that everyone addressed as "Your" was now classed as an outsider. But it could, strictly speaking, be justified. They were "his people," whether as Chief or as Prime Minister, and everyone on the *aboura* knew it, and wanted to hear it.

8

Dinamaula did not speak for long. Other people had done that; he was the one man who did not need to. Addressing the vast meeting alternately in Maula and in English, he bade them all welcome. He told them that this was the greatest day in the history of Pharamaul, and that there would be other, greater days in the future.

Yesterday Pharamaul had been a *farela*—he translated this as "a small creature," though to David Bracken and most of those present it meant, actually, "A little dog," and was a term of insult. Today Pharamaul had become a lion. Tomorrow, if they all worked faithfully as one people, following their leaders, no one could say what Pharamaul might not become.

He promised them equal justice before the law. He promised freedom to all who worked honestly to make this a single nation. He promised them "one colour"—the colour of Pharamaul. There was now no past, only the future. He wished them fine crops, great herds, and rain.

The last word, "*Ahsula!*" was the end of the speech, and the signal for a fantastic ovation. Dinamaula stood stock-still, smiling slightly, as the uproar swelled to its thunderous climax; and there it seemed to hang, a fierce and stormy shout ringed round by the hyena-calls of the women; a shout which went on and on, as if caught in the eye of its own hurricane. It was an African greeting, violent, full-throated, and loving; and it was not quenched until Dinamaula raised his arms again, in the same signal of command.

Lucky was the Prime Minister, thought David Bracken ruefully, who had *that* sort of following.

As Dinamaula sat down, the Earl of Urle leant across the gleaming bared knees of his countess, and said: "Good show, old boy!"

The moment had come for the flag-raising ceremony.

First the Union Jack had to be lowered, for the last time; and as the band broke into "God Save the Queen," David Bracken, stiffly saluting, was conscious of a sudden ache in his throat. He had known this was going to happen; he had even mentioned it, jokingly, to Nicole. But damn it all!—it wasn't such a bad old flag, it had done well by this country, and a hundred others besides. One need not be ashamed of sadness at seeing it go, deserting Pharamaul for ever after a hundred and twenty-six years. . . . Then, to interrupt this mood of mourning, there came a hitch.

The band had already finished the anthem while the Union

Jack, snagged by a twisted halyard, was still only halfway down. There it stuck fast. A nervous silence fell, as the police sergeant in charge of the "flag detail" wrestled with his problem, and with history.

When this had happened before, thought David Bracken, still at the salute, another Royal Personage with a readier wit than most had murmured to the incoming Prime Minister (it had been Kenyatta of Kenya): "You can still change your mind." But Pharamaul's day was different from Kenya's day; this had been an uneasy ceremony all along, made more uneasy still by the way Dinamaula had stolen the show, and there was no one here to bridge an awkward moment with cheerful irreverence.

They all waited, while the halyard was unravelled and the Union Jack finally lowered. Then the band struck up again, and another flag began to rise.

The band was playing a rather jolly tune, Pharamaul's new national anthem. Originally composed by the organist of St. Boniface Cathedral, and now scored for trombones, trumpets, tubas, clarinets, flutes, piccolos, cymbals, and big bass drums, it had a definite lilt; and as the flag rose and the music blared, Bobo Urle's comment could be clearly heard: "Oh, I like this number! It could be a real swinger!" Then the flag, fluttering in a chance breeze, spread its wings suddenly.

It was Dinamaula's own design: Dinamaula's, aided by David Bracken and by a young man from Port Victoria Museum who had access to various books on heraldry. It was chequered, in four different colours: black for the people, blue for the sea, yellow for the earth, and red for "progress." It had not been seen before. As it rose taut to the top of the flagpole, David Bracken heard a whisper behind him: "Bloody thing looks like a dishcloth!" followed by a giggle and a penetrating "Sh'h!"

There was bound to be somebody like that, thought David Bracken angrily; and, in drink or in sneering disdain, there were going to be plenty of such remarks, before this thing settled down. . . . He considered turning round, to glare at the offender —he had recognized the voice easily enough; but then he thought better of it. Let it go, let it go. . . . He stood firmly braced at the salute until the anthem ended.

Now there was only one more item to come, and one way to end the proceedings: the March Past and Salute. Everyone had wanted to get into the March Past; David Bracken had had applications, and indignant protests when they were turned down, from the Port Victoria football team, the small but militant Orangemen's Lodge, the Stevedores' Union, the Life Boat Society, the Port Victoria Sailing Club, the Physical Culture Union (weight-lifting and karate), the Beach Rescue Brigade (including scuba divers who wished to march in their flippers), and the mixed choir of St. Boniface Cathedral.

Faced with a program which might have gone on till nightfall, David had taken refuge in the formula "military units only," and when this was challenged, since Pharamaul had no military units, had amended it to "para-military." He had been left, at the end, with the Boy Scouts, the British Legion, the Fire Brigade, and the Royal Pharamaul Police; and it was these contingents which now advanced, to the music of "Colonel Bogey" and the cheers of the crowd.

The Boy Scouts straggled; the British Legion was its usual boozy blend of patriotism and picnic informality; the Fire Brigade, their faces grinning under the absurd brass helmets, were inclined to clown. But the police, bringing up the rear, supplied the corrective to all this. They marched like soldiers, eight platoons under white officers; they gave an "Eyes Right!" to the saluting base which was sharp enough to snap a dozen vertebrae; they looked as tough and businesslike as anything in Pharamaul that day.

Their commanding officer, Major Crump, watched them with steely eyes from the dais; but he was proud, as everyone else was proud; and even the *sotto voce* contribution of the man who had made the silly remark about the new flag, now singing "Bollocks! And the same to you!" to the accompaniment of female giggles, could not spoil it. The music blared and roared, the men marched in compact squares and saluted the flag as if they believed in nothing else. When David Bracken leaned across to speak to Major Crump, he could only find words of praise.

"Congratulations, Keith. They're very smart."

"They'd better be," growled Major Crump. But he was pleased, and so was almost everyone else, whichever side they were on. This was law and order, plain for all to see; something not to be despised, something to be glad of, something which certain other countries had lost track of completely. . . . A lot of things might be going to change in Pharamaul, but the Royal Pharamaul Police would still be holding the ring, the guardian of change itself.

. . .

Once inside the magnificent grounds of Government House, the four hundred invited guests, the *élite* of Pharamaul, left their cars and streamed across the baked lawns towards the receiving line. It was a long line, winding backwards from the tall white portico halfway down the drive, then skirting the flower-beds where the cannas and poinsettias blazed, then making a prudent detour out of the burning sun and into the shelter of the flame-trees.

The line moved very slowly, and the reason for this soon became obvious; it was, as David Bracken overheard someone behind him complaining, because "that bolshy bastard's holding up the drill." It was painfully true that the Earl of Urle was making a meal of the occasion; whereas the royal cousin shook hands swiftly and wordlessly, and the Governor-General's lady could not have been more offhanded if she had been dishing out cloak-room tickets, the Governor-General himself, playing the expansive host, was having the time of his democratic life.

His aide-de-camp, Paul Jordan, stood close at his elbow, briefly cueing him in on each new arrival; and as the Governor-General heard the key words—"Town Councillor," "Head of the hospital," "Bank manager," "Export-import"—he swiftly changed his own role, and almost his own face.

Everyone was accorded a personal greeting, with a couple of technicalities thrown in; and even though this process was limited to about four cheery sentences, four sentences on hospital staffing, and four sentences on the exchange-differential with the South African *rand*, and four sentences on dredging operations for the new harbour, added up to a lot of words and a very slow procession indeed.

It would have been very well done, if His Lordship had been canvassing on the eve of poll. As it was, it was simply a traffic block under an insufferable sun. Before long, the receiving line began to look like a section of snarled interior gut, with a most unhealthy bulge between the first brisk handshake and the second slow-motion one.

Thirsty men, eyeing the distant champagne tent, licked their lips in torment; but it was as far away as ever. Others, shifting uneasily from one foot to another, had to slip away to wash their hands. Already tongues, male and female, were buzzing mutinously.

"If this is independence, old boy, I don't think much of it."

"These Labour people never know how to behave."

"I've got a good mind to make a break for the bar."

"Can't do that, old boy. Etiquette."

"What sort of etiquette is this, then?"

"Oh, *come on!*"

"Just look at the Governess's skirt! It's up round her neck!"

"Probably trying for the Order of the Garter."

"Wouldn't mind a bit of 'O Come All Ye Faithful' myself."

"Now George! Eyes in the boat!"

"I *won't* curtsey to that woman. I simply *won't!*"

"Dinamaula's got fatter, hasn't he?"

"Must be raiding the till already."

"If I don't have a cucumber sandwich soon, I'm going to die."

"Wish I'd brought my flask from the car."

"What's in it?"

"By now, hot martini."

"Sorry, chaps, I've just got to leave you. Nature calls."

"Do one for me, will you?"

"Oh, *come on!*"

The voices buzzed and blurred, rising and falling like a long sea swell. Across the lawn, the Police Band played the *Merry Widow* waltz. The Governor-General's voice and laugh rang out with great heartiness; he was greeting the American Consul, and acting out a role of transatlantic fellowship. The clogged line shuffled forward a pace or two. Slowly, very slowly, the Vice-regal Garden Party got under way.

The champagne tent was besieged from the start; the day was hot, people had been kept waiting, they had grown bad-tempered, there was only one thing to do. . . . A jostling crowd butted continuously against the long bar; none of the white-liveried Maula servants could take two paces out of the tent with a loaded tray before it was snatched bare of glasses. One could feel no remorse, on a day like this. It was just someone else's bad luck.

Under the trees, the women in their long party dresses waited patiently for their husbands and the promised drinks. In the meantime, they envied the flowers, which a staff of eight gardeners had brought to summer perfection; they complained about the heat, which made the whole scene shimmer; and they united in their hatred of the Countess of Urle.

Paul Jordan, the aide-de-camp, released at last from close attendance, made his rounds, noted the imperfections, and decided, as usual, that there was nothing much to be done about them. Garden parties were always the same; they were a kind of charade, not meant to be enjoyed, simply to be performed with the traditional gestures, like some stiff-jointed morality play without a single joke.

It was always difficult to get a drink. Blacks and whites didn't mix, even on such a notable day as this. The consular corps only talked to each other, never to "civilians." The band played the same *bloody* tunes (soon it would be time for *Ruddigore*). There were never any girls, just wives.

Resplendent in his white naval uniform with the gold-tasselled aiguillettes, he circled discreetly to the back of the champagne tent, signalled to the Government House butler, and secured two privileged glasses of champagne. Then he made his way back to Bobo Urle. She was undoubtedly the best bet of the afternoon. In fact, she was the only one. And it *was* in the line of duty.

Apart from the consular corps, there were four other centers of aloofness, and David Bracken, making *his* rounds, touched each of them in turn.

Withdrawn even from their own people, the three northern chiefs—Murumba of Gamate, Banka of Shebiya, and Justin of Fish Village—stood alone at one corner of the lawn. They had bowed with great dignity to the child of the Queen; they had bowed—though less politely, and with a certain directness of gaze—to the Earl of Urle; they had somehow contrived to greet the Countess as if she were not really there. They had sipped, once and formally, at this ridiculous fizzy drink, fit only for pleading children, which the Europeans seemed to favour.

Now they simply stood their ground, in their splendid embroidered robes and bright-coloured caps, unsmiling, not talking even to each other, a still and solemn part of a scene which was otherwise frivolous.

Murumba and Banka were oldish men, growing past their prime; Justin (a Catholic mission child) of the go-ahead Fish Village was young—as young as Dinamaula had been when first, twelve years ago, he became Chief of all Pharamaul. But the three were alike, in authority and the habit of command. They had been brought to power by the voice of the people; now they ruled by its consent, and by their own showing.

They were proud to be there on this great day, but they were

14

not happy. Happiness did not lie in the soft south of Pharamaul, in the city talk and the city ways; happiness lay only in the true north, where the true men grew, and their crops and cattle with them. The spine of this country was the northern spine. . . . It was an ancient division; it had sometimes been a murderous one; and even now, when the country was newly knit together, it still lurked in the bloodstream, like anger, like lust.

They respected Dinamaula, because he was the proclaimed Paramount Chief, and had proved himself; above all, he was a Gamate man, born and bred, the son and grandson of the Gamate line. But there was still room for doubt. Would he now become a Port Victoria man, and lose the edge of honour? Would he become a talker, a boaster?—worse still, would his new power, proclaimed by the Queen, take him along certain paths of corruption, as had happened to other men in other parts of Africa?

On a day like this, the future could look bright. But this day was the first day. The days which would follow might have different colours altogether. And though there were no such doubts as yet among the people, it was the part of a chief to be the first to doubt, the first to give warning, and the first to act.

David Bracken, a man of whom they had no doubts at all, came across to greet them. It was a formal greeting on both sides, suitable to men of rank who had watched each other at work, and found no fault.

To Murumba of Gamate, the arch-conservative, David gave the conservative salute, wishing him rain—that rain which, in a parched country, embraced all human hopes. To Banka of Shebiya, eternally plagued by wife-trouble which stemmed from the jealousy of his twenty sons, he said: "I wish you all tranquillity, Chief." To Justin, an energetic young man who would have been a highly competent shop-steward if he had not been Chief of Fish Village, he used a word which had come into vogue among the younger men—"*Warriah!*"

It meant something between "All together now!" and "Let's get organized," and was much used at football matches, particularly by supporters of the losing team.

Then he spoke briefly of their homes in the northland, where they doubtless wished to be at this moment.

"When will you next visit Gamate, Mr. Bracken?" asked Murumba presently.

"Soon, I hope," answered David, and meant it—the sprawling

"native capital" of Gamate had captured him, ever since he made his first tour there. "But I do have a lot of extra work here just now. At the moment I'm really very busy."

"Everyone is very busy in Port Victoria," said Chief Banka, looking round him. He did not sound impressed by the fact.

"Anyway, I expect His Excellency will be making an official visit to the north soon," David added.

No one said anything to that.

David moved on. His way took him past the towering elm-tree under which all the "black wives" were sitting, and he gave them a cheerful salute which was answered by a sudden display of dazzling teeth from the whole group. But they were having a wretched time, as always happened at parties. Their husbands—civil servants, town councillors, members of the Legislature—had all the brains and did all the talking, and were not afraid to mix on an occasion like this. Their wives *were* afraid, and all the world knew it.

They were scared of the European women, who were so smart and always knew how to behave; and they could have nothing to say to a white man, particularly a white man at a glittering *aboura* like this. So they withdrew, as they always did, into a fenced group, and sat there in patient embarrassment, staring at the enemy scene and waiting for release.

Unfairly, they were "cooking-pot wives," married too soon to husbands not yet optimistic of their own future. The husbands knew this, and resented it, and would have given much to set the clock back and start all over again with (to put it politely) different ideas.

Sometimes, in private, they chided these wives bitterly for disgracing them, for being so stupid and fearful, for never enjoying themselves. But it was worse, a thousand times worse, when the cooking-pot wives made an effort to keep up.

David Bracken, after touching the peak of his cock's-feather helmet towards the group, did not stop. He was no use at entirely one-sided conversations—and there was a family convention that Nicole was "awfully good with the wives," and did more than her share. That took care of that. He moved on to the next enclave, and this time it was the Press.

Not many of them had flown in for this occasion, which was becoming a routine African assignment. Pharamaul had no special problems save poverty; nothing was likely to go wrong on

Independence Day, and therefore there could be no worthwhile story. The only possibility in this area was Bobo Urle, who might decide to kick up her heels. But one did not need to fly a man out to Africa to catch that sort of performance.

London was full of badly-behaved "show people," with their public love-affairs and semi-private parts. A bus to Chelsea saved £285 on the air-fare to Africa.

David Bracken was relieved at this drought. Pharamaul had had its fill of the Press at the time of the "Sign of the Fish" trouble, and Dinamaula's exile; even now, years later, the memory was still sharp and the taste awful. Today, as things came full circle, and the "hated colonial masters" were quietly pulling out, there was only a man from the South African Press Association, a stringer for *The Times*, and a cheerful young Negro from Tanzania who called everyone "brother."

These had all made their number already at the Government Secretariat. But the party under the tree was five, not three; and when David drew near, it was to find that he knew the two extras. One was good news, the other bad. One was Tom Stillwell, editor of the *Times of Pharamaul*, who had done as much as anyone to prepare the ground for this day. The other was an old enemy, Tulbach Browne of the *Daily Thresh*.

David had not known he was coming, though he might have guessed it; and he was conscious of a pang of dismay, of the sort which he should have grown out of long ago, when he ceased to be afraid of little growly dogs standing in the way. Tulbach Browne, famous or notorious as the *Daily Thresh* roving executioner, had made the Pharamaul story his own, at the time of its acute crisis; in fact, there would probably never have been an acute crisis, and possibly no story at all, if he had not flown in and started to operate.

But he was that kind of man; he recognized the entrails from afar off, like a senior vulture, and if the entrails were not yet producing the requisite stench, he speedily injected poison of his own, to start the ferment. He was a story-maker in the worst sense, an operator without conscience, a manipulator of secret grimy strings.

In Pharamaul, on that first visit, he had done everything to deride authority, to stir up discord, and to provoke Dinamaula to a pitch of rebellious despair. The result had been murderous chaos.

Now he was back again, and it would not take Pharamaul long to learn the reason why.

Twelve years ago, thought David, Tulbach Browne had been taunting British officials with "stuffy, blockheaded colonialism," and screaming at them to get out of the country. Probably he had now changed sides, and would charge them with leaving the sinking ship, with being irresponsible cowards, arrant rats. . . . David said hello to the other newspapermen in turn, and nodded finally to Tulbach Browne. Ludicrously insincere, he found himself saying, of all things:

"Welcome back."

Tulbach Browne had not improved. He was smaller, sharper-beaked, more rumpled than ever—things he could not help. He was also quicker to pounce, readier to disbelieve, and more offensive all round, and these were his own improvements.

Now his nose wrinkled. "Bracken," he said, and it sounded like the beginning of a music-hall joke. "I thought I recognized that hat. . . . Let's see—what are you now?"

"Chief Secretary," answered David Bracken, very curtly. It might not mean much in Fleet Street, but it meant a hell of a lot in Pharamaul, and that was where they were now. As he spoke, he forgot his brief stab of nerves. He had been young when he first met Tulbach Browne, and the man had made rings round him. Now he had better weapons. "Are you still on the same paper?"

Tulbach Browne grinned sardonically. "I think that's pretty well known, wouldn't you say? . . . Chief Secretary. . . . You're the one that's staying on, then."

"Yes."

"Now why would you want to do that?"

The others were watching them, aware of a tension they had known nothing about.

"Why not?" asked David. "I've been here for years. I've come to think of it as my own country. Naturally I'm staying."

"For how long?"

"That depends on how things go."

"Oh, we all know how they'll *go*," said Tulbach Browne unpleasantly. "Right down the chute with the rest of the rubbish."

"I don't think so."

"Well, it's always nice to meet an optimist." Tulbach Browne gestured round him with his champagne glass. "What's the point of this picnic, anyway?"

18

"Independence Day celebration." David stared at him, not concealing his dislike. "As you know quite well, since you're here."

"I mean the *point*, the actual meaning behind all the nonsense. Blacks and whites all chums together. Is that it?"

"I don't know what you're talking about."

The *Times* man had edged away, seeming to recognize an unsuitable climate. The reporter from Tanzania was watching David closely, as if he really wanted to find out something important. The SAPA representative, an Afrikaner who had his own views on blacks and whites being chums together, stood ready to pick up any plums which might fall. Only Tom Stillwell, edgy and dedicated, looked as though he were eager to break a lance—any lance—in defense of all ideals.

Tulbach Browne sighed gustily. "Maybe you've been here too long. . . . Maybe you don't read the newspapers. *All* the new countries have started out with these cosy ideas, and all of them have blown them sky-high. This sort of racial-harmony guff doesn't mean a thing."

"Pharamaul is different."

"I'd like to know why."

Tom Stillwell chipped in, as David Bracken had known he would. "Race relations have always been excellent here," he said fiercely. "They really work!"

"They weren't *excellent* when I was here last. They were bloody awful."

"You took good care of that," said David unwisely.

Tulbach Browne seemed to dart at him like a wasp. "Can I quote that?"

"I don't mind what you do with it."

But Tom Stillwell had a more serious intent, and was going to pursue it. "That was years ago," he declared. "It's absolutely different now. This is a united country. There's full representation at almost every level. We've had a mixed legislative assembly —black and white, elected members—for nearly five years."

"How long will that last, now?"

"There's no reason at all why it shouldn't last. In fact there's another election coming up in a few months."

"There usually is," said Tulbach Browne sarcastically. "You know what they say—'one man, one vote, *once.*'" Suddenly he waved his arm round again, taking in everything—the gleaming white façade of Government House, the long dresses under the trees, the parasols, the massed flower-beds, the band tootling away at a Sousa march. He even seemed to include, somehow, David's uniform, his plumed helmet, his polished sword-sheath. . . . "Oh well," he said, "it's good to see the end of all this rubbish, anyway."

David turned on his heel without a word, and walked away. Behind him he heard Tulbach Browne's voice again, on a barking note of command: "Boy! Bring more champagne! Chop chop!" Then there was a step behind him, and it was Tom Stillwell, almost running to catch up.

"What was all that about?" Stillwell asked, surprised.

"We don't like each other," said David shortly.

"Oh, I guessed that. . . ." The other man grinned. "Chop chop!" he mimicked. "Would you believe it?"

"I can believe anything of that man," answered David. "I've seen him in action before."

"When was that?"

"Long time ago. I'll tell you some time." Suddenly David relaxed, pushing it all away again. He did not want the day spoiled, by Tulbach Browne or anyone else. In fact, it was not going to be spoiled. "But not now. . . . I liked your leader this morning."

"Not too radical for you?"

Stillwell grinned again as he said it, since this was an old joke, part of an old argument which no longer mattered. When, years before, the *Times of Pharamaul* had changed hands, and young Tom Stillwell had arrived to take charge, there had been some immediate changes, and European Pharamaul did not like any of them.

Stillwell, a shock-headed north-country radical with few graces and no inhibitions at all, had come into quick collision with almost everyone, from Government House to the local storekeepers. He was "moving too fast," according to the moderates' argument; he was "selling out to the niggers," in the more explicit version of the conservatives.

But Tom Stillwell had stuck to his guns, and he had won. He had "africanized" certain sections of the printing side of the paper, in the teeth of violent opposition from the old-guard union concerned. He had loaded the paper with news in which "most people" were interested—and most people, of course, were Maula. He gave the Maulas their own social column, complete with photographs, to the derision of the whites and the enormous pride of class-conscious Maula citizens. He had, in his own words, "cut down on news about two-headed calves in Gamate, and given people a look at the horizon instead of the earth."

Several times he had crossed swords with David Bracken on such things as farm prices, which were heavily loaded in favour of the white farmers, and had won some unwilling Government reforms. Above all, he had tripled his circulation in three years, and made the *Times of Pharamaul* pay handsomely. Grudgingly, the critics had to admit that the "radical rag" was a necessary part of the new scene, and had come to stay.

Thus, David was able to answer: "No, not too radical," and to answer the smile as well. He went on: "I thought the tone was just right. There's a hell of a lot of hard work ahead for everyone —that's the main point."

"It was *not* a point made by His Excellency," said Stillwell grimly. "He made it sound as if we've only to press the independence button, and everyone comes up smelling of violets. 'A land flowing with milk and honey'—what a load of tripe!"

"He was trying too hard to please," David agreed. "Of course, the Maulas don't like that sort of thing at all. In fact, they've got a wonderful phrase for it. They call it '*rau bacha*.' It means 'tail-wagging,' but rather more rude. More like 'bottom-waving.' Very expressive."

"Bottom-waving," repeated Tom Stillwell. "That just about covers both of them, doesn't it?"

David laughed. "Some bottoms have more appeal than others."

"If either of them overdoes it, there's going to be trouble."

Tom Stillwell went on his way, while David, hot and sticky in his tight-collared uniform, stayed where he was under the shade of a big flame-tree. The party was thinning out now, but there was still a long way to go before he could doff his plumed helmet for another half-year. . . . Then he heard his name called, from the opposite side of the tree, and when he turned it was to find the only man he really wanted to talk to, on this special afternoon —the Prime Minister.

Dinamaula was standing alone, the last of the aloof men. Earlier he had been thronged by well-wishers, crowding in to shake his hand, and his tall robed figure topped by the ceremonial lionskin cap was for a long time the hub of the afternoon. But now the formalities were done, and he had become a monument rather than a man. For some reason he seemed to have grown remote from the day, and people understood this, and respected his honourable solitude.

His wife was with the women, and he did not wish it otherwise.

But inside him, beneath the somber mask of his rank, was a great well of happiness and pride. He felt, with special awareness, that when this day had dawned he had come a long way, even though he had been born a chief. . . . He could remember, years ago, the laborious teaching of his first tutor, intoning syllable by syllable the very first lesson he had to learn by heart—his own style and pedigree:

"Dinamaula, son of Simaula, grandson of Maula, Hereditary Chieftain of Pharamaul, Prince of Gamate, Son of the Fish, Keeper of the Golden Nail, Urn of the Royal Seed, Ruler and Kingbreaker, Lord of the Known World. . . ."

Dinamaula had last heard it, fully proclaimed, when he was installed as Paramount Chief. It had sounded outlandish then, even ludicrous, yet proudly so. Now it was all summed up in a western version, simple but of enormous consequence to him: Prime Minister of Pharamaul.

It was as Prime Minister that he called out to the man he had once thought of as his enemy, and who was now his friend:

"Shall we drink to it, David?"

David Bracken, though taken by surprise, did not have to think twice. He joined the other man readily, and took the glass of champagne which Dinamaula, with a single stately signal, had conjured from a passing Maula servant. Then they nodded to each other, and drank, and smiled.

"That's my fourth," said David. "I think it had better be the last."

"This is not a day for counting drinks," said Dinamaula, and tossed off his glass with a second hearty swig.

"I have a position to keep up," said David, and smiled again. It was really extraordinarily pleasant, champagne or no champagne, to be alive on this day, and talking at ease with a man one trusted. "I liked your speech very much. It really was a success."

"Against such terrific competition," said Dinamaula, with an edge of sarcasm.

David took the thought. "He wasn't very good, was he? In fact he wasn't *any* good. I hope"—he realized that he was talking with unusual freedom, but it seemed an excellent day to do so—"I hope that he's going to fit in here."

"He will learn. Anyway, Pharamaul has survived worse things."

"Not recently." The phrase "worse things" recalled something else, and he added: "By the way, I just met an old friend. Tulbach Browne. Remember him?"

"I saw you talking to him," answered Dinamaula. He was looking at the middle distance now, wrinkling his eyes against the glare, somber again, thinking serious thoughts. "He was no friend of mine."

"You'd like him even less now."

David believed this to be happily true; and he could be happy also to believe that Dinamaula now saw Tulbach Browne for what he was, and thought that the other man had brought him nothing but trouble. The declaration recalled to him how very well Dinamaula had behaved while in exile, and later when he had been allowed to return to Pharamaul; he had shed all such dubious backers, he had struck no attitudes, in London or anywhere else; he had borne no public bitterness and joined no cliques, although ardently wooed by "progressives" in search of a talkative martyr. In exile he had kept silent, and worked steadily for his law degree; and when he returned home, with no sort of fanfare, he had ruled as chief without incident or drama of any kind.

Of course he must have been thinking hard about independence all the time, and working towards it with a single-minded purpose. But why not? That was the way the world was going; and compared with certain ratty little countries which had been handed their freedom on a plate, and had then proceeded to kill it stone-dead and to gorge upon the corpse, Pharamaul and its Prime Minister seemed to deserve a high priority.

Now Dinamaula asked, in the same serious way: "Why do you say I would like him even less now?"

"Well," David began, and paused. He did not really want to go into the details, with their embarrassing allusions and all their inherent insult. "Are you going to talk to him? Or have you talked to him already?"

"No," said Dinamaula. "He did try to start up an interview, as soon as he arrived this afternoon. I said that this wasn't the time for it, but he could have an appointment tomorrow. He said he was leaving tomorrow. I said what a pity. He said that it probably didn't matter anyway." Dinamaula recited the exchange without special emphasis, as if he had not been involved at all, not even in the final impertinence. Then he added, holding his neutral tone: "He was allowing you a rather longer audience, as far as I could see."

"He was being very offensive," David answered. "He seems to have made up his mind about our independence already."

"That it will fail?"

"Exactly. . . . That was a very good guess, Prime Minister."

"It was a very easy one, Chief Secretary. . . . As a matter of fact I still read the *Daily Thresh*, as soon as it gets here. To keep up with trends of fashion in Fleet Street. At least, that's the official explanation. Actually it's a marvellous paper. You devour it, and don't believe a word of it. . . . So I know more or less what Mr. Browne is thinking. In the old days, he could not grant Africa its freedom quickly enough. Now he wants to take it all back again." Dinamaula smiled, as if he were more than strong enough to endure such nonsense. "All the same, he might have given Pharamaul more than three hours' trial."

"He wanted to know why on earth I'm staying on."

"For the money, of course," Dinamaula shook his heavy shoulders, like a man shedding an unpleasant load. Then he said, echoing David's earlier thought: "Forget it, as the Yanks say. It will take more than Tulbach Browne to spoil this afternoon."

"Day One," said David. "I'm damned glad to be here to see it."

"On Day One Thousand," said Dinamaula, "we will drink to it again." His voice and tone and manner had grown suddenly formal, as if he were saying something he had saved up for a long time. "It means a great deal to me that you are staying on. . . . Let us make this a *real* country."

The fierce sun was declining, and the garden party with it. Cars were moving out of the grounds in a clogged stream, and people who had come on foot began their slow trudge down the drive and out on to the broad avenue leading homewards. Royalty had retired with a touch of the sun, and the Governor-General, after escorting him inside, himself withdrew to the colonnaded cool of his private balcony, put his feet up, and dozed off, well content with a flourishing start.

The band played "Auld Lang Syne," hopefully, and then sat in silence, their repertoire exhausted, their uniforms wilting, their tongues like hot sand. There began a final onslaught, by the true, getting-their-money's-worth stayers, upon the champagne tent.

David Bracken, passing close by, overheard a snatch of conversation. It came from the man who had made an offensive fool of himself at the ceremony, the man who had been drinking warm martinis most of the afternoon and had now spent two hours dowsing them with champagne. His name was Terence Woodcock—"Splinter" Woodcock to his friends; a beefy red-faced ex-planter, a past-president and pillar of the Port Victoria Club, and (as far as David was concerned) a boorish nuisance.

Now he was propped up against the central tent-pole, talking to one of his cronies—Biggs-Johnson of the Universal Bazaar, the city's only department store. Splinter Woodcock's face was sweaty and sagging, his glass slopping over, his pink glazed eyes bulging like boiled sweets. But the voice was as loud as ever, and the theme unflaggingly the same.

"It's no bloody good arguing with me, George," said Splinter Woodcock—and it was clear that some long meandering discussion was reaching its peak. "I tell you, there's only one way this country will go, and that's down the you-know-what. Straight to hell on a bloody wheelbarrow. Stands to reason. Look at all the others."

"What others?" Biggs-Johnson, a smart hand in the counting-house, was not at his best in general discussion. He was a small yellowish man, sandy all over, from pointed nose to freckled neck; when brought up short, as now, he looked like a puzzled ferret. "Other wheelbarrows?"

"No, you clot! I mean, other *countries*. Look at bloody Ghana. Look at bloody Nigeria. Look at the bloody Congo, for Christ's sake! They all went the same way, didn't they? Talk about rack and ruin! They're just shit and small stones! It'll be the same here. You mark my words."

David Bracken, in spite of a wish to keep clear of all such scenes as this, had paused to listen. What he was overhearing contrasted so unpleasantly with what he had just heard from Dinamaula that he felt compelled to witness it. It was part of his job now, just as a dead dog in the road was part of a street-sweeper's.

"Oh, I agree about all those other places," said Biggs-Johnson. "You can scrub the whole lot out, as far as I'm concerned. But Pharamaul's not like that. It's civilized. Chaps like you and me."

"It *won't* be chaps like you and me. That's just what I'm *saying!* It'll be a lot of black-arsed bastards with their shirts hanging out of their trousers, *giving the orders!* It'll be Mr. Bloody Dinamaula, telling *us* what to do! It'll be some kaffir who can't add up two and two, running *your* business and robbing you blind as soon as you turn your back."

"I'd like to see him try."

"You'll see it." Splinter Woodcock swallowed a fresh draught of champagne, and then let his head flop back against the tent-pole. In the process it lolled sideways, and he caught sight of David Bracken, standing a few paces off. His look changed, from incipient torpor to a spiteful concentration. "And there's one of the bloody crooks who's selling us out," he growled. Then he raised his voice. "Hello, David! . . . Don't just stand there scratching yourself. . . . Come and drink to glorious independence!"

It was a contact David would have preferred to avoid, but that was hardly possible. He crossed the few steps between them, and became an unlikely third in this raffish group. Then he said:

"I'll drink to that, any time."

"I bet you would," said Splinter Woodcock unpleasantly. He stuck his chin out like a fat wet prow. "Most of it was your idea, wasn't it?"

"Most of what?"

Splinter Woodcock waved his hand round. "All this poop. Independence. Selling out to the Maulas, I call it."

"Steady on, Splinter," said Biggs-Johnson nervously. He had to deal with Government at several levels—import licenses, rates of customs duty, work permits, even loading-zones for his lorries—and he wanted no black mark on a day such as this.

"You don't have to put it like that."

"I'll put it any way I please," Splinter Woodcock retorted. "In fact I'll put it right up, if I have to! It's time a few people round here stopped saying 'Yes sir, no sir, three bags full,' and said what they think."

David Bracken looked down at him, feeling the onset of anger, controlling it from long habit. "I gather you don't like the idea of independence."

"I think it's a lot of tripe."

"You're entitled to your opinion." But that was as far as David felt he could go. Now he spoke as curtly as he could. "But you're not entitled to be insulting about it. I didn't think much of your contribution at the ceremony, and I don't think much of it now. Independence is here, whether you like it or not. We've got a new constitution—"

"Who's 'we'?" Woodcock interrupted rudely.

"We in Pharamaul. You should give it a try. We've also got a new flag and a new national anthem, and you'd better respect them both."

"Respect them!" said Woodcock loudly. "I'll piss on them if I feel like it!"

Heads were turning in their direction, including female heads; it was a wholly disgusting moment. Never argue with a drunken man, thought David ruefully, and knew that he should not have started this, however strongly he felt. Now he could not possibly answer, without a first-class row which might lead any-where, even to a public brawl. In silence he turned away, and left the tent. Behind him he heard Splinter Woodcock's fruity voice, raised in triumph:

"That settled *him!* Did you see that? He couldn't answer! He knew I was right!"

"Splinter," began Biggs-Johnson pleadingly, "I don't think—"

"Oh, balls! I told you, you've got to stand up to these bastards.
. . . Let's have some more champagne. I feel better already."

"Darling," said Nicole, when David Bracken finally found her, sitting alone on a swing-seat, "I've just had a lovely session with Paul Jordan. I haven't laughed so much for years."

"How nice for you," David answered shortly. He was still bad-tempered after his encounter with Splinter Woodcock, and not yet in the mood even for family exchanges. "But shouldn't he have been working?"

"He had been. That's what was so funny." Nicole looked up at him. "What's the matter?"

"Nothing much."

"Well, what?"

"I just had an argument with Woodcock, that's all."

"That frightful man." Nicole wrinkled her nose. She had had her own awkward encounters with Splinter Woodcock, on a dif-ferent plane, in the past; and though he had long stopped "being a nuisance," the thought of his furtive pawing on the dance-floor could still make her skin crawl. "I hope you told him off for behaving like that at the ceremony."

"I did," answered David. "Then he began to argue the toss, and since I didn't want a row in public, I had to leave it. I'd like to have kicked him out of G.H." Suddenly David grinned. "Good

God—Splinter Woodcock! Why should we let that oaf get us down, on a day like this? Have you had a drink?"

"Several," answered Nicole. "Well, two. Is my nose all right?"

"Bang in the middle," said David, with ritual family wit. "And hardly shiny at all. . . . Tell me about Paul."

Swiftly Nicole examined her face, in a mirror as neatly palmed as a conjuror's ace of spades. She said: "I think it'll just last the course," and then: "Poor Paul. He had the most terrible time with the Governess."

"That sounds very unlikely."

"Wait till you hear. He thought he ought to spend most of the time looking after her, because she's only been here a couple of days; but she seemed to think that he was—you know, trying to seduce her or something." Nicole's forehead furrowed briefly. "Actually, he probably *was* trying to make a good impression, and enjoy himself at the same time, because these parties are pretty dull for the young. But he wasn't *serious*."

"H'm," said David.

"Of course he wasn't!" said Nicole, slightly scandalized. "He's much too nice. . . . Well, anyway, there he was, trying to be agreeable, but whatever he said, the Governess twisted it round so that it sounded—you know, suggestive. When he offered to fetch her another drink, she said: 'Are you trying to get me loaded? What's on your mind?' And when they were talking about the ceremony, and Paul said something about there being almost too many children in Pharamaul, she twisted it all round again and said: 'Why don't you ask straight out? Of course I'm on the pill!' Isn't that *terrible?* But it was like that all the time. Honestly, Paul was absolutely terrified! It's his first posting as aide, and he only got it because he's been ill. Now he can't wait to get back to sea!"

"I don't blame him," said David. "Bobo Urle. . . . I prophesy that we'll have plenty of trouble with that one."

"I think she's awful," said Nicole forthrightly. "And you should hear the women going on about her." Then she giggled. "Oh, I forgot something else. At the end, when she said she was going indoors, Paul offered to escort her, and she said: 'Down, boy! It's not your night to howl.' Poor Paul—he was still shaking when he told me about it."

"It's an occupational hazard."

"But not so *obviously*. . . . We must find him a really nice girl.
. . . Do you think Bobo Urle is attractive?"

"If you like that sort of thing."

Nicole looked up at him. "That's not very reassuring. You *do* like that sort of thing."

"Only from you, my darling."

"Good old champagne. Shall we go home?"

"I think we might. This is pretty well over."

"I'm longing to hear how the children enjoyed themselves. And how they got on at the tea."

"Sick as dogs, I shouldn't wonder."

David Bracken, as Chief Secretary, occupied a "government bungalow" acquired, decorated, and furnished by the Office of Works when in its most frugal mood. It was square, unadorned, red-roofed, white-painted; it stood in a square, unadorned, and normally bone-dry garden; both were perpetually menaced by armies of soldier-ants, a lowering climate, and the yellow dust which blew in steadily from the arid foothills to the north.

But it was home. Nicole had refused to be daunted by its original ochre walls, dark mahogany woodwork, and furniture embalmed in that official pattern which had been repeated all the way round the colonial world since the mid-1800s. Though "Linden Lea," so christened by some homesick patriot of long ago, could never be distinguished, nor even handsome, it had been improved wonderfully by painting and polishing, and by prudent furniture-buying whenever David notched up another "annual increment."

They had lived there for eight years; one of the children had been born there, and most of the family crises resolved within its four shabby walls. It was home.

On the wide red-tiled *stoep* which ran round two-thirds of the house, and gave grateful shade from noon till sundown, Simon the faithful houseboy waited to greet them. It needed no detective work to see that Simon the faithful houseboy was barely sober; an unmistakable odour of crude kaffir beer hung round him, and his fat face was set in the vacant, benevolent smile of a man who could see no vice in the entire world.

But why not? thought David, surveying Simon without sternness; this was something which only happened about three times a year, and there could have been no better day for it than the day of independence. . . . Simon was a U-Maula from Shebiya, up north; he had first brought them their morning tea twelve years ago, when David was a District Officer and Nicole a not noticeably blushing bride. Today, four thousand morning teas later, he was still their longest link with the past, and treasured for many other reasons.

Now he stood at the top of the steps, barefooted, rocking slightly, and welcomed them home.

"*Jah, barena.* You enjoy party?"

"Very much," answered David. "Did you get a good place at the *aboura?*"

"Oh yes, *barena.* Right in front. See everything. See *barena.* See Chief."

"The Prime Minister," David corrected him.

Simon smiled widely. "I mean, *my* chief, *barena.* Chief Banka from Shebiya. Very fine."

"He is coming to see me tomorrow," said David. "He will be glad to speak with you."

Simon shook his head, disbelieving, delighted. "Ow! Chief Banka! What time he come, *barena?*"

"Eleven o'clock," answered David, and gave him a warning glance. "Be careful you are in good health."

The wide-eyed look was slightly overdone, which meant that Simon had taken the point. "I go to bed early," he said, and suddenly gave a wild giggle, and vanished kitchenwards while his luck still held.

They went through into the sitting-room.

The two children, Timothy and Martha, were side by side at the table, looking at their joint stamp-collection; the two corn-yellow heads, close together, made a bright focus of colour in the evening shadow. It continually astonished David, and it did so now, to see how the next generation had firmly established itself, before he was aware of it at all. At one moment there had been nothing; and suddenly there they were—Timothy and Martha, aged ten and eight—to prove how the years had raced by and vanished, while he was looking down at his desk or up at the shimmering horizon.

They were a worry and a delight, like most other children. They were loved, and scolded, and very welcome all the time. But there should be some sort of public warning that childhood, achingly slow for children, was for their parents a brief encounter indeed.

Martha looked up quickly as they came into the room. "We saw you, Mummy," she said excitedly. "You looked smashing!"

"Thank you, darling," said Nicole, and took off her hat—her flowered, preposterous hat—with relief. "We saw you, when the Prince was speaking."

"How about me?" asked David.

"You looked smashing, too," said Timothy loyally.

"It's the uniform," said Martha. "I told you. . . . We did wave, lots of times, but you didn't see."

"We couldn't have waved back, anyway," said David.

"Why not?"

"Because it was *official*," Timothy chipped in. "I told you. . . . Shall I help you off with your sword, Daddy?"

"All right."

"Have you ever stabbed anybody?" asked Martha.

"It's *ceremonial*, silly," said Timothy scornfully. "I told you."

"That'll do, children," said Nicole. "This isn't the day for arguments. Did you have a nice tea-party?"

Martha looked at Timothy, who was suddenly engrossed in unhooking the sword-scabbard from its ring. Finally she said: "It was all right."

"Is that all?"

Martha almost whispered: "Timmy had a fight."

There was a hiss of "Sneak!" from somewhere beneath David's left armpit. But Martha had her counter ready. "It's all right to tell. It was *honourable*."

"What was honourable, darling?" asked Nicole.

"The sort of fight. He was defending me."

David, freed of his own weapon of defense, stretched out in the armchair by the fireplace. From there he looked at Timothy, still standing in the middle of the room, wearing that inward look which meant that he was imagining himself not to be there at all. "Let's have the story," he commanded.

"It was nothing," said Timothy. But he saw from his father's look that "nothing" would not be enough. He swallowed, and began: "There was a big tea-tent, and long tables. The food was there already. We could hardly get in, it was so crowded. All the schools. But natives mostly. We tried to sit down, and someone —a girl—sort of pushed Martha so she had nowhere to sit."

"They were so rude," said Martha primly. "They never said please and thank-you. They just snatched!"

"How about that fight?" asked David.

Timothy took up his tale. "We were just standing there, behind the people sitting down. So I reached over to try to get some sandwiches. A boy tried to stop me, so I pushed him. Then I got a sandwich, and gave it to Martha, and I tried to get another one for myself. Then another boy stood up and pushed me away. So I pushed him back, hard."

"What happened then?"

"He fell into some jelly."

Quite a climax, thought David, and managed to hide his smile. He had rather enjoyed the picture, in short snapshot sentences, of a boy and girl starving in this unfair wilderness. But there were other parental comments to be made.

"You shouldn't have done that," he said. "Especially if they were native children. They were probably—well, hungrier than you."

"But it was *our* party," said Timothy rebelliously. "Not just for them."

"We were jolly hungry," said Martha in support.

"Hungry or not, you've got to learn to share."

"But *they* weren't sharing. They were taking everything."

The ethics of the situation were not clear-cut; perhaps it would be best to leave them. Nicole, with the same thought, asked:

"What happened then? Didn't you get anything to eat at all?"

"Not much," said Timothy. "A teacher came and took us to another table by ourselves. The table with all the lemonade jugs on it. Everybody was staring at us. . . . We had some lettuce sandwiches, and then they said the cake was all finished, *and* the jelly. So we had some more lettuce sandwiches. Then we found Gloria, by the clock tower, like you said, and we came home."

"Is this all absolutely true?"

"Yes, Daddy."

"All right," said David after a moment. "Case dismissed."

Timothy beamed instantly. This was the most welcome family phrase, as far as discipline was concerned: borrowed, he knew, from the days when his father had been the magistrate and sole law-giver up at Shebiya. It lifted all burdens, blew away all clouds, because it meant exactly what it said. . . . He rejoined Martha at the table, gave her a not-more-than-brotherly elbow nudge in the ribs, and bent to the stamp-collection again. Presently he raised his head:

"Daddy?"

"M'm?"

"Will we have some new stamps for Pharamaul?"

"Yes."

"When, Daddy?"

"Soon. In about three weeks. They're on their way from England."

"What will they be like? Will they have the Queen's head on them?"

"Yes. And pictures as well."

"What sort of pictures?"

"Let's see. . . . One has a *katlagter* bird, one has a crayfish, and one has an Afrikander bull." David knew the importance of detail to a collector. "There's a fourpenny, a ninepenny, and a one-and-nine."

"Gosh! That's two-and-ten altogether. . . . Can I have a set?"

"We'll see."

"Smashing! But why do we only have three stamps?"

"Because we're only a small country."

"But Ghana had *nine* when they had their new set."

"That's up to them."

"Who decided for us?"

"There was a committee."

"Were you on it?"

"Yes. . . ." David looked up at the clock. "Isn't it about your supper time?"

"Supper time," said Nicole loyally. "And then bed. Go and find Gloria."

There was less than the usual chorus of protest; it had been a long, hot, and tiring day. Martha, coming up behind her father's chair to kiss him goodnight, said:

"Daddy, you've got a pond."

"A what?"

"A pond." She touched the top of his head. "A pond in your hair."

"Oh. . . . How big is it?"

Martha considered. "About a sixpence."

"Tell me when it gets to half a crown."

Nicole, returning later from the kitchen, found David in an

agony of contortion, trying to look at the top of his head in the mirror at the same time as he made a gingerly exploration with his forefinger. He straightened up, slightly shamefaced, when he saw her.

"I'm going bald, damn it."

"It suits you," said Nicole, without thinking too carefully.

"What do you mean, it suits me? I'm *not* going bald! It's just one tiny little patch. It's the top of the parting, actually."

"That's what I meant, darling. It's perfectly natural. I wonder where on earth Martha got that word 'pond.'"

"Made me feel like some wretched old monk." David sat down again, and stretched out wearily. "Oh well, I *am* forty-three. . . . God, what a day this has been!"

"But a good one."

"Oh, yes. The best yet, in a way. You know, I suddenly felt, this afternoon, that we really had taken a step forward, that we'd made a bit of worthwhile history. Except for a few silly bastards like Woodcock, I think there's enormous good will over this whole thing."

"I felt the same way. . . . Did you notice, when Timmy was talking about the stamps, he called them *our* stamps? He said, why are *we* only going to have three? It sounded funny when he first said it, and then it sounded just right."

"Even after that sad tea-party."

"Especially after that."

The lights burned late in the Port Victoria Club, falling alike on marble pillars, shabby red carpeting, panelled walls, and the rows and rows of monarchs, governors, pro-consuls, club presidents, and visitors of note, whose photographs, spotted with age, faintly autographed in violet ink, lined every available corridor. Normally the bar closed at eleven o'clock; but on this auspicious day there could be no question of such calamity, and an impromptu extraordinary general meeting, duly convened round the mantelpiece, voted itself the necessary powers to stay open indefinitely. Attended by yawning, drooping club-servants who were also voted a grudging bonus of two shillings a head, the bar trade was still thriving at one A.M.

Foremost among the late contributors, Splinter Woodcock held court at the center of a sweating, boozy group which was now on its fourth bottle of Scotch. Coats had long ago been discarded,

34

and ties loosened to mid-chest; under the slow-turning punkahs which gently scythed the gloom above them, the leading solid citizens of Pharamaul took their ease and their pleasure.

Biggs-Johnson was there, drinking in the shadow of his leader; and Binkie Buchanan, whose ancient Rolls-Royce decorated every gathering of consequence in Port Victoria; and half a dozen others, good fellows all who could never have missed this sort of celebration, even though there was, in fact, damned little to celebrate tonight.

As an honorary member for the day, Tulbach Browne was also one of the group, drinking at his leisure while his tiny lapel microphone did all the work, lapping up in the process some absolute gems.

Splinter Woodcock, a very old campaigner whose rocklike head concealed the fact that he was now monumentally drunk, had told and retold the story of how he had "ticked off that chap Bracken," who in the end "hadn't had a word to say for himself." They all agreed that this had been a notable victory, worth another round any day, and that David Bracken, for some very funny reasons, seemed to have gone absolutely native. The talk was now on the future, and the gloomy horizon which independence was mapping out for them all.

"I'll tell you something else," said Splinter Woodcock, who had already told everyone a great deal. "There'll be black members of this club, before the year's out. I'll bet you anything you like!"

"Dinamaula's a member already," said Binkie Buchanan, a bluff character who had made all his money—which was a great deal— out of one ship which plied to and fro between Cape Town and Port Victoria. "So it's hardly a bet."

"Don't count him," said Splinter Woodcock. "We had to let him in, I suppose. The old Governor put him up. But I mean, *hordes* of natives. Swamping the place. They did it in Nairobi, I happen to know. They just couldn't keep them out. Now they have a bunch of black loafers sitting up at the bar like a lot of dummies, with one glass of beer between them, and six straws. They make it last half the day! You can't run a club like that!"

"You can't keep them out, though," said Biggs-Johnson. "Not now."

"How about Rule Eighteen?" asked a voice from the outer fringe.

"What's Rule Eighteen, for God's sake?"

"Balloting for new members. Two black balls exclude."

There was a roar of laughter. Splinter Woodcock wheezed: "That's a bloody good one! Two black balls!" while the impassive Maula servant at his elbow emptied his ashtray. Tulbach Browne, though he had heard the joke before, smirked his approval dutifully. It often seemed to him that he had heard *all* this before, wherever the British were packing up and leaving: the same alarm, the same readiness to take failure for granted, the same sick relish with which they awaited defeat. And, always, the same reaching for the same bottle. . . . He decided to probe a little further, and in the silence after the burst of laughter he asked:

"I suppose you'll have a native legislature as well?"

"Got it already," said Splinter Woodcock promptly. "Half of it, anyway. And a useless bunch of bastards they are, too. I'd like to put 'em up against a wall and shoot the lot."

"Steady on, old boy," said Binkie Buchanan. He glanced towards Tulbach Browne. "Strangers present."

"Oh, he's all right. He's one of us. . . . Anyway, what's the use of hiding things? Of course we'll end up with a black house. A hundred-per-cent Maula zoo. And a bloody awful job they'll make of it, too!"

"Well, you're on the blasted council, old boy. Do something about it."

Woodcock stuck out a belligerent chin. "What do you mean, do something about it? What the hell can I do?"

"Get reelected, for a start. You and all the others. Make sure there's still a fair-sized bunch of whites in the legislature."

"You mean, *electioneer*? Hold meetings? Go round P.V. scratching up votes?"

"Why not?"

"I wouldn't canvass these bastards if you paid me ten quid a head," answered Splinter Woodcock contemptuously. "Who do you think I am—a bloody commercial traveller? If they want me in the legislature, let them go ahead and elect me. If they don't, that's *their* bad luck, not mine."

"But you'll get slung out if you don't put up a show."

"Then I'll get slung out." He brought his fat palms together with a sharp slapping sound. "*Bar!* Bring another round. Pronto!"

"Not for me, thanks," said Tulbach Browne, and stood up. "I've got some work to do. And some sleep to catch up as well."

"Are you going to write something about Pharamaul?" asked Biggs-Johnson.

"Well, I might. . . . These independence things are pretty well routine by now."

"You're damned right they're routine," said Woodcock. "And what happens afterwards is routine, too." He gulped enormously at his new drink, and set down the glass with a crash. "*One,* they take over. *Two,* they chuck away all the money, or steal it. *Three,* they go broke. *Four,* there's a revolution, or an army take-over. *Five,* the whole thing starts up again with a new lot."

"Is that your forecast for Pharamaul?" asked Tulbach Browne.

"That's my forecast, and you can have it buckshee. Give it a couple of years, and this country will be flat broke. We all will, unless we're smart and get out while the getting's good. I'll bet you anything you like"—he pointed a pudgy, wavering finger at Binkie Buchanan—"that they'll nationalize your ship, and then let it rot alongside the quay."

"She's up for sale, anyway," said Buchanan, and winked broadly.

"Then you'd better hurry up and find a buyer, before they bloody well swipe it. And I'll bet you another thing, too—yours'll be the last Rolls-Royce in Pharamaul."

2: DESPITE THE DIFFICULTIES OF THE PAST

TULBACH BROWNE's piece in the *Daily Thresh* was well up to standard. It covered a full half-page; but it was chopped up into those short, bite-sized sticks of prose which, like sugar-coated cornflakes, the *Daily Thresh's* readers found easiest to digest. It was, all knowing hands agreed, well worth T.B.'s having missed his deadline.

PORT VICTORIA, PHARAMAUL. (*Delayed.*)

"Delayed" is a polite way of saying that Pharamaul, the latest of our emerging paradises, is not yet geared to a working newsman's schedule. "Come back tomorrow" might be the local motto. But no matter. Time in this sluggish part of the world is never vital.

Pharamaul—so say the experts on the spot—will not go away. Not for a couple of years, anyway.

I witnessed today yet another in the interminable series of "Independence Days," celebrating the "end of slavery" for some and "kowtowing to the niggers" for others, when a new country sets out on the highroad to freedom, with a golden handshake from the British taxpayer.

This time it was Pharamaul; and if you are not entirely sure where—or even what—Pharamaul is, then you may join the club.

In fact it is a half-asleep island off the west coast of southern Africa. It is small, it is hot; it grows gaunt cattle and catches small fish. It has 200,000 inhabitants, which makes it about the size of Plymouth or Harrow.

As from today, this African Plymouth/Harrow is an independent country; and if you suspect that it might not be a

38

viable one—the current jargon for being able to stand on its own two feet without resort to the begging-bowl—then you may, once again, join the club.

But who are the people who will be trying to make a go of it? Whom do we leave behind, with the white man's burden and the best of British luck?

At the top, for the moment, is the Governor-General, the Earl of Urle. I say "for the moment," because these ungrateful countries have a habit of kicking out the Queen's representative at the first opportunity, and electing their own president instead.

But for the moment, the Earl it is; the Labour peer whose last speech in the House of Lords besought us to "give homosexuals a fair deal." His speech at the Independence Day ceremony was on a loftier plane. It besought the good citizens of Pharamaul to "march forward together towards a happy and prosperous future."

Judging by his Lordship's reception, the good citizens would much prefer to stay right where they are, squatting on their hunkers and waiting for that happy future to drop into their laps.

The noble lord will be assisted in his labours by the Countess of Urle, whom he married in a Mexican ceremony last year. She is better known to the swinging world as Bobo Tempest, high priestess of the Rhyming Rudery, whose very personal "O Come! All Ye Faithful" sent clerics into a tizzy, and several other great and good friends scurrying for more cover than they seem to have enjoyed in the past.

There was no doubt at all about *her* reception. Except for a handful of stuffy old-timers, who still thought that, at an official vice-regal ceremony, Her Excellency's skirts should at least reach the knee, the good citizens, black and white, thought she was a dish.

Next on our list of assorted top people is the man of the moment, Pharamaul's first Prime Minister, Dinamaula. Pharamaul loves him dearly; it may be that the British Government loves him a bit less dearly, since in 1956 they exiled him for five years for general misbehaviour, and only allowed him back to his native land seven years ago.

However, tastes change, governments switch their options, and all is now forgiven. Dinamaula is now at the top of the heap, with official blessings and best wishes. Since he did not afford me the courtesy of an interview, I am unable to report how his improved fortunes have affected him.

However, he looked happy enough, as well he might. He now has power, money in the bank, and a free hand.

Last on this list is the British-appointed Chief Secretary, Mr. David Bracken, c.m.g., m.c. I first met Mr. Bracken twelve years ago, when he was a junior member of the Governor's staff in Port Victoria. Time, as they say, flies. But junior or not, he had some very senior ideas, even then.

He didn't like the Press, and one must admit that the Press didn't like him. It was his appointed task to persuade us that Dinamaula deserved his exile; and when we tried to probe a little deeper—such as asking "Why?"—Mr. Bracken's reaction was dramatic, not to say hysterical.

It was all our fault, he told us, for "stirring up trouble." Without the Press to poison it, Pharamaul would have been paradise itself.

Since, when I tried to talk to him today, he was curt to the point of rudeness, it is safe to say that he still feels the same way.

However, it *was* a hot day; and a sword, a high tight collar, and a helmet adorned with cock's feathers is not exactly the gear guaranteed to improve the disposition.

Back in 1956, it was no coincidence that Mr. Bracken was chosen as the "conducting officer" to accompany Dinamaula on his flight into exile—i.e., to see him safely off the premises. He had been the official hatchet-boy from the start. Now Mr. B. is staying on, as the head of Pharamaul's civil-service machine.

It is a curious choice; and not the least curious part of it is Dinamaula's agreement. One would have thought there would still be plenty of bad blood between them. However, neither of them could or would enlighten me on this point. Nor, indeed, on any other.

I was left to enjoy the delirious pleasures of a Government House garden party, a stuffed relic of the Victorian era, which was a depressing kickoff for Pharamaul's coming-of-age.

I had more luck later on in the plush mausoleum known as the Port Victoria Club. There, they at least had the guts to speak their minds, even if some of those minds seemed nearer, in size and scope, to pickled walnuts than human brains.

I heard stern talk of putting the Negro members of the legislature up against a wall and shooting them. True, this does happen in other parts of Africa, but it was odd to hear it from a white elected representative, Mr. Terence Woodcock, o.b.e., known to his friends as "Splinter."

Mr. Woodcock was in no doubt about Pharamaul's future. The country, he prophesied, would be broke within two years.

Would he be standing for reelection to the legislature? "If they don't elect me," said Mr. Woodcock, "that's their bad luck. They'll finish up with a hundred-per-cent black zoo."

Worse still, in his view, there were going to be black club-members, right here on the premises. Horrors! The whisky flowed like water as the company contemplated this frightful prospect.

As I left, "Splinter" Woodcock was solemnly warning one of his fellow-members: "You are driving the last Rolls-Royce in Pharamaul."

I do not know what will happen to Pharamaul after we have packed up. It seems likely that its future, like the life of man in the seventeenth century, will be nasty, brutish, and short.

That word is brutish, not (as you might suppose) British.

But if this is all we leave behind us, after 126 years—a sodden wake, a tear-stained Rolls-Royce, a forlorn show of cocked hats, and a Chief humiliated, sacked, and then re-imported as Prime Minister—then why in God's name were we ever there in the first place?

We were there in the first place, David Bracken thought irritably, as any bloody fool knew, because no one else wanted to take Pharamaul on, at a time when it was being reduced to chaos and ruin by tribal warfare. True, Britain had some minor trading interests there; and there had been a vague idea, when first the island came into the news, that if anyone was going to walk in it had better be the British rather than the Germans, who, once installed there, would be squarely astride the sea-routes to the Cape.

But the Germans, like everyone else in the scramble for Africa, were there for loot rather than strategy; and this latter concept had only been someone's stray tea-time thought on a Foreign Office memorandum, *circa* 1840. By and large, Britain had gone in to restore order, an abiding national passion long before and ever since.

David laid aside the three-day-old Secretariat copy of the *Daily Thresh*, and, his thoughts reaching for the past rather than the present, opened one of the lower drawers of his desk. From it he took out a dog-eared yellowing sheaf of papers bound with pink tape, blew the dust off the top sheet, and laid the pile in front of him. It was Andrew Macmillan's ancient, never-to-be-finished *History of Pharamaul.*

When David Bracken had first come out to Pharamaul, Macmillan, the Resident Commissioner up at Gamate, had been his chief mentor and friend: a wise, cynical, set-in-his-ways colonial administrator near the end of a career dedicated without stint to this unrewarding corner of the world.

As a first briefing on the country, he had given David his manuscript to read, though almost shyly; and when he later died, in despair and defeat, brought down by the bloody violence which had made Dinamaula's exile essential, David had promised himself to finish the book—because of all that the other man had done for him, and especially because of the way Andrew had died, beaten by Pharamaul.

But in fact he had never added a word to it, and sometimes he was ashamed of the fact. He was ashamed at this moment, as he looked down at the messy, forlorn stack of pages. Macmillan had been writing the book, or trying to write it, for the last fifteen years of his life; it was to be his testament, the best he could do, by way of judgement and witness, for the country which had shackled him. The crabbed writing of the first paragraph, which David knew nearly by heart, was thus more than twenty-seven years old:

The Principality of Pharamaul came into official existence on the fifteenth day of April, 1842, by Royal Decree. A company of Her Majesty's Foot Guards having been brought in to quell an insurrection which threatened British trading interests, both at Port Victoria and in the interior, they stayed to ensure public order; and thereafter a Lieutenant-Governor, Sir Hugo Fortescue-Hambleton, was appointed (in the words of the proclamation) "to re-establish the rule of law, inculcate the principles of good administration, and work towards such degree of self-determination as the inhabitants' best endeavors, and Her Majesty's Government, may from time to time decide." From that moment, Pharamaul was a British Protectorate under the Crown.

Well, they had kept their word, thought David, and now they had gone the first full step beyond it. Without Britain, Pharamaul would have been nothing; now at last it was something. It was on the map as a separate country, where before it had been two half-starved warring tribes, eternally at each other's throats, fighting murderously for goats and sand.

The process had taken a long time, and cost the lives of many good men: generations of the younger sons of England, pitchforked into this waste and told to get on with it. Willing or not, content or rebellious, they had got on with it to good purpose.

To show for their labours and lives and deaths, Pharamaul had achieved some modest blessings which, in the light of the grim past, were more like modest miracles. Most of the tropical diseases had been conquered; enteric and hookworm no longer doomed men to lie down and die; the Medical Officer of Health had replaced the witch-doctor, after a long, patient, and cunning battle; and cow-dung was not now the specific ointment for raw wounds.

There was much more to eat. Water conservation had trebled

the crops and multiplied the livestock; the huge wandering herds of goats, which had once been the sole measure of prestige in Maula life, and which could strip a hillside bare in a day's grazing, had been culled to reasonable proportions. Though Tulbach Browne's dig at "gaunt cattle" was still fairly near the mark, the breeds had been improved; meat was now a staple food instead of bizarre luxury, and the hides, exported from the abattoir at Port Victoria, made a profit and paid men's wages. An entirely new crop, groundnuts, was being pressed for oil and cattle-food.

Most Maulas still lived on the land, and clung to it, and believed in nothing else. But there were three thriving sawmills to support a logging industry; there was the big fish-canning plant up at Fish Village, now branching out into such exotic fare as tinned crayfish tails. The harbour had been deepened and improved; the repair dockyard could take ships up to 5,000 tons. Most exotic and incomprehensible of all, a satellite-tracking station had been set up on a hilltop on the west coast, and there strange mad men from England and even America watched the heavens and talked to each other all night.

Half the people could read and write. Half was not enough for a literate election, and the coming contest would still be fought under signs instead of names. Yet fifty per cent was better than most of Africa, and, with big new schools and big new hospitals to back them up, the children of Pharamaul were marching steadily towards their privilege, pushing the percentage up every day.

It was not dramatic, any of it; the "colonialist" taunt was still heard from the sophisticates whenever Pharamaul was mentioned, as if the pace of Africa, traditional and stubborn for a thousand years, could be shoved through the sonic barrier just by wishing it so. Yet motives and methods had changed immeasurably over the years; Britain, having come to pacify and discipline, had remained to educate and develop; and she was now, in all good faith, handing over the result as a modest going concern.

Because of the size and structure of the country, there had been deep misgivings about it in London, and the pace had been set deliberately slow, so that Pharamaul could grow into freedom rather than swallow it whole at the touch of a wand. If it had to come, let it have a fair working chance. . . . Bringing back

Dinamaula from his exile had been the first step, and with that, David Bracken had been intimately concerned.

He could still remember making the flight back from London with Dinamaula, an exact reversal of the strange and awkward journey of five years earlier, when he had "conducted" the exiled chief out of Pharamaul. Then, he had had a bitter young man on his hands, a young man who felt, in his own words, that he "had been treated like a little boy," and hustled out of his homeland as the scapegoat for his country's troubles.

On the return journey, they had both been wary of each other. So much depended on how this thing went; a careless word might estrange them, and a careless act might harvest a whole new crop of troubles. But they had got on well, as they usually did in private; in the five-year interval they had both grown up, more than enough to recognize that the past was the past, and that an old grudge, like an old suspicion, could with forbearance be buried for ever.

The flight had proved exhilarating for both of them; and the uproarious, triumphant welcome home had been Pharamaul's confirmation that (as David Bracken had reported, times without number) the Maulas would have Dinamaula as their chief, and no other man.

It might have turned his head, or given him that touch of overconfidence which grew into rashness or arrogance. But it did not. Dinamaula had settled down to work with sober determination. There were no backward glances towards London, where he had once been lionized, and where a cheaper popularity was always waiting for him.

He had come home to stay; his heart and mind and both his feet were in Pharamaul, and nowhere else. Very soon after he arrived, he had married a Maula girl from Gamate, as if embracing with her, once and for all, his own country and people.

David's job had been to watch him, and to report on the prospects for the future. Going well beyond this, he had thrown all his weight on the side of independence for Pharamaul, with Dinamaula as the only possible choice for Prime Minister.

Official misgivings had not lessened with the years. There had been many discouraging talks with David's old chief, Sir Hubert Godbold, head of the Scheduled Territories Office, which still held Pharamaul's future within its cautious hand. Godbold, a wise and liberal civil servant who had watched, and in his time initiated, some mighty changes in Britain's colonial holding, could not bring himself to be hopeful about the future.

"I still don't like it," he had said on one occasion, when they were sitting in his room, long after office hours, going over the prospects for the hundredth time. The view outside was a world away from Pharamaul; in place of the crystal-clear air and the harsh sunlight, there was only Whitehall on a Friday evening—gloomy, wet, tired out, beset by the rumble and roar of home-going traffic. "I agree with you that the pressures on us to make a move are tremendous—this is the way the world is going, and we'd be damned fools to try to stop it. Particularly in Africa. But Pharamaul! How on earth can they ever make a go of it?"

"I think they have a good chance," answered David. He cared enough about this to be unusually stubborn, in a way he would never have dreamed of, a few years earlier; and nothing made him more stubborn than to be thousands of miles away from Pharamaul, fighting its battles on what now felt like alien ground.

He missed his adopted country all the time; even after a short week's leave, London seemed artificial, and unconcerned, and damnably overcrowded. Wherever he went he felt like the classic colonial visitor, standing in odd clothes at the corner of Regent Street and Piccadilly Circus, homeless and bored and lonely. He wanted to be back at work; back in Pharamaul, the only place which was real. . . . "Of course it will need help," he went on. "But it really has a better chance than lots of other places. It's more—more compact, more manageable."

"It is also a great deal smaller," said Godbold. "Pharamaul will need at least two million pounds a year for the next ten years—not as a loan, either, but a direct grant. That is dependence, not independence."

"It's costing us something like that already."

"Maybe it is. But at present we know exactly where the money goes, and we can control it."

"We could still control it, in a way."

"How?"

"By refusing it, if we think it's being wasted."

Godbold smiled bleakly. "And be branded as hardhearted and ungenerous tyrants? My dear David, I can see the banners now.

'Britain Deserts Pharamaul.' 'Down with Colonial Dictatorship.' 'No Strings.' We've been through all that before, I think."

"But sir, it *needn't* happen like that. We may have nothing to complain of at all, as far as spending is concerned. And if everything goes the way we hope, Pharamaul will start to make its own money."

"Out of fish and scrub cattle?"

"That would have to be the basis. But of course we'd start thinking about secondary industries."

"Plastic knobkerries, I suppose." Godbold really was in a bad mood tonight. "Well, we'll see, we'll see. At the moment, I'm afraid, you must count me among the opposition."

David was stung to indiscretion. "Sir, if that's so, we'll *never* get it."

"Who is 'we'?"

"I mean, Pharamaul."

Godbold was looking at him sharply. He seemed to be on the verge of a rebuke, since David's remark had switched the whole topic into a kind of personal framework, with more than a hint that Godbold had an unfair advantage which he would not scruple to use. That was the way people earned their permanent black marks, and ended up in the low, low reaches of the Archives Department. . . . Godbold was tapping impatiently on his desk with a silver paper knife shaped like a cutlass, looking quite ready to use it against such sulky mutineers as this. Then suddenly he relaxed, and laid the ominous weapon aside, and asked:

"If it went through, would you be prepared to stay on in Pharamaul?"

"Oh yes." There could never be any doubt about that.

"Well, in spite of what I've said, I would envy you."

It was clear that Godbold meant it, though he did not look at all like a man willing to serve again in a new and chancy country. He only had a year to go before his retirement, and his face was now grey and weary. The years of service had taken their toll; and all he would have to show for them, after four decades at the center of affairs, would be a brilliant, untarnished reputation within the narrowest of circles, one or two modest directorships, a decoration round his collar on state occasions, and a pension of one-half—or, as the Civil Service Commissioners preferred to phrase it, forty-eightieths—of his final salary of £6,500 a year.

As between Britain and Sir Hubert Godbold, K.C.M.G., there could be no doubt who had had the best of the bargain.

"Well, let us drink to the future, whatever it is," he said, and rose from his chair. Godbold kept a modest bar in his room, and did not care who knew it; if there were those who thought that the Permanent Under-Secretary for the Scheduled Territories should not have a drink whenever he felt like it, then that was just too bad. . . . "Sherry or gin? Or whisky?"

"Gin, please. Gin and tonic."

"That we can do." Godbold busied himself with glasses. Over his shoulder he said: "How's the leave going?"

"All right, sir. I'd rather be back."

Godbold laughed. "That's what Andrew always used to say. He thought London was a perfectly terrible place, compared with Pharamaul."

"I know just how he felt."

That had been three years earlier. David Bracken had returned to Pharamaul empty-handed and depressed, to report to Dinamaula, among other people, that things were still "very sticky." But then the gears moved again, and the car of state with them. Suddenly the whole subject of Pharamaul's independence was stamped "Approved in principle"; and though the weasel words could mask a decade of niggling argument, at least the basic signal had been given. After that, it was a matter of hard facts, hard bargaining, and hard work.

A new constitution was hammered out, after consultation at every level, from the Council of Chiefs in Pharamaul to the Law Officers of the Crown in darkest Strand, W.C.2. Since all this had happened before, from British Guiana to Zanzibar, there were plenty of constitutions to choose from; the one selected, David thought irreverently at the time, was probably marked "Small & Slender"—an 850-cc. constitution, tropic-tested, with modest acceleration and really good brakes.

Once it was settled, there followed an inevitable procession of events, labels, and targets, sounding as dull and dusty as legal parchment, but disposing, as legal parchment did, of the flesh and blood of living, hopeful, and yearning men.

Entrenched clauses to safeguard the future. Setting up a Legislature (twelve appointed members, twelve elected). All new

District Commissioners to be Maulas. Full-scale elections to be held within six months of independence (one man, one vote, all twenty-four members to be elected by ballot). No upper house. Defense and foreign affairs to remain in British hands. A Governor-General to represent the Queen, acknowledged as Head of State. "Reserved powers" for the Crown in case of armed insurrection or public violence. Police, civil service, and judiciary to be "Maularized" at a suitable pace, starting now.

This technical bread-and-butter, in such large quantities, had been barely digestible within the time allotted. Before long, independence, which had seemed such a slow process, had come to look, to David Bracken, more like a rush job. However hard he had worked, and however swift had been Dinamaula's cooperation, the loose ends seemed to multiply, like a fraying rope which would not come under control. The longest and loosest end of all had still to be dealt with, as independence dawned. It was the coming election.

This was going to be difficult enough anyway. The vast majority of adult Maulas and U-Maulas, totally unsophisticated, would have no idea what it was all about. They could not read. They had a hereditary chief already. What was this election? Was it to bring his rule into question, as had happened before? Or was it a cunning way of increasing taxes?

For David Bracken it seemed to hold the seeds of every kind of headache. The direst of all was the idea of an "official opposition," with official blessing. To the average citizen of Pharamaul, opposition meant seizing a spear and quenching it in an enemy, preferably between his shoulder blades. A man either fought, or he was at peace. Yet now they were being invited, by implication, to pick such a quarrel artificially; to choose, if they wished, a man who would go down to Port Victoria and defy their chief. If this was what the Old Queen wished, was she then against Dinamaula? What was a man to think?

The only true basis for an opposition party would be a division on tribal lines, the old North and South split which had once brought the country to ruin, and was the very last thing to be revived.

As one looked at other, torn parts of Africa, David thought, it was doubtful whether the polite and stately rules of the Mother of Parliaments were really suitable for export. It might be that,

49

with the noblest of motives, they were inviting Pharamaul to go the same way.

Dinamaula had once taken him aback, when they were talking about the future Legislature, by remarking: "Well, we have plenty of candidates for Black Rod!" Dinamaula was so rarely ribald that this slur upon a noble office had a double edge. If the Prime Minister himself couldn't take Black Rod seriously. . . .

The phone on his desk rang, and it was the man he had been thinking about. But the Prime Minister's first words were something of a shock. The slow, heavy voice inquired:

"Can I speak to the official hatchet-boy?"

"What's that?" asked David, taken by surprise.

There was a laugh from the other end of the line. "Don't tell me you haven't read your *Daily Thresh?*"

"Oh, that." David suddenly remembered, with a slight embarrassment. "Tulbach Browne. . . ."

"He was in splendid form, didn't you think?"

"I'd like to wring his neck," said David. Then he remembered the courtesies. "Good morning, Prime Minister. I'm glad you're not too annoyed about the article, anyway."

"I was ready for it," said Dinamaula, "and so were you. Now, presumably, he'll leave us alone for a bit. God knows we've got enough to do, without any barracking from the spectators."

"He won't come back till something goes wrong. So he won't come back."

"What a pleasant thought. . . . There are one or two things I want to talk about. Nothing special. Are you busy at the moment?"

"Well, I have some of the Chamber of Trade people coming to see me. But——"

"No, don't change anything. Let's have lunch instead."

"I'd like that," answered David. "Shall I meet you at the club?"

"That should make Mr. Splinter Woodcock very happy," said Dinamaula, on a sudden grating note. "*Black* members!"

So he had been made angry, after all. David put as much force as he could into his answer:

"I've a damned good mind to have Woodcock up before the committee!"

"What for?"

"Discussing club affairs with a non-member. It's absolutely un-heard of! It's against all the form."

"I think you'll find," said Dinamaula, "that Tulbach Browne *was* a member. Just for that day. So technically . . ." he paused, and then his voice changed. "Oh hell, what does it matter, any-way? Black skins are thick as well. Any scientist will tell you. . . . I'll see you later, David."

"One o'clock?"

"One o'clock." Dinamaula's voice changed again, to a very fair imitation of the Earl of Urle's demoniac tones. "Let us march forward together towards a happy and prosperous lunch."

3: UNDER THE WISE GUIDANCE OF

WITHIN THE PORT VICTORIA BRANCH of Barclays Bank (D.C.O.), all was quiet and drowsy and peaceful. The sunlight, slanting through slatted blinds, fell on the black-and-white tiled floor as gently as a caressing hand; the big punkah fans murmured like doves. It was mid-morning, and customers were few; the nine-o'clock depositors had been and gone, the noontime housewives had not yet arrived to collect their spending money. Solemn as church, solid as quarried marble, kindly as Juliet's nurse, Barclays was keeping its daily rendezvous with history.

The two old men who shuffled in through the swing doors were like a thousand other old men to be seen on the streets of Port Victoria. They were barefooted, but that was nothing new in a land where the earth was warm and shoes cost good money; their dusty blankets and yellow beehive hats were the time-honoured uniform of Pharamaul.

They looked a little out of place in a bank; but, like misers who dress in rags and yet have seventy-five thousand pounds in their current account, they were acceptable, whether in disguise or not. When they walked up to the teller nearest the door, no one gave them more than a second glance.

But soon all Barclays was looking at them, because in the silence their voices were loud and their words unusual. Arrived at the counter, they said, in firm and perfect unison:

"Give us money."

The bank teller, an alert young man who sometimes pictured himself as a hero at a moment of crisis, with swift promotion to follow, came to attention instantly. But the new arrivals were not armed, nor menacing in any way; they were just two old men with their hands held out. The teller asked, as he had asked a hundred times before of tourists and other strangers:

"Have you an account here?"

The two old men looked at each other, as though confronted by some absolutely strange thing; then the elder, whose wisp of white beard gave him authority, asked:

"What is account?"

To a large and rapt audience, the teller answered: "It means, do you have money here? Are you a customer?"

The spokesman shook his head. "We have no money here, *barena*. *You* have money. That is why we ask."

The beautiful logic of this was not to the teller's taste. He answered firmly: "If you have no account, then of course you cannot draw money from the bank."

"But we have seen it done," the old man explained patiently. "We have watched the Europeans. When they want money, they come here and ask for it, and you give it to them. Now this is our country. The chief told us so. So now it is our money."

The teller leant forward against the mahogany counter, friendly, helpful, almost confidential. With equal patience he explained:

"The Europeans are given the money because it is theirs. Each one has an account."

The younger of the two old men asked again: "What is this account?"

"It means that they have put money into the bank. So now they can take it out."

"Why do they put it in, if they wish to take it out again?"

Privately, in the case of certain small and whirling accounts, this had puzzled the teller also. But he knew the textbook answer:

"That is how a bank works. You give money to the bank to look after, and when you want it, you ask for it, and it is given back to you."

"We can look after it ourselves," said the leader, "if we have it."

Some subdued giggling from the typing section at the back of the room warned the teller that the scene had gone on long enough. He stood up straight again.

"I'm sorry. There is nothing I can do about that. There is no money for you in the bank."

"Is this true?"

"Yes, it is true."

The two old men watched as, at the very next wicket, a red-faced man in a silk suit and jaunty panama said: "I'd like two five-pound notes and five singles," and was given his money straight away. They looked at each other. There was something here which was difficult to understand, which was not to be believed without great faith in the white man's word. In the meantime, it was a moment for courtesy. They touched their beehive hats, and the elder man said: "We will return when we have talked of this." Then they walked out of the bank again, their manner betraying nothing, their dignity still theirs.

Not till they were outside did they begin to shake their heads.

Far up-country on the Oosthuizen farm, which had seen such fearful bloodshed in the old days, there was another episode of the same sort; but the rural version had a cruel note to it, and was not to be solved so amicably. Oosthuizen's was now farmed by the cousin who had inherited it, another South African called Piet Vermeulen, and Vermeulen had a curious story to tell when next he came down to the Port Victoria Club. There he found an attentive audience, which had a special interest in this kind of thing.

"Those bloody *kaffirs!*" he began, in that deep guttural voice which was more at home in Afrikaans. "You never know what they'll get up to next. Like a bunch of bloody kids! D'you know, some of them actually trekked in and settled on my land! Two whole families of them, about sixteen kids, with goats and chickens and God knows what. They just moved in, without a word to anyone, put up a couple of *rondavels*, and planted a mealie-patch as if they owned the place!"

"I hope you kicked them out, good and hard," said Binkie Buchanan, as Piet Vermeulen paused to take a swig at his beer. "There's a damned sight too much of that sort of thing, these days."

"You're damned right, I kicked them out," said Vermeulen, "but it wasn't as easy as all that. To start with, they'd been there more than a month before I heard anything about it. It's a bit of worthless land up where the high veld begins. All scrub and cactus. You have to walk a mile for a bucket of water from the *spruit*. To tell the truth, I never look at it, from one year's end to another, and I wouldn't have known a thing if one of my herd-boys hadn't mentioned it. He thought I must have given them permission."

54

"What happened then?"

"I went along double-quick and told them to bugger off. D'you know, they actually had the sauce to start arguing! There was one of them, a great big sweaty buck who seemed to be the boss, telling me the tale. Christ, I can hear him now! 'This is our land. Dinamaula said so. We're free to settle down anywhere we like.' Pretty rich, wouldn't you say?"

"I'll bet you told him a thing or two," said Binkie Buchanan, outraged.

Piet Vermeulen grinned. "I did my best, by God! In the old days, I'd have been after the lot of them with a *sjambok*. Or my ridgebacks would have seen them off the premises, minus the seat of their pants. But this is a bloody democracy! First I had to argue, then I had to send for the police. *They* soon moved them on, I can tell you. But honestly, would you believe it?"

"I'd believe anything, these days."

"Disgraceful!"

Yet it still had not been easy, even with the police. The intruders would not move for the law, any more than for Piet Vermeulen. They said, again and again: "This is our country, so this is now our land." They claimed that the police were wrong, that there were many new laws which said that a man could now do this and that. They said that the police must protect their rights, not drive them away like dogs.

They said that the police should drive the white man away, since this was not his land any more. . . . They would not yield to reason, they would not give way to threats. There was a new law, they shouted desperately, even as they warded off the blows, and the land now belonged to any man in Pharamaul who needed it, and would work it.

In the end, four of them were taken off to jail, and the rest of the squatters were pushed and shoved out beyond the farm boundaries, with their women and children and goats. They were flicked with oxthongs, and told to keep moving till they reached their own village again, and not to come back. The *rondavels* with their thatched roofs were burned down, and the mealie-patch left to the crows.

After the first brave defiance, there was only ragged shambling retreat, and women wailing, and a half-grown boy calling out: "Then what is new in this country?" before he ran away.

• • •

Simon the cook-houseboy had a shameful secret, and only Gloria the nursegirl knew it. Gloria, a sophisticated Port Victoria girl whose getup on her "day off" was positively startling, had always looked down on Simon, the U-Maula country bumpkin with the slow wits which all southerners laughed at; after her discovery, she positively despised him.

It was a simple secret, which she had found out by accident. Simon was terrified of the Hoover—so terrified that he could not bring himself to use it.

Gloria had been in the garden one day when she heard the Hoover going in one of the bedrooms. By chance curiosity she glanced through the window, and saw something which made her laugh out loud. The Hoover was going, all right, in the sense that it was switched on; but it was purring steadily to itself, tucked away in one corner, while Simon was on his knees brushing the carpet by hand.

She was ready with a derisive greeting when he returned to the kitchen.

"Old man," she said, "what is the Hoover for? Do you think it is a radio, to listen to? Does it play your tribe's music? Is that how they have a party, up in your stupid village?"

In Shebiya, women did not talk to men like this; in fact they did not talk to men at all, unless they were asked a direct question. But this was Port Victoria, where the women chattered freely, like jays, and behaved shamelessly, as if they were equals like the Europeans. Gloria could always make a fool of him; and now, it seemed, she had come upon a new sharp weapon, to make him feel a fool always.

He said: "Hold your tongue. I have work to do." But his head was hanging low already, and he had great fear of the future.

"Work with the Hoover?" Gloria inquired sarcastically. "That should be very quick work. That should be finished in a minute, the way you use it."

"I do not like the machine," said Simon. "The brush is better."

"Have you told the missus so?"

"She does not need to be told," said Simon, gruff with anxiety. "As long as the work is done."

"We will see," said Gloria. "I have to think what is right. The missus hears the Hoover going, and she says to herself: 'Ah,

56

the old man is working well, he is doing what he is ordered.' But all the time, old man, you are deceiving her. Should she not be told?"

There were seeds here of endless small blackmail, and Simon knew that he was powerless to withstand it. He said again: "The brush is better. I work better with the brush."

"Then do not switch on the Hoover. Do not waste the electricity. What about the master who pays all the bills? Should he have to pay for electricity that does nothing, that is used for music?"

Simon said nothing.

"I will have to think about this, old man," said Gloria. "While I am thinking, I will have some tea."

"It is not time for tea."

"It is time when I say it is time," snapped Gloria. "Make me some tea. And do not make it on the Hoover. Use the kettle and the stove." As Simon, dispirited, turned away towards the sink, her voice came threateningly to his ear: "Perhaps *that* is what they use the Hoover for, up in that stupid village."

Up in that stupid village, under a dry and dusty thorn-tree which had sheltered a generation of men and a thousand gatherings, adult education was in progress. There was, as evidence of this, a blackboard borrowed from the school, and a large and attentive audience, and Tannoy loudspeakers so that they could all hear, and a teacher—the District Commissioner himself—to give the instruction. His subject was simple: "How to vote."

Charles Seaton, the District Commissioner for Shebiya, was a tall young man in a white bush-jacket and white shorts—the only tolerable dress in the glaring heat which the thorn-tree hardly tempered at all. At the moment he was standing, chalk in hand, drawing animals, and birds and other pictures on the blackboard. By his side sat old Chief Banka, and behind Chief Banka stood a good selection of his twenty sons. Close at hand, and necessary because Charles Seaton's command of the Maula tongue was not equal to this occasion, was the interpreter. He was the son of the official interpreter at Gamate, Voice Tula, and was known, inevitably, as Small Voice Tula.

Charles Seaton drew, with some labour, stylized versions of the symbols which in this election would stand, not for parties but for men. There were eight such pictures, for the eight candidates

57

who had come forward: a cock, a horned ox, a spread eagle, a horse, a domed mud-hut, a water pot, a spear, and a three-legged stool. When he had finished his drawing, Seaton began to speak, pausing at the end of each sentence so that Small Voice Tula could translate. The process took a long time, but in Shebiya there was always plenty of that.

"This is a choosing," he began, and the Tannoy speakers echoed his words raggedly, as if in some vast boxing arena. "It is a choosing of men for the great new council in Port Victoria. Shebiya is to send four men to the council, which will rule all Pharamaul, and you will choose them, out of the eight men who have come forward. These are the eight men"—and he pointed to the drawings on the blackboard.

This earned a quick laugh, which was not at all what Charles Seaton wanted. His orders from the Chief Secretary had been firmly summed up in a single phrase: "Make them take it seriously," and, as a wide-awake young man with his eye on a certain job in the Scheduled Territories Office, he was determined to do exactly as he was told, whether he believed in it or not. So he frowned at the laughter, and raised his hand for silence, and went on:

"I should say, these are the signs for the men you will choose. I will give you a list of the men now, with their signs. It will be repeated here on the *aboura* every day until the day of the choosing. If you forget the list, or if you are not sure which sign is for a certain man, then come to the Government office and ask."

Now Seaton picked up his bamboo swagger-stick, and pointed at the blackboard. "Listen carefully. Chief Banka—the cock. Benjamin Banka, son of the chief—the ox. Matthew Banka, son of the chief—the eagle. Pele Matale, Government clerk—the horse . . ."

He went on down the list until he had finished it. It was heavily loaded in favour of tribal authority, he realized, but there was nothing to be done about that. Chief Banka was, for a dozen sound reasons, an essential candidate, and his two sons deserved their chance because of their rank, though it had been the devil's own job to stop *all* the sons coming forward, and thus flooding the market completely. The twenty sons of Chief Banka were, beyond doubt, the prime nuisances of Shebiya. Some put on insufferable airs, some chased after other men's wives, some drank beer all day and snored like pigs all night. None of them ever did a stroke of work, and all of them quarrelled constantly, prodded and poked forward by their jealous wives and competing mothers.

Charles Seaton had had to plague the life out of Chief Banka, already plagued beyond endurance, before weeding out the non-starters and bringing the number of his family candidates down to two.

When he had finished the list, and waited for Small Voice Tula's translation, he took up his tale again.

"On the day of the choosing, you will come to the school. Do not come all together. Come at any time during the day, until the sun sets. At that time, a bell will be rung, and that will be the end of the choosing. When you come to the school, you will each be given a paper. On the paper will be these signs." He pointed to the blackboard. "When you have decided who to choose, you will take a pencil and make a cross—so—against the sign of the man you choose. Remember, you are to mark four of them, and no more. If you mark more than four, your paper will be thrown away."

He paused again, not only for Small Voice Tula but to allow all this to sink in. He wished above everything that he could have left Shebiya before this nonsense started. He did not believe in any of it. He liked Pharamaul, and the U-Maulas were good chaps, most of them, and he had enjoyed his time in Shebiya. But an election. . . . It was coming about a hundred years too soon, and the childish charade he was now acting out was proof of that.

Cocks and eagles and horses. . . . What these lads needed was reading and writing. Then a literacy test. Then the vote. Not in a hundred years; it wouldn't take as long as that. But twenty would be about right. When the new generation had grown up and knew what it was voting for, that was the time for elections.

In twenty years, perhaps, he, Charles Seaton, would be remembered in village folklore as the D.C. who drew pictures on the blackboard and tried to make people vote for animals instead of for men. But in the meantime—he raised his swagger-stick again, to cut off the murmur of comment from the crowd, and said:

"Now. Is there any question you want to ask? Is there anything you have not understood?" He turned to the old man sitting by his side. "Chief?"

"It is clear to me," said Chief Banka after a pause.

"It is clear to me," said his son Benjamin, unasked.

The second son, Matthew, a fat young man who liked the lime-light, asked: "Why is it only four men from Shebiya?"

Well, that wasn't too silly a question. . . . Seaton turned back to the microphone. "I have been asked, why is Shebiya to send four men? The answer is, it has been decided according to the number of the people. Port Victoria will send eight men. Gamate will send ten men. Fish Village will send two."

After the translation, there was a sudden surge of talk from the crowd. Then an old man in the front row called out querulously: "What chance have four men of Shebiya against ten men of Gamate?" and there were voices of approval all round him.

Seaton put it as simply as he could. "It is not *against* Gamate. It is *with* Gamate. Together, all the twenty-four men in the council will rule Pharamaul, for the good of all."

There was more loud talk at that. Shebiya had never been *with* Gamate. Gamate, an ancient enemy, was at best a suspect neigh-bour. But the point was not made in open debate. It was a mat-ter for private words, for nighttime murmuring in huts when wood-smoke and suspicion and jealousy could mingle in the dark-ness without a man having to account to authority. It was not a matter for the District Commissioner. Instead, there was a second question, not quite as rational as the first:

"If the men we choose go away to the council, how will we hear what they say?"

Perhaps it was rational after all, thought Seaton; it was the normal absentee-member-neglecting-his-constituency complaint. He answered as best he could:

"From time to time the men you have chosen will come back to Shebiya, and tell you what they have said, and what new laws have been passed."

A young man at the back shouted: "How will we know if they speak the truth?" and there was a burst of laughter.

Seaton decided that he had better step on this straight away. "They will speak the truth because they are the men you trust. That is why you will choose them. . . . Now, are there any more questions?"

After a long silence, the old man who had spoken already asked:

"You say, we make four marks on the paper, for four men. But can we make four marks for one man? If we do not like a certain man on the paper"—and he looked with the utmost disdain to-ward Benjamin Banka—"can we then give his mark to another man?" He rose, and bowed suddenly. "Can we, perhaps, give four marks to the Chief?"

"No," answered Charles Seaton, when all this had been translated. "You will give one mark to each man. But if you wish to, you may make only one mark."

"Yet you told us, four marks," said the old man, accusingly.

"I said, not more than four marks." Seaton, realizing that he had not said this at all, was angry with himself, and impatient with the whole thing. This was all so bloody complicated. . . . "You may choose one man, or two men, or three, or four. But not more than four."

The old man had not finished. "Then how many times can we go to the school and make our choosing? Can we return a second time if we have a strong wish to choose a certain man? How many pieces of paper will there be for each one of us?"

Charles Seaton sighed again. Once more, he wished he could have left before the election, before independence itself. This was like a kindergarten, it was like one of those obedience schools for dogs. And, within a few months, his successor as District Commissioner was going to be a Maula. . . . He said firmly:

"Each man can choose only once. His name is written on a list, and when he is given his voting-paper the name is crossed off by a policeman." It might be a good moment to stress the rules. "If anyone tries to choose twice, he may go to prison, or he may lose all his cattle." That was probably the best note to end on. "No more talking today," Seaton said. "If you have a question, come to the Government office and ask it. Or come here each day for the announcement." Then he touched his swagger-stick to his forehead, which was a salute they all knew, and spoke the traditional closing words: "*Aboura i faanga.* The *aboura* is ended."

As the crowd, buzzing with talk, began to melt away, he turned to Chief Banka.

"Thank you, Chief," he said formally. "I think that was a good start."

The old man, who had a sense of humour behind his grave authority, inclined his head. "Thank you, Mr. Seaton. Let us say, the longest journey starts with a single step."

On a bare hillside, across which the night wind blew soft and chill, the band of men stood guard by their net. It was a huge net, strung taut on stakes eight and ten feet above the ground; it had been spread and tended each night for more than two years, ever since it had been noticed that the same great bird came flying in each day at dawn.

One day, it was believed, that bird would fly low instead of high, or it would drop from the sky because of failing wings; and then it would flutter into their net and there lie still, and it would be theirs for ever, with all its power and magic.

The net-men had built a cave of loose stones near by, and there, well screened from the sky, a fire burned all night to give them comfort. But there were always men awake and on watch under the net, in case the bird came early. These men looked upwards through the net, straining for sounds, watching the moon on its slow journey past the stars.

When, towards dawn, heavy dew fell on the net, the moonlight glistened on it strangely, sending confused gleamings and shafts of light across the great trap. Then one of the watchers would get up, and walk all round the stakes, shaking the net; and the dew would drop down like cold misty rain, and their sight would be clear again.

The pale light which was the dawn began to make an arc in the east. The men on watch strained to listen, and then one of them, whose hearing as a hunter was famous, said: "It comes." The tiny throb of sound, coming also from the east, gained strength even as they listened; and they called softly to the men lying by the cave-fire: "It comes," and within a moment shadows moved and grew together in the half-light, and the space under the net filled, until all the net-men were at their posts.

The throbbing gained power till it was a steady droning. Presently, over the crest of the bare hillside, the bird itself could be seen, moving across the sky towards them; it had flashing lights, green and red, which were its fearful eyes, and sometimes its breath could be seen, streaming away behind it as it soared in flight.

It seemed perhaps a little lower at this dawning, and the men under the net clenched their hands, and prayed that *this* might be the day. The noise was very loud, the drumming of the wings like thunder, the flashing eyes as clear as jewels. But once more, the huge bird's flight was not low enough to bring it into their trap; once more, their net was empty as the prey passed overhead. The bird had escaped them again.

The newspaper plane from Windhoek droned and snarled away to the south, dropping towards Port Victoria. As its eyes disappeared and its breath faded, the net-men sighed, and rubbed their stiff limbs, and went back to the cave and the fire. Another chill night had passed, another sunrise was at hand, and another chance to catch the bird and fill their empty net was gone for ever.

But there would be other dawns, and they were bound by the strictest oath to watch them. One day they would catch that bird, a bird so strong that it could fly like the wind, yet so stupid that it flew the same patch of night sky on every journey. One day they would catch it, and eat it, and steal its power with its blood.

All they need do was keep their net in good repair, and tend it faithfully and cunningly, and wait for that great day.

2

"Of course," said the Earl of Urle, in those strangled, declamatory tones which many of his opponents thought of as the wakeful curse of the House of Lords, "I think it's absolutely monstrous that we didn't give Maula *women* the vote!"

There was a thoughtful silence from his audience, the liqueurs-and-coffee male half of a Government House dinner party. It was the kind of silence imposed when the words spoken are so large a piece of nonsense that it is not possible to make any useful comment, without overstepping social boundaries altogether. The Governor-General, lounging deep in his high-backed chair, and now drawing contentedly on a cigar, must be allowed his point.

They had sat down sixteen to dinner—Dinamaula and his wife, the Anglican Bishop of Port Victoria and his, a visiting American senator and what he called his "little lady," the Brackens, the Crumps, the Stillwells, Paul Jordan the aide-de-camp, and the Government House social secretary, Sybil Bartholomew.

At the top of the table, the Governor-General presided with relentless bonhomie; at its foot, the Countess of Urle gave a sketchy caricature of the First Lady of Pharamaul. As far as neighbours were concerned, she had done slightly better than her husband, sitting between the Prime Minister, whom she always proclaimed "a doll," and the senator, from whom sonorous and gallant sentiments flowed as readily and weightily as Niagara. The

Earl of Urle had been stuck with Dinamaula's wife, who was speechless throughout the meal, and the senator's little lady, a large woman so intent on protocol and table manners that she met every conversational opening with a wild and worried stare.

The Government House dining-room had been at its splendid best, from the handsome Georgian silver (the gift of the first Governor, a man of taste who carried his own notions of civilization with him wherever he went) to the elegant, mirror-like Hepplewhite table; from the pale Aubusson carpet to the servants who stood at attention, their white frock-coats crossed with scarlet-tasselled sashes, behind the brocaded chairs. There was a footman to every two guests, presided over by the formidable Government House butler, in whose white-gloved hand a silver-topped wand of office weaved like a magic baton.

The service had been flawless, the six-course dinner excellent, and the wines (sherry with the *hors d'œuvre* and the soup, white Burgundy with the fish, claret with the roast duck, champagne with the *Bombe Surprise*, and Tokay with dessert) beyond reproach.

When the Urles, whose taste for democracy was coloured by a sense of drama, had first moved in, an effort had been made to "simplify" Government House entertaining, in tune with the levelled times. Servants were dismissed in droves, cars laid up, and meals cut down to glorified snacks. Even the peacocks were offered to the Zoo. But the spartan experiment had not lasted long.

Every Maula in the household found this meager living disgraceful and unworthy; it had precipitated such a mutinous uproar, such sulks and frowns even from the gardeners, and so steep a decline in service, that the Governor-General, against all his sacred convictions, had been forced to capitulate.

He let it be known that things were to be "just like the old days." Peace swiftly returned, and with it a standard of opulence which would not have disgraced the Washington *corps* at its most ambitious.

But this evening, for all the grand *panache*, the dinner had not been a success. There were too many blank spots round the table. The dumb wife of the Prime Minister, and the flustered elephant who owed allegiance to the senator, could contribute nothing; the consort of the Bishop, an avid *protocolaire*, considered that she and her husband should have had precedence over the senator and his wife, honoured guests though they were, and had been in a brooding, fretful rage ever since she observed the table-placings.

David Bracken was dead tired, after a day's wrestling with the upcoming budget. Mrs. Stillwell, a pretty north-country girl who liked to see everyone happy, had dropped a social clanger by assuring her hostess, too early in the evening, that she had *loved* her book. (She was not to know that Bobo Urle liked at least an hour's stiff-jointed social minuet, with all the servile trimmings, before anyone could take off their shoes.) The Countess herself, bored, belligerent, and slightly drunk, was at her most obstreperous.

In the past four months, the Governess (a *sotto voce* term which infuriated her) had kept in motion a ground swell of gossip which, though it never quite achieved a breaking wave, was good for a swirl of boiling foam, laced with gasping fish, at any party in Port Victoria.

She could conduct herself with perfect decorum, or she could behave like all hell. Gatherings at Government House might be models of polite, constrained formality; or they could well finish up with half the room scandalized, the other half tripping over the furniture in hazy pursuit of a refill at the bar, while their hostess, reclining on the lionskin hearth-rug, let fly with selections from her unpublished verse which set the very chandeliers shivering like a nunnery disturbed.

She was just as likely, as many startled guests found out, to change back from Diamond Lil to Queen Victoria, at the flick of a wayward switch. This was a matter of moods, and the moods were unpredictable.

It was her strength that she could always catch people out, and it had become her favourite sport to do so. She liked to have things both ways, like certain other young women of exalted rank; she wanted everything that went with the word "Countess" and with her husband's position, and all the joys of bad behaviour as well. There was a third pleasure here, a dividend from the other two combined.

When people were too formal, she could say contemptuously: "Oh, don't be so stuffy!" When they grew careless, and seemed to presume on friendship, she would set them back on their heels with a crisp reminder of protocol.

She was sweetness and informality itself, until one thought oneself an intimate and was lured into going too far. Then the poised guillotine fell. Suddenly she would freeze, as if drawing on a spectral pair of long white gloves; and an icy draft would blow through the silenced room as she gave the withering directive: "Please address me as 'Your Excellency.'"

Even Nicole Bracken, with years of training behind her, and her husband's career always in mind, had been caught flat-footed by this same technique. Very soon after the Urles' arrival, she and Bobo Urle had gone downtown together, on a guided tour of the leading shops. They got on well with each other, had a cheerful, gossipy cup of coffee at the restaurant which was part of Biggs-Johnson's Universal Bazaar, and resumed their window-shopping.

Bobo Urle's attention was suddenly caught by something she seemed to covet—a suit of black open-work "lounging pyjamas," of the kind worn by film-starlets who later complain of rape. They were, in Nicole's view, too tarty for words, and when her companion exclaimed impulsively: "Those are for me!" she gave her own opinion in a would-be diplomatic way, but yet, it seemed, too carelessly. She said:

"But you can't very well wear that sort of thing *now*." The slight emphasis made her meaning crystal clear.

Lady Urle gave her a steely look, equally clear in its meaning. She had then frozen into complete silence, walked towards the Government House car which was following them around the town, stepped into it, and had herself driven off without a word. Nicole was left on the pavement, feeling a fool, but possessed of a healthy rage as well.

She did not tell David about it; he had enough worries already. Instead, she decided to call the bluff. There was really nothing to lose; David was much too important in Pharamaul for this sort of row to affect him seriously, and she herself needed Bobo Urle far less than Bobo Urle needed her—as a guide, a counsellor, and perhaps as a friend. When the expected peace overtures were made, Nicole ignored them completely.

Telephone calls were cut short—she had "something on the stove." Shopping trips were declined—she was really far too busy. Invitations were turned down; there was a constant clash of engagements. In chance meetings, it was Nicole's turn to be wordless and distant. In the end, the Countess of Urle gave in. One morning, the post included a heavily crested Government House card, with the words, in a large sprawling hand: *"I'm very sorry. Bobo Urle."* After that, Nicole at least had no more nonsense to put up with.

But there was plenty of other nonsense; and Paul Jordan, in the direct line of fire, had to deal with it as best he could.

Bobo Urle, the ex-hippy, was used to moving on; now she was stuck in Pharamaul, and Pharamaul, with all the perquisites of office, was dull as ditchwater. She had taken to roaming: the city's three nightclubs and two superior bars now knew her well; and since it was inconceivable that she could wander about on her own, it fell to Paul Jordan to escort her.

He loathed the job, which was increasingly unpredictable and embarrassing. He was having enough trouble already with the Social Secretary, a fat scatty girl who had wangled the job as a distant cousin of the Governor-General's, and could not have kept it on any other basis.

Sybil Bartholomew was an ungainly thirty-five, and her prospects of marriage, never bright, were now the subject of terrifying odds. Paul Jordan's office was in Government House, and he had to be there most of the day. He must be "in attendance" nearly every evening also. Sybil Bartholomew had him cornered, and she never gave him a moment's peace.

But it was still Bobo Urle who was the real menace. She had a taste for sitting about in bars—not at a table, but high on a stool at the counter, chatting it up with the barman. She liked to spend hours in nightclubs, listening to dreamy music and getting loaded on plain gin-and-water. She liked to talk to strangers, and ask clarinet players over to her table. Sometimes, towards dawn, she liked to recite.

The Maulas could make nothing of this sort of thing, except that the Governor-General must be either a fool or a fairy. White Port Victoria was shocked to its marrow; Lady Urle was letting the side down, with a thump unequalled since the fifth Governor (1892–5) used to keep his carriage, its coat of arms gleaming under the red lamplight, waiting outside one of the downtown brothels. The idea that they were expected to bow or curtsey to this *creature* set their collective teeth on edge. And she was always with that goodlooking aide-de-camp. . . .

That goodlooking aide-de-camp was being driven up the wall.

Whenever he ventured any advice, or the mildest remonstrance (as when he said that she really *mustn't* recite that sort of thing in public), he was given the "Don't be stuffy!" treatment; for the rest, Bobo Urle had established a kind of intimate legend that he was wildly in love with her, and must be constantly pushed away to arm's length.

Paul Jordan, like a harassed junior diplomat, had to examine every sentence for hidden meanings before he dared say a word. His style of dancing, never very dashing, grew positively vicarish as he strove to avoid that display-case bosom, those mobile thighs.

Once he had confided to David Bracken, in desperation:

"Sir, she's so *awful!* Honestly, I don't know what to do sometimes. We were at Ricardo's last night, and she had a bunch of American tourists sitting with us, and one of them said something about cowboy pictures, and she said: 'I used to be known as the quickest drawers in the West.' I was the only one who didn't roar with laughter—in fact, I didn't laugh at all—and she leant across and said: 'Don't look so sulky, darling. It gives people the wrong impression.' What *can* you do?"

"You'd better marry Sybil," said David unfeelingly.

"Oh God! . . . You know," Paul said wistfully, "I really *am* well enough to go back to sea."

When the Countess of Urle had given the signal for the ladies to leave the table that evening, she had called out to her husband: "Don't be too long, darling. It's so dull." The ladies, thought Dinamaula, must make what they chose of that one. . . . But he found it a great deal more pleasant to draw the chairs together and settle down to a male conversation, even though the Governor-General talked such rubbish; he had had enough of his female neighbours—his hostess whom he thought despicable, even when she had not had too much to drink, and the Bishop's wife, who was furious about something or other, and could scarcely manage a civil word.

The talk flowed easily enough, arriving by and by at the coming elections. It was when the Governor-General made his fatuous remark about giving the vote to Maula women that Dinamaula wondered if anyone would bother to take it up. The silence grew awkwardly long; finally the American senator—a Southerner, as Dinamaula had established earlier—made bold to break it.

The senator, a ripe old charmer from Georgia, had his own steely view on access to the ballot-box; it scarcely included Negro men, let alone their womenfolk. But with a left-wing lord, his host, on one side of him, and a black prime minister on the other, he had to steer a rather close course.

"That's very interesting, your Excellency," he said. His manners had been punctilious throughout the evening. "But I'm just wondering about the larger issues. . . . Would you say that the women of this country were *quite* ready to exercise that precious gift of the franchise? Wouldn't you say it was a little too early?"

"Not at all," said the Earl of Urle promptly. "What's the difference between men and women?" He gave a high whinny of laughter. "Before I get any rude answers, I'd like to amend that question. I mean, as far as the vote is concerned. If we have universal suffrage for men in Pharamaul, then why not for women?"

"Because, as I understand it, they have so far taken no part in public life at all."

"Then the sooner they make a start, the better. How can they learn otherwise?"

"I should have thought," the senator began cautiously, "that a qualifying period——"

"Oh, nonsense!" said the Governor-General cheerfully. "That's the oldest excuse in the world for doing nothing. Suppose"—he searched round for an analogy, and found one which must hit right home—"suppose there had to be a *qualifying period* before Columbus set out to discover America. Suppose he had to pass an examination, or something silly like that. He would never have started at all!"

"And we would have been deprived of one of our great national holidays," said the senator, who knew the value of a timely jest. "But it's my understanding that Columbus had spent over twenty-five years at sea before he made that particular voyage." He turned sideways towards Dinamaula. "What would you say, Mr. Prime Minister?" he asked courteously. "Votes for the women of your country?"

Dinamaula, who had been studying his brandy glass, looked up. He did not want to be involved in this silly subject, but it was not possible to ignore the direct question. "I agree with you," he said slowly, "that it is too early to extend the vote to women. To begin with, it would go directly against tradition. Women have

69

never shown the least interest in tribal affairs. That is the man's job, and both sides are quite content to have it that way. Women really have no wish to get involved."

"Then they must be made to," said the Governor-General firmly. "I've absolutely no use for that sort of attitude. . . ." He looked down the table, towards Tom Stillwell, the editor of the *Times of Pharamaul*. "What about it, Stillwell? Let's hear the voice of the radical Press!"

Stillwell had his answer ready; it was something he had thought about a lot. "I think it would be much too early," he said. "In fact, maybe this whole election is too early. It's depressing, but I don't believe the average Maula or U-Maula—the man on the land—has the slightest idea what this is all about. He is loyal to the chief— pardon me, the Prime Minister," he corrected himself, with a smile towards Dinamaula, "and he's happy in a vague sort of way about independence, principally because it was a hell of a good party. But that's about as far as it goes."

"What an extraordinary attitude!" said the Governor-General. He leant forward, wagging a forefinger in his best debating style. "But doesn't that mean that your newspaper isn't doing its job? If the average Maula——"

"The average Maula cannot read."

David Bracken caught the eye of Keith Crump. The policeman was listening, and frowning at the same time; he had a contribution to make, but the habit of silence was ingrained. A policeman, like a soldier, took orders and carried them out; if he had to think for himself, he thought according to the book, and the book didn't allow for questions of "why," only of "how." The word "why" was a civilian privilege, and a prime luxury into the bargain.

But in the silence which followed Tom Stillwell's curt disclaimer, he decided to make a point, if only in self-defense.

"I wouldn't know about Maula women," he began. It was a stupid sort of start, and he realized it, and went on quickly: "But my lads have had a lot of work to do, organizing this election, and the reports aren't very encouraging." He nodded towards Tom Stillwell. "Most of them still don't know what it's about; if they're interested in that sort of thing at all, they're interested in what the local chief and the headmen do in their own backyard, not with a new sort of council miles away in Port Victoria. Of course it's different down here; there's a lot more talk about it, and

70

they've seen the legislative assembly starting to work, and they can read the paper. But in Gamate, and worse still, up in Shebiya, it just isn't getting through to them."

"It's only the first election," put in David, who was finding all this very depressing. "We're just laying out the guide-lines with this one."

"Oh, I agree. But don't expect any miracles. Charles Seaton, up at Shebiya, says some of them still think it's something to do with the poll-tax. They won't get themselves on the voting list, because they're afraid of having to pay double for it."

"Education!" exclaimed Lord Urle. "That is the key. Schools. A great university. Adult education classes. Occupational training. Seminars. Discussion groups. Exchange students. Travelling scholarships, so that people can visit other countries. Educational broadcasts. Educational *television*——"

"In fact," Dinamaula cut into him, in full flight, "we'll need a grant of about twenty million a year instead of two." He was smiling, but there was a brooding discontent in his eyes as he looked at the Governor-General. "We could certainly spend it. But where do we get it from? From Britain? It was made pretty clear in London"—he glanced across at David Bracken—"if I'm not giving away any secrets, that there was a fixed limit to what we could count on, and that we had to live within our means."

"Would you expect otherwise?" asked the senator, with a certain silky disdain.

"No," answered Dinamaula curtly. He wasn't standing any nonsense from this old mountebank, who had that disgusting trick of pronouncing "Negro" as "nigra," thus keeping within the limits of decency while still having his private fun. "No, I wouldn't expect Britain to do more for Pharamaul than she does for any other commonwealth country of the same size. But that doesn't mean that we wouldn't *like* more."

"It's an extremely interesting structure, that commonwealth of yours," said the senator, shifting ground with the ease born of a hundred political brawls. "Let me see—you are retaining your allegiance to that great institution, the monarchy?"

"Yes," said Dinamaula.

"Yet you could become a republic, if you wished?"

"Yes."

"It's a matter of simple choice," said Lord Urle, who had made an early reputation by denouncing the monarchy as snobbish, outdated, and riddled with privilege, and had been countered by a fellow peer who labelled him—in a phrase which stirred the House of Lords into genteel uproar—"a stupid twerp." "And of course, it makes no real difference at all. Pharamaul would have a president instead of a Governor-General, like India or Zambia." He smiled round the table. "I should find myself out of a job, I'm afraid. But that wouldn't be the end of the world, would it?"

By God! thought Dinamaula, it wouldn't. He glanced down at his watch. It was still only ten o'clock; there was another whole hour to go before that sacred knell of 11 P.M., when he could make his escape from this dull farce. He had had enough of the Urles, after four short months; enough of the drunken exhibitionist who was the first lady of Pharamaul, and enough of this silly boob who was, to black and white alike, simply a figure of fun.

If Urle was the best that Britain could do, by way of vice-regal presence, then it was money down the drain, a swindling sideshow which should be taken off before it gave the whole circus a bad name.

They joined the ladies, who seemed, as a group, in rather poor shape. Nicole Bracken, talking dutifully to the Prime Minister's wife, was showing signs of strain, after a monologue which had lasted nearly an hour. The Bishop's wife was alone in one corner, looking at a photograph album with an expression of grim distaste. Mrs. Stillwell had paired off with Mrs. Crump, and they were doing well enough; but the Social Secretary, eating her heart out for male company, was in sulky argument with the Countess of Urle, whose third scotch-and-soda had been, she complained, an itty-bitty thing, not worth a damn.

The senator's wife, staring at her as if she could believe neither eyes nor ears, was clearly homesick for Georgia, more dependable company, and the American way of life.

As the men filed in, in that slightly shifty way which meant that they had stayed away longer than they should, had done better without the women, and had just been to the lavatory, their hostess's voice rose loud and clear:

"I'm *bored!*"

The Governor-General, with a year of practice behind him,

took his cue swiftly. "I'm sorry, darling. I'm afraid we were rather a long time."

"It's not that."

The Bishop sat down beside his wife, and they were soon in earnest, whispered conversation. The other men hung about, awaiting that adroit, skilled disposal of their bodies ("Senator, I know you'd like to talk to Madame Dinamaula"—"David, do tell the senator's wife about your plans for children's playgrounds"— "Mr. Stillwell, Sybil was asking me about soil conservation—I know you can explain it far better than I can") which any good working hostess had ready, simmering on the fire, against the moment of reunion.

But it was not forthcoming. Though the moment had arrived, the hostess was not in working order. She was stoned.

"Put on the LP of 'O Come! All Ye Faithful,'" she commanded, breaking a long silence.

"Darling, I think the record-player is broken."

"Get it fixed, get it fixed. . . . Then let's go to that terrific nightclub."

"What nightclub is that?" asked Major Crump, who liked to keep track of such things.

"The Colour Bar." Bobo Urle turned towards the Prime Minister with a giggle. "Oh God, listen to *me!* So sorry, old boy. It's just a little joke of a place, but cute. Run by a couple of South African queers. You'd love it!"

"Darling," said the Governor-General, "I don't think——"

"Oh, don't be so stuffy!" snapped his wife. She lolled sideways, and the loaded ashtray on the arm of her chair crashed and spilled its contents on the carpet. "What idiot put that there?"

David Bracken, who was nearest, started to clear up the mess.

"Well, we can't sit around like a lot of dopes," said the Countess of Urle. She looked directly at the Bishop's wife, whose bosom, armoured by a massive acreage of brown lace, was already heaving like a flight deck in a storm. "Come on!" she called out. "Let's all get smashed!"

3

A few people, not liking the omens, had packed up and left already. Certain traditional faces were now missing from the lunch-time martini sessions at the Port Victoria Club; the most noticeable gap was left by Binkie Buchanan, who had sold his small freighter to Alexanian's, the export-import firm, shipped his Rolls-Royce to Cape Town *en route* for Rhodesia, and announced that he was going to resettle in a civilized country.

His farewell party had been a truly sensational bash, even by southern African standards; but now he was gone, and a bit of authentic colonial history had gone with him.

The survivors, huddling together round the waterhole, had been downcast for a short while; but it had not lasted long, since there were no more such thunderbolts. Even the election to the club of eight Maula members, mostly elderly civil servants, had not proved the ghastly fiasco which had been foretold. The "New boys" behaved practically like human beings.

Life went on, almost the same. Though old members, accustomed to shouting "Boy!," were now asked to amend this to "Steward!," the tone of voice was unaltered. The Port Victoria Club, at least, was standing up well to the jolting of progress.

Of course, there was still the coming general election to reckon with; but there were not thought to be any serious problems about this. Splinter Woodcock, seeking reelection in one of the downtown Port Victoria wards, was the spokesman for those who proclaimed that there were certain members whom Pharamaul could not possibly spare.

"It stands to reason," he told his audience on one occasion. "They would never chuck me out. Not with my record. How could they? I've given the best years of my life to this bloody country, and they know it. I've had chaps practically with tears in their eyes, coming up and saying: '*Barena*, we need you now more than ever!' Only last week, one of my stable-boys said: 'What shall we do if the *barena* takes away his horses?' I tell you, when it comes down to it, the old Maula knows the real issues."

"He knows which side his bread's buttered, more likely."

"Same thing. Of course, it's all a lot of bloody nonsense. Why should they get the vote in the first place? They don't want it. It's like giving them caviare when all they want is mealie-porridge. But if there *has* to be an election, then by God I'm ready for it!"

"Made any speeches, Splinter?"

"I put my name on the list of candidates. That's quite enough."

"What's your symbol, old boy?"

Splinter Woodcock's chins began to wobble, ready for laughter.

"Should have been the cock, and plenty of it. But actually it's the bull. So stand by with your shovel!"

To David Bracken, at their daily meetings, the Prime Minister sometimes seemed preoccupied, and less talkative than usual. It was true that he had a lot on his mind; they both had; the joint work-load was pressing harder with every day that passed. But often it seemed as if Dinamaula were building up a private fund of reserve thoughts, which he did not choose to share. His attention seemed to have settled in two layers: there were the things he said, and the things which were occupying his mind at the same time; and they were not always faithfully married to each other.

It was not double-dealing, nor anything like it. It was double-feeling, like that of a man who, negotiating a bank loan in a chill forbidding office, daydreams of the snug country cottage it will buy, even as he studies the small print.

Yet this was only a small cloud on a happy horizon. The two of them got on well together, because of their common purpose; out of the checkered past, something had been forged which was now showing a profit. They met every morning for about an hour; much of it was routine business, but sometimes their talk ranged into the future. It was on one of these occasions that Dinamaula returned to the subject of a republic, which had first come to the surface at the Government House dinner party.

His thoughts seemed to be moving towards it, and David found it rather hard to argue with him. He found it, also, difficult to define precisely where his own loyalty lay: to the Queen, in the odious person of Lord Urle, or to Pharamaul itself, with the Prime Minister at its head. There was one thing certain: Dinamaula was making up his own mind about it.

"I can't honestly see what function the Governor-General fulfills," he once said. "Or rather, I see the function, constitutionally, but I can't see the point of it. He's really only a passenger, isn't he? And she behaves so badly. . . . What would we lose if we were a republic, inside the commonwealth?"

David, sitting in an armchair in the Prime Minister's study, hesitated before answering. There were hardly any factual arguments to use. He could only give his own feeling on the subject.

"It's a matter of personal belief, really," he said at last. "I happen to believe that countries which keep the Queen as head of state, technically, are better off than the ones that cut the tie and elect a president. It's a kind of status symbol, nowadays, I suppose, but I think it's a good one. It gives people someone else to serve besides—well, a politician."

"But it's the country they serve—if they do serve it at all—not the person at the top."

"All the same, it still appeals to me very strongly. I think it makes people behave better. Like dressing for a dinner party."

"But if people see it in those personal terms, then they see Lord Urle as the one they're serving, not the Queen." His heavy brows drew together. "Don't you think they'd rather work for me than for him?"

"If you were president?"

"If I were president."

David smiled. "I'd like to feel my way past that one, but I honestly can't. Of course, there's no question whom this country thinks of as its leader. It's you, every time. But that goes back to the tribal structure, doesn't it?"

"It goes back to me," said Dinamaula, rather curtly.

David was going to say: "And your father, and your grandfather," but he changed his mind. If Dinamaula were in the mood to think of himself as a Prime Minister chosen entirely on his merits, without benefit of ancestry, then it would take a brave Chief Secretary to argue with him. . . . Instead he cut several corners, and asked:

"How would you go about a move to a republic? By a referendum?"

"Or by a vote in the new legislature. It would be within our province."

"Substantial constitutional change. You'd need a two-thirds majority."

Dinamaula nodded. "We'll have to see who gets in, first. For all I know, they may all be royalist to the core. . . ." He looked up suddenly. "Would you oppose it yourself?"

"Not in any serious sense. It's not my job, anyway."

"Well, that's all in the future, obviously." He shuffled some papers on his desk. "Oh, there's one other thing, David. You remember we were talking about fishery protection, and I said we ought to have some sort of ship to take care of it."

76

"A minesweeper, to be exact."

"Yes. Well, I've been thinking about it again, and I've decided not to push for it."

"I'm sure you're wise."

David spoke with a careful lack of emphasis, but he was secretly relieved. The idea, at this stage, of setting up the nucleus of a Pharamaul Navy, with money borrowed from the World Bank, had been so ludicrous that when it was first advanced he found difficulty in treating it seriously; it was only when he saw that the Prime Minister was in earnest that he had begun to marshal some arguments against it.

He had had to go carefully, he found, in an area suddenly tender; prestige was involved, and the first flexing of brand-new muscles. He had concentrated exclusively on the money side, and left the rest unsaid.

In the past few months he had been able to curb several such extravagances, ranging from new Government offices, which they did not need, to a change-over to the decimal system, which would have been a long and costly headache. The minesweeper had been the biggest project, as well as the most bizarre, and he was very glad to have scotched it. After the Royal Pharamaul Navy would have come the Royal Pharamaul Air Force, and after that—he smothered a grin, and took his formal leave.

The outside world was becoming interested in Pharamaul. As the newest, and one of the very smallest, of the emerging nations, it had a certain popular appeal, like a blue baby in an incubator. Would it live? Would it die? Bets should be placed before it was too late. . . . But there was something else, beyond vulgar specu- lation. There was interest at a different level altogether: official interest, diplomatic interest, and some commercial inquisitiveness as well.

Here was a brand-new country, just out of the egg, which could in certain circumstances be of great strategic importance. It was anchored off the coast of South West Africa, that contested area of white supremacy, and of South Africa itself, that inter- national outcast waiting patiently for its liberation by a hun- dred million brethren near by. It seemed to promise a grandstand view of whatever was next on the menu for this uneasy continent.

Suddenly, "our man in Pharamaul" became a useful man to have.

There had always been a consular corps in Port Victoria, taking care of modest trade interests, bailing out drunken sailors, and helping them to catch up with their ships. These envoys had ranged from the representative of West Germany, an earnest young man who was interested in groundnut oil and, more genuinely, in butterflies, to the Honorary Consul for Poland, an ancient aristocrat who claimed to wear the only monocle south of the Sahara, and was revered among the Maulas as a special kind of magician, with access to a third eye.

But now the trend was more professional. A full-blown diplomatic corps was in process of formation, and requests for accreditation were coming from many different directions.

The Chinese were actively interested. Eight European countries had signified their intention of sending ambassadors. Half a dozen new African countries were already on the scene. Russia had sent a "technical mission," headed by an expert in cattle-breeding and crop rotation. Latin American interests were in the hands of the Argentine Ambassador, a man of round-the-clock physical appetite whose last appointment, to Paris, had terminated in what were delicately called "circumstances of debatable propriety."

The only two countries now content with mere consular representation were South Africa, which kept her mission downgraded as a matter of policy, and the United States, where the State Department was currently being harassed by a Congress intent on cutting expenditure overseas.

As a gesture, the Consul-General whom they appointed was a Negro. This carefully-planned compliment had however proved valueless. Maula opinion, perversely, concluded from the appointment that America was not taking their country seriously.

There had been many discussions about this diplomatic invasion between David Bracken, the Prime Minister, and Lord Urle, who was principally concerned with this area of development, since Britain retained responsibility for Pharamaul's external affairs. The Governor-General's attitude seemed to be a cheerful "Let 'em all come!," and his dispatches on the subject were more concerned with problems of accommodation ("I envisage a completely new 'diplomatic village,' to house the entire corps in circumstances of comfort and harmony") than with the effect which this inrush, or certain aspects of it, might have on Pharamaul.

David Bracken was soon to learn, within his own office, what these "certain aspects" might be. Almost overnight an edge of a curtain lifted, and he was brought face to face with what could be in store for a country which was a new playable piece, however tiny, on the colossal chessboard of world politics. It puzzled him; it also made him angry; but neither puzzlement nor anger were of much help.

There was a man in the Chief Secretariat named Joseph Kalatosi who had worked there as a clerk for many years, and who had been, in the process of "Maularization" now fully underway, an obvious candidate for advancement. He was a hardworking young man who was always there when he was wanted, always eager to learn, always ready with an answer, and always taking an interest, not only in his own department, but in other people's departments as well.

He was already, officially, the Number Two man, and, in a way no longer vague, David had now begun to think of Kalatosi as his successor, on that day, dimly glimpsed, when he could, with a good conscience, hand over the Civil Service of Pharamaul as a going concern. But that day was not tomorrow, nor anything like it. Joseph Kalatosi still had to prove himself not only a busy know-it-all (though that was an essential part of the job) but also the man of judgement, compassion, and truth who would run the Chief Secretariat as the honest empire it ought to be.

David Bracken had found out, by accident, that Joseph Kalatosi might well be looking for a short cut.

One morning Dinamaula had to cancel their usual meeting, and David Bracken went straight to his office instead of calling at the Prime Minister's on the way. This meant that he drove into the Secretariat car-park at nine o'clock instead of ten, and as he did so he was surprised to see there an easily recognizable car— the black chauffeured Mercedes belonging to Spedkhov, the Russian head of mission. No appointment with him had been arranged, and when David got to his office he found that his secretary knew nothing of the visit either.

He was about to telephone Joseph Kalatosi, whose office was down the corridor, when something made him decide to wait. He dealt with his mail instead, and kept an eye on the waiting Mercedes at the same time. At nine forty-five two men left the Secretariat by the side entrance, and walked across the parking space towards the black car. They were Spedkhov, the Russian, and another man whom he recognized easily—the Zambian envoy, Luanda.

Spedkhov and Luanda. . . . It didn't make sense at all, and he summoned Kalatosi immediately. When the other man came in, he was obviously disconcerted. He was small and neat, elegantly dressed in pale tussore silk; but for once his manner did not go with his appearance.

"You're early, sir," he said as he came forward.

"Yes," said David. "I see you've been having visitors."

"Visitors, sir?"

David stared at him hard. "Oh, come on! Mr. Spedkhov and Mr. Luanda. Presumably they've been seeing you."

"Oh, they . . ." When Kalatosi was flustered, as he was now, his English sometimes slipped a notch. "Yes, they did us the honour of calling."

"Us? They called to see you, didn't they?"

"Well, yes, sir."

"By appointment?"

"An appointment was made, yes."

"Why wasn't I told about it?"

"I did not want to bother you, sir. It was just a courtesy call."

"They have both made their courtesy calls already. In fact you met them both, with me, in this office."

"This was at a lower level, sir," said Kalatosi, with a small in-gratiating smile. "They professed to be interested in our administrative side. So I undertook to tell them something about it."

"You should have let me know."

"I did not think there was any harm in it." His eyes widened, as if some awful thought had suddenly struck him. "*Could* there be any harm in it?"

David looked at him for a long moment. The effect of appalled innocence had been rather overdone. "I don't know," he said finally. "Russia and Zambia. . . . Why the sudden interest? They're not exactly our best friends, are they?"

"I would prefer," answered Kalatosi, rather primly, "to think that we can *make* them our friends. By showing them friendship."

"That's not really your business, is it?"

It was a curt enough rebuke, but Joseph Kalatosi made an effective comeback. "Is it then your wish, sir, that I do not have any contact with members of the diplomatic corps?"

"I didn't say that at all," David snapped. But he was not sure what he really did want to say. He had been surprised and annoyed by the visit, and the planned secrecy which seemed to have surrounded it; but if it had involved anything really sinister, Spedkhov and Luanda would scarcely have walked into the Secretariat in broad daylight. . . . "Let's leave it like this, Joseph. Of course you can make what social contacts you like. But when any high-ranking visitors call at this office, I want to know about it."

"I will certainly remember that, sir."

David could not resist making an extra point. "Particularly when I am expected to be out."

"Sir," said Joseph Kalatosi, now deeply injured, "I hope you do not think—"

David cut him short. "Let's leave it, shall we? I'm sure we've both got lots of work to do." Yet he was still annoyed, and from long habit he chose to show it, instead of keeping it hidden. He was the Chief Secretary, not a rabbit. . . . "But when next you meet Mr. Spedkhov and Mr. Luanda," he finished coldly, "tell them how sorry I was to miss them."

He might have forgotten it before very long, except for the small cautionary notation which must now go into Joseph Kalatosi's file; but something which he learned about a few days later ensured that it became a permanent feature of his private blacklist. It rose from a chance conversation with Keith Crump.

He had met the policeman for a drink at the Port Victoria Club, before going home; and as they were leaving the club again, the black Mercedes car, with its hammer-and-sickle pennant flying, drove past them. It recalled to David Bracken the recent incident in his office, and he outlined the details to Crump.

He noticed that, from the very beginning, the other man was listening to him with unusual attention; and when he had finished, Crump said, unexpectedly:

"Well, I'm damned!"

David looked at him curiously. "It was a bit of a surprise, I must say."

"It's more of a surprise to me," answered Crump. "Now I'll tell you *my* story."

He had been driving home late, he said, a couple of nights previously, and his route had taken him past the house which was the combined embassy and residence of the Zambian Ambassador. The lights were still on, and he could make out a car standing in the drive. When he slowed down for a closer look, he found that it was one of his own police cars, a Land-Rover, waiting empty by the side door.

"I could see its number," Crump told David, "and of course I knew whose it was. It belonged to my Sergeant-Major."

"Mboku?"

Crump nodded. "Sergeant-Major Mboku. And due to be Lieutenant Mboku next month, by God! He's the first chap I'm promoting, under the new scheme."

"I suppose he's earned it," said David. But there was some doubt in his voice. Mboku was one of the few policemen he did not like at all: a big hulking man whose body seemed always to be straining out of its uniform, whose voice invariably sounded louder than it need be, whose manner reflected something between confidence and arrogance. But he had proved his worth in the past; and, as the senior police N.C.O., his promotion to the forthcoming vacancy could hardly be challenged, except on vague instinct.

"Oh, he's earned it all right," Crump agreed, "though he wasn't exactly earning it the other night. I thought he'd mention his call the next morning, because these embassy things can be important, but he didn't say anything about it. So out of curiosity I sent down to Records for the Land-Rover's logbook. You know they have to enter full details of every journey each car makes. It takes care of joyriding, among other things. Well, the logbook was right up-to-date, but there wasn't anything about the Zambian Embassy. It just said: 'Routine patrol,' with the time out and in, and the mileage."

"What did Mboku have to say about that?"

"Nothing much." They were standing in the sunshine at the bottom of the club steps, and Crump looked round him before he went on. "In fact, he was too bloody smooth about it altogether. He said it *had* been a routine patrol, only that Luanda had asked him to call round, so he was killing two birds with one stone. But why had Luanda asked him to come round? No special reason, according to Mboku. Just social."

"A courtesy call, in fact," said David.

"Exactly. Well, I gave him a rocket, because I like to know about these things, and it's not part of his job anyway. Then I asked him if he'd made any more courtesy calls. And he said yes, but only one."

"Don't tell me," said David.

Crump nodded. "Comrade Spedkhov, U.S.S.R."

"Well, I'm damned," said David, repeating Crump's earlier words. "What the hell's going on?"

Crump shrugged his shoulders. "Nothing, for all I know. It may be quite innocent, though you and I don't particularly like it. It can just mean that some of the dips are making friends with the right people."

"We're the right people," said David stoutly.

"Yes. But for how long?"

"Till we're ready to hand over."

"Oh, I agree on that. And I think by now both my Sergeant-Major and your Mr. Kalatosi know it. But you can't blame them for wanting to jump the gun."

"I can," said David, "because I still don't like the implications. If they want to start getting chummy with the diplomatic corps, why don't they try the Americans or the Italians? Why does it have to be Russia, which is always shouting the odds about neo-colonialism, or Zambia, which seems to hate our guts?"

"I'm a policeman," answered Crump. "Those delicate political shades are for you."

"Of course, we could"—David gestured—"you know, keep an eye on them."

"On our chaps?"

"No. I meant a sort of diplomatic security watch. On Spedkhov and Luanda, for a start."

Crump shook his head. "That's almost impossible. We haven't had anything like this before, and I'm just not geared for it. Ordinary security, yes. I've got lots of good detectives, and lots of informers as well. But who's to keep an eye on an ambassador? And don't forget—before very long, both Mboku and Kalatosi will have access to all the files."

83

"But these files would be secret. They couldn't possibly disclose them."

"That depends on where they think their loyalty lies."

David sighed. "Oh, damn all this! Why can't people behave themselves properly? . . . I wonder if I ought to tell H.E. about it."

"Save your breath. His Excellency loves all mankind."

"Or Dinamaula."

Major Crump tucked his swagger-stick under one arm, preparing to take his leave. "Just for the moment," he said, "I suggest that we don't tell anyone."

4

One of the most delightful people in the life of the Bracken family, and of Port Victoria itself, was a man called Alexanian, head of the import-export firm which bore his name. He was a middle-aged South African Jew, charming and cultured, a man who seemed at ease in many worlds; it was sometimes difficult to imagine why he had chosen this particular one to live in.

Anyone who could talk, with such authority and perception, about money in Switzerland, politics in the Middle East, ballet in Russia, literature in Paris, sex in Sweden, and cooking in Mexico, must surely be less than completely at home in Pharamaul.

David always thought that there must have been, in the past, some vague "trouble" which had taken Alexanian into this partial exile; Nicole Bracken preferred the idea of a fatal woman somewhere in the background—a ravishing creature who had spurned him, or betrayed him, or died in dreadful circumstances, leaving him bereft and hopeless. But whenever Alexanian was asked about it, he only waved an elegantly manicured hand and answered: "I like it here," and with that they had to be content.

Though he travelled a great deal every year, Pharamaul was indeed his home, and "Alexanian's" his abiding interest; over the years he had turned the quay-side trading post set up by a distant relative into the island's premier commercial link with the outside world. Alexanian's now imported everything, from plastic toys to heavy farm equipment; and they were the main agents for the returning tide of beef, hides, timber, groundnut oil, and processed fish, with which Pharamaul tried to balance its budget.

Alexanian himself was a favourite visitor at the Bracken home;

the children in particular adored him, in two guises—as a smashing storyteller, and as a rich adopted uncle who must have many a warehouse full of chocolates, and walnut cake, and crystallized fruits, so lavish was he with such presents. Nicole sometimes protested that he was spoiling them, but he always had his answer ready.

"I've just had a shipment in," he would say. "I want someone to try them." At that magic, romantic word "shipment," the children would come to wide-eyed attention. A shipment! A whole ship full of butterscotch! What an uncle!

He came to dinner on the eve of the election, and, as usual on "Uncle Alex nights," Timothy and Martha were very slow to go to bed. "Tell us just one more story," they begged, even up to the final deadline. "Tell us something from the Bible." Surely *that* would get official approval.

"What from the Bible?" asked Alexanian. He seemed somewhat preoccupied this evening, though he had become, as usual, part of the family as soon as he entered the house. "What sort of story?"

"Tell us about Moses stopping the water, and all the Jews walking over the Red Sea."

"But you've read that in the Bible, lots of times."

"You tell it better than God," said Martha.

"Now just a minute," said her father. "That's not a very nice thing to say, is it?"

"It was meant to be polite," said Martha.

"No more stories," said Alexanian diplomatically. "I've used up all my brains today. Tell me how you're getting on at school."

"All right," answered Timothy. But he did not sound at all enthusiastic. "We're *mixed*, you know."

"Don't you like being mixed?"

"Not much. It's so crowded."

"They smell funny," said Martha.

"Now, darling," interrupted Nicole, "you mustn't say things like that. It's not very polite, and it's not true either."

"But they do smell funny," said Timothy, backing up. "Though we know they can't help it. It's pigmentation."

"Pigs have it," said Martha.

"Perhaps you smell funny to them," said Alexanian, shortcutting a complicated trail.

85

"Uncle Alex, that's *rude!*" said Martha, scandalized. "We *don't* smell! Do we, Daddy?"

"You smell of butterscotch to me," said David, "and now you really must go to bed."

When, disconsolate, they had finally been maneuvered from the room, Alexanian shook his head. "'You tell it better than God,'" he quoted. "That is something like a testimonial."

"I'm sure Martha meant every word of it," said David. He was crossing to the side table. "How about another drink before dinner?"

"Have we time?"

"Just," said Nicole. "It's one of Simon's Spanish omelettes, cooked exactly for seven-thirty."

"Does he really call it a Spanish omelette?"

"Good heavens, no!" answered Nicole. "I just say garden eggs, and that's what comes up."

Alexanian sipped at his Dubonnet. Then he said: "There's a rather funny American story, about that Red Sea crossing. Moses says to his public relations man: 'Here's my plan. I'm going to raise my right hand, and divide the waters. Then we'll all walk across, dry as a bone. Then I'll drop my hand, and the sea will come rolling back again and drown all the Egyptians.' The P.R.O. said: 'My God, Moses! That's almost impossible! But if you do bring it off, I can get you three pages in the Old Testament.'"

"Well, really!" said Nicole, laughing. "You're as bad as Martha."

"Then I'm in very good company."

But later, over dinner, Alexanian grew more serious, and the reason for his early preoccupation made a very curious story.

They had been talking about Government contracts, which Alexanian handled on a substantial scale.

"I'm starting to get some rather odd inquiries," he told them, "and I can't quite make up my mind whether to take them seriously or not."

"Inquiries?" asked David. "Who from?"

Alexanian hesitated. Then he said: "Well, I promised not to give anyone that particular piece of information. But you can take it that they're official."

"What sort of inquiries, then?"

"About things that we can't really afford, in my view. And things that we won't need, for a long time. Specialized loading gear for the docks. Automatic road-laying equipment. Double-decker diesel buses. Air-conditioning units. A fire-fighting tug." He smiled as he saw their expressions. "No, I'm not making this up. There's a . . . a section of the Government which is starting to have some rather exotic dreams."

"Well, I'm not," said David promptly. "I never heard such rubbish in my life. We haven't a penny to spare for things like that. Damn it, this is a *poor* country!"

"Exactly." Alexanian took a sip of his wine before asking: "Have you heard anything about buying new aircraft?"

"No," answered David, "and as far as I'm concerned we're *not* buying new aircraft. We have a perfectly good Viscount which has still got years of work in it. For a twice-weekly service to Windhoek, it's more than enough. The mail delivery and the newspaper run are done much more cheaply by charter."

"Yet it has been put to me," said Alexanian, speaking with particular care, "that it would be a good idea to exchange that Viscount for a DC8. Or even two DC8s."

"Good God!" David exploded. "What on earth would we do with a DC8? Over a hundred passengers? It would never be more than a quarter full."

"I think the idea is to step up Pharamaul Airlines, make them an all-Africa line instead of just a local."

"But that's impossible," said David. "Who would use it? It would simply be a phoney prestige thing. We'd go bankrupt, just in the process of setting it up."

"How much does a DC8 cost?" asked Nicole.

"Two million pounds," answered Alexanian promptly. "Or second-hand, about one million." He spread his hands, in a caricature of a Jewish trader making the very final offer. "For you, Mrs. Bracken, a special price. I can let you have four five-year-old DC8s for three and a half million. Terms to suit your budget."

Nicole laughed. "Alex, you're just showing off. Can one buy a DC8 on hire-purchase?"

"Certainly."

"But is this really serious?" said David.

"I think it could be. Whether I become involved in it is another matter."

"It just isn't possible," said David again. "Good heavens, when I first came out here Pharamaul Airlines consisted of one old

Dakota! And we did very well with it. To begin with, we would need a whole new airfield. Or two new runways, at the very least."

"Don't forget, I sell concrete as well," said Alexanian. Then he turned serious again. "But as I said, for me it's a question of getting involved or not getting involved. I've always handled the major share of Government contracts, as you know, and it's becoming obvious that this might develop tremendously. I could be a very rich man, in the short run. But at some point it would begin to be based on funny money."

David looked at him sharply. "How do you mean?"

"I mean, it would be money which did not really exist, or ought not to exist. What's the good of that sort of development, most of it on credit, if it leads to bankruptcy? What's the good of my business growing, if it gets so big that they can't pay me, and one morning I wake up and find I've been nationalized." He sighed. "There are all sorts of fake fortunes to be made in Africa. *Still* to be made, even at this late stage, when everything is meant to be organized and controlled. But Pharamaul is my home. I want to live here, not skim off the cream and make tracks for Acapulco."

"There's no question of being paid in funny money," said David, rather crossly. "Pharamaul isn't going to be that sort of country."

"But it might be, if it started buying things like transatlantic jets."

"And *that* isn't going to happen, either."

Alexanian shrugged. He did not want to pursue the point, if it was angering David, or depressing him; but the long friendship of the past gave him leeway, and he did not see why any subject should be barred, on this evening of accustomed honesty.

"Who really has the say on that?"

"The Government, of course. If you're talking about the spending side of the budget."

"I'm talking exactly of that. Spending. At the moment, David, you are there, like a really tough bank manager. If you say No, or London says No, then the answer is No." He smiled. "I'm sure there's a very good short story to be written about this. It would be called 'The Last Days of No.' But there's an election tomorrow, and a new Government on the way. Possibly quite different. Probably republican. Certainly much more independent and freewheeling. After tomorrow, I have the feeling that Pharamaul is going to be a 'Yes' country." His voice took on a sudden, entirely foreign bitterness. "It will say 'yes' to everything. If it wants to, it will set up Pharamaul World Airways, fully equipped with empty jet planes, their tires rotting in the sun. It will have marvellous seventy-mile-an-hour roads leading into the bush, and a colossal deserted hotel with hot water coming out of the air-conditioning. It will be an utter sham."

"You've no right to say this," said David sharply.

"I am a Jew," said Alexanian. "We deal in facts."

Nicole, chin on hand, absorbed in this sad recital, came to attention. "Alex, is that the real reason why you're not standing for reelection?"

Alexanian nodded. "Just so. A very minor piece of market research showed me that I would not have a hope in hell." He sat back. "My dear friends, I am sorry to borrow your section of the Wailing Wall. But I feel the tide going out tonight, and you are the only people in the world I can tell."

After he had gone, Nicole, busy setting the room to rights, asked:

"David, what *is* all this about jet aircraft, and things like that? Who could have been making those inquiries?"

"Dinamaula, obviously."

Nicole turned and stared at him. "But that's ridiculous! He would tell you all about it. You'd be the first to know."

"I'm not so sure."

5

On the morning of the election, Tom Stillwell moved his *Times of Pharamaul* editorial from the inside leader page, promoted it to page one, and bordered it with thick black type. It was a short piece, for a reason which was made clear in the opening paragraph:

"This is our very first General Election Day, and the *Times of Pharamaul* salutes it with pride and pleasure. May it lay the foundation of a happy, stable, and prosperous country! Much has been said and written of the various issues, and nothing remains for this newspaper to do but express our hopes for a big turnout. The vote is the very essence of a free democracy, and should never be allowed to go to waste.

"Yet there is one point which we wish to stress, on this significant, perhaps dramatic day. A great deal has been said of changes in Pharamaul, and they are certain to come. But not all change is worth making. Not all new things are good, and not all old ones bad.

"This applies to men as well as things. There are respected councillors in Pharamaul who have given long service and wise leadership to their country. Their experience is valuable, their wisdom precious. They should *not* be rejected by the voters because they are identified with the past, or with a different Pharamaul. There is room for the old as well as the new, in this our new nation."

In some of the country districts the counting was slow, and it was three days before all the results were known. But the trend, begun in Port Victoria, was obvious from the start. Not one of the former "appointed members" was successful; and to the new Legislature, of twenty-four members, no single white man had been elected. "This our new nation" was new indeed.

"Good grief!" said Splinter Woodcock in disgust, surveying the world and the election returns from his usual vantage-point. "Just look at these chaps' names! They're all called Boola-Boola!"

4: A REPUBLIC WITHIN THE COMMONWEALTH, YIELDING TO NONE IN LOYALTY, YET

PRESIDENT DINAMAULA sat in the shade of a vast spreading elm tree, sipping a tall glass of lager beer, and looking out across the lawns towards the great façade of Government House. He was well content. He liked everything he saw, from the noble white columns of the portico to the new flag of Pharamaul moving gently at the masthead, and the Presidential standard over the front door. He liked the banked flowers, and the ice-cold beer, and the feel of the frosted glass in his hand. He liked the white-robed servant, watching him from a window in case of further command. He liked his cushioned bamboo chair, fit for any ruler.

He liked everything, and especially the fact that all this domain was his; for this was the very house in which, years ago, the official order sending him into exile had been read out to him, by a flustered, embarrassed Governor. President Dinamaula could be well content on this day, and on any day thereafter.

It was mid-morning, the time when he always took his ease in solitude, before callers were admitted. The callers themselves made up another item which he liked—the fact that Government House was the core, and himself the center, of a constant to-and-fro, not only of men on state business, but of important visitors and suppliants as well.

It was always flattering to see their respectful faces; to listen to the careful compliments; to watch them as they maneuvered themselves and their words closer to the matter in hand—the favour of a Government position for a relative, the favour of the President's help in a complicated dispute over tribal boundaries, the favour of a contract, the simple favour of support from a powerful man.

Many arrived with money ready in their hands, and were rebuffed. The diplomats were more subtle, as well as more flattering; they wanted nothing except the friendship of Pharamaul, though perhaps—in some far-distant future—certain small generosities by way of reciprocal support might be looked for. It was a matter of His Excellency's *attitude*, nothing more. . . . Since Pharamaul had become a republic, a number of competing countries had shown warm and urgent interest in its future.

Who would have thought that the Russians wanted to study the soil structure of northern Pharamaul? Who would have thought that the Portuguese were interested in an exchange of cultural missions? Who would have thought the British Council so eager to make definitive records of its folk-songs? Who would have thought that the Chinese had ever heard of the place?

Dinamaula, aware of problems interlaced like tendrils in a rain forest, stirred himself, set down his empty glass, and signalled languidly to the watchful servant. Almost before his hand had dropped in his lap again, the man was walking towards him, wearing a smile, bearing a tray. This was, indeed, one of the happiest hours of the day.

The change to a republic had been served up to him on another tray; the calendar had scarcely swung before the departure of the Urles became a matter of public necessity, and their replacement by a second emissary of the Queen unthinkable. The Governor-General and his awful wife had done the trick, all by themselves. . . . Dinamaula would always remember the last few weeks of their weird tenure, when a remorseful Earl of Urle, feeling the chill wind of disapproval blowing about his ears, from quarters as far apart as Fish Village and Whitehall, had suddenly become a model of decorum and duty; while Bobo Urle, raging in public and in private about everybody's "stuffiness," had embarked on a wild series of parties, pub crawls, exotic free-verse recitals, insults, tantrums, crying jags and cruel hangovers.

It had been brought to a head by a wonderfully scandalous scene, when she floated out of a nightclub as the morning cocks began to crow, had insisted on driving the Government House car home, to the terror of her chauffeur, and had bashed straight into a market gardener's cart, carpeting the entire street with an assortment of pumpkins, melons, avocado pears, and squashed passion-fruit.

She had leant out of the Rolls-Royce, surveyed the horrid mess of split rinds and entrails of pulpy fruit, murmured "Icky!" and promptly driven off again, pursued by shouts and by a police Land-Rover which had happened to be cruising by. The police car had tailed her, every tire squealing like a wounded hyena, to the very portico of Government House. At this point she had staggered out of the Rolls, tipsy as a lark at dawn, and, her sense of universal brotherhood slipping a notch, could be heard bawling up at the façade:

"Eustace! This bloody nigger's trying to arrest me! *Do* something!"

After that, tempers had grown really short, coded telegrams flew to and fro like hooded bats, and Bobo Urle was put firmly into purdah until the time of departure. At the final leave-taking, the Police Band had played, as a matter of tradition, the somber air of "Will Ye No Come Back Again?" It was clear that the answer was an emphatic echo of "No!"; but, to drive the point home as the aircraft taxied away, the band had then swung into a jaunty, "high life" version of something different.

It was an old favourite of many continents, "I'll Be Glad When You're Dead, You Rascal You!" and was very well received by all concerned.

The rest had fallen neatly into place; it had been like pressing a button marked "Republic," and waiting for the medal to drop. But even so, not everyone had liked the change—and the malcontents were by no means all drawn from the main bar of the Port Victoria Club. Of course, there had been plenty of loyal howls from that quarter; but it had been the two northern chiefs, from Shebiya and Fish Village, who had led the opposition, carrying their people with them and causing something like a split, on straight party lines, within the new House of Assembly.

"What do we want with this new republic?" old Chief Banka had thundered, in the course of a debate which had been tempestuous and emotional by turns, as if men suddenly saw their true enemies for the first time, and knew that such enemies might be lifelong. "Why are we turning our backs upon the Queen? Why are we cutting these bonds, which have been our pride for a hundred years? Who is to take the place of the Queen, and receive our homage, and be sure of our love?" He looked with cold disdain towards Prime Minister Dinamaula, sitting with lowered brows a few yards from him. "We know well who it is, we know which man has been foremost in thrusting this change upon us. . . . It is the man whom we are glad to call Prime

Minister, whom we were glad to call Chief in the past. *But*"—he suddenly crashed his wrinkled palm on the desk in front of him, and in the silence which followed asked, in tones of measured spite: "But are we now to call him king?"

Dinamaula, remembering that moment, and the ugly scene which followed it, with fists shaken across the floor of the House, and a drunken young member from Fish Village making a pantomime of a man kneeling in homage—Dinamaula stirred himself again, this time in quick discomfort. He would never forgive Chief Banka of Shebiya his speech, and the cunning insult which lay in that last question. . . . At the time he had answered with a matching insolence:

"If and when the day comes, you will call me Mr. President. I will then choose whether to answer, and what to call *you*."

His supporters had roared their acclaim at the thrust. But the wound to himself was still there, salty and throbbing, even as he laughed at the old chief, and outfaced him. He had never wanted to be called "king," and it was unworthy to charge him thus. It was not to be borne. Could not a man become President, without these shrill and mangy dogs barking at his heels?

The bill had been voted through, in an atmosphere thick with suspicion and ill-temper, though the later "Dinamaula for President" referendum had been a rousing success—one colossal week-long party, during which the beer flowed like a river, and work became almost a treasonable word. On the morrow, a few more people had sold up and left—the kind, thought Dinamaula, who could best be spared; and the northern districts of Pharamaul had settled down to a sullen, watchful silence.

It was the first quarrel of the new nation, and it seemed likely to last, and perhaps to revive the ancient tribal division between north and south. The brief honeymoon was over—and with that thought, a black cloud on a sunny day, the President's mind swerved away from politics, and centered with grim, furtive distaste upon his own bed.

Lieutenant Paul Jordan, Royal Navy, His Excellency's principal aide-de-camp, stood in his dressing gown by an open window on the first floor of Government House, looking down at the garden and at his master under the elm tree. The dressing gown, a splendid silk affair embroidered with hearts and flowers, had been a Valentine's Day present from Sybil Bartholomew, the Social

Secretary, who had personally helped him to try it on for the first time.

He still squirmed when he remembered the scene, and the way she had gambolled round him like an arch shire-horse, with many a whinny of joy, many a cry of "Just like Casanova! . . ." But now that she was gone, he could wear it with genuine satisfaction. It was much more expensive than anything he could have afforded himself.

Paul Jordan could only see the lower half of the President—the skirts of his robe, and the elaborate tasselled sandals below them; the rest was hidden by thick-leaved branches. But it was enough; it told him where Dinamaula was, which was something he liked to know even when, as now, he was off-duty. It was when the chap started prowling about the larder, or skipping up to the maids' bedrooms, that one felt a bit of a charlie. . . . But it was all part of his job, the job he did not want and had hoped by now to escape.

When the Urles had left, he had expected to leave with them. But, for a reason he now understood, Dinamaula had put in an urgent plea that Paul Jordan be retained as a presidential aide; and he had been able to pull it off, at any rate for a limited period. Dinamaula, Paul now knew, had insisted on keeping him because he was not at all sure of himself in his new surroundings, in the magnificence and state of his new position.

He was afraid of making silly mistakes; thus he needed continuity, and a good deal of discreet guidance; and he wanted it, not from someone like David Bracken, who was quite enough of a father figure already, but from a younger man, whose junior position was beyond question. So the request had been made, and the strings pulled; and Paul stayed where he was, an essential prop not too superior to be told to see that the ice-buckets were topped up and the ashtrays emptied.

It wasn't a bad job, though it seemed further than ever from the sea. Paul was able to get quite a lot of free time: like this morning, which was a half-day off, in preparation for another dreary thrash that night—a dinner in honour of the Japanese trade mission, which was trying to flood Pharamaul with their funny little cars. The snag was that, even after the disappearance of the senior and junior banes of his life—Bobo Urle and Sybil Bartholomew—this was a slightly miserable household to work in.

The trouble was still the eternal trouble—good old sex. But

this time it was sex that didn't take. President Dinamaula, after seven years of marriage, was still unable to father a child, and he was getting bored with trying.

Tradition in Pharamaul still favoured the idea that this could only be the wife's fault, and her abiding shame, and in former times it had been sufficient excuse for sending the disgraced and barren bride back to her father's hut, the dismissal to be followed by a lawsuit, which might last a generation, over the return of the goats and cattle making up the dowry. But obviously this would not suit the second half of the twentieth century; and it was out of the question for the President of a modern "emerging nation," eager to show the world how up to date it was.

Dinamaula therefore had three choices: to divorce his wife, who was called Mayika, daughter of a Gamate tribal elder; to give up his hopes of an heir; or to keep on trying.

The first two were not to be entertained; the divorce of a wife who was connected, in one way or another, with half the ruling clique of Gamate would have been politically hazardous; and an heir, born to the royal line of Maula the Great, was essential for much the same reason. Thus, with decreasing enthusiasm, he kept on trying.

But he kept on trying in his own way, and it was this that Paul Jordan found forlorn and slightly irritating. Dinamaula slept with Mayika whenever he could summon the energy; he practiced assiduously on the female staff of Government House, and their relatives and friends, all of whom remained obstinately childless; and he took counsel with what could only be called the confidence men—a troupe of witch-doctors, quacks, wise men, soothsayers, casters of spells, herbalists, makers of strange medicine, and manipulators of flesh, all of whom claimed to have the one infallible answer.

It was sad, and silly. He and Mayika should of course have gone straight to a gynecologist, taken the necessary tests, assigned the blame, and worked out the answer—if answer there was. But instead the President had returned to the dark past, to the ancient myths of Africa which had always infected this topic.

Government House—or part of it—now resembled a sort of crazy bazaar. There was a continual coming and going of hucksters and quacks whose absurd wares and astonishing treatment seemed to combine a magicians' catalogue with a sixteenth-century medical convention. Dinamaula was dosed with love potions, aphrodisiacs, powdered rhinoceros horn, bits of toad ground up with menstrual fluid, Spanish fly, and oysters laced with red pepper.

Incantations were recited over the marriage bed, spells laid upon the pillow, and bones cast to determine copulation's lucky hour. He was exposed to mascots, jujus, fertility charms, thermal baths with rank ingredients, and ritual dances of an explicit kind. His private parts were encouraged by the application of tattoo needles, and lightly whipped with that Biblical toy, a bull's pizzle. He was counselled to crow like a cock at the moment of ejaculation.

Paul Jordan learned all this from the Government House butler, an expert in this area, who maintained that it was only a matter of time, while taking a steady rake-off from every such caller admitted. Dinamaula said nothing about it; and poor Mayika, who rarely said anything anyway, never spoke a word nor cracked a smile. The big moon-faced girl, now running to fat, had settled back in mournful shadow—a true cooking-pot wife whose compulsive interest was in fact eating.

She must have felt deeply ashamed, but she was not yet bitter. She remained placid, expressionless, and greedy. It was becoming her habit now to miss official functions, taking her enormous meals alone in her room. Dinamaula went to most parties by himself. Government House had become a brooding, slightly scandalous bachelor's lair.

There was a tendency now to call it "the Palace"—Dinamaula himself sometimes did so; and there was no doubt that the Palace was becoming an expensive place to run.

It was to be expected, Paul thought, that at the beginning the newly-elected President should give things a bit of a bash; he had something to celebrate, and he liked celebrating. No harm in that. . . . But the late-night parties for his cronies were now almost a daily feature, and the catering, which no one bothered to control, had grown extravagant and wasteful.

Great tubs of meat, spoiled vegetables, and half-loaves of bread could be seen every day at the back door, waiting for the refuse-men. An army of "Friends of the Kitchen," as Paul Jordan called them, hung round the back quarters, and was fed daily by an openhanded chef. Champagne was the staple diet at the President's supper parties, and brook trout which had to be flown in from the Northern Transvaal, and crayfish tails, and perhaps a small mound of *pâté*, and caviare spread on digestive biscuits. . . .

It was funny, in a depressing sort of way. One did not need to be a snob to appreciate that the standard of living of those close to the throne had taken a dramatic upswing. Alexanian, who was the principal supplier of "luxuries" to Government House, must be making a minor fortune.

In one respect, this high living had a clear, unsubtle connection with the past. At one of these parties, Paul had heard Dinamaula giving, with huge enjoyment, an imitation of Sir Elliott Vere-Toombs, the former Governor, reading out his exile order, while occupying the very chair in which the President now sat. It was a popular turn, and went down very well. The party that night be-came riotous, and the collection of empty bottles next morning was something like a record.

One could understand *that*, too; if the past still rankled, the present could be made to square the account. But how all this was going to be paid for was another matter.

The noise of a motor car coming up the drive drew him closer to the window. It turned into the forecourt with a defiant swish of gravel, and could be recognized as one of the fleet of six black Cadillacs which had been put at the disposal of senior ministers. That was another £24,000 on the score-sheet. . . . Paul Jordan watched as the occupants got out, assisted by a chauffeur in maroon uniform and a braided cap, and started to walk across the lawn towards the President.

It was the Heavenly Twins—Joseph Kalatosi, who was now Deputy Chief Secretary, and Captain Mboku, newly promoted, of the Pharamaul Police.

It was they who now made the daily calls on the President, instead of David Bracken and Major Crump. Of course, this was Maularization, as promised. . . . Paul watched as the three came together in one group, and two servants with laden trays began to walk swiftly in its direction; and then he stood back a pace, and settled down to wait.

In a little while it would be time for the Vulture Parade, the morning rush. He was not involved in the receiving line today, thank God, but it was always worthwhile keeping an eye on such callers. All sorts of odd people were getting chummy, these days.

Even six months after "Republic Day," no one was working very hard. The holiday mood persisted, just as it had done after

Independence; the national party went on, and anything or nothing was an excuse for keeping it going. Since they were now their own masters, it was felt and said, why should they have to behave like servants, as in the old days? Indeed, why should they work at all? Only a fool *ordered* himself to work.

So there were freedom rallies, and celebration marches, and solidarity demonstrations, and firework displays, and good-natured strikes when the mood was so inclined. Football teams and swimming clubs multiplied; the newest craze was for street picnics, when traffic was barred from four o'clock onwards, and a colossal brew of beer made, enough to last through an evening and half the night. The resulting sore heads always needed a second day for recovery.

Dockers stopped work when the sun was hot, leaving the quays idle and goods hanging in the cargo slings. The factory up at Fish Village had to be closed for a month, because a key maintenance man drank himself to sleep on the job, and failed to notice an overload which ruined most of the assembly line. Shops put up their shutters, while the assistants sunned themselves on the pavement outside.

Official exhortations, in and out of the Legislature, fell on ears not exactly deaf, but bemused by a lazy contentment. There always seemed to be enough to eat—and why not? Was not the food all theirs now? Then there was this new thing called Assistance—small, but enough to keep a man happy, especially if he had been blessed with children. And why not, again? It was *their* money, and *their* country, and above all *their* freedom to do what they liked with it.

In this matter of freedom, the *Times of Pharamaul* was beginning to take a sour line:

"It is time to wake up!" [Tom Stillwell commanded his readers, after Budget Day in the Legislature had disclosed some unmistakable danger signals.] "Yesterday's national accounting was something which should make all of us alarmed, and some of us ashamed. The President's own words, 'We must all work a little harder,' were something short of the truth, and something less than an inspiring battle-cry.

"*We must all work a lot harder*, and that is a stark fact

which no amount of soft soap or soothing syrup should be allowed to hide.

"Strikes, unofficial holidays, absenteeism, slacking on the job—these all add up to one thing, which yesterday's budget figures make clear: we are simply not earning our keep. Pharamaul is still celebrating its 'freedom,' instead of getting down to the task of making itself truly strong and truly independent.

"There is only one road to that goal. It is the road of hard work.

"There is another danger, which those in authority often seem to disregard. It is the danger that, as a country, we are trying to run before we have learned to walk. Ambitious schemes and costly projects are all very well, but the time for them is not yet. Let our plans be modest and properly thought out; let us get things in the right order. And once again, let us *work*, to translate plans into reality.

"With hard work must come thrift, both individual and national. At this stage, there are many things this country cannot afford. We look to our leaders to set us a good example.

"There is one particular aspect of this, to which this newspaper draws early attention.

"There have been reports that Pharamaul is to become a member of the United Nations, with a full-blown delegation going to New York in the not-too-distant future. To some, it will seem early days for us to embark on such a big undertaking, early days to think that we can really contribute to this world forum.

"But if we do become a member, let us proceed with care. Let us remember our stature as a nation. Above all, let our delegation be a modest one, and its expenditure in keeping with a small country which, if it were a family, would travel by bicycle rather than by the smallest motorcar.

"There is nothing to be gained, and much to lose, by 'showing off.' We are not millionaires, and without stringent economy and—once again—*work!* we have no hope of ever becoming so."

• • •

But then, who cared about the *Times of Pharamaul*, even when it was thundering?

"It's all very well for that bolshy bastard to talk," said a loud voice at the end of the bar. "A lot of it's his fault. Of course he's whining about conditions *now*. He should have thought of that, before he started shoving independence down our throats."

"I don't need Tom Stillwell to tell me my troubles," complained a second voice. "What did he think was going to happen to this country? Who ever heard of a Maula doing a stroke of work, without a good sharp kick up the backside?"

"All the same, Dinamaula isn't going to like that article."

"I won't lose much sleep over that."

"Boy! I mean, steward!"

"Come on, Weekes! It's your last chance, you know."

It was another farewell party at the Port Victoria Club.

This time it was for a retired army Major called Weekes, who was returning to England after fifteen years in Pharamaul, "absolutely defeated," he said, "by all these changes." Towards the end of a long evening, he had reached a stage of snuffling incoherence, in which the phrases "Given my life to this country," and "My wife can't stand it any more," were becoming blurred and intermingled, like a faulty sound track.

No one really liked Weekes, who was a bore without enough money to make him palatable; and his wife had well earned the concise nickname of Boadicea. But tonight, Weekes was the hero of the hour. He was one more white man driven out of his own country by the enemy, one more of the garrison who could ill be spared, but who must be allowed his honourable retreat, marching out of the beleaguered fort with a comparatively fixed bayonet.

"Though why you want to go back to England, beats me," said Splinter Woodcock, the eternal center of all such gatherings, frowning at his glass as if it might sneak away before he had drained it. "The welfare state! Jack's as good as his master! Income tax! They'll rob you blind, just to give free false teeth to a lot of layabouts."

"Oh, I don't know," answered Weekes vaguely. "Old England, you know. Never changes."

"I've got news for you."

Biggs-Johnson, the loyal supporter, laughed dutifully. "I certainly wouldn't go back *there*. Not at any price. All the same, sometimes I've a good mind to sell up, myself. The outlook for taxes——"

"You sell up," Splinter Woodcock interrupted him. "You sell up while you can. Try South Africa. Try Rhodesia, or Portuguese East. They've got the right idea there. Alexanian would buy you out, any time."

"At a price."

"Well, he's a Jew, isn't he?" Woodcock spread his hands, palms upwards. "Give me mein pound of flesh, eh?"

"Oh, Alex is all right. And you know, he still believes in this place."

"I should damn well think he does, the rate he's going. He'll end up by owning half the island. And much good that'll do him."

"How do you mean?" an outer voice inquired.

"Because they'll kick him out of the country, as soon as he gets too big."

"But he'll still have the money, won't he?"

"He'll have the money in blocked Pharamaul sterling. That'll be about as much use as a sick headache. In the end, they'll pay him off in seashells. If they pay him off at all."

"Alex is smarter than that."

"He'll need to be." Woodcock spread his hands again. "Oi, oi! I've been robbed! . . . He'll be lucky if he gets out with his season ticket to the synagogue. But what can you expect, if you put a bunch of stupid coolies in charge of the whole works, and give them a free hand?"

There was a sudden, embarrassed murmur of "Sh!," and some backward glances towards the fireplace, where a late-staying party of Maula members were quietly taking their ease.

Splinter Woodcock came to instant, bristling attention.

"Don't you shush me!" he snarled belligerently. "This is *my* club! Christ, I was a member here when most of these *gentlemen* were sticking their backsides out and doing it in the street!"

"You mean, last week?"

A wave of barking laughter spread along the bar, making all well again. Then, like a boozy Greek chorus, the voices rose once more, led by a wavering Major Weekes:

"That's why I'm pulling up stakes! This whole place has gone native! My wife can't stand it any more!"

"Have another drink, old boy. It's your last chance, you know."

"After giving up my whole life!"

"Of course, old Splinter did get had up for widdling against a lamp post outside the club. Don't you remember?"

"It was quashed."

Woodcock, overhearing, bellowed out: "It wasn't quashed! Just a bit bent, that's all. But don't tell the wife."

"If she doesn't know now, she never will."

"Of course, he's dead right about the way this country's going."

"Well, *I'm* staying on."

"Good for you."

"Did you hear about the slogan for Brotherhood Week in the Congo?"

"What was that?"

" 'Take a missionary home for dinner.' "

"Can you imagine us going to the United Nations?"

"Does it matter a damn who goes to that bloody place?"

The decision to sponsor Pharamaul for membership of the United Nations, to pay her annual dues for some years to come, and to underwrite, substantially, the cost of her delegation to New York, caused fewer headaches in Whitehall than the flurry over Rhodesia; but it was nonetheless very trying, very trying indeed. It was not a question of money, though that aspect was far from satisfactory; it was a doubt as to whether this fledgling country, so fresh out of the egg, should belong to UN at all.

Pharamaul, on independence, had come under the wing of the Commonwealth Office. But, by one of those exercises in musical chairs which, in Whitehall, went by the label "Economy," all the staff of the Scheduled Territories Office made redundant by the "new nations" leaving the nest were transferred, man by man, to the parent organization. Thus the same people, though in slightly different hats, were now looking after Pharamaul as had advised and controlled her in the past.

It was Hubert Godbold's successor, Sir Goronwy Griffith, who had to deal with the latest turn of events; and his distaste for it had stirred up a very rough patch of water indeed.

Griffith, a small, elegant, rather jumpy Welshman, son of a schoolmaster, grandson of a postman, had worked very hard to get where he was; and he was disposed to take good care that everyone else climbing the ladder, whether they were juniors in his cipher room or the heads of small nations, should work very hard too.

There was little he could do about Pharamaul and UN, once the proposal was squarely on the table; the reins of tutorship were now so loose that they hardly existed at all. All he could manage was to advise delay; to urge President Dinamaula to allow what he called, in an unfortunate phrase, "a decent interval" to go by before pushing for membership.

To this end, he used his talents for persuasion, which were legendary, and his capacity for obstruction and delay, which was notorious. The lengthy dispatches multiplied; the complicated, minutely detailed estimates of cost were solemnly batted to and fro, each time with tiny amendments clinging to them like leeches.

David Bracken, in a series of private letters, was ordered to use his best endeavours to see that the idea was scotched for at least five years, while Pharamaul got on its feet. Finally, Dinamaula was invited to London for "talks"—that beloved euphemism, which might cover anything from amiable waffle to the most peremptory directive.

Inclining towards the latter, Sir Goronwy Griffith found he had come up against a man at least as tough as himself, and in a much stronger position altogether. President Dinamaula listened to him with good-humoured politeness—it was so nice to be in London again, and his suite at Claridge's was all that a man, even a head of state, could wish. Then, leading from lazy strength, he made two points crystal clear.

If Britain did not want to sponsor Pharamaul, someone else would. If Britain did not want to pay for the exercise, someone else would do that too.

Across the width of a handsome mahogany desk, suitable for a Knight Commander of the Most Distinguished Order of St. Michael and St. George, Sir Goronwy Griffith looked at the man who had suddenly become an adversary. He had met Dinamaula many times before: at the time of his exile, at the bargaining which preceded his return to Pharamaul, at the close negotiations for independence, and at later meetings of the Commonwealth Secretariat, always a good time for "talks." But he had not met him on this sort of ground, nor in this sort of mood.

"My dear Mr. President," he said finally, his tone lapsing into that lilting Welsh asperity which his staff knew as "the Druid's revenge," "I hardly think we need look beyond the *present* elements of this discussion."

"I was not doing so, Sir Goronwy," Dinamaula answered. He took the last two words very slowly; he found "Sir Goronwy" almost as difficult to say as "Sir Dinamaula," though the latter was not likely to become a problem. "I was simply mentioning some alternatives. If you do not wish to sponsor us——"

"We are perfectly prepared to sponsor you," Griffith interrupted him, with sharp determination. "But it must be at what we regard as the proper time."

"If you do not wish to sponsor us," Dinamaula went on equably, borrowing a technique, endured many times in the past, which was purest Whitehall, and best summed up as *Accept, Ignore, Continue,* "then clearly we must look elsewhere. In the course of *looking elsewhere"*—he repeated the key words with elaborate care, as if they were part of a spelling lesson—"we have received a number of alternative offers of help."

"May I ask, from whom?" Griffith asked.

"Certainly." It was not too long after lunch, and Dinamaula, fresh from Claridge's splendid restaurant, was at peace with all the world. But he was not fooling, and he had all his cast-iron facts, and he produced them now with a poker-player's relish for a packed hand: "Russia, Zambia, the United Arab Republic, and France have all given me assurances that they would be glad to sponsor Pharamaul. In addition, China and West Germany have signified their willingness to"—he waved his hands gently—"to underwrite the cost of our membership, as soon as it goes through."

Sir Goronwy Griffith had to admit that it was extremely well done; the phrase "Have given *me* assurances" was particularly effective, a superior exercise in personal effrontery. The list of countries was authentic, and perfectly damnable. Also involved in this operation was that familiar piece of twentieth-century blackmail, which America especially had to contend with, in a score of gruesome confrontations: "Give us the money, or we'll go communist." But this time, the net was wider, and skilfully spread.

For all sorts of reasons, the inclusion of France was a master stroke, by both sides.

After an overlong pause, Griffith said: "I must congratulate you on having so many good friends."

In the circumstances, it was something less than a penetrating shaft, and Dinamaula did not feel he need do more than incline his head.

"*But,*" said Griffith, after waiting, "do you really wish to commit yourself in this way?"

"Commit myself?"

"Place yourself under an obligation to another country which has helped you financially." He picked out the least complicated one. "West Germany, for example."

"I would be under no more obligation to West Germany," said Dinamaula, "than I would be to you."

Sir Goronwy Griffith winced—a concealed Whitehall wince which, on a thousand such occasions in the last twenty-five years, had masked the pain of man's ingratitude. This was take-it-or-leave-it in its most wounding form; even if they paid the piper, apparently, they were not to call the tune—nor even know its name. He made some scribbles on the blotter in front of him; presently, persistently, they turned out to be arrows, pointing in different directions. Not much help there. . . . Annoyed, suspecting mismanagement somewhere, he said:

"I would certainly hope that, if we sponsor Pharamaul, and make these generous financial provisions, we can expect loyal co-operation, to say the least."

"Surely the United Nations serves world rather than sectional interests."

In his more exasperated moments, Sir Goronwy Griffith sometimes wished that he was an ardent Welsh Nationalist, blindly dedicated to one tiny segment of human aspiration, free to turn awkward, free if need be to tell the rest of all mankind to go to hell. This was one such occasion. He was not doing well with President Dinamaula; in fact he was not doing anything with President Dinamaula; already he knew that he would have to backtrack on all the recent past, all the committee work, all the wise counsel, and let the other man have what he wanted.

If not, he would be breaching one of the cardinal rules of the club, hopefully enclosed in a global girdle which stretched from India to Nigeria: the rule that Britain's graduate children—industrious, gifted, plus-eleven-plus—must always merit special consideration, and receive at least half a dozen free scholarships to help them towards the bright horizon of the future.

In sum, they had now received hundreds of millions of pounds, loyal backing, and patient forbearance in the face of insolence.

The myth still persisted that they were thereby fashioned into staunch supporters of the Commonwealth; and it was not his job, alas, to point out the rents and tears, the myriad moth-holes in such mythology. England now, like some ancient insured person, expected very little from her dutiful, prompt, and inflated premiums. . . . Griffith stopped doodling, and stopped casting round for valid arguments, or any arguments. Instead, he said:

"I need a little time to think about this. Shall we say, tomorrow morning?"

"By all means."

The tone was so bland that Sir Goronwy Griffith was stung to match it with a little acid. "Normally I would ask if we could do anything to make you more comfortable. Theater tickets, and so forth. But of course, you know London well, don't you?"

Dinamaula, who had been prepared to coast down a most favourable slope, decided after all that this was a bit too much.

"I know London *quite* well," he answered, allowing the words rather than the tone to make their own sarcastic point. "I was sent into exile here. I was here for five years. I had an allowance of ten pounds a week, and I lived in a bed-sitting-room in Acton." He smiled with cold irony. "Acton is one of your western suburbs. Now I am staying at Claridge's. Suite number four hundred and five. It costs thirty-two pounds a day—though of course I am not paying that. *You* are paying it. The only question which now arises is, how much more do you wish to pay?"

"Now, just a minute—" began Griffith.

Dinamaula had once slept with a Welsh girl, to their mutual enlightenment. "*Prynhawn da,*" he said cheerfully. "See you tomorrow."

On the morrow, he got all that he wanted, as any fool might have foreseen. But it was ungracefully done, leaving another smeared fingermark on this small windowpane of history, a fingermark which could have been avoided with a little clean common sense. As it was, no one was really happy. Dinamaula returned home with his grudged prize; and Griffith remained, in possession of a singularly barren field.

For many days afterwards, "the Druid's revenge" was a fearsome reality among his staff.

Though Sir Goronwy Griffith kept a voluminous private diary, in anticipation of his planned memoirs, he made only one brief entry on this occasion. Against the notation of Dinamaula's final appointment, he wrote, in thin red ink:

"Still bitter."

There was so much he could say that David Bracken found himself almost speechless. The chaotic mass of accounts which someone had slid into his In-tray, early that morning, was not simply appalling; it was accounting gone mad, and spending gone mad also. When Joseph Kalatosi came in to see him at half-past ten, it was difficult not to glare at him, to start lacing into him from the very first word.

Though it was not really Kalatosi's fault, yet he seemed to David to represent the people whose fault it was, and he had probably done his share in promoting the kind of extravagance which these wretched schedules had laid bare. By all accounts, he always did himself well, up at Government House. . . . David looked up from his desk, and said curtly:

"Good morning, Joseph."

"Good morning, David."

The small exchange reflected their changed status, now well established. It did not mean, David thought grimly, that Kalatosi had learned any more sense. He slapped his hand down on the file, and said:

"This is ridiculous."

Joseph Kalatosi opened his eyes very wide. Then he made a show of peering across the desk. "What papers are those?" he asked.

"The accounts," said David briefly. He decided to dive in straight away. "The bills are starting to come in, and they show that we're wildly over the estimates. As you must know already. We've overspent by at least £250,000 in the last half-year. A quarter of a million pounds." He stopped abruptly, and took refuge in colloquialism. "Don't you think that's a bloody awful way to run a country?"

Joseph Kalatosi also took refuge, in a bromidic phrase which he had used many times before. "We are at an experimental stage," he said mildly.

"Rubbish," snapped David. "We're just getting in a hell of a mess. Don't you understand? Doesn't anyone understand? We've gone over our budget by at least twenty per cent, *in six months.* Where's the money to come from?"

Kalatosi did not seem at all put out, either by the tone or the facts. He had sat down in an armchair, crossed his legs comfortably, and lighted a cigarette. Then through a cloud of smoke, gently expelled, he answered:

"From various sources, I imagine."

"There aren't any *various sources*," said David, almost savagely. "Money doesn't just grow on trees. It either has to be earned, or it has to be borrowed, and then paid back. What on earth's the good of having estimates, if we don't stick to them?"

"Perhaps they were not good estimates."

This time, David Bracken did glare at him. "I prepared them." Kalatosi gave him the wide-eyed look again. "Oh, I did not mean *that*. They were *excellent* estimates, in their own way."

"What's that supposed to mean?"

"I mean, they were just estimates, weren't they? What is it the Yanks call them? *Guess*timates. There is so much to be guessed, at this stage, so much that we cannot foresee."

"I foresaw everything that common sense told me was necessary, and unavoidable. What I *didn't* foresee"—David flipped over some of the papers in front of him—"was six Cadillacs at £4,000 each. What I didn't foresee was a thirty-per-cent increase in civil-service salaries. Or houses for ministers—£72,000. Or an admiral's barge, £16,000. Or twenty-four electric typewriters for £4,800. And what I *particularly* didn't foresee was that it would cost £5,000 a month to run Government House."

"You must appreciate," said Kalatosi, "that there has been a great deal of official entertaining."

"You're damn right there has! A hundred and fifty cases of champagne, at £30 a case, for a start." David stared across at Kalatosi. "How is the champagne—officially?"

Kalatosi was silent for several seconds. But he was staring directly back, David noted, and it was unusual for him to do this in any circumstances. It was therefore less than astonishing when Kalatosi answered, in cold withdrawal:

"You have no right to use that tone."

There was a first time for everything, thought David, and this was the first time that Joseph Kalatosi had ever steered a collision course, and held it, without swerving, to the moment of impact. Perhaps it was the first time that he had needed to; David could not remember a row like this ever having happened before. For an obscure reason, he felt rather glad about it, and pleased with

Joseph Kalatosi for standing his ground. But he was not pleased enough to change his nature overnight. He snapped back:

"I'll use any tone I like. These figures are disgraceful, and you know it."

"It was not necessary for you to become personal."

Perhaps that was true, thought David; Kalatosi might have grown fond of champagne, but he had not drunk eighteen hundred bottles of it. On a milder note, he said:

"All right—let's forget it. But don't you see, Joseph, this sort of thing is hopeless. Pharamaul will never get on its feet, if it doesn't live within its budget."

"Neither can it grow, if it is in a straitjacket. That is as bad as the old days."

The mild appeal had not touched Kalatosi at all; he had taken his ground on the champagne issue, which had nettled him, and his tone made it clear that a quarrel still lay between them. David said:

"All right. Have it your own way. But it's silly to talk of straitjackets. How can you possibly run a country, without strict accounting?"

"Perhaps we are going to find out. At least, we will be making our own mistakes."

"You've certainly got off to a good start."

The retort had been irresistible, and David was not sorry to see how Kalatosi fired up as soon as he took it in. If toughness did not work, and mildness made no impression, then at least toughness was more enjoyable. . . . Kalatosi, breathing hard, said:

"You are sneering! I will tell everybody, everybody!"

"I am not sneering at all. I'm explaining the facts of life. This sort of spending is absolutely out of the question."

"That is not for you to say. You do not authorize. Only the President, as Minister of Finance, can authorize. After a debate, and a vote. And that is only for the elected members."

"But I'm here to advise you! God damn it, I *know* about these things!" David turned back to the files. "Look, let's go through a few of the figures, and I'll try to show you what I mean. The original estimates——"

But Joseph Kalatosi had suddenly stopped listening. His eyes dropped without concealment as he consulted a gold wristwatch. Then he said:

"I'm sorry. I must go. I have an appointment with the President."

"This is more important."

"The President would not like to hear you say that."

"But we *must* settle this! You're off to New York in a couple of days."

"That is why I should keep my appointment with the President. We are discussing the details of the delegation, and what we do when we get there."

David sighed, and sat back in his chair. They were not making any progress, and they were not likely to do so, in the present atmosphere. There would have to be another time, and probably another kind of approach. He said, on a note of dismissal:

"Well, whatever you do when you get there, for heaven's sake stick to your budget. You know exactly how much you have to spend, and the Commonwealth Office simply won't stand for any more."

"We are most grateful for their contribution."

"It isn't a contribution! It is a direct annual grant, to cover the whole of your UN expenditure. But you'll have to watch how it goes, all the time. Living in New York can be very expensive."

"So I understand."

"You shouldn't be going with them, really. It's not your job at all."

"We are so short of qualified men."

"We're short of qualified men, right here in the Secretariat."

For the first time Joseph Kalatosi smiled, a gentle and infuriating smile.

"With the Chief Secretary left behind as a watchdog, how could we lose a moment's sleep?"

"The children love the new stamps," said Nicole.

"I'm glad somebody does," said David. It was the end of a long day, and his bad mood had not yet left him. "I still prefer the Queen's head."

"But he photographs quite well."

"So does Twiggy."

Nicole looked up from her sock-mending. "Good heavens, David—what do you know about Twiggy?"

"I know she has a friend called Engelbert Humperdinck."

"Darling, *no!* That's another one. *Her* friend is called Justin de Villeneuve."

"That's what we should have called Timmy."

He was smiling slightly, which was something new for that evening, but the smile did not do much for the tight lines round his eyes, and the grey smudges of fatigue. Nicole looked at him for a long moment before asking:

"Tired?"

"Just a bit. There's an awful lot of work at the office, and friend Joe isn't doing much of it. He's too tied up with this UN jaunt."

"How did he get on to the delegation?"

"He has a friend. . . . Actually, it's not a bad idea that he is going. He's been getting on my nerves lately. We had a bit of a row this morning."

"What a shame. What was it about?"

"Money. Spending. But that's not the main part of it." David sat back in his armchair, frowning, tapping his pipestem against his teeth. "Joe Kal is getting a bit too eager. The take-over has really started."

"But isn't that the whole idea, that he should take over?"

"Not in three easy lessons."

Nicole laid aside the finished mending. "Justin de Villeneuve needs some new socks."

"*Who?*"

"Timmy."

"Oh. . . ." He shook his head. "Sorry, darling. I'm not really with it this evening."

"You need a holiday, David. Can't we go across to Cape Town, or along the Natal coast somewhere, and forget all this for a bit?"

He shook his head. "Not possible. Particularly with things in the state they are. It's more and more obvious that we're getting ourselves into the most awful mess. That's how the row started this morning."

"The money?"

"Yes. They're being so extravagant, it's hard to believe some of it. Things are simply getting out of hand. Of course, it's Dinamaula's fault, not Joe's. He's been buying the most absurd things, and I'm sure he's planning a lot of other damned nonsense as well. And Government House is just becoming a racket. . . . I'll have to read the riot act before long."

"Can you do that?"

"Not really. But I'll have a damned good try. He can't go on like this."

"Alex says they're putting in a private cinema."

"I know. . . . Maybe I should read the riot act to Alex as well."

Nicole looked up, very surprised. "Darling, why?"

"I get the impression that he's making things a bit too easy for them. The extravagance, I mean. Do you remember when he was here, he said something about not wanting to get too involved, or taking on too many Government commissions, because in the end it would all be based on funny money? Frankly, I think he's changed his mind about that. I think he's collecting all the money he can, as fast as possible, before it does turn funny."

"But darling, how awful to have a row with Alex! And after all, it is his living."

"He can make a perfectly good living, without selling admiral's barges, or importing brook trout from Magaliesburg. He did make a perfectly good living, before all this nonsense started."

"I suppose so. . . . What a shame. . . . Everything's so unsettled. . . ." She put her hand up to her cheek. "Which reminds me. I'm terribly afraid that Simon wants to go home."

"He can have a holiday if he wants."

"No. It's more than that. You know how he talks, round and round in circles. But I think he wants to leave for good. Go back to Shebiya."

"Why on earth?"

"He said something about a U-Maula being a stranger here."

"But he's been with us thirteen years!"

"It's no good if he's miserable."

David got to his feet. "Oh, God damn it! What's gone wrong with this place?" He was striding about the room in a surge of restless irritation. "Everybody's starting to quarrel. Nobody trusts anybody. The north thinks the south is getting away with murder. The south thinks the north doesn't deserve anything better. And down here"—he stopped suddenly, and swung round to face her—"it's shaping up into something even worse. We're starting to split up, before we've even got started. It's beginning to be us against them."

"Who's 'us,' exactly?"

"Me and Keith Crump. Chaps like Stillwell. And on the other side, Dinamaula and Joe Kal and Mboku. It sounds like a colour thing, but it isn't! It goes far deeper than that. It's two entirely different ways of running Pharamaul. One of them is honest, the other is crooked. Or stupid, anyway." He shook his head, in violent disagreement with something within himself. "Maybe it's *me* that's been stupid. I used to know what was going on in this country. I could see things coming, and do something about them. I could smell trouble ahead, the way Andrew Macmillan could. Now every damn thing that happens is a surprise. Like you being unfaithful. Like *me* being unfaithful. Like bumping into a tree that simply wasn't there the day before. Maybe Dinamaula was just a big bad guess in the first place."

"David, that *can't* be true! Anyway, what about the people in the middle? Chief Banka. And the people up at Shebiya and Fish Village. They don't all agree with Dinamaula."

"Far from it. In fact they're on our side, basically. But they're getting fed up. Just like Simon. They want to turn their back on the whole thing—pull clear, go home again, grow mealies, and forget the glorious republic. And by God I can't blame them!"

Nicole rose suddenly, and put her arms round him. "Oh, darling. . . . It can't be as bad as that. Not after all the work you've done."

"Maybe not. . . . I'm sorry. . . . It's been a bad day. But sometimes I can just see the whole thing sliding down hill." He kissed her. "Oh, well. As long as *we're* not sliding down hill."

"We're sliding into bed," she said.

"Total defeat?"

"You speak for yourself. . . . Darling, *really* it may not be as bad as you think."

"Perhaps not."

"Whatever you said to Kalatosi may do some good."

"I hope so."

"And you'll be talking to Dinamaula. . . . Perhaps they'll all learn some sense at the United Nations."

"H'm."

5: THE DISTINGUISHED DELEGATE FROM

IT WAS VERY COMFORTABLE at the Ten Eyck Hotel. They had an interconnecting suite on the eighth floor, with a splendid view, across the treetops, of upper Fifth Avenue and the green acres of Central Park. The four bedrooms and the sitting-room, carpeted in yielding scarlet, sumptuously furnished in cream and gold, were a most agreeable base for official operations.

Meals involved no more trouble than the lifting of a telephone receiver; secretarial, messenger, and valeting personnel were on hand, at the touch of a button. The Ten Eyck service was impeccable; and it was a very good address. In this New World paradise, the delegation from the Republic of Pharamaul was now happily installed.

They were four: President Dinamaula, Joseph Kalatosi, Benjamin Banka, and Paul Jordan.

We must seem a funny lot, Paul Jordan had once thought, self-consciously, when first they arrived to set up house; but the feeling had not lasted long. New York was used to funny lots, and took them in its stride, in a fashion almost disappointing; and the Ten Eyck, which could have played host to a pygmy cricket team without batting an eyelid, was politely unimpressed.

Even on formal occasions, when Dinamaula wore his embroidered robes, young Banka wore robes *and* a lionskin, Joseph Kalatosi wore a black tailcoat and gleaming top hat, and Paul Jordan his white naval uniform with the gold aiguillettes looped round the left shoulder, they passed through the lobby with scarcely a ripple.

The simple took it for granted that they were foreigners; the sophisticated thought that, with Paul's aid, they were on their way to advertise something whiter than white. In either role, they were no more fantastic than the sum of New York itself.

Yet for Paul Jordan the Pharamaul delegation remained an oddly assorted bunch, none the less.

President Dinamaula was really quite impressive; he moved in this world of strange people and novel customs with an impassive, unhurried dignity which, like a really good performance of Prospero, was a pleasure to watch. In a sense he was on show, and he knew it; but the figure he wished to cut was not theatrical, like certain other heads of state—it was more nearly regal.

On this much larger stage, he could not possibly be the sole focus of attention, as he was at home. Yet if calm assurance could attract favourable notice, then he had chosen the right way to go about it.

Joseph Kalatosi, on the other hand, had promptly become very busy, very full of affairs, blossoming out like a fight-manager whose boy is suddenly on his way up. He was everywhere at once, making quick friends ("Call me Joe!"), claiming the widest acquaintance; bouncing up and down in the General Assembly, table-hopping in the restaurant, back-slapping in the delegates' bar; edging himself on to minor committees, arranging meetings, fixing up small parties for congenial people.

He talked continuously, he ran from one group to another, he laughed uproariously at important people's jokes. Yet no one could look more mysterious, nor glance more cautiously over his shoulder, when secrets were in the wind and the exchange of views fell into whispering.

He was undoubtedly the delegation's big operator, and he had seized upon the part with snapping appetite.

The third member was, just as certainly, their problem child. Benjamin Banka, son of Shebiya's chief, was a lazy young drunkard who should never have been chosen in the first place; they had had a taste of his quality on the plane coming over, when he had plunged into the complimentary martinis to such effect that presently the captain had to be called, to suggest and then to command a good deal more decorum.

Dinamaula had chosen Benjamin Banka for two reasons: to annoy his father, and to make some political friends among the young men of Shebiya. Chief Banka continued to be a considerable thorn in the flesh of the House of Assembly; and he had initiated a violent row over this very subject of the UN delegation, claiming that it was far too early for Pharamaul to aspire to such heights.

In the debate, Dinamaula had taunted him with a sneer at "those who wished to see us small for ever," and Chief Banka had countered with another unmistakable reference: "We shall never be bigger than the small men who rule us." It had developed into a royal set-to, the second major clash in the Legislature; and it had given the President solid, spiteful pleasure, a few days later, to clinch it by announcing Benjamin Banka as the third member of the delegation.

Young Banka had to be carried, sometimes literally, but it had been worth it, to see his father for once so flustered and deflated. There was nothing the old man could do about it; and even if he could have forbidden the journey, the resulting row with Benjamin Banka's mother, and his wife, and the gleeful gloating of all the other mothers and other wives, would have made his home intolerable.

Chief Banka had sat speechless and trembling, while the President's party—now the National Party—had laughed their heads off.

Paul Jordan's own role in New York was harder to define. He was not an accredited delegate; he was there as the President's aide-de-camp, for much the same reason as had kept him in his post at Government House—because he was needed, to supply a continuing background and give helpful hints on the way things were done.

He was always close at hand in the United Nations building, where the session was now halfway through; and he made himself generally useful outside it—keeping track of Dinamaula's appointments, running errands, getting theater tickets, organizing meals, fixing up secretarial help, and ordering the Rolls round to the front entrance.

He did not mind these rather insignificant chores, since they were part of his job, or could be stretched to look like it, and it was a lot more interesting than watching the goings-on at Government House. It was only when he had to do something distinctly domestic, like checking over the laundry with the valet, or serving midnight drinks to a crowd of Joseph Kalatosi's new cronies, that it grew irksome.

Occasionally he would stop in his mental tracks, and ask himself: "Why should a Royal Navy lieutenant be fetching brandy and ginger ale for an idle little bugger like Benjamin Banka?" Let the distinguished delegate from Shebiya slouch across to the sideboard himself. . . . But then Paul would think again, sometimes with the nagging suspicion that he might be feeling this way because Banka was a Negro as well as a useless layabout; and, still with reservations, he would pour out the customary whopping drink and carry it back to the layabout himself.

This odd servitude would not last for ever; and in the meantime, life was full of novelties and excitements, and he loved New York.

It was the most fascinating city he had ever been in; even quite ordinary things, like window-shopping after dark, or taking the ferry across to Staten Island, seemed to have a special flavour, as sharp and clear as neat vodka. Window-shopping meant wandering through colossal caverns of steel and concrete and glass, where, miles above the glittering windows and the thunderous, demented traffic orchestra, tiny stars could be seen pricking away at the night sky, as remote as the simple life itself.

The Staten Island ferry was exciting, not because it was the only occasion when he could get aboard a boat (though that was important, in a foolish sort of way), but for the return journey, when New York's fantastic skyline rose out of the mist as if uplifted by giant hands, and the lofty pointing fingers of its architecture could be seen, in a single glance, as one fabulous frieze hammered into the sky.

The food in the restaurants seemed the best he had ever known, whether it was the bulging mounds of a *sauerbraten* and dumpling dinner, or the small and vital elegances which went into the French disposition of a chicken. Gibes about American cooking seemed, in this city at least, to be slanderous for a special reason.

"Of course, there's no American cooking," a New York friend with whom he sometimes dined had admitted. "Unless it's chickenburgers, or those damned jellied doughnuts. But if you want to eat in Paris or Berlin or Copenhagen or Calcutta, just walk down a New York street till you come to the right place."

"What about London?" Paul had asked.

The American could not stretch his loyalties too far. "There must be a suet pudding joint somewhere," he answered, "but I haven't found it yet." He grinned cheerfully. "As a matter of fact,

I'm not looking for it. Come on, let's go down to Luchow's again! Bismarck herring with sour cream! Noodle soup! *Knackwurst!*"

Paul, though grateful for skilled guidance, would rather have been wandering this paradise hand-in-hand with a beautiful girl. But that had not happened yet. He found that there was little time for serious girl-watching, even at the United Nations, where a most complex range of beautiful girls, shipped in from a hundred different countries, was constantly on view. At UN, he had other things to watch, by special instruction.

"Keep an eye on them," David Bracken had commanded him, at their last meeting. "Write to me personally, at my home address. I shall want to hear what's going on, all the time."

What was going on, in one area, was exactly what David Bracken did not want to hear. The delegation from Pharamaul, whether demolishing jugfuls of Daiquiri in its Ten Eyck suite, or being whisked downtown to Forty-eighth Street and First Avenue in a rented Rolls-Royce, was living on a scale which must be far above its budget.

"It doesn't seem to worry them" [Paul wrote to David Bracken in one of his reports] "I mean, in terms of actual cash. Joe Kal, as well as signing all the cheques on the New York account, has a briefcase full of £10 notes which he keeps in a safe in his room. He brings it out quite openly when they need some extra spending money.

"They call it the Consolidated Fund—it seems to be a sort of joke between them. I've paid some pretty big bills for them, out of this cash, though I have to change it into dollars first at the currency exchange at Rockefeller Center. I must be their best customer!

"Apart from that, there's nothing much to report. B. Banka continues to be a bloody nuisance; duty-free liquor must have been specially invented for him. Joe Kal is busy making friends—and rude remarks about you. Dina is the best of the bunch, of course, but even he is showing signs of reacting to the VIP treatment.

"He made a pretty good speech, a bit narky in parts, and

after that the whole circus of promotion and flattery went into action. It's enough to turn anyone's head.

"The trouble is, what this place—I mean, UN—does to all of them. I mean, the Afro-Asians. Whatever they are in their own country, and whatever their own country is, when they get together they think they own the earth. At any rate, they think they can run it.

"I hope Timmy has already seized on the UN stamps from this envelope. I paid for them myself!"

President Dinamaula had taken enormous care in the preparation of his first General Assembly speech, which was a contribution to one of the debates on the surviving examples of neo-colonialism still disfiguring the globe. He had made it short, modest, and moderate in tone; his theme was reconciliation rather than recrimination, and he did pay tribute to Britain for the way in which she had progressively and promptly "freed" most of her colonial empire.

But the speech contained half a dozen phrases which some of the British newspapers picked up, and which caused comment among other UN delegations. Speaking of this process of liberation, Dinamaula had declared:

"Freeing the slaves must always bring a warm feeling of self-satisfaction: the feeling of the philanthropist who inherits a zoo and frees the animals. But it should not be forgotten that this liquidation of the British Empire was a forced liquidation, under the pressure of history, and any self-satisfaction must be tempered by the thought of what might have happened if freedom had been denied; since, in fact, the zoo was falling to pieces anyway, the bars were coming loose, and many of the cages were in ruins.

"Forced liquidation is only bankruptcy under another name—in this case, bankruptcy of thought, feeling, and common humanity. So it is not for us, the newly-free, to touch our hats in gratitude to our late masters. It is for us to tell them two things, in unmistakable words: not to be too smug about it, and never to do it again."

Since that speech, a great deal had happened to the President of Pharamaul.

It began with a note, sent across to his desk as soon as he returned from the rostrum, from one of the Zambian delegation:

"Excellent!" it read. "Congratulations on a brilliant start. We would like to offer you a *vin d'honneur* this evening, to celebrate the occasion. Please accept!"

A *vin d'honneur* was a new one, and at this particular moment he could afford to admit it. Dinamaula, in that warm and exalted glow enjoyed by all speakers as soon as they had got it off their chests, leant back to Paul Jordan, who was sitting behind him, and showed him the note.

"What's a *vin d'honneur*?" he asked, in a whispered colloquy.

"Just a drink party. With you as the guest of honour."

"Should I accept?"

"No reason why not. . . . That was a jolly good speech, sir."

"Thank you, Paul."

"Sir, I think the British Ambassador is trying to catch your eye."

Dinamaula leant forward again, peered down the rows of seats, found the British delegation, and watched as the ambassador, clasping his own two hands together, went through a pantomime of congratulation.

He smiled back, and bowed. But part of his brain, still sharp from the glare of exposure, thought: You kick them, and they still wag their tails.

President Dinamaula was in a very happy mood as, later that evening, with Joseph Kalatosi in tow, he entered the private room for the promised party.

There were already about forty people gathered, all Negro or Asian, and it was a few moments before their arrival was noticed. Then their Zambian host, a small elegant figure in a white Palm Beach suit, came forward, almost at a run.

"*Cher collègue!*" he exclaimed—and it was the most unexpected greeting Dinamaula had ever heard from anyone. His host shook hands as if they were devoted friends meeting after a long parting. "All the congratulations in the world! That was a splendid speech —absolutely splendid!"

"Thank you," Dinamaula answered formally. He did not much care for the effusive approach, but it was nice to be loved, very nice indeed. "It is kind of you to entertain me like this."

"My dear man, you deserve it, a hundred times over! And we have a mutual friend, of course."

"Who is that?"

"Victor Luanda. Our man in Pharamaul."

Joseph Kalatosi said: "Good old Victor! One of my very best friends."

"So I've heard," said the Zambian, and winked merrily. "Now, come along. You must meet *all* your admirers."

The other guests, moving gently like a well-drilled school of fish, had already formed a semicircle round the room, and Dinamaula and Kalatosi were introduced to them one by one. The smiles were broad, the handshakes warm, the greetings always complimentary.

An Indian, who looked like the late President Nehru and sounded like an English cavalry major, said: "Good show, old boy! Ripping to have you on our team!" A Nigerian delegate, pumping his hand almost savagely, exclaimed: "The cages of the zoo, eh?" and went off into peals of laughter. A tiny Japanese, bowing with doll-like precision, assured him that his speech had been "a most fundamental piece of oratory."

It was all very flattering, and when, at the end of the introductions, silence was called for, and his health proposed and drunk, the President of Pharamaul felt at peace with at least half the world.

With the formalities disposed of, Joseph Kalatosi immediately set off round the room again, talking to everyone, addressing the backs of their necks if necessary, while Dinamaula stood still near the center, champagne glass in hand, and let them come to him. His speech was still the subject of comment and congratulation.

"Some of your remarks about Britain were really very generous," his host told him. "Especially after what they did to you."

"Did to me?" Dinamaula queried.

"I mean your exile." The Zambian looked at him coyly. "Or don't we talk about that any more?"

"I certainly don't think about it much."

"Well, by God!" said his next-door neighbour, a huge Jamaican who carried himself like a prizefighter, "if they did that to me, I'd never forget it! And I'd take damned good care that they never forgot it, either!"

"Perhaps that would not be a very productive process," said Dinamaula.

"Nor is being kicked out of your own country. I'd have been a lot tougher, in your place." The Jamaican was looking at him rather searchingly, eyeing his robes. "You still prefer the old getup, eh?"

"It is the way I always dress," Dinamaula answered coldly. He sipped his champagne, and then lapsed into silence, listening to the crisscross of voices round him.

"Smug! He's quite right. That's what they are, the whole lot of them."

"The only tolerable part of New York is this building."

"It's the only tolerable bit of America, as far as I'm concerned."

"We've got to keep plugging away at Vietnam, till they learn some sense."

"Who ever heard of the Israelis telling the truth?"

"I was in London last year. Just awful! And they're so damned stuck up."

"New Zealand sitting on the fence as usual. They're as bad as the Canadians."

"Oh, it's no good talking to him. An absolute blockhead. No wonder Australia is in such a mess."

Dinamaula smiled suddenly to himself. A vague echo from somewhere else had been tugging at his memory, puzzling him, but now he had placed it, and it was very near home. It was the Port Victoria Club.

When, after an hour or so, he was saying his farewells, the Jamaican asked him:

"How long are you staying at UN?"

"Another six weeks, I think. Then I must get back."

"You have your own aircraft?"

"Not at the moment."

The Jamaican shook hands. "Well, see you again soon. We'll make you one of us yet!"

The tone was very friendly, and Dinamaula, who had had his reservations, found himself reacting to it, and warming suddenly to the whole evening. He did want to be one of them, very much. The talk in this room might have reminded him of the Port Victoria Club, but this time it was *their* club, their very own, and that was going to make all the difference.

Already he was in love with the whole United Nations setup, with its air of being the center of affairs, manned by important people, and even with the building itself. There was something about the towering mass of glass and concrete, and its thirty-nine storeys soaring, like its hopes, to the sky, which took the imagination.

Even to walk along its corridors, as he had done on the night of his arrival, and glance into the various rooms and offices and places of assembly, with their magnificent lighting and colour and decoration, their striking emblems of origin, was to have the spirit lifted instantly.

The special woods from Scandinavia, the marble walls, the blue and gold tapestries: the black pebbles from Greece, limestone from England, teak from Burma, rugs from Turkey and Afghanistan, gifts and materials from almost all the known world—all these, which now surrounded and adorned his working day, made him feel almost arrogantly proud of Pharamaul's membership, and his own.

For the first few days he had felt very much the new boy; even the pleasure of using the delegates' private entrance was always overshadowed by the daunting size of the organization itself. It was difficult to take it all in; it was hard to realize that four thousand people worked in the Secretariat alone: that there were fourteen special agencies, their interest ranging from food to the weather, from world money to world health, toiling away all the time, in addition to the Assembly meetings, and the endless committees, and the tentacles of communication which must reach round the world and back again.

One could be baffled by the initials alone—FAO, WHO, UNICEF, ICAO, and a score of others—which long-term delegates reeled off like the superior contestants in a spelling-bee. There were the names of countries he had scarcely heard of, even though they belonged to his own continent—Mali, Dahomey, Gabon, Burundi, Upper Volta, Chad; and other mysterious ones even farther away, making the map almost too big for a single brain—Costa Rica, Guatemala, Iceland, Luxembourg, Chile, Peru, Mongolia, Honduras. . . . It was another daunting thought that more than a hundred-and-twenty heads of mission must have exactly the same feelings, the same bafflement, about Pharamaul.

Yet this was a wonderful thing to belong to—and that gave President Dinamaula a certain nagging regret for the past. At his reception—his *vin d'honneur!*—he had said that he never thought much about his exile. But it was also true that, if it were not for that wretched uprooting, and the five-year sojourn in the wilderness, he and Pharamaul would have been installed at the United Nations long ago.

Time had been wasted, he himself had been wantonly delayed upon his pathway. He was today the newest of the new boys, still disguising his awe and uncertainty, when, had things gone the right way, he might now be at least a candidate for a term as President of the General Assembly.

When the Jamaican delegate had assured him: "We'll make you one of us!" Dinamaula had glossed over, in his thoughts, the slight disparagement, the idea that he was *not* one of them, and known only the pleasure of being thought worthy to join the gang. A few weeks of the current three-months' session at the UN had given him a glimpse of the power which lay in that gang-membership.

Joining the gang, making the gang bigger and stronger, meant eventually taking over the reins; and it was to be an Afro-Asian take-over—a largely cynical operation, wherein the pleasure was in being on the winning side, and the profit limitless.

We (Dinamaula now inevitably thought of the gang as "we") could make this place our own, while *they* were still being polite, still playing by the old rules, and still asleep.

It was a matter of simple arithmetic. The old rules said that everyone had one vote: two hundred million Russians had one vote, and fifty-five million Britons, and two hundred thousand of the sons of Pharamaul, and sixty thousand Malis. One had only to multiply these small nation-members, take good care that they were "us" and not "them," and the whole organization would fall into the Afro-Asian lap.

The idea, Dinamaula knew, had progressed far beyond the hopeful or speculative stage; it was already common talk, which he had heard at half a dozen heady sessions in the bar, or at parties outside, or in committee rooms when a few men with the right ideas lingered on afterwards to talk of this and that.

Basically, it was the idea of the club-within-a-club; the small clique which grew into the large one, the large one whose members, armed with their precious votes, gradually took over the committees, and the organizations, and would finally alter all the rules to suit their own purposes, and vote the white opposition down the nearest drain.

It was actually happening, and "they" did not seem to have caught on yet—or, if they had, they were too polite to say so, too traditionally-minded to cut off the flattery and the finance, or else powerless to make a stand and reverse the process. New members were being elected in droves; and though sponsored and often paid for by "them," they could all be counted on as "us." The United Nations, established a quarter of a century ago in an atmosphere of benign authority, was being refashioned entirely, and the atmosphere was frankly opportunist.

"We'll make you one of us," the Jamaican had said. It was the only thing to be. The so-called "corridors of power" no longer wound to and fro along those dreary stretches of Whitehall, which Dinamaula had come to know so well. They were not in the Elysée Palace either, nor the White House, nor even the Kremlin. They were here in New York, in this gleaming complex of buildings whose image and influence and hard cash now stretched all the way round the world.

Power lived here, delivered into the hands of the club-within-a-club; and some of that power—a tiny slice, yet magnified stupendously by one invaluable vote—was now Pharamaul's.

Inside were all the courtesies of diplomacy. One Distinguished Delegate, writing a note to another Distinguished Delegate, would think himself very remiss if he did not conclude: "I avail myself of this opportunity, my dear colleague, to assure your Excellency of my highest consideration."

Inside, similar refinements of the verbal minuet ensured that even the most rustic cultural attaché could feel himself part of the high plateau of manners.

Inside were all the privileges of diplomatic rank. Agreeable marks of status made life simpler at the social level; a minimum of two cocktail parties a night were available, for those who trod with relish the regular circuit. Diplomatic immunity solved all traffic problems save the vulgar jam itself. Duty-free alcohol made it a pleasure to entertain instead of purgatory to pay for it; duty-free goods of all other kinds stretched the salary very happily.

Inside, this same privilege provided, for the astute, a substantial second income. A case of Scotch whisky, imported at its basic price of £6, was worth £22 10s to any diplomat who chose to enter the retail trade or dispose of it to a friend. A Mercedes, similarly imported duty-free, could show a profit of 30 per cent if retained for exactly the right number of months, and lodged with the right agent.

Just inside the delegates' entrance was the key to this easy paradise. Just outside it was the waiting Rolls-Royce, with the national flag flying bravely at its silver jackstaff.

Just a little farther outside, however, a tougher world took over, and it was Benjamin Banka's bad luck to find this out, at first hand.

It started, as did most things in the life of Benjamin Banka, whether they were sweating hangovers, knife affrays, furious quarrels with his wife, or the careless fathering of children, with a party.

It was given in one of the huge, compacted honeycomb of flats known as Central Park West, and his host was a young Nigerian diplomat who was also finding duty-free alcohol an acceptable cure for homesickness. His chosen tipple was vodka, and Benjamin Banka made it his own.

He drank it with great freedom from nine o'clock that night until four in the morning, in forms as far apart as vodka and tonic, vodka and pineapple juice, and vodka and cold *consommé*. When the time came to depart, with most of the other guests felled, and all the girls either bespoken or already betrayed, Benjamin Banka was near the limit of his staying-power.

"Get you a taxi," his host said, and made for the house telephone with an uneasy lurch. But on the short journey he tripped over a quartet of legs protruding from beneath the piano, crumpled to the ground, and made no effort to rise again.

"Don't bother," said Benjamin Banka, after waiting a few moments. "Get it myself. Good night. Many thanks." Then, with movements as carefully planned as a piece of battle strategy, he let himself out of the flat, summoned the elevator, and after a journey to the top storey, and a floor-by-floor descent, negotiated the front lobby and the barred doors, and found himself outside.

One or two cruising taxis passed him, but in spite of imperious signals they did not stop to pick him up; there was something about his whirling robes, and trailing lionskin, and the cap askew on top of a moonstruck black face which, at four o'clock in the morning, was not reassuring.

Twenty minutes' boycott passed, and he was left, a baffled,

slightly disconnected figure, still on the pavement. After patient calculation, he began to walk, first south along Eighth Avenue and then, with the idea of making a short cut, diagonally across Central Park itself.

In spite of setbacks, he had recovered his fine spirits, and was still at the crest of that dizzy peak which comes before the letdown. He sang songs and hummed a little, he followed winding footpaths in the general direction of the Ten Eyck Hotel, past groves of trees, over small slopes, round corners pitch dark and others well lighted.

The two agile young figures who trailed him for a hundred yards, and then jumped on him out of the bushes, could not have had an easier target. Banka was hit in the stomach with a fist, and then on the back of the neck with a wooden cosh. It was all done in silence, with methodical skill and rehearsed brutality; and in silence he was kicked twice in the ribs, stripped of his robe and his lionskin, robbed of the wallet in his waist-belt, and left senseless at the side of the pathway, in convenient shadow.

Benjamin Banka was a tough young man, in spite of a wide range of excesses, and when he came to, after an hour, he was still mobile. His shattering headache was not much worse than a routine hangover; the aching ribs and villainously stiff neck had come his way before, at various brawls and booze-ups in Shebiya. The fact that he was penniless, and covered with early morning dew, and naked except for a pair of red-and-white striped underpants, was all in the night's work.

He rolled over, and was sick on the grass. Then he levered himself up, first on his knees, and then to his feet. Sunrise was on the way; the birds were singing, and the traffic stirring beyond the trees. As soon as he had made out the right direction, he took up his walk again, at a slow shambling pace. He could no longer match the birds in song, nor even hum a tune, but the vodka still buoyed him up, and the tall buildings beckoned him to safety.

He had got as far as Fifty-ninth Street, almost within touching distance of the Ten Eyck, when the police car at the edge of the curb barred his way. After that, the scene deteriorated swiftly.

There were two blue-uniformed men in the police car, and if they were surprised by the sight of a fat and nearly naked young Negro in a pair of striped underpants waiting to cross Fifty-ninth Street, and swaying slightly as he waited, it did not delay their reaction. One of the policemen leant out of the front window, and said crisply:

"Hey you! Come here."

Benjamin Banka looked back at him haughtily, but he said nothing. Instead, he turned on his heel and made a move to cross the road. The policeman got out quickly, while the driver picked up his microphone and spoke a few words into it. Within moments, Benjamin Banka found his way barred, for a second time.

"O.K.," said the policeman, who was large and determined, and armed with a revolver. "Get in."

Benjamin Banka swayed again, and grimaced as a spasm of pain shot from the top of his head to the back of his neck. But he was still sure of his position.

"I am going home," he said grandly, and pointed down the street to the Ten Eyck. "I live there."

"You heard me," said the policeman. "Get in the car. We want to talk to you."

"Do not speak to me like that," said Banka. "I am a diplomat."

A London policeman might have reacted to the word and the tone; but a New York policeman, no.

"Yeah," said the officer. "You're a diplomat, all right. Wandering around in your shorts, six o'clock in the morning, and"—he placed an enormous flat hand against Banka's bare chest, to steady him—"more than a bit drunk, I'd guess. Get in the car, like I said."

"But I've been robbed!" Benjamin Banka protested. "And beaten! It is disgraceful! You are here to protect me."

The policeman waved an arm towards the three or four early risers who had collected, and were listening. "Get going," he commanded. Then he turned back to Benjamin Banka. "Robbed, where?"

"In the park."

"You been walking across the park in your shorts?"

"They took all my clothes."

"What clothes?"

"My robe. And my lionskin."

"O.K.," said the policeman. "Let's start again. You been walking across Central Park, at night, by yourself?"

"I couldn't get a taxi. I made signals! I was walking home after a party."

"What party?"

"A diplomatic party."

"In lionskins?"

"It is my national costume."

"Walking home from a diplomatic costume party," said the policeman, as if transcribing some interior notebook. "Well, well. . . . Haven't you got any sense?" he inquired, sharply and suddenly. "You're a diplomat? Don't you read the papers? People get themselves knifed every day. . . . We'll sort all this out at the station. Get in the car."

"I will not get in the car!" Benjamin Banka answered vehemently. "I am going to the Ten Eyck. You cannot touch me! I have diplomatic immunity."

"We'll sort that out."

"You are worse than brigands!"

Behind him, the police driver called out: "Put him in, Joe."

The first policeman laid his hands on Banka's arm and naked shoulder, in an expert and painful grip.

"It's like this," he said, still reasonable, but firm as a rock. "If you're a diplomat, you're coming to the station to file a complaint. If you're not a diplomat, you're under arrest. Drunk. Acting suspiciously. Indecent exposure," he added, with an eye to Benjamin Banka's sagging underpants and gaping fly. "Get it?"

The struggle was very brief. Inside the car, Benjamin Banka screamed: "Take me to the Ten Eyck Hotel at once! They will identify me!"

"I wouldn't doubt it," said the driver. "But all in good time. We'll make a little routine call first."

It was a silent journey, with Benjamin Banka sullen and silent in the back seat. But underneath, his temper was beginning to seethe as his throbbing head caught up with these disgraceful events; and once at the police station he made a wild scene, and tried to break free. He was subdued, handcuffed and locked in a cell; and there he promptly passed out, and slept peacefully for the next six hours.

It fell to Paul Jordan to sort all this nonsense out, and he had never known a more embarrassing assignment. In response to a confused telephone call which reached him in the UN lobby during the afternoon, and which included the ominous phrase: "I need clothes as well!" he sped up town in the Rolls, calling at the Ten Eyck on the way to collect Benjamin Banka's second-best robe, his diplomatic passport, and, just to be on the safe side, a thousand dollars in cash.

All he knew was that Benjamin Banka, missing all night, seemed to have spent most of the day in jail. It might be nothing new in Shebiya, but in New York the context, like the rules, was different.

He had a foretaste of how different it might be, when he stepped out of the Rolls-Royce. The first man he met was not the expected policeman inside, but a reporter waiting on the front steps; a reporter who, as soon as the Rolls drew up, skipped towards it as if recognizing a very easy clue.

He was young, and untidy, and smiling, with eyes as sharp as his tongue presently proved to be.

"Lootenant Jordan?" he asked.

"Yes," said Paul. "Who—er—?"

"John Marsh, N'York *Observer*. You come to bail this UN guy out?"

Paul Jordan, taken by surprise, could only ask: "How did you know that?"

Reporter Marsh had his answers ready, as well as his questions. "I was there when he made his phone call. . . . Has he done this sort of thing before?"

"What sort of thing?"

John Marsh gave him a knowing look. "Well, he *is* in trouble, isn't he? Is it true he was wandering around Central Park naked?"

"I don't know anything at all about that."

"Well, what do you know?"

"So far, nothing."

"Came as a shock, eh?"

Paul Jordan made an effort to push past him, but the other man was agile, and the pavement narrow. Brought up short, he said:

"Please let me pass. I really don't know what this is all about."

"It's about one Benjamin Banka," said Marsh, still smiling. "UN delegate. Picked up on Fifty-ninth Street in his shorts. Claims he was mugged in Central Park. But *they* say he was drunk. And resisted arrest. That's about enough, even for a dip, wouldn't you say?" He glanced at what was under Paul's arm. "Are those the clothes he asked for? Can I have a look?"

"No."

"Where's the lionskin?" And as Paul did not answer, Marsh added: "Doesn't have a spare, eh?"

"Let me pass!" said Paul, much more sharply. He was taller than the other man, and with a little maneuvering and plain shoving he found his way no longer barred. He began to climb the steps to the police station.

"You pleading diplomatic immunity?" the reporter called after him. "Or amnesia?"

Paul said nothing.

"You guys can get away with murder, can't you?"

It was a view which seemed to be shared by the police. Paul, having established his identity, was able to insist that the interview with the sergeant in charge should take place in a private room, and not in the "front office" whither the reporter had followed him; but there the atmosphere of accommodation seemed to be suspended, while a grim scepticism took over. The sergeant, a burly fellow with a strong creased face and hair like a grey steel brush, was turning Benjamin Banka's diplomatic passport over and over in his hands, as if he did not believe it and did not want to believe it.

His expression when he had first studied the photograph had been incredulous. Now it was one of cold dislike. Banka had already been sent for, and in the meantime his official credentials were receiving the maximum of scrutiny and the minimum of approval.

The sergeant flipped over a few pages, and then paused. "Pharamaul," he said, pronouncing it very slowly, like a child exploring syllable by syllable. He had the usual Irish accent, but it was tough Irish, not charm Irish. "Where would that place be?"

"It's a small island off South West Africa," Paul answered, and wished he could make it sound more important.

"Africa. What sort of a place is it, then? Would you call it civilized?"

"Oh, certainly."

"Well, it sends some funny people to New York." Paul did not answer, and the sergeant, detecting disapproval, decided to make his point clear. "I'm just going by what's on the sheet," he said, tapping the papers in front of him. "Walking out of Central Park in his underwear. Refusing to cooperate with the police. Unsteady in his walk, probably drunk. Resisting police. Abusive language to police. Trying to escape police custody." He looked up at Paul, his eyes uncompromising in their contempt of this behaviour. "What sort of a civilized diplomat is that?"

Paul Jordan had a job to do, little as he liked it. He made his main objection:

"They had no right to take Mr. Banka into custody, since he *is* a diplomat."

"The officers didn't know that. How could they? *Mister* Banka had no identification, and not a cent on him. They had to go by the look of him, and that was terrible."

"But he'd been robbed, hadn't he? He said on the phone——"

"He said a lot of things," the sergeant interrupted. "The officers didn't believe any of them. Nor would I, when I got a sight of him this morning." He looked at Paul, taking in his smart uniform, his air of competence and discipline, his quality. His tone changed, becoming scornful: "Now why would you want to work for a feller like that?"

In the open doorway, Benjamin Banka's voice rang out, in a sudden snarl:

"Don't say such a thing! It is insulting! Why should he not work for me?"

As they both swung round, it did not take Paul Jordan more than a few seconds to see the point of the sergeant's question. Benjamin Banka, even in a clean white robe, looked awful. His eyes were bloodshot, in a face puffy with drink; he was scowling in ferocious ill-temper; he blinked continually, and he had to steady himself against the doorpost.

He looked exactly what he was—a dissolute young man in trouble. The usual thought crossed Paul's mind, and was instantly dismissed. A white man, in this state, would have looked just as horrible.

The police-sergeant surveyed Banka with a cold eye. "Good afternoon, *Mister* Banka. You had a good sleep?"

"Never mind my sleep!" Banka snapped. He advanced into the room, in two unsteady strides. "Tell me what you meant when you said——"

The sergeant waved him to silence. "Never mind about that, if

133

you please. I was talking to the lootenant here. Now let's take your case. We've just been informed, which we didn't know before, that you're a diplomat. In the circumstances, all this"—he motioned, with distaste, towards the papers on the desk—"is washed out. Which means you're free to go."

"I *told* you I was a diplomat! I told the police at the time."

"But you couldn't identify yourself. Isn't that so?"

"They should take my word."

The sergeant looked him over sardonically. "They have to go by appearances."

Benjamin Banka leant over, and thumped the desk with a crashing fist. "I shall tell people what you said!" he shouted. "I shall tell everything! I was attacked and robbed! Nothing was done. No police protection!" He was working himself up into a blind rage. "Instead, I was arrested. Put in prison without trial. With handcuffs! There was police brutality——"

"Now just take it easy," said the sergeant swiftly. "What brutality was that?"

"They twisted my arm."

"But you were resisting arrest."

"They had no right to arrest me."

"The officers didn't know that. They had a right to bring you in for questioning." He was suddenly very emphatic. "I don't want to hear anything about police brutality. My men don't work like that."

"I shall make a full report. It is a disgrace——"

Paul Jordan stepped forward, ashamed and exasperated. "Now look, why don't you just leave it?"

Banka rounded on him. "Don't speak to me like that! I am a chief's son!"

"Funny thing," said the sergeant. "So am I. Chief O'Sullivan, Boston Police. Thirty-eight years on the force. Clean record all the way through. Never got drunk in public. Never walked around in his striped shorts. Never had to be handcuffed——"

"You are insulting me again!" said Banka furiously. "Just because of colour! I can tell! You have kept me in prison for eight hours——"

It might have gone on for ever, but at that point the sergeant stood up, and standing up he was a commanding sight. Banka fell silent.

"You were here for eight hours," said the sergeant, "because we couldn't wake you up for six of them. You were out cold. . . . Mr. Banka, you're free to go."

"I demand an apology!"

There was silence for some moments. Then the policeman said formally:

"I am sorry for any inconvenience."

"That is not enough!"

"*But*," the policeman went on, "it was your own fault, and that's what my report will say."

"Do not fear! *I* shall be reporting! Reporting to the highest authorities!"

"That's your privilege. *Sir*."

When they were gone at last, the sergeant went out into the front office again. One of the arresting policemen, standing by the door, turned round.

"O.K., sergeant?"

"We'll see. Let me have that expanded report, anyway."

"O.K." The policeman nodded towards the open doorway. "Did you see the car?"

"No."

"Rolls-Royce. Must have been a block long."

"Mine's a Chevvy," said the sergeant. "Six years old. Chief's son, too."

"Huh?"

"Never mind."

President Dinamaula, who had few illusions about Benjamin Banka, would have preferred to let the matter rest where it was, in spite of Banka's cries of outrage. But a horrid piece by John Marsh in the *Observer*, headed "Down to his Last Lionskin," which made the point that, were it not for diplomatic immunity, the culprit would have been tossed into jail forthwith, set the UN corridors buzzing; and Dinamaula felt compelled to do something about it.

He lodged a formal complaint with the Protocol Section, and demanded an official apology for Benjamin Banka's arrest.

The machinery was put in motion, though unwillingly, since Banka had made himself a small but squalid reputation already, and the newspaper comment on the affair had been too explicit, as well as too funny, to be reassuring. But there were meetings, and a departmental inquiry; witnesses were heard, submissions made, and, when action lagged, more protests handed in.

The Afro-Asian Mafia went into action, on behalf of a mistreated colleague whose only crime was his colour. It was urged that the United States, whose record on race-relations was so despicable, could hardly afford . . .

Finally, under heavy pressure from bodies as far apart as the State Department and the Harlem Housing Brotherhood, the Police Commissioner of that long-suffering host, New York City, agreed to the publication of a written apology. Though it was couched in terms of minimal regret, it was still an apology; and the Secretary-General backed it up with another one, at the same time taking the opportunity to assure the Distinguished Delegate from Pharamaul of his highest consideration. Honour had been satisfied; indeed, in the circumstances, it had been gorged.

More than ever, thought President Dinamaula, as he closed the correspondence, was it clear that this gang-membership was the only thing to count on.

Paul Jordan found himself acting as a combined go-between, messenger-boy, and loyal supporter in all this. He played the part with so little relish that the girls in the Protocol Section, he was to learn later, nicknamed him the reluctant dragon. He hated the whole thing; the vulgarity of the episode was only topped by the absurdity of wringing an apology from it.

Yet in the end it came out wonderfully right, as far as he was concerned. For among those girls in Room 201, it turned out, was *the* girl, the one he had been looking for all these weeks. Fantastically, she was Chinese.

Her name, he had soon discovered, was Frances Hoy, and in strict accuracy she was Chinese-American, one of a third-generation immigrant family from San Francisco. But neither the hyphen nor the seeming dilution of race could alter the allure and mystery which she held for him, from the very beginning, when he first spoke to her across the width of a counter.

In speech she was completely American, in manner not at all; she was very quiet, very graceful in her movements, soft-voiced and gentle all the time. In looks, Paul thought, she was ravishing. Her pale oval face was framed in raven-black hair which reached to her shoulders; below her calm brow those marvellous

136

eyes, slanting like tiny bird's wings, seemed to look out upon the world, and all the men in it, with a special kind of message.

I am Chinese, the eyes seemed to be saying, all the time; I am different, I know different things. . . . A single look, a single mingling of their glances, had been enough to transport Paul Jordan a thousand miles away, up a slow-moving yellow river, through a forest of interlaced branches, towards a bamboo house hidden in that same forest where, behind slatted blinds which moved to the sound of bells, this girl would seem to glow in the darkness as she waited for him to strip and lie with her.

Such had been his absurd dream when first he dreamed of her. In waking, it persisted as a permanent reverie, though in a format rather more sedate, rather more UN. He simply thought that she looked terrific, and he longed to take her out to dinner and, in due course, to tell her so.

For the rest, she was tall, and slim as a wand; the silk *cheong-sam* which she sometimes wore, with its discreet yet eye-riveting slit to midthigh, made a western mini-skirt seem truly vulgar. She should, he decided, have been called Lotus Blossom or Dawn Flower Petal—something like that. But if she was called Frances Hoy, then that was all right too.

Knocked silly by this adorable creature, Paul multiplied his visits to Protocol, far beyond the call of duty. Presently Frances Hoy became the girl who always walked up to the counter when he appeared, and took the letter or the message or whatever it was, and lingered for the brief exchange of sentences which was all that Paul, under the sharp eyes and within the hearing of a dozen other girls, could manage without blushing scarlet.

But soon, too soon, Benjamin Banka's awful case was settled, and Paul had no more excuses to drop in on the Protocol Section. Room 201 was virtually out of bounds.

It was nearly a week before he met her again. Then, in a corridor full of hurrying people, he suddenly caught sight of her coming towards him, not hurrying at all, walking Chinese (as he thought of it) with flowing, almost liquid grace. His heart skipped, and his face brightened as their eyes met; and—wonderful to see—so did her own.

"Hello, Lieutenant," she said, and stopped.

"Hallo, Miss Hoy."

The to-and-fro of people eddied round them like a thrusting

137

whirlpool, and without speaking they drew to one side, and stood close together, protected by a huge black velvet curtain which reached to the ceiling. Against this backdrop, her slim white-clad body and pale face stood out deliciously, as if in high relief, startling the eye even as they enraptured it.

She said: "Please call me Fran. Everyone else does."

"Not Frances?"

She smiled. "Sometimes Frances."

"That's the one I like." Because it's beautiful, like you, he thought, but he would never have had the nerve to say so. She, and the chance meeting, and this moment all seemed far too fragile to risk. "Did you know Frances means free and brave?"

"Now how in the world would you know that?"

"I looked it up." He felt he must turn it into a joke. "I just happened to be passing a dictionary."

She laughed gently, watching his wary face. "What does Paul mean?"

He said: "It's silly. It means—well, it means little."

"Perhaps you were a small baby. . . . Why haven't you been to see us again?"

"Well . . ." He shifted on one foot, in a very unseamanlike manner. "You see, when our case was all wrapped up . . . I couldn't think of an excuse to come round," he finished, in a rush.

"You should just stop by. This is America!"

"I'll remember that."

"Particularly after your boy won," she said, and pulled a face. "We needed cheering up. Mr. Benjamin Banka. He sounded just awful!"

"He is."

"I thought you must feel that. . . . You know, I'd heard quite a lot about you already."

He was very surprised. "Who from?"

She was smiling again. "A *great* friend of yours, called Sybil Bartholomew. She works here."

"Oh God!" exclaimed Paul, and looked round him involuntarily.

"It's O.K.," said Frances Hoy. "She's on leave in England, I happen to know. But didn't you and she nearly get married?"

"No."

"That's not the way I heard it."

"It wasn't even mentioned," said Paul desperately.

138

"That sounds even worse."

"Now just a minute——" Paul began, and then saw that her beautiful eyes, pretending to be stern, were not stern at all, but full of laughter. "You shouldn't say things like that, even in fun," he went on, greatly relieved. "Sybil Bartholomew was no laughing matter."

"What sort of a girl is a laughing matter?"

"That would take too long to explain." Suddenly he was very brave. "Would you like to have dinner with me sometime?"

She put her head on one side, coolly considering, in control of this and all else besides. "Well. . . . Let's begin with a drink, shall we?"

"When? Tonight?"

"All right. But quite late. I just *have* to change, after a whole day here. How about eight o'clock?"

"Wonderful," said Paul, so enthusiastically that she began to smile again. "Where would you like us to meet?"

"You choose."

"What's near you? Whereabouts do you live?"

"The St. Regis is near," she said. She glanced down at the watch on her slim wrist. "Gosh, I must get moving, or they'll be screaming for me. Eight o'clock, then." Now she was looking directly at him again, in a way almost mocking. "Perhaps *not* in your white uniform," she murmured.

"All right. But why not?"

"People might think you were Lieutenant Pinkerton," she answered, and took off, laughing, before he could even begin to work it out.

But he had worked it all out, by the time they met again. He was waiting in the lobby of the St. Regis Hotel as she came through the doorway, and he walked towards her with a joyful, whirling heart. It was her *cheong-sam* night, thank God, and she looked beautiful enough to turn every head in sight. His own was lost already. . . . Standing in front of her, he began straight away:

"Firstly, Lieutenant Pinkerton was an American, not an Englishman."

She was watching his face, amused. "Go on."

"Secondly, Butterfly was Japanese, not Chinese."

"All this makes a difference?"

"I should damned well think it does! There's no connection."

"That's a very rude way to put it."

"Oh!" She could disconcert him at any time, and she had done it again. "What I meant was——"

"All right, Paul," she said, and put her hand on his arm. It was sweet to feel her touch, sweeter still to hear her speak his name so softly. "Chinese-American joke. I was only fooling. It wasn't my idea, anyway. One of the girls said it."

"Is that how girls talk?"

"Of course. It's how men talk too, isn't it?"

He smiled. "Not Englishmen."

"Tell me more."

They went downstairs to the pint-sized bar, and found a table. The precious process of learning began.

She was one of eight children, she told him, between economical sips of an Old Fashioned and greedy nibblings at the St. Regis Hotel's insidious cocktail biscuits. Her father owned a restaurant in San Francisco, and that was where she had grown up.

"In Chinatown, near the waterfront," she told him, her eyes alight. "That's *real* San Francisco! And the restaurant is *real* Chinese, too. Just try asking for chop suey. You'd risk your life!"

"Why?" asked Paul, already out of his depth.

"Because it's a fake! Like vichyssoise, which isn't French at all. It was invented in America. So was chop suey. It means mixed bits, literally. But no one in China has ever heard of it."

"Then I promise not to ask for it," said Paul.

"Not in dad's restaurant, anyway. But he's a wonderful man. Eight children, and mother died when I was three. So he had to bring us all up. Now two of my brothers are lawyers, and one's starting to be a doctor, and one helps in the restaurant, and my three sisters all are married. So that leaves me, and you know all about me."

"I don't know anything about you," said Paul. "Except the way you look, which is marvellous." Alcohol, freeing his tongue, was prompting a dozen new questions at the same time. "I don't even know how old you are."

"Twenty. Isn't it terrible? I've had this job for two years."

"Where do you live?"

"Round the corner. I share an apartment with another girl."

"What does she do?"

"Secretary. I'll tell you about her, sometime. You're twenty-six, aren't you?"

"Yes."

"It's all in Records," she explained. "If you know where to look." Seeing him still surprised, she went on: "Well, you looked up my name, didn't you? What's it like, being a sailor?"

"Not much fun, at the moment. Because I've really stopped being one." He glanced down at her hand, resting on the table, and wished he could take gentle hold of it. Round them was a constant coming and going, a constant rise and fall of other people's voices; but theirs had become a most private world. "I used to get a lot of sea time—I was first lieutenant of a frigate—but then I was ill, so they put me ashore and made me into a stooge."

"What was the matter with you?"

"I started to have an ulcer. Then it cleared up completely. But they *still* won't give me a ship."

She looked at him with concerned eyes. "You shouldn't have an ulcer at your age. In fact you shouldn't have an ulcer any time. Ulcers are for jumpy Americans. Salesmen and advertising people. Didn't you know that?"

He smiled. "Ulcers are also for first lieutenants worrying about a brand-new ship full of fantastic gadgets. . . . I wonder if Pinkerton had an ulcer."

"He surely deserved one."

"But he only fell in love."

"Love shouldn't make you cruel. Love shouldn't make you go away. . . . I always cry at *Butterfly*. . . . What did you mean about turning you into a stooge?"

"These sort of diplomatic postings. Government House was quite fun, but this is"—he gestured—"not really a job at all. Just running errands. Still, it's better than a pusser's desk in Pompey."

"Chop suey!" she exclaimed suddenly. "Vichyssoise!"

"What?"

"You'll have to explain *your* language. What on earth is a—whatever you said?"

"Sorry. . . . It means, a desk job in the barracks at Portsmouth. That's our big naval base."

"Have you always been sailors?"

"No. As a matter of fact my father was a soldier. He was killed in Korea." Paul was brought up short by the word. "Oh! That's rather odd, isn't it?"

There were not many things that needed explaining to Frances Hoy. "But Korea's not China," she objected. "It's quite separate."

"Sorry," he said again. "Sloppy thinking. I always think of them all as 'that part of the world.' Insular. English."

"Worse," she joined in. "Imperialist! Neo-colonialist! Phooey!"

He felt brave enough to take the plunge. "What do you say *now* to having dinner with me?"

She smiled back at him gravely, holding his glance for a delicious moment which made his heart thump. "Oh, that was settled long ago."

"When, exactly?"

"When I didn't have any lunch."

Frances Hoy studied the Twelve Caesars' colossal menu, ribboned in royal purple, a production so ornate, so baroque, and so bulky that in most other countries it would only be found in the manuscript section of the local museum. Hers were not the shape of eyes to widen satisfactorily, but she was clearly astonished by what she read, perhaps already stricken with remorse. She turned to Paul, and almost whispered:

"When I said yes, I'd love to come here, I didn't know about the prices. Eight-fifty for steak. . . . Can you really afford it?"

"It's all right," Paul reassured her. He had been taken aback himself to note that his favourite lobster cocktail, which would have been a satisfactory appetizer, would cost him the equivalent of twenty-nine shillings. But as one sat side by side with this girl, it was easy to make a brave show of courage—unthinkable, in fact, to do anything else. "I've been saving my pay."

"But you're living at the Ten Eyck."

"That comes out of the Consolidated Fund."

"Now what's that?"

"I'll tell you. But first, choose what you would like to eat."

"Well, it's just awful," she said. "But I do love steak."

"And what before it?"

She sighed. "How lovely to meet a rich Englishman, for a change."

She chose smoked trout, and Paul opted for *pâté*—wild boar

pâté at a mere three dollars, rather than *foie gras* at eight. Then, having ordered, he asked:

"What did you mean, 'for a change'?"

"Well, whenever I go out with Englishmen," she told him, striking him to the very heart with the most instant, vilest jealousy he had ever felt, "they seem to be counting the pennies all the time. Literally. And when they're in a taxi, they don't have any time for the girl. They're too busy watching the meter. You can feel them shiver, every time there's a click."

"But it's a question of dollars," explained Paul, suppressing all sorts of bloodthirsty thoughts with an enormous effort. "Normally, we just can't get hold of any. The ordinary travel allowance is absolutely miserable, and the Treasury has kept it like that, as a matter of policy, for the last twenty years."

"Then the Treasury is being stupid," said Frances. "Because it's really given the English a terrible image. As if they were all mean, as if they were just spongers. . . . I'm sorry," she said, seeing his face, "but it *is* true. Americans tend to think of the English as poor relations anyway, and when they come here, and stay in private homes for nothing, and practically have to be given cigarette-money to help out, it's pretty gruesome to watch. So tell your Treasury that the saving just isn't worth it."

"I'll do that, first thing."

"Now what was that, about a consolidated fund?"

He explained its strange but most convenient workings, while Frances demolished her smoked trout at a speed which confirmed that she had indeed missed lunch, just for him. Yet she was listening very carefully, nonetheless.

"But it must be some kind of racket," she said at the end. "Bags full of money! I never heard such a thing, outside of the mobs. Where does it all come from?"

"Taxes, I suppose. Or bribes, even. All I know is that Joe Kalatosi never seems to run short."

"I think that's just typical," she said, almost fiercely.

"Typical?"

"Typical of the UN. Or parts of it. It's as if there's a perfectly respectable front organization, but behind it all sorts of rotten, mean things are going on."

"But I thought you liked it, liked working for it."

"I used to." Now she was momentarily sad. "When I started, I

143

had ideals running out of my ears. But it's so different when you know about it. Everyone's so selfish! Honestly, it makes me so mad! There are times when I feel Chinese, proud of being Asian, and times when I feel so American that I could spit in their eye!"

"Chop suey," he said. It was wonderful to share a secret word already. "You'll have to translate. Whose eye?"

She opened her mouth to say something, and then seemed to change her mind. "I'll tell you, sometime," she said instead. It was the second time she had used the phrase, as if she were not yet ready to confide more than a limited range of her thoughts and feelings. But it did not worry him. It meant, at the least, that she took it for granted that they would meet again, and there could be no more agreeable prospect than that. "I'm not going to spoil this fabulous food by getting angry," she went on. "And I'm not going to ruin a first date by talking UN politics, either."

"What should one talk about, on a first date?"

"Each other, of course." She suddenly reached over and, quite naturally, quite marvellously, put her hand in his. "You have to tell me what a dreamy doll I am, and I have to sit here and eat it up."

"We don't use the phrase 'dreamy doll' in England," Paul said. Her hand was still in his, and he gave it a gentle answering pressure. "But putting it in *my* language, I'm bound to say that I think you're absolutely beautiful, and I'd rather be sitting here with you than lying naked on a cloud in heaven."

"Perfect." She sighed. "Are all sailors like this?"

"Just concentrate on me."

"You're making that pretty easy. . . . Now tell me how many girls you've had, and what they were like. But *don't* make me jealous. They were all awful, weren't they?"

"Hideous. All two of them."

"Do go on."

Afterwards, making for her flat on Fifty-sixth Street, they wandered hand in hand up Fifth Avenue, window-shopping as companionably as any old married couple. "Hand in hand" had come about perfectly naturally; Frances had taken his, to draw him towards a jeweller's window, and after that they kept the clasp intact.

It brought to Paul's mind certain ambitious thoughts, which

close contact with this slim, beautiful, and utterly desirable girl would have provoked in the most dedicated pilgrim lifting his eyes to the skyline of the Vatican.

What would happen now? Nothing? Everything? Did she or didn't she?—the advertising cliché inevitably occurred to him, as urgent and exciting as if it had been newly minted that evening. Dinner had been lovely, and her companionship entrancing; it was the nicest thing that had happened to him in New York, perhaps the nicest ever.

But dinner was one thing, and making love another. Then, halfway in between, there was plain and fancy kissing. He decided that he would settle for that. In fact he would settle for anything, if only he could see her again.

He wondered what she was thinking about. Girls were always meant to be thinking about sex, even when they were pricing curtain materials on Fifth Avenue. Was she thinking about it now? Had she made up her mind? Or wasn't she that kind of girl at all?

Perhaps the Chinese were very formal, very reserved, and the dividing line between holding hands and lying in bed together was governed by mysterious ceremonies of behaviour, inviolate, innocent, deeply honourable, a thousand years older than the crude western strategies of intercourse.

By the time she said: "Here we are," and checked their forward steps, his head was in a hopeless whirl, and his body hovering in suspense between instant manhood and the most feeble abdication.

Perhaps she knew all about this, for she took charge of the moment with quiet skill.

"I can't ask you up, I'm afraid," she said. "It's only a tiny place, and Stella will probably be asleep. Rich folks live in Ten Eyck suites, ordinary people share little boxes on Fifty-sixth Street. O.K.?"

"Of course," said Paul. "Er . . ."

They were standing outside the lighted entrance of a large, rather shabby apartment block; within the lobby, a porter reading a newspaper could be seen, sitting by the elevator. The omens were not promising. If they went inside, they could not possibly kiss there, under such a sardonic professional eye. If they said good-bye on the pavement, it wouldn't be much of a good-bye. It would have to be next time, Paul thought, and held out his hand.

"Thanks for a lovely evening," he said. "It was just perfect."

"Thank *you*," she answered. She had taken his hand, and was looking at him, smiling a little. "Fabulous dinner. And all the sweet talk as well. It made me feel like a million dollars."

"You are."

She laughed out loud. "I can see I shall have to watch you all the time. Well, beauty sleep for me. Good night, Paul."

"Good night, Frances."

He stood irresolute, still holding on to her hand. They might have stood thus for ever, but she solved the doubtful moment in her own direct way. She moved forward until she was touching him, leaning against him so that he could feel the warmth and outline of her body.

Then she kissed him, and he kissed her, and she drew back and said: "I told you—this is America!" But she was gone before he could think of putting his arms round her, and holding her close, and not letting her go.

There was a whole week of such meetings, a time of exclusive devotion which she seemed ready to offer and eager to share. They went to the theater, they dined off spaghetti as well as *coq au vin*, they walked through the iron canyons of the city, and took the tourist boat round Manhattan Island, and went to the Central Park Zoo and the Museum of Modern Art and Upstairs at the Downstairs.

They kissed often, with increasing freedom. But he never took her up to the Ten Eyck suite; their closeness was something he wanted to keep entirely private, away from Distinguished Delegates' eyes. She never brought him to the Fifty-sixth Street flat, either. Perhaps it was for the same sort of reason.

Occasionally he felt jealous, and suspicious, about this lair which she shared with someone else, someone he had never met. Two girls living together? What might that not mean? And Stella? —surely a dubious name, conjuring up visions of an iron-jawed female executive, probably nicknamed Butch. Or perhaps Stella was not Stella at all, but a man. . . . It could be that Frances Hoy had her love-nest already, fully furnished with rich athletic playboy or virile left-wing intellectual, a seasoned performer now on holiday who might come back at any moment, lusting for his share of the bed.

But no, she could not be a lesbian, nor in love with another man, and still look at him like that, and hold him as she did, and light up her face with that sweet brand of happiness as soon as she caught sight of him. There was too much ready kissing between them, even though it was only kissing in taxis, or dark sidestreets, or restaurants so dimly lit that a struck match glowed like a Roman candle.

She could not be in love with anyone else, and kiss him as she once did, one specially exciting time, in the darkness of the deserted UN committee room which they had found by chance, and slipped into, in a sudden, mutual conspiracy of hunger.

There in the darkness she clipped herself to him as if she would print the whole contour of her body on his; she kissed him long and lovingly, she allowed his hands to wander where they would, over her breasts, down her slim flanks, along her thighs which presently began to move in urgent rhythm, first against his body and then with it, as if the two of them were truly making love.

It was all so fluent, so skilful, so wildly exciting that for him it could only be a brief flare-up. He was stormily spent while she was still clinging to him, almost crying, and whispering: "I wanted to do that for you. . . . Oh, I am so slow," in tender yearning for the same release.

So she did want him after all, he thought, as he held her gently and felt her hungry body tremble into quietness again. She wanted him as much as he wanted her. Yet he was still never asked to that Fifty-sixth Street flat, the only place where they could have turned the wanting into giving and taking.

But within twenty-four hours he was rather glad that they were not yet lovers, because of something he had to involve her in, something so shoddy and second-rate that he was deeply ashamed of ever having taken it on.

He had reported it jocularly to David Bracken, at the end of a long letter reciting the trials of Benjamin Banka. But in reality the taste was horrid.

"Dinamaula has now got himself a permanent girl," [he wrote]. "Or rather, I got her for him, under instruction. Her name is Lucy (might be Loosey!) and she is in fact a call girl with whom D. has become so stricken that she is installed here, down the corridor, officially as a secretary. I'd hate to rely on her shorthand! He has even hinted that he may bring her back with him to Pharamaul, which will make for a really wonderful atmosphere at G.H. See you before too long."

It had begun with an unusual talk between Paul Jordan and President Dinamaula. Paul knew that Joseph Kalatosi had found himself a girl; he knew that Benjamin Banka had found several, though he usually collapsed before he could do them any harm. It seemed to be established that Dinamaula, the most reputable member of the delegation, was giving this particular activity a rest, for the duration of their stay.

But it now turned out that Dinamaula was, after all, as susceptible in New York as he was in Port Victoria. He wanted a girl, he told a startled Paul out of the blue, in phrases which, though explicit, were delivered weightily, as if they concerned Vietnam or the International Monetary Fund. He wanted a girl who would not be a nuisance—that was, she was to be available when she was needed, out of sight at other times. He wanted her promptly; time was wasting. Paul Jordan would be kind enough to fix it up, if possible for that evening.

Paul was taken aback, and rather embarrassed. "But sir," he said, feeling his way in a delicate situation, not yet clear, "I'm afraid I don't really know any girls."

"This would not be a girl that anyone knows."

"Oh. . . ." Good God, Paul thought: he wants a call girl! "Sir, I don't know anything about girls like that, either."

"It should be quite simple to find out."

They were alone in the sitting-room of the suite, the President installed in his favourite armchair, Paul standing uneasily by a window. The quiet elegance of their surroundings, and the privileged view across the park, made this transaction seem all the more odd. Paul did not like it at all—pimping for the President was *not* one of his preferred jobs as aide-de-camp—and he made a determined effort to disengage.

"It really is a bit out of my line," he said firmly. "I honestly don't know how to go about it. Wouldn't it be better if you asked one of your friends on another delegation? They've been here longer than we have——"

Dinamaula was equally firm. "That would not be suitable."

"Or Mr. Kalatosi. He seems to know a lot of——"

"I would prefer you to do it," said Dinamaula, rather distantly. He was assuming his grand manner, Paul noted, probably because he felt a little ashamed of himself. But a little shame was not going to stand in the way of this particular appetite. "I know you will be discreet about it."

Paul did not feel at all flattered. All he felt, in fact, was a sort of old-maidish shock at the very suggestion. But he wondered how far he could go, in trying to get out of the assignment. He was there to do as he was told; that was one essential part of his job. The other was the obligation to take care of the President's needs, and this project certainly belonged to that category, in the most intimate way. He made one more effort.

"I suppose I could ask a cabdriver," he said, trying to make it sound infinitely distasteful. "Or one of the bellboys here. They're always supposed to——"

Dinamaula held up his hand, in an immediate gesture of command. "You will *not* involve the hotel in any way," he said. "I told you to be *discreet* about it!" He stood up, and now he was at his most haughty, as if they were discussing some major stroke of policy, disposable only at the Presidential level. "You're making far too much of this, Paul. It is perfectly simple, if you find the right contacts. Please get to work on it at once."

"Yes, sir."

"Money need *not* be a consideration," said Dinamaula grandly, and stalked out of the suite, leaving Paul in fuming disarray.

Jack Barber, his New York eating guide who was probably an expert in this department also, was out of town for the weekend. After some feeble indecision, Paul took his problem to his only other confidante, Frances Hoy.

Following the morning coffee-break, which seemed to bring UN to a daily standstill, and turn the United Nations building into one vast frieze of clacking tongues, sipping lips, and crooked little fingers, Paul and Frances played truant for a few minutes longer. They sat in the sunshine on the paved terrace overlooking the East River, with the tugs and barges moving slowly by, and the brave flutter of flags making a bright-coloured curtain behind them, and talked. Before long, Paul took the plunge, with the words:

"Darling, I've got an awful thing to ask you."

It did indeed sound awful, when he gave her the details, but she did not seem put out by his request, only surprised and perhaps disappointed that he should have become involved in it. Her manner when he renewed his apologies was almost offhand. She said:

"Oh, people are always sounding us out about girls. Usually they make a play for us first, and then they ask for telephone numbers. It's quite an industry."

"How horrible!"

She was looking at the river, her face turned away from him. "It's the United Nations," she said. Suddenly she became factual and businesslike, which was even more discouraging. "But of course I'll help you. What sort of girl does your President want?"

"Good God, I don't know!" Paul exclaimed. He was hopelessly embarrassed already, and angry with himself for ever considering Frances as a source of help. She should have been the very last person in the whole world. . . . "Just a girl, I suppose."

"They do come a bit cheaper."

"Darling, let's forget about this," he said desperately. "I'll find someone who——"

"We are here to assist the delegates," said Frances, ridiculously formal, and stood up. "That's chapter one, paragraph one, rule one of the charter. It makes us do some funny things, and it makes *you* do some funny things too, doesn't it?" She added, in quick and sad farewell: "I'll leave a message in the box," and then she was gone, taking all the sunshine with her.

The message, when he got it half an hour later, could not have been more precise, nor more depressing to him. It gave a Lexington number, and then the words: "Just ask for Lucy."

It took Paul quite a long time to summon up the courage to ask for Lucy. He kept putting it off, all that afternoon; he sat alone in the Ten Eyck suite, drinking gin-and-tonic at a steady pace, morbidly downcast at this horrid situation which had suddenly sprung up all round him, like rank weeds in a gloomy forest. His position, he thought, was entirely false, and very unfair.

Constrained to do what President Dinamaula wanted, he had

in the process obviously offended Frances Hoy, even though she had agreed to help him. He had thus put their relationship in danger, just when it was sweetly balanced on the edge of fulfil-ment.

He did not want to telephone call girls. He wanted to talk to Frances. He wanted to be *with* Frances, watching the play of feeling and thought crossing her beautiful face, instead of sitting alone in this suite at five o'clock in the afternoon, sweating with nerves because he had to make contact with some terrible tart and fix up a deal for someone else.

But Dinamaula had said: "This evening." It really would not wait any longer.

The voice at the other end of the telephone was, unexpectedly, English, with a slight offbeat accent—Lancashire or the Midlands. He put his request as delicately as he could, not knowing this particular language of love, and he felt a complete fool as he heard himself using the phrase "inquiring for a friend," like a girl sounding out an abortionist. But Lucy was very easy, very matter-of-fact. All she wanted to know was the time.

"Any time after eight o'clock," said Paul.

"Eight o'clock," repeated Lucy, as if—and it was probably the case—she were making a diary entry. Then she asked: "Do you know this address?"

"He wants you to come here."

"Where's here?"

"The Ten Eyck."

The reaction was immediate. "Jesus, I can't come there!" she exclaimed. "It's asking for trouble! They've got rules!"

"It's all right," said Paul. "We have a suite with a sitting-room."

"So what? The house detectives watch that sort of thing all the time. That place must be strict!"

"Also we have diplomatic immunity."

"I haven't got diplomatic immunity."

"But they don't know you here, do they?"

She laughed shortly. "No, they don't exactly know me at the Ten Eyck. . . . Diplomatic, eh? Well, I suppose it's all right. . . . Eight o'clock, then. And it's two hundred dollars. Sure it isn't for you?"

"No. Someone else."

"Pity. You sound all right."

He hung up, and made for the sideboard and the gin bottle, almost at a run.

Lucy, when she arrived at eight o'clock, was not at all what he expected. He had formed a mental picture of a New York call girl, even one with a Midlands accent; she would be blonde and tough, her face dreadfully stamped by experience, her body bearing the marks of unmentionable excesses; she would have stiletto heels like stilts, and lots of lace or feathers round her neck. But the reality, the girl who came into the suite, and smiled, and said: "Hi!" was more like the ideal younger sister than any sister ever was.

She was young—about eighteen—and very pretty indeed; soft waved brown hair framed a calm and innocent face, on which the only lines were the classic ones of good humour and vitality. Her skirt was very short, but so were all the skirts; and her legs were really worth showing—straight and slim, with that coltish grace which was the sensual badge of quality.

In fact she looked a damned sight more acceptable to the Ten Eyck Hotel than most of the women who came through the swing doors of the lobby, and Paul Jordan, bemused by gin and jumpy with nervous tension, could only beam foolishly as he closed the door after her and followed her into the room.

Then they began to talk, and that spoilt it all, within a few seconds. She might have looked like a comely young angel, but there was no doubt that she was a tough customer after all. Not the pretty package, but the professional filling, was the real girl.

Paul, flustered, could think of nothing except to ask her name.

"Lucy Help," she answered, and looked at him invitingly. "You know—call for Help." She must have made the joke a hundred times before, and when Paul laughed she gave only the briefest smile in reply. Then she glanced round the room. "Say, this is quite a setup!" The Americanism, delivered in the authentic accents of Middle England, sounded highly unlikely, as though a dove had let go with a raven's croak. "I heard this place was smart, but my goodness!"

"Do sit down," said Paul. "Er—my friend isn't quite ready yet." It sounded atrociously crude, as if Dinamaula were limbering up in a back room, and Paul felt himself blush scarlet. "You're English, aren't you?"

"Born in Birmingham. Good old Brum." She had sat down, and

the shapely legs, now revealed nearly to her hips, became an immediate focus of attention. She saw him staring at them, and followed a natural train of thought: "Are you sure this isn't for you?"

"No. I told you on the phone."

"O.K., O.K. People get nervous, that's all."

"Would you like a drink?"

"Not when I'm driving," she answered, and gave him a look of such lecherous intensity that his discomfiture was complete.

He crossed to the sideboard, and helped himself to another liberal measure of gin. Over his shoulder he asked: "How did you —er—come to America?"

"I won a contest," answered Lucy Help. "Miss Sutton Coldfield. The prize was a trip to the World's Fair, Montreal. Then I came down here with a friend. He got me a job with Staff Expander."

"What on earth's that?"

"They supply girls to offices, when there's too much work for the ordinary staff."

"And what happened to you at Staff Expander?"

"The staff got too big." She gave him another of her explicit looks. Probably that was a favourite joke, too. "So one thing led to another." She looked at her watch. "Can we get going? I want to be back by ten."

It was eight-fifteen, the time when Dinamaula had said that he would be fancy-free. "All right," said Paul. "It's just down the corridor. Room 87A."

She stood up. "You said something about the diplomatic. Who is this, exactly?"

Paul felt no obligation to conceal the details. "He's the leader of our UN delegation. The President of Pharamaul."

"Where's that when it's at home?"

"Southern Africa."

"Oh." She turned back from the door. "Is he—you know—black?"

"Yes." Seeing a frown cross her face, he asked: "Do you mind?"

"Not really. But my mum was very strict. . . . Oh well." She gave him her brightest smile. "Don't forget now—if you're in the mood, call for Help."

"I've got a girl already, I'm afraid." Some stupid, drunken impulse made him add: "She's Chinese."

"Well, good for you!" Lucy Help's expression became totally lewd. "Is it true?"

"No," he said miserably. "I mean, I don't know."

"I'll bet!" she smirked. "A big strong boy like you. Well, so long."

Then she was gone, with a swaying of those trim hips, a lithe flicker of long legs, which should have done for him what she claimed to have done for Staff Expander, but which, in all the circumstances of this day, only multiplied the horrid taste of betrayal.

He had planned to phone Frances that night, as soon as he was free; but by now it was too late for a meeting—and, in the present context, insultingly so. She would know exactly what had held him up. By now, also, he was in poor shape for meeting anyone, least of all a girl so precious; the gin-and-tonics had taken their toll, leaving him thoroughly disorganized and none too steady on his feet.

Above all, he was ashamed of himself, for allowing this crude enterprise to touch Frances at all; the contrast between their own tender feelings, and the cash-and-carry deal which he had just promoted, was enough to turn the stomach, without benefit of alcohol.

His guilty self-dislike reached its peak when, passing No. 87A on his way to his own room, he heard the unmistakable sounds of man, glorious man, at the moment of achievement. He stumbled to an early bed, feeling as if he had just been taken on at the zoo.

But morning brought relief, because it brought him Frances Hoy again. There was a note waiting for him in the delegation's "box," a note which gave him the wildest surge of joy he had ever known. It began, astonishingly: "I am sorry, my darling," and after that there were only seven more words: "Please meet me at Franco's at eight." But the seven words were enough to keep him joyful all day, and the meeting itself was a miracle of happiness.

Franco's, which boasted twenty-seven different kinds of *pasta* and "the best Chianti west of Tuscany," was also the darkest of their evening rendezvous; and there they settled down, and held hands immediately, and she said again what she had written in the note:

"I'm so sorry, darling. Forgive me."

He kissed her. "What for, for Heaven's sake?"

"For being bad-tempered. I ought to have realized it was something you *had* to do."

"Well, yes, in a way it was. But I should have had the guts to refuse. And it was awful to bring you into it. I was so ashamed about that. I still am."

Squeezing his hand, she tried to reassure him. "I told you, it's happened lots of times before. It's part of the job. That's why I shouldn't have been angry. . . . What was Lucy like?"

"Awful."

"But pretty?"

"Yes. Very pretty. But awful all the same. And two hundred dollars."

"Diplomatic prices," Frances said disdainfully. "It's all part of this place. It's the new system. Like your consolidated fund."

"How do you mean?"

"Throwing other people's money away. Two hundred dollars for one of those girls! Only diplomats would pay that kind of price."

"What ought it to be?"

"I'm not even going to tell you!"

They ordered their favourite *tagliatelle verdi*, and then, as if steering a deliberate course away from Lucy Help and towards more general woes, she said:

"When I started at the UN, I thought it was all so wonderful. I used to *believe!* Now it's all gone wrong."

"But why?"

"Because it's become a sort of privileged racket. I said I'd talk about this some time, didn't I?"

"The first night."

"And this is the ninth." She squeezed his hand again. "How faithful we are. . . . I think I began to worry when I saw how the delegations were throwing their money around. It's just like children showing off—playing at being rich men when the countries they represent can hardly subsist. Little backward countries where the people are desperately poor—but in New York the envoys all live it up as if they were dollar millionaires, without a care in the world."

"We have a Rolls," said Paul. "Fifteen dollars an hour."

"You would. . . . Yet half these countries are way behind with their UN dues. Honestly, it's like pulling teeth, getting them to pay up. I *know*. They say: 'This is *our* show, *our* organization.' Then they say: 'But we're a little strapped for cash right now. *You* pay for it.'"

She ate for a while, with a fierce zest which was half hunger, half irritation. Then she went on:

"The next thing was, watching all that foreign aid going down the drain. Millions of it, every day. Supporting people we shouldn't be seen dead with! Propping up a lot of rotten, corrupt thieves who just steal it!" She smiled when she saw him watching her. "I'm sorry, darling—but honestly, it makes me so *mad!* All that money, made by *our* brains and *our* hard work, coming out of *our* taxes, given to kids to throw out the window, or to crooks to stash away in Switzerland. Do you know, Ghana owed nine hundred million dollars before Nkrumah was kicked out? *Nine hundred million.* Most of it came from us. But do you think we'll ever see a cent of it again? In a pig's ear!"

Though his mouth was half full of delicious green *pasta*, Paul laughed out loud, garlic dressing and all. The resulting fit of coughing sent hollow echoes through the gloom of Franco's, as if somewhere in this cave there were a hermit dying.

"Serve you right," she said severely. "This just isn't funny."

Recovering, he said: "Of course it isn't. But oh, darling Frances, you're so wonderful! I didn't know you took this so seriously."

"You don't know anything about me," she said. "But you will, you will. . . ."

"As a matter of fact, that sort of thing is going on in Pharamaul. Not on the same scale, of course. But it *is* beginning, with British money."

"Then you'd better watch out," she told him. "Or you'll have to write the whole lot off, *and* bail them out again. And don't hold your breath till they say thank you. It's their *right*—didn't you know that? Give us a big loan"—she was mimicking a whining suppliant, with unexpected spite. "But no strings attached. Don't expect anything in return. And hold still while we spit in your eye."

"Chop suey," he said. The intricacies of foreign aid had not been one of his studies. "What do you mean, spit in your eye?"

"Because in spite of all we do for them, they still think they can say anything they like about the West, fire off any kind of insult. Look at you and the Zambians. Look at us and India. Or Egypt. They take our money by the cartload, and then they curse us out for being so filthy rich. It's so dishonest!"

He felt that there was a flaw in this somewhere, or some aspect of unfairness. He said:

"But they *are* poor, aren't they? They do need our help."

"Oh yes," she agreed. "And of course they deserve it, in a way, for what we've done to them in the past. The slaves, all the plundering. We've got plenty on our conscience." She smiled. "I'm not being very Chinese tonight, am I?"

He suddenly dropped his hand, and pressed her thigh against his own, so that he could feel its whole warm length quickening his flesh. She let it stay there, while she looked deep into his eyes. Her remark about "being Chinese" had started Paul on a very different train of thought. Between them, "being Chinese" had come to mean sharing with him the sensual side of her nature; she was "being Chinese" whenever they kissed, and memorably so when she had drawn him into the dark committee room, and moved her body against his with such freedom and such shattering effect.

When he said, still touching her thigh: "You're very Chinese for me," the message travelled swiftly. She turned sideways and leant against him, so that he could feel the soft contour of her breast.

"I'm glad," she answered. "But that wasn't what I was talking about, and you know it." She straightened herself with prim formality, picked up his hand, and put it firmly on the table. "All right, Mr. Pinkerton. I'll tell you one more thing, or two more things. Then we'll talk about something else, or do something else."

"I can't wait."

"This is about one of the African delegates," she began straight away. "He left the text of a speech behind in Protocol, by mistake, and I read it. I thought he must have delivered it already, so it wouldn't matter. And he *had* delivered it already—or one version of it, anyway. Because it was actually two speeches on the same subject, prepared for the same debate, clipped together. They were about aid, as usual. Speech Number One was pro-American —how generous we were, how disinterested, what a constructive approach, how much his country loved us. Speech Number Two said what twisting Scrooges we had turned out to be—neo-colonialists, imperialists, the lot. How we grudged even the tiniest loan unless the Afro-Asians did exactly as they were told in return." She expelled a long breath. "He was simply going to wait, you see, until America announced its aid program. Then, if his country got a good cut, we were angels. But if he came out of it badly, then we were no-good bastards."

"Which speech had he used?"

"The one that slammed us. Because we only gave him a miserable twenty million dollars to build a dam."

"Well, at least he *was* going to say thank you."

"Sure. At fifty million dollars a word."

Paul had been intrigued, in spite of those other urges which had flared up a few moments before. He prompted her: "Tell me some more."

"Oh, there's so much. . . ." She pushed her hair away from her eyes. "There was one that really made me laugh, a couple of months ago. A Nigerian marched in and complained that he'd been insulted in a supermarket. It seemed that he'd run over a child's foot with his shopping cart, and the mother had bawled him out for being careless, and when he reported it the manager had refused to do anything about it. He was absolutely furious! Gave us all hell. Said we weren't even civilized. At the end he said: 'This could never happen in Nigeria!'" She laughed at the memory. "Honestly, I nearly blew my top. Nigeria. . . . Their last two Prime Ministers were only shot or hacked to death, that's all. They only slice people up and throw them down the nearest well, because they belong to the wrong tribe. And *we're* uncivilized!"

"These things are relative."

"These things make me sick! . . . Of course, some of them are only little things. Pinpricks. But there are plenty of big ones. And it's the general attitude I hate." She seemed to be brooding in melancholy. "If men behave stupidly or selfishly, so do nations. I can tell you, a lot of people at the UN are getting fed up with it. Some of us feel it's hardly worth working there any more."

"That's very sad."

"Isn't it?" She shook her head. "So you have your awful girl, and I have the Afro-Asian bloc." Then suddenly her face cleared. "We also have each other, my darling, and it's really silly for *us* to be sad."

"Be Chinese instead," he said.

"I'm Chinese now. Instant Chinese." Then she murmured: "Shall we go home?"

Paul's heart jumped at the words, and at the look—shy, yet almost naked in candour—which went with them. But he could still hardly believe. "What about Stella?"

"She's away."

The dream began. As they went up in the lift, they could only stare at each other, on the edge of a private rapture which suddenly, for no reason at all, had come fantastically near. Words were no longer their currency, only looks and, in a few moments, the clamorous excitement of touching each other. Her hand was shaking as she turned the key in the lock; then they were safe inside, and the door shut behind them, and she was in his arms, and he said—almost shouted:

"Oh God, I love you!"

The swift pictures multiplied. The tiny hallway became the sitting-room, a warm and quiet shell isolated from all the outside world; the sitting-room became the drink trembling in his hand as soon as she was gone. The drink became her voice calling out: "Darling," and the voice the embracing twilight of her bedroom, and then the bed in which she was lying, and the brown arms stretched out towards him, and her shining black hair fanned out across the pillows, the focus of all desire and all the thudding of his heart.

He looked down at her. "My Chinese," he said.

Her face was beautiful, softly sensual, beginning to be radiant; above the high cheekbones, her eyes shone for him alone. She leant forward, and the clothes fell away as she had intended, and there, offered to him, were her smooth shoulders and her small, marvellous breasts, uptilted as if they already sought his lips.

She said: "I'm very Chinese tonight." Her voice was low, determined in the need to touch him with her desire. "I'm Chinese all over. Inside, too. Come." Then all the pictures slid away for ever, and the focus blurred to nothing, as she said again: "Come. Come quickly!"

But she had summoned him too potently, too exactly altogether; he did come quickly, and the first time was a silly, boyish fiasco. He had dreamed and planned that it should be wonderful for both of them; but their evening together, with its swift change of current, had taken him far towards high tide before he even lay down beside her. He had wanted her so much, for so long, that as soon as he felt her slim naked body alongside his own the uncontrollable rhythm began, not to be checked, impossible to hold back.

There was hardly time for anything except the first ecstatic entry before it was all over; he was gasping in release, and she, with a single tender cry, was left in hungry, lonely solitude again.

He felt a sad fool, a cheat in love already, and as soon as he found his voice and could summon his thoughts, he told her so, with deep humility.

"Oh darling, I'm so sorry!" he said. He was still breathless, as if the race had been long instead of stupidly cut short. "That was so selfish. But I just couldn't help it."

"It doesn't matter," she answered, almost in a whisper. "I understand."

She was still lying back where she had welcomed him, only a moment ago; her body was motionless, her eyes staring at the ceiling. Guiltily he thought of it as the classic pose of woman left out upon a limb. He touched her hair, and then the soft warmth of her cheek. He said again:

"I'm so sorry. You were too strong for me, too wonderful. It was the way you felt. I just couldn't stop. I'd been thinking about it so much. And then, being with you, close to you, all evening——"

"Lie still," she told him. "Rest. Don't think about it any more."

"But I feel so useless."

She turned towards him. There was enough light for him to read the gentle message of desire in her face. "You didn't feel useless to me. . . . I was glad I could make it happen so quickly, even if . . . A girl can be proud about that, you know."

"But there was hardly anything for you."

"There was enough. There was holding you, feeling you so

160

strong." She smiled, in secret assurance. "Do you think you won't have another chance?"

There arrived another chance, and a potent one, before the clock had half gone round again; and this time, he thought, it is to be you, only you, and he told her so in words, and his body told her so in the strong, loving care, the triggered intensity with which he sought to carry her with him, ahead of him, separate from him and yet deeply engaged in the same search for her delight.

Slowly, strand by strand, the first dream he had ever had of her began to come true. At last he was journeying up that sinuous river with its slow rhythm, through the yielding screens, into the secret house where wild pleasure was waiting for his hands and body and thundering heart; but it was waiting for her also, as her flowing movements and small cries of delight soon told him.

Within a little while she was all movement, all passion, all tormented eagerness; she was calling out: "Oh stay, stay with me!" as if the thought, the danger of his leaving, had now become a source of terror. He whispered: "I will stay for ever, if you want it," and with those words she seemed to move out upon a sea of loving confidence, a sea where she could float in languor, or swim with any stroke, or strive with shuddering effort for the divine further shore.

Then for a long moment she was poised, and silent, and still, almost as if she were listening, or waiting for a final summons; and then she cried out, in wonder and astonishment: "Oh, it is happening!" and the turmoil he could feel in her body became a wild clenching, and with another cry she had reached home.

She said, immediately, breathlessly: "You?" and he nodded, and with no more signal than that, no more than a single stroke, he topped the crest of his last wave and was home also.

They lay in rapturous harmony as all the waves fell back, and left them loving castaways.

Somewhere in the deep of that long night, Frances said:
"There's no Stella."

He was half asleep, in the hazy twilight which lay between exhaustion and contentment, and he only took in the word "Stella." He said:

"What about Stella? When does she come back? And where does she sleep, anyway?"

Frances turned over, and pushed some admonishing fingers against his shoulder. "After all I've done for you, and you won't even listen. I said, there *isn't any Stella!*"

He came fully awake. "What? How do you mean?"

"I invented her, a long time ago. The roommate that never was."

"After all I've done for *you*, you tell me these terrible lies. . . . Why, darling?"

"She was my insurance."

He understood. "That's rather sweet. And clever."

"But now I don't need any insurance."

"You never did, with me."

"Oh, there were one or two times. But not really, no. That's why I love you."

They were two murmuring voices, voices in their private night, sundered by darkness, closely bound by recent contact. He said: "Tell me another reason."

"Because you're so beautiful. And everything."

"Everything was wonderful."

"I surely loved you *then*. Did you guess that was the first time it ever happened?"

"Yes. You were so surprised. I adored you, at that moment. And felt terribly happy. And proud too."

"Why not? It wasn't the first *time*, of course."

"No."

She waited, but he did not ask. "I've only had one other lover," she told him. "About two years ago. It didn't work out, though it went on quite a while. He really wanted a girl who looked different, to take out. You know—Chinese food to take out. That was me."

"Darling, don't."

"Oh, it's long gone. . . . Then he got bored with it. It was like I wasn't news any more."

"What an awful idea!"

"I can understand it. It's true for you, isn't it, in a way?"

"No."

She leant across and whispered in his ear: "Aren't I the chink in your armour?"

162

"Frances!"

"I'm sorry, darling. I've been saving that joke for *years*."

"I wish I could feel honoured."

"You *are* honoured. I'm in bed with you."

"Why didn't that happen before? Why all the thing about Stella?" He felt her stiffen, and he said: "Darling, I know it's a wonderful idea. But it doesn't seem to apply to us. We felt just the same, almost from the beginning, didn't we?"

There was a long silence. He could not tell whether she was thinking, or whether she did not want to answer. Then she said:

"I held back, just because we *did* feel like that. How can you start something which has to die? You were going away. You *are* going away. We have to say good-bye. Soon." She moved swiftly, until she was lying against him, and her long legs were once more entwined with his. But it was the need for comfort, rather than any other hunger, which brought her so close. "Last night, it suddenly seemed the best reason in the world for *not* missing it. But oh love! Oh darling! If I weren't in bed with you, I would be crying already."

She did cry, early that morning, when they said good-bye; the coffee she brewed for him might have been compounded with bitter tears, for that was the true taste of their farewell. In grief which was the forerunner of what lay ahead for them, she clung to him with shaking sobs, as if the end of their night had become the end of their world, and they were now destined for different planets, different zones of time and space. The last view he had, before he closed the flat door, was of her head bent forward until her hair became a dark curtain for her face, and her shoulders beneath the blue-patterned robe trembling as the hopeless tears seized full possession again.

He would have gone back, if going back could have done anything to stem such scalding sorrow. Every line of her body beckoned him; yet every line also told him that such particular sadness, conceived by two people, must be borne by one alone.

But during the course of the morning they both took a firmer grip. Though they did this independently, it turned out to be the same grip, the same plan to salvage whatever time was left to them.

They met at the coffee-break, and wandered out to their favourite vantage-point on the East River terrace. It was a bright day, but windy; the same breeze which ruffled the grey-blue water stirred her hair, making it glisten as it caught the sunshine. All around them was the usual activity: the to-and-fro of people, the droves of sightseers, the snaking queues of tourists waiting their turn to be led like wondering sheep through the UN building.

But neither sheep nor people were an intrusion, on this bright day. When one was in love, it was with all the world.

Paul stared into her face, loving all of it and all of her. The faint smudges under her eyes, the fatigue of love, made her seem especially dear. He said:

"You look a little more than a day older, since yesterday."

"Thank you so much," she murmured. "That's all that a girl wants to hear, at a time like this. . . . Darling, I'm sorry I cried."

He touched her hand. "You were crying for both of us."

"Maybe so. But there's plenty of time for that. Shall we be brave again?"

"Yes. And I've had a wonderful idea."

"So have I." She looked away for a moment. "Paul, how much longer have you got?"

"About three weeks."

"Can you get some leave?"

He stared at her. "Hey, that was *my* idea! Yes, I think I can. There's nothing going on, as far as the delegation's concerned. We're really wasting our time here. Even more than usual. But can *you* get leave?"

She nodded. "Yes. I've lots saved up. I've checked already. How long should we take, do you think?"

"Let's try for two weeks, starting tomorrow. Will you want to go away?"

"There doesn't seem much point. Come and stay at the Hoy Hotel."

"I hear the service is terrific."

"Propaganda," she said. "The service is only just starting. You know these country girls. Practically peasants. But it will improve. I promise you."

"Room service?"

"Particularly room service." She stood up, and the crosswind caught her hair again, so that it became a moving, shimmering frame for a lovely face. "Come on, Paul—let's start things going right now."

It was indeed easy for Paul to take his holiday, since, even if the session itself had not been petering out, the distinguished delegation from Pharamaul appeared to have ground to a standstill, as far as work was concerned. Dinamaula seemed to be in bed all the time; Benjamin Banka had discovered the joys of strip-tease, and was a daily and devoted customer from opening-time onwards —which, in certain select establishments in the sleazy warren round Times Square, was at the grisly hour of 10 A.M.

Only Joseph Kalatosi could be said to be working, and he was working very much on his own, in some specialized area involving dozens of visitors who arrived at the Ten Eyck suite with bulging black briefcases, and were then ushered for further conference into his own room.

Whatever he was cooking up, thought Paul, was a very personal affair. From the look of the callers, it seemed to have sharp undertones of commerce.

Securing his leave was a simple matter of asking Dinamaula, who replied pleasantly: "Of course, Paul. Take some time—you've earned it. Just leave your address." Leaving his address ("I'm staying with friends") involved a short conversation with Joseph Kalatosi, who said, straight-faced: "Fifty-sixth Street, eh? Would that be the Chinese Embassy?" and then went off into roars of laughter. Trust Joe Kal, the compulsive know-it-all, to have got wind of this as well. . . . But nothing could spoil the loving freedom which was theirs the following morning, even though it trembled all the time on the cutting edge of farewell.

Without another word to the world, they dived into their private paradise, and drew the covers over their heads.

There they did nothing, and they did everything. Life at the Hoy-Hilton, as they came to call the flat, was a mixture, intensely happy, of talking, listening to music, loafing about in old clothes or in none, reading, watching ancient films on television, eating, drinking, and making love. Her cooking turned out to be delicious, with certain surprises built into it—he was, for example, astonished to find that a magnificent dish compounded of crab meat, onions, mushrooms, bamboo shoots, tomatoes, and soy sauce went by the guileless name of Egg Fu Yong.

Once he said: "It's my turn tonight," and, attended by the good luck which was theirs all the time, he dished up a prime specimen of what the Navy called "cheesy-hammy-eggy."

"I didn't know sailors could cook—this is perfect!" Frances told him, her mouth inelegantly full.

"Sailors can do anything," he assured her. "I once sewed a piece of a man's ear back on! He was fooling about with the ammunition hoist——"

"Darling, please!" she interrupted. "Could it wait till after dinner?"

"All right—I'll tell you in bed."

"The only thing you'll tell me in bed is that you love me."

It was true that this was almost the only thing he told her in bed. Their life was now geared, above everything else, to love-making, and in this realm all fears had vanished, and the map of its numberless highways was spread for their delight.

It was she who had given the signal for this, very near the beginning of their retreat. She had been making their mid-morning coffee, and he had come into the kitchen and put his arms round her waist, and she had turned instantly and wrapped him in such a loving embrace that, like the simplest exercise in mathematics, it could only have one answer.

"Hardly worth getting dressed, was it?" she said, between tender kisses, and the searching, questing movements of her body which had already begun. "Darling I want to make love all the time! Isn't it awful?"

"No." He held her close. "Like now?"

"Certainly! The coffee isn't perking yet."

"Then the coffee's in a minority."

"Oh darling! Quickly!"

"You mean slowly."

"Very slowly. Like"—she turned her head, and whispered in his ear.

"Miss Hoy, I've told you before, that's very rude."

"I don't care. That's what it feels like."

Like many other things, the connection between sailors and lighthouses had been early established. All he had to do was to keep on proving it—the least arduous job any sailor ever had.

Yet for all her eagerness she remained, when in the very lists of love, curiously submissive and humble; there were times, he once

166

thought fancifully, when she seemed to be saying "My lord," not with her lips but with her body, so subject to his own had it become. There might indeed have been a tiny hotel called the Hoy-Hilton, whose aim was impeccable service, given by our highly trained staff, our skilled chef. . . . In fact, she was so good, so wonderful, so inventive in love that there were moments when he felt suspicious, and jealous of the past. She had learned all this from one love affair which "didn't work out"? Perhaps it was just as well that it hadn't.

But he preferred, in daydreams, to think that her skill was a race-inheritance, mysterious, hidden deep in sensuous oriental blood, or that certain secrets of delight were passed on from one generation to another, imparted by slant-eyed old women whispering in an inner chamber, old women who knew all the duties which a young girl owed to the marriage bed.

It was part of Frances's fantastic appeal that she could give him these foolish thoughts, and almost make him believe that some ancient "lore of the east" was being practised upon his enraptured flesh.

Towards the end, when time was racing away, and they were counting in hours rather than days, they grew, not sad—"I cried at just the right time, at the beginning instead of the end," she told him once—but more serious, more practical. Did all this really have to disappear, and go to waste?

He wanted to marry her, he said, and meant it with all his heart.

She had been thinking of it too, she told him, without artifice. But how would it work out—not between the two of them, but with his job, and his family? "What does the Navy think of foreign wives?" she asked him. "Funny ones, too."

"The Navy doesn't mind foreign wives," he said. "Not Americans, anyway."

"Take a look," she said, turning a thoughtful face towards him. "I'm not *quite* American, am I? How would I go down at—what's that silly name? Pumpy?"

"Pompey. Portsmouth." A vision of Frances Hoy, teacup in one hand, buttered scone in the other, doing battle with one of those awful admirals' wives, reeling under the weight of the social broadsides which they so enjoyed, rose up to plague him. "Oh, the

Navy's not as stuffy as it used to be," he assured her, and himself. "England isn't so insular, either."

"It's sad that there should be anything to be stuffy about. And what about your family? Your mother?"

He smiled. "She'd get the shock of her life. She wants me to marry a girl called Angela Dartington-Coombs."

"You go ahead."

"I want to marry you. . . . Then mother would think it over for a bit, and then she'd accept it. She's very"—he was about to say "broad-minded," and then he realized how insulting it would sound. "Very proud of never being surprised by anything," he finished. "She would say: 'Oh, is she Chinese? I hadn't noticed.' Darling, let's think about this really seriously!"

"I will, I will. But you have to go back now, don't you? We have to say good-bye."

"I'm afraid so."

"For how long, in Pharamaul?"

"I don't know. It depends on Dinamaula. When he feels he doesn't need me any more, he'll say so, and I can move on."

"Then it might be sooner than you think."

"How do you mean?"

"I get the impression," she answered, "from what people are saying, that your Mr. Dinamaula is becoming *very* sure of himself, very inspired." The word, as she spoke it, had a discomforting ring. "That's what the UN does to people, sometimes."

"Good," said Paul promptly. "Then I'll be released, and posted to Washington, and we can be married in a shower of cherry-blossom."

"All same Butterfly. But you want to go back to sea, don't you?"

"Then you can live in Portsmouth, and knit things, and wait for me to bring you back a parrot."

She sighed. "Bliss! I can't wait for either of you. . . . Oh darling, I don't mind what Dinamaula does, as long as he lets you go."

Suddenly it was the last weekend, and then the last full day; the time had come, for all of them, to wrap things up, and say their various good-byes. The Distinguished Delegates from Pharamaul must now join the home-going tide which marked the end of the session.

On this last day, President Dinamaula was enjoying a slow stroll with his friend from the Zambian delegation, up and down the broad terrace which flanked the Conference Building. This was privileged territory, and the two robed and capped figures, walking at their ease, seemed a natural part of this privilege, a pair of patrician Roman senators taking the air in a modern Forum. If they were conscious of being stared at, they gave no sign. Rank carried such burdens, and after a time one became used to it.

"That was a really splendid party last night," said the Zambian. "I enjoyed it immensely. The Ten Eyck does these things very well."

"I was glad you could come," answered Dinamaula. "There are so many of these farewell parties just now."

"And they are sad, so sad, even the best of them. New York when the session is adjourned is like a desert! But I suppose you will be glad to get back. Three months is a long time to be away from things, however capable the people one leaves behind."

"It is certainly time I went back. David Bracken—that's my Chief Secretary—is very efficient. But as a civil servant, of course, he has his limitations where political matters are concerned."

"Ah yes, David Bracken." The Zambian pronounced the name with special care. "Victor Luanda mentioned him in one of his dispatches. I remember seeing it. How long will he be staying in that post?"

"I have not made up my mind."

They had reached the farther end of the terrace, and turned in unison, their robes swinging gently outwards as if in a movement of dance. There was a big white tourist boat going by, up the East River, and they watched it for a space in silence. Then the Zambian took up their talk again:

"I only asked because I have heard some comment. Victor reminded me, among other things, that Bracken was the man who saw you off into exile."

"He was the conducting officer, yes."

"Conducting officer! What a monstrous picture that conjures up! . . . It was a long time ago, of course," the Zambian went on, seeming to choose his words carefully. "But I would have thought that as long as he remained in Pharamaul—apart from serving as a reminder of the past—his new status would be something of an anomaly." He paused, but Dinamaula said nothing and gave no sign of reaction. The Zambian continued: "However, I am sure you have these things under consideration, all the time."

"The arrangement was that he should stay as long as he could be of use to me."

"Quite so." The Zambian glanced sideways at his companion's face, and found it, as usual, grave and somewhat uncommunicative. "Thus, the inference, as long as he is there, is that you need a—how shall I put it?—a British coach, to use a sporting term."

"He is not my coach," said Dinamaula shortly.

"Of course not! Please don't misunderstand me. I mean that there is an *appearance* of having to depend on outside advice, outside help. A kind of tutorship. There is that young naval officer, too. . . . However, I would not dream of influencing your judgement. We shall miss you here, that is really what I want to say. Tell me, what are your plans for a permanent delegation in New York?"

"That is our next step," said Dinamaula, glad of the change of subject. "I shall be recruiting five or six suitable people, as soon as I get home. At the moment we are leaving Benjamin Banka behind, to make the office arrangements and to form the nucleus of a permanent staff."

"Benjamin Banka," the Zambian repeated, and wrinkled his nose delicately. "Yes, well. . . . As long as you consider him sufficiently *protocolaire*."

"It is not necessarily a permanent appointment."

"Quite so. You know what I feel about our representation here. It must be kept at full strength, all the time." He spread out his hands in a wide gesture, as if claiming all that he saw. "This is *our* century, *our* world, and no one is going to take it away from us again! But we cannot relax for a moment—those people are much too smart—and so we count on every like-minded country pulling its full weight." He smiled. "Well, that is the end of my lecture, *cher collègue*. I must say good-bye—I have a committee."

Dinamaula, slightly chagrined to realize that in some ways it *had* been a lecture, subtly directed, nevertheless smiled in return, and held out his hand.

"Good-bye. I hope we meet again before too long."

"I am counting on it," the Zambian answered. "In the meantime, I trust you will allow Victor Luanda to keep in close touch."

The man who almost bounded into the bedroom at Joseph Kalatosi's bidding was like a score of other men whom he had welcomed, during the past few weeks; a brisk, balding, sharp-eyed, youngish-oldish man, a little thick around the jowls, his grey face creased into a permanent smile, his hand outstretched a full yard ahead of him. Behind the outstretched hand was a second focus of interest—the bright blue bow tie which instantly signalled confidence, buoyancy, and drive. Before the man had said a single word, his hand and his tie seemed to have said it for him. The message was a simple and direct declaration: I am your newest and firmest friend. I have something to give you. You *must* accept it, with my best compliments!

Joseph Kalatosi, in the course of the past three months, had become used to such swift pressures, whether they were those of friendship or of competition. He did no more than register that his caller was energetic and determined, before the runaway avalanche was upon him.

"*Your* Excellency!" his visitor began, in a throaty voice which was a prime example of whisky-laced good fellowship. "Ken Calhoun—and thanks a million for seeing me at such short notice! But you people move about the world so fast—we have to catch you on the wing, or we're likely to lay an egg." He burst into barking laughter, and switched it off almost before the first echo had twanged into silence. "I'll come straight to the point, because you distinguished people have no time to waste. Don't I know it! I often say, the business rat-race has nothing on the diplomatic grind. We only deal in products, but you deal in human beans— and human beans, by God, are what makes this planet tick! Do you know, just while I've been talking, more than half a million human beans have been born?" He held up a fat hand. "But don't blame me, for Chrissakes—I've been on the pill since they invented aspirin!" The barking laughter came and went, like Mirth itself breaking the sound barrier. "Briefly, Mr. Kalatosi, *Your* Excellency, I'm Ken Calhoun, and I'm here to sell you light-bulbs. If possible by the million!"

Joseph Kalatosi had not wasted his time at UN, or anywhere else in New York. He had trained himself to resist the hard sell, and the soft sell, and the no sell—that cunning ploy which nudged the buyer into active business by hinting, in the nicest possible way, that he was not quite the class of customer who would appreciate, and could afford, the product on display. Ken Calhoun had initiated the hard sell, and the only thing to do with the hard sell was to step back and allow the pressure to subside.

Joseph Kalatosi, who had shaken hands rather limply, showed himself perceptively remote in the face of the onslaught. "Please sit down," he said coldly. "I would like to offer you a drink, but of course I do not keep anything in my bedroom. Now, as to light-bulbs—I am not sure that this is quite my concern. Perhaps you will tell me what you have in mind."

Ken Calhoun could take the temperature as quickly as any other man, and could react to it with rare speed. On the instant, his expression and his manner changed. He ceased to smile; he became decorous, even statesmanlike, and his voice as he answered was positively devout.

"Your Excellency," he said, "I think I can persuade you that light-bulbs *are* your concern, in a very direct way. Light-bulbs are used by the human beans we were talking about, and human beans are your special interest, as a high administrator. Isn't that so?"

Joseph Kalatosi allowed several daunting seconds to pass before he answered: "Please go on."

"Well," said Ken Calhoun, with a little more assurance, "human beans are *my* special interest, too. They're more than customers—they're flesh and blood *people*. Their health and happiness is *my* health and happiness. And one of the most precious things about good health is—good eyesight! Isn't that the truth? Mr. Kalatosi, sir, I told you on the phone that I represent Nu-Lite——"

"To be frank," said Joseph Kalatosi, still deliberately cool, "I misunderstood you. I thought that Nu-Lite was something in the educational field."

"Ah, but so it is! Deeply educational. Reading. Books. Newspapers. The spread of knowledge. As soon as dusk falls, what happens? It all comes down to the light-bulb! Isn't that a fact? One of the biggest blessings in the whole civilized world is the simple, household——"

Joseph Kalatosi had no scruples about interrupting him again.

"So it concerns light-bulbs," he said, as if he were speaking of chewing gum, or even fertilizer. "But how am I involved? Surely you sell them through the ordinary commercial channels?"

"Well, we *have*," Ken Calhoun agreed. "Up till now. But I want to improve on that, for our mutual benefit. What I'm proposing, for you good people in Pharamaul, is a Government monopoly."

Though he was coming to have a rare affection for the last two words, Joseph Kalatosi was still startled to hear them in this context. After a long pause he asked: "How could that possibly be justified?"

"Easily." Ken Calhoun leant forward in his chair, scenting blood already. He was over the first and biggest hurdle of all: he had the client asking questions. "You're a very senior Government official—right? You are concerned, every day and every night, with the people—their health, their happiness, their efficiency— right? Given an inferior product in the shape of a light-bulb, the people's precious eyesight could well be in danger. It might become a permanent national affliction. Given a superior product, that's impossible! The nation's health is safeguarded!" He paused dramatically, and then a wagging finger came up, like the probing dagger of truth. "If every light-bulb used in Pharamaul went through your hands, Mr. Kalatosi, you would not only be taking care of that sacred trust. You would be in control of a really important sector of public life. Think of it! Government offices. Stores. Business houses. Private houses. Street lighting. Hotels. Schools—especially schools! All lit by Government-approved bulbs. All of the same dependable quality. All channeled through one central buying agency. And all in the hands of one department— in fact, one man!"

After another long pause, Joseph Kalatosi said: "On second thoughts, perhaps we *might* have a drink. I recall that I have a little whisky which I was keeping for the journey." He got up, crossed to his wardrobe, and drew out a king-size, leather-covered, silver-topped flask which held a guaranteed fifteen ounces of any liquid. There were glasses above the washbasin. There even chanced to be a bowl of ice on a side table. He poured out two substantial drinks, and turned. "A little bourbon on the rocks might help our discussion," he said. "But it's only fair to tell you that one of your competitors has already been to see me."

If Ken Calhoun recognized a familiar gambit, he gave no sign.

Instead, he took a hearty swig of his drink, said: "That's Jack Daniels' Sour Mash, by God! You diplomats certainly learn our ways fast!" and put the glass down again. Then he went on: "We like to think that we have *no* competitors, Mr. Kalatosi. Which outfit was it?"

"Best-Lite."

"Best-Lite!" Ken Calhoun assumed an expression in startling contrast with the one which had followed the whisky. "I guess that would be Jim O'Leary."

"Yes."

Calhoun sighed. "Well, God knows I've nothing against Jim O'Leary, and nothing against Best-Lite except that their product stinks. Do you know what they say in the trade? Buy Best-Lite— and keep it dark!" After a single syllable of laughter, his eyes grew sharp. "If I may ask, what exactly did you tell my friend Jim? Did you make a commitment? Is the deal zipped up?"

"Not exactly."

"Well, if it's not zipped up, it's still open for business. As the girl said to the sailor." He coughed. "Excuse me, Your Excellency. I guess that just slipped out."

Joseph Kalatosi countered: "As the sailor said to the girl, eh?" and grinned with unmistakable zest. After that, progress was much more swift.

"In Pharamaul," said Calhoun, reacting briskly to the altered climate, "we were doing business through Alexanian's. But they seem to be going sour on us. Our man in Johannesburg—that's where we operate from—seems to have run into a roadblock. Alexanian himself, in fact. One of the chosen race—and he's stopped choosing us. Don't get me wrong. I've nothing against the Jews except that they seem to own half New York and can make life very difficult for the rest of us. But that's the way it is, and that's why I'm here."

"What was the trouble between you and Mr. Alexanian? He handles a great deal of Government business, as you know."

"He handles *all* of it, as far as I can see. . . . Oh, he was complaining about the product. Maybe he wasn't getting a big enough cut—who knows? Anyway, he said the bulbs burned out too quickly. Said they cost too much. Said he couldn't involve the Government in such disgraceful waste and extravagance. You'd have thought he wanted to slow up business, instead of promoting it! Anyway, between him and your Chief Secretary, who seems to have the say-so—can't remember his name——"

"Mr. David Bracken," said Joseph Kalatosi.

"That's the man!" Calhoun looked across the rim of his glass at his companion, and something he saw made him take a chance, on an entirely new tack. "Mr. Bracken seems to have your country sewn up, good and tight."

"That is not so, by any means."

Calhoun shrugged. "Well, he sure cancelled *us* out, as far as our Government contract was concerned. It looked as though he blew the whistle, and Alexanian stopped the game. Or maybe the other way around."

"Mr. Bracken has not the kind of power you describe."

"He could have fooled me."

"Of course, he is a senior civil servant. But he only holds his post as an interim measure. During the process of transition. After that, who knows?"

Ken Calhoun grinned. "After that, according to my spies, a certain Deputy Chief Secretary will take over. And a damned good job too! Mr. Kalatosi, can we make a deal, along the lines I've suggested?"

"It is not impossible."

"That's what I want to hear!" Now Calhoun seemed to be growing, almost visibly; in his hand, which only held a glass, an invisible order-book manifested itself, swelling page by page until it filled the entire space between them. "I needn't tell you how big this thing can be, volume-wise. I believe you're going to extend your electricity supply northwards, around Gamate and the other villages—right? That's the march of progress—and you can't beat it! We calculate that the average person makes use of five light-bulbs, every day of his life. Every night, rather. So the market's there, that's for sure."

"How long do these bulbs of yours last?"

Ken Calhoun grew suddenly solemn. "Mr. Kalatosi, I'll be honest—I can't give you the exact figures. They vary with the power supply, the climate, the number of times the bulbs are switched on and off, and God knows what else. That's quite apart from the actual time they're burning. Let's say that the Nu-Lite bulb lasts a *reasonable* time. Then of course it has to be replaced, like everything else in the world, from a car to a can of beans. I'll make no secret of it, at Nu-Lite we regard the light-bulb as a consumer item, and we work out all our specifications with that in mind."

"I see," said Joseph Kalatosi.

"That's what makes the world go round," said Calhoun, without further elaboration. "Well, let's see now. . . . Do you have any particular purchasing agent our man in Johannesburg should contact?"

"In this case, he should contact me direct."

"Right! Would you like to know about prices, at this time?"

"No," said Joseph Kalatosi. "We can go into the details when I have some idea of the—of the scope of this transaction." He studied his glass with particular care, at the very same moment that Ken Calhoun began to study his. "What I would like to know, of course, is what *general* financial arrangements you make, when Government contracts of this kind—very valuable Government contracts—are awarded to you."

"That's very simple," said Calhoun promptly. "We set a price, an overall price, for the supply of the initial consignment. Then we set a price for the replacements, as and when they become necessary. Then, since this might be a very big operation, we give a rebate, on each and every consignment."

"A rebate?"

"A cash rebate. You might call it a commission. You might call it a price reduction on bulk supplies. In any case, it's payable either to the department concerned, or to the individual who initiates the contract with us."

"How much?" asked Joseph Kalatosi.

For the first time in some moments, Calhoun looked at him directly. "Twenty-five per cent."

"Payable in cash?"

"Like I said. Payable in cash to you personally. Or it can be placed to your credit in a bank here. It would then be available when you are in New York on United Nations business."

"I would prefer it in Pharamaul."

"Couldn't be easier. Our Johannesburg agent will make a personal call, every time that the Nu-Lite order is renewed."

Joseph Kalatosi rose, and made for the table with the flask and the ice on it. "You would like another drink, I expect. I look forward to meeting your man from Johannesburg. . . . I wonder what exactly he will do when we meet. . . . Just to clinch the bargain, Mr. Calhoun, I would like a little demonstration. Show me what your agent will do, when he comes into my office in Port Victoria. Give me—shall I say?—a *sample* of that meeting. A really reliable sample."

He was smiling, and Ken Calhoun was smiling, and then they were both roaring with laughter, the first genuine laughter of their day, as Kalatosi held out a candid hand, and Calhoun, reaching into his hip pocket, drew out a bulging wallet.

In the bland, agreeable gloom of the downstairs bar at the Ten Eyck, Paul Jordan was killing time until he knew that Frances Hoy would be back at the flat. He could not have been in lower spirits; he had spent the afternoon packing, which was a bore at any time and today had seemed the saddest task in the world. Now there only remained their last evening together—a blissful, awful evening which he longed for, and hated, and feared. Time, as she would say, had at last run out on them.

He was sipping his unwanted gin-and-tonic, and staring into space, when a voice beside him said:

"Mind if I join you?"

It was Lucy Help, dressed to kill in a mink coat which was very like the mink coat he and Frances had seen in Lord & Taylor's window on Fifth Avenue—priced at $3,000. Lucy was still the prettiest girl to be sighted in the neighbourhood, but he did not like her any more than he had, at their first meeting. Perhaps he liked her rather less; he could never help feeling, now, that she was either just going to get into bed with Dinamaula, or had just climbed out of it, and either way the idea had no appeal whatsoever.

But there seemed no escape, at such a moment. He was not very cordial.

"If you like," he answered. "But I've got to leave in a minute."

"O.K., O.K. Let's have a quickie."

He refused to react to the inviting look. "What would you like to drink?"

"A brandy Alexander."

The horrid concoction was brought—who in their senses could want to drink a mixture of brandy and curaçao with a topping of semi-curdled cream?—and Lucy Help sipped it sparingly, almost nibbling at it. "I love this stuff," she told him, "but I've got to watch my figure all the time." Her figure, alluringly displayed from perky breasts to marvellous legs, seemed to come front-and-center even as she said this. "Well," she asked, horribly cheerful, "are you all packed and ready to take off?"

"Pretty well."

"I suppose you're glad to be getting away?"

"No, not really."

She was looking at his withdrawn face, but it did not deter her. "Did you make out with that Chinese girl?"

"No. Of course not."

"I believe you. Thousands wouldn't. . . . Do you know, I may be coming out to Pharamaul?"

"I heard something about it."

She took another sip of her drink. "The trouble is, I can't make up my mind. The price is right, I can tell you that! But I dunno. . . . What's it like out there?"

"Hot. Sunshine all the time. Very dry. Dusty. There's not much to do."

"Do you think I ought to come?"

He stirred uncomfortably. "It's up to you. You do know that the President is married?"

"Yes. But he says she's no good. He says she probably won't be there anyway."

"I didn't know that."

"Oh, he's got it all fixed. . . . The trouble is, he's not much good. Know what I mean?"

"Not exactly."

"Well, I can tell you. It's not true what they say about the blacks. No, sir! It's all bark and no dog. I've seen better whatnots in a cigarstore. And he's all mixed up, anyway. He's got too much on his mind. Did I ever tell you about Tony Lazzarotti?"

"I don't think so."

"You know, the mass murderer. He robbed a bank, about a year ago, and shot about eight people. Well, *two hours* before he did all that, he was doing me! Tucked up in bed with little Lucy! In like Flynn! Would you believe it? He was all keyed up. Like he was working up an appetite. Like he was doing it to the bank instead of me. Only it didn't pop—he couldn't make out. That's what Dinamaula reminds me of. Too much on his mind and not enough on the—well, you know. What was it we used to have in England? A minister without portfolio. Well——"

"Look, I'm afraid I must go," Paul said, and stood up. "I'm late already."

"O.K., O.K. I'm glad somebody's portfolio is in better shape. See you in Pharamaul, eh?"

He left the Ten Eyck in a kind of sick rage, and charged down Fifth Avenue under the weight of a worse misery than he had ever known. It was so *awful!* Dinamaula need only snap his fingers, to have this crude little bitch shipped wherever he wanted her; while he and Frances, babes in their concrete wood, had known no future beyond the next twelve hours.

All they had—and it was now at hand, it was now *here*—was the privilege of saying good-bye.

The residue of their tremendous bill at the Ten Eyck had been paid. The Rolls-Royce had been dismissed, with fat tips all round. An accommodation had been reached, with British help, regarding certain unpaid dues at the United Nations. They had taken the opportunity, once again, to assure the Secretary-General of their highest consideration. Now they sat—President Dinamaula, Joseph Kalatosi, and Paul Jordan—in one of the VIP lounges out at Kennedy Airport, waiting for their boarding call.

The plane was delayed—"for technical reasons," the cooing hostess had informed them—and there was nothing to do but sink back into BOAC's very comfortable armchairs and enjoy the free drinks. They were the only first-class passengers, and had the lounge to themselves.

The girl, who had been listening on the telephone, put the receiver back and stood up. "I'm *so-o-o* sorry," she told them, in truly heartbroken tones. "There will be a further delay of one hour."

"What's the trouble now?" asked Joseph Kalatosi.

"Just technical reasons."

"You mean there's something wrong with the plane?"

"No, no, no! A loading delay, I expect. Or perhaps your beautiful lunch hasn't arrived yet. Would you like another drink while you're waiting, sir?"

"Yes, please," said Kalatosi.

"And one for me, too," said Dinamaula, who had been in a

brooding bad temper about something, ever since they left the hotel. "I do think we might have been warned about this earlier."

The girl said again: "I'm *so-o-o* sorry for the delay, really," and served them their drinks. Then she crossed to Paul, sitting alone on the other side of the room. "What about you, sir?"

Paul, who was absorbed in reading a letter, looked up vaguely. "What?"

"Another drink for you?"

"Oh—no, thank you."

Silence fell once more, and Paul went back to his letter. It had been handed to him, with some ceremony, as soon as they arrived at the airport, and already he knew it by heart—by sore heart.

"My darling," [it ran] "this has been rushed out to you by special courier, pretending to have diplomatic urgency. It is the first time I have ever cheated the UN, and I will make it up to them somehow. But I had to send you my last love, knowing how you must be feeling. I am the saddest girl in all the fifty, if that is any consolation.

"I shall miss you tonight—your darling weight, and your voice saying: 'Now.' I shall miss you every night. But Paul, we will have it all again, and more! And that is all I have time for, except to swear to you my dearest love, and to say—if you could ever doubt it—that I am American till I see you again. Hoy-Hilton now closed for winter of discontent. Frances."

He wanted to cry, but he would have to leave that to her. Instead he crossed to the writing-desk, and sat down to scribble a reply. Just his thanks and his love—it could be posted when their flight was called. Behind him he heard Dinamaula heave a deep sigh, and then growl: "This is really ridiculous, this waste of time." He heard Joseph Kalatosi, as bouncy as ever, answer: "You know what they say—it's quicker by BOAT," and then go off into a series of giggles, probably directed at the girl. Then he heard Dinamaula's voice again, in surly determination:

"The first thing we do when we get back is to buy our own aircraft."

6: CERTAIN ECONOMIC AND OTHER MEASURES HAVE NOW BEEN PUT IN HAND

THE HUGE BUILDING was beginning to take shape. Modelled on the U.N. General Assembly, the circle of its gleaming white walls was already up to roof level, and the roof itself, in green tiling specially imported from Italy, was also starting to sprout here and there. It would have a honeycomb of offices, facilities for press, radio, and television, conference rooms, dining-rooms, five bars, a cinema, and a vast semi-circular hall to seat two thousand people. It was designed to house next year's Pan-African Congress, for which Port Victoria would be the host.

Facing it, a hundred yards away across the newly-planted palm trees of Dinamaula Square, was the half-finished new hotel—two thousand bedrooms, two thousand bathrooms, air-conditioned throughout—which would accommodate the delegates, or the convention visitors later on, or the floods of tourists who would doubtless be flocking to the newest of the faraway places, the Republic of Pharamaul, as soon as they heard of its charms.

Across town, the new sports stadium was also a-growing; it was being built to full Olympic standards, fit to house the Pan-African Games, or the Afro-Asian Games, or even the Olympics themselves, if they could be wrested from the grasp of greedy older countries. Nearby was the extended runway of the airport, which had already felt the weight and heard the thunder of Pharamaul World Airways' own DC8, as well as the smaller Presidential plane, a Beechcraft converted into a "flying office," which was Dinamaula's latest toy.

Even the harbour had a new five-hundred-foot breakwater, and the principal school a new science laboratory, as yet unstaffed. The southern end of Pharamaul, in fact, was being given a tremendous face-lift, geared to a new, mysterious optimism. Only the waterside slums and the Port Victoria Club remained the same; the one as crowded, raucous, and violent as some timeless football match, the other a solid, faded, most comfortable monument to certain aspects of the past.

In fact, David Bracken thought, as he waited in the colonnaded bar for his guests, Alexanian and Keith Crump, the Port Victoria Club was just about the only thing in Pharamaul which could still make him feel even moderately happy. He must be getting *really* old.

They lunched in the high-ceilinged, panelled dining-room, under the mottled portrait of Queen Victoria in the prime of her comfortable widowhood; in spite of club rules, this favourite corner of his had come to be known as the Chief Secretary's table. The food was as traditional as ever; today's lunch centered round a vast complication of curries, just as tomorrow's would pay homage to roast saddle of lamb. The service was smooth, watchful, and highly skilled; perhaps it was a little less deferential than it had been in the past—the new stewards were younger, better paid, and did not take things quite as seriously as their elders.

But, thought David Bracken, as the young man serving the soup actually grinned at him, one did not have to come to Pharamaul to find that out. For the past quarter century, from London to Singapore, Boston to Sydney, it had been the subject of much senior snorting.

The colour of the dining-room, and some of its atmosphere, had certainly changed. More than half the club's members were now Maulas: Maulas who had swiftly come out of their shell, and who talked faster, laughed louder, and argued more readily than the staid breed of whites. There was no harm in that, either.

If they were going to take over, let them do it in their own style, cutting out the pomposities, the clubland snobbery, the old-boy exchanges, the hallowed rituals of hushed voice and portentous small-talk—just so long as the Chief Secretary could get a decent lunch and a half-hour nap in the surroundings he loved.

Their conversation was interrupted for quite a long time by the traditions dispensing of the curries. It took four servants, bearing a relay of eight silver trays, to set before them the basic beef, lamb, chicken, prawn, and egg, and then the heaped mounds of satellite dishes—chapattis, pappadums, mango and lime chutneys, sliced bananas, ground coconut, almonds, dhal, and rice. The food spread across their table like a flooding eastern tide; it even became necessary to remove the bowl of flowers.

"I think Tuesday is my favourite day of the week," David said with a sigh, as he surveyed the riches set out before them. "When I get home, Nicole always swears she can see curry oozing out of my forehead."

"How is the family?" asked Alexanian, who had been holidaying in South Africa for the past month. "It seems an age since I saw them."

"They're all blooming," David answered, "and longing to see you. But I'm afraid the way the children put it is: 'What do you think he'll bring us?'"

"This time it's a new kind of chocolate cake. . . . Is Simon still hanging on?"

"Oh yes. But he's very depressed, as usual. It beats me that we've been able to keep him from trekking home to Shebiya, the way things are going. This country's being turned upside down."

Keith Crump, who had been marshalling his chosen dishes with a policeman's command of detail, nodded. "I was driving all round town this morning, checking the lads on point duty and the patrols. Honestly, the amount of building that's going on! How's it all being paid for?"

"By borrowing," David said shortly.

"But why should so many people want to lend us money? It must run into millions."

"It does. . . . In the last year, apart from what we get from the U.K., we've been given loans by the Russians, the Chinese, the Americans, the French, the Swiss, and the Portuguese. Even the Zambians, who are flat broke themselves, have come across with something."

"But why? As an investment?"

"In a way. A sort of golden handshake between friends. Or would-be friends."

Alexanian, who had been eating with the close attention he always gave to food, looked up.

"I would say that the investment side is not very serious. It's more a matter of buying influence. They must all know by now that a great deal of the money is being wasted. But it's worth writing it off, if they finish up with a lien on our friendship."

"It's being wasted, all right," David said grimly. "Some of

the things we're buying are absolutely grotesque, apart from all these new buildings which are likely to turn out complete white elephants."

Alexanian looked across at him, his thin face watchful. "I am not so much involved in these affairs now, as you know. I am still Alexanian the Jew, and sometimes the palms of my hands itch a little, but when I see such foolishness. . . . Do you remember when you gave me that stern talking-to, that official rebuke——"

"Unofficial." David smiled. "The official one is a real stinker."

"I told you, then, that though I was doing very well with the new Government contracts, it was nothing to the thousands of pounds I *might* be making, if I said Yes to everything. I think I saved you quite a lot of money in those days, by being discouraging, or making difficulties, or saying that such-and-such goods were not available. I believe I did something to control the situation. But that, alas, is not true any more. They are starting to bypass me—and why not, if they are being blocked by a crazy Jew who doesn't want to sell to them? As if I were not having enough trouble down at the docks, anyway!"

"What's the trouble with the docks?"

"They are becoming extremely slow and inefficient," Alexanian answered decisively. "In fact, in some respects they seem to be running down altogether. I really cannot see the point of building a beautiful new breakwater, if there's no one there to man the cranes, and no one who knows how to rig cargo slings, and only one clerk who can check a manifest properly. We had an excellent Port Captain in George Trefusis. Now he's gone, and instead of George Trefusis we have his replacement, Mr. Kintera. Mr. Kintera is stupid. I mean, stupid in the very worst way: a blockhead pretending to know the answers. I do not say that because he is a Maula. He would be stupid if he were a blond rabbi." He sighed. "The troubles of an import-export merchant, chapter six."

"But how did you mean, you're being bypassed?" Crump asked him.

"Because the powers-that-be are turning to other people who are not so finicky. They are placing contracts direct, instead of through my firm. Incidentally, they are buying a great deal of rubbish in the process. It's my belief that before the year's out, we'll see a State Trading Corporation, or something like that, which will handle everything, exports and imports. Then *I* shall be bankrupt, as well as Pharamaul." He looked across at David. "But I suppose you know all about that, as Chief Secretary?"

David helped himself to more of the cinnamon-scented dhal before answering: "As *Joint* Chief Secretary, I know *something* about it. About half what I should, in fact."

"How is that scheme working out?" Crump asked him.

"I wouldn't recommend it, as a job."

There was something in his tone which discouraged further probing. "Well, God knows I've got my own troubles!" said Crump, though he sounded rather cheerful about them. "How would you like a big brute like Mboku breathing down your neck the whole day?"

"I would not like it at all," said Alexanian delicately. "In fact I should keep walking south, rather fast, all the time. But Captain Mboku is efficient, is he not?"

"In a tough way, yes. In a very tough way. . . . I've been hearing rather a lot of complaints—well, more like hints, actually—about police brutality. Arrests being carried out too roughly, interrogations going on too long and too forcefully. . . . It's the very last thing we want to start here! Our reputation has always been so good. As far as the public is concerned, we have by far the best police force in Africa"—he grinned—"and I don't care who knows it. But that could all disappear in a week, if the strong-arm boys took over."

"They won't, as long as you're here," said David.

"You're damn right they won't! As long as I'm here."

He sounded suddenly cagey. Perhaps, thought David, he's feeling the draught worse than any of us.

Alexanian looked from one to the other. "Well, before we all start crying into our curry—our delicious curry—let's take a look at the bright side. We are not exactly puppets on a string, are we? I am Alexanian the Jew, big importer. You are Major Crump the policeman. You are Chief Secretary Bracken, the *beau idéal* of the civil servant. Are we without strength? Surely three influential citizens——"

"But it all goes with what Keith was saying," David interrupted. "How long are we here for? We've all done our best. We'll go on doing our best until the tide runs out. God knows why! But the tide *is* running out. Oh, *hell!*" he exploded, so suddenly and loudly that heads turned in their direction from all over the room. "Let's forget about it. This is Tuesday! Alex, there are four more prawns in that dish in front of you, and since I happen to know that your religion forbids them . . ." He reached out his hand. "Comfort me with prawns," he commanded. "And you can have the last of the curried eggs. And now let's talk about something cheerful. How was South Africa?"

"Ah, that cheerful country. . . . Well, let's see. I began by driving along the Garden Route, eastwards from Cape Town. . . ."

Tom Stillwell of the *Times of Pharamaul* read through the short galley-proof of what he had written that morning. He made an occasional alteration, but only to his punctuation; he had known exactly what he wanted to say, and it had come out as he had intended, direct, pointed, and explicit. It was the toughest leader he had ever written for any newspaper, and he meant every word of it.

"On certain occasions in the past, this journal has felt that it had a duty to sound a note of warning, concerning various aspects of public policy. Sometimes they have been gentle warnings, sometimes loud and clear; sometimes they have been heeded, sometimes not.

"Today it is our intention to warn the nation again, in unmistakable terms, and as bluntly as possible.

"The time has come to call a halt to the extravagance, waste, and corruption which is bringing this country to the edge of ruin.

"The extravagance is plain for all to see; the corruption is not yet in the full public view, yet it is there all the time, eating into the very heart of our national life. It is so freely talked about, and indeed so much taken for granted at certain levels, that it has become a national scandal.

"More than this we cannot say, under the present laws of libel; but the culprits—there is no other word to use—may rest assured that the *Times of Pharamaul* has ample evidence, not only of official waste and incompetence, but of official misconduct as well.

"The tentacles of extravagance and greed now involve some of the very highest in the land. We make a direct appeal to the President to set an example of integrity and thrift; to discipline himself and his administration; and to place the most stringent curbs, both on Government expenditure and official misbehaviour.

"Otherwise, the first will bring Pharamaul into bankruptcy, and the second into utter disgrace."

Too strong? Not a bit of it. . . . Feeling almost triumphant already, he took it along to the composing room himself.

Some three hours later, when Stillwell should have been listening to his favourite music—the hum and clatter of the presses at the far end of the corridor—he became aware that he was hearing nothing of the sort. In fact, he was hearing only silence: a strange and total silence which seemed to have fallen upon the *Times of Pharamaul* offices like a surgical blight. There were no voices, and no action of any sort. There were not even footsteps.

All his staff—two sub-editors, three reporters who could have been out, one secretary, one advertising manager, one quick-footed child, and six men in the composing and printing rooms —might have been eight feet underground, for all the evidence of life now available.

He gave it five more minutes, which made them nearly a quarter of an hour late. Then he called through to his secretary next door:

"Maria!"

She came in—a tall pretty Maula girl, an "experiment" which had worked out extremely well. She had replaced a middle-aged, ladylike character who, like many another such in Port Victoria, could not abide the way things were going, and showed it by sniffing from morning till night at any evidence of "Maularization." Now she had been Maularized herself, and Maria the substitute had become Maria the gem.

Usually Maria smiled, but this afternoon she did not. "Yes, sir?"

"We seem to be running late. Where's Mr. Henshaw?"

Henshaw was his senior sub-editor, who usually gave the order to start the presses.

Maria said, again in the same blank way: "He's along in the printing. I think there's been an argument."

"What argument? What about?"

"I don't know." For some reason she was now sounding almost sullen, as if she did know, and did not like it at all. This was so unusual with Maria, the cheerful Girl Friday, that Tom Stillwell found himself staring at her in honest perplexity. If Maria was sad, then the world was sad indeed. . . . "Shall I get him for you?"

"Yes, please."

Presently Henshaw came in. He was an ancient battered Englishman, grey and forlorn; he was really much too old for his job, and there was nothing so depressing as having an antique sub about the place, but Tom Stillwell had kept him on, an inheritance from the past who would never rise but who seemingly would never fall. It was Stillwell's belief that every newspaper should have at least one man who was an institution, as long as the institution worked—which Henshaw did, though so slowly and painstakingly that he might have been just learning to write.

Henshaw always looked glum, so the expression on his face was no surprise. But his words certainly were.

"We're running late," Stillwell told him. "What's the trouble?"

Henshaw cleared his throat, and even that had a melancholy sound. "They won't start up," he answered.

"Did you get the electrician in?"

"No, I mean the men won't start the run. In fact they won't do anything."

"*Won't start the run?* Why on earth not?"

"It's that leader," said Henshaw.

Tom Stillwell suddenly saw the light. It was a clear light which even explained the sulky Maria as well. . . . "*What bloody sauce!*" he burst out. "You tell them from me to get cracking, or there'll be ructions they won't forget!"

Henshaw shook his gloomy head. "It's no good. I've tried. They won't print the paper, and that's that. They want to send a deputation."

"Oh, rubbish! I'm not seeing any deputations, today or any other day. Send Jackson in to me, and tell him to jump to it."

Henshaw turned, and went on down the corridor, in search of the printing-room boss. He was gone a long time, while Tom

Stillwell waited, fuming. Then a step sounded outside, and he whipped round. But it was only Henshaw again, his face now almost ready for burial.

"Where's Jackson?" Stillwell demanded.

"They won't let him come."

"*What?*" Stillwell's shout nearly split the building. "What the hell *is* this?"

"They say it's got to be a deputation, not just the head man. At least three people, and two of them must be Maulas." His lips suddenly cracked into the tiny ghost of a smile. "They say that's proportional representation."

"Good grief! What's that supposed to mean?"

Henshaw's expression was now back to normal. "Because the shop has four Maulas to two ordinary folk." He had certain old-fashioned modes of speech which it was too late to change. "So it's two to one, isn't it?"

Tom Stillwell looked at his watch. They were half an hour late already, and there was a train to catch, and lorry deliveries to be made before the hated word "overtime" became operational. He was in a corner, and he wasted no time on inventing fancy steps to get himself out.

"All right," he said. "Send three of them in. And for Heaven's sake let's make it quick."

He spent the next few minutes, while he was waiting for the deputation, trying to forecast which particular men would be on it. Jackson must almost certainly be one of them, whichever side he was on, since it was his own department which was causing all the uproar. But of the four Maulas who worked in composing and printing, he could only guess who the malcontents would be.

They had all been there for more than two years, and had done a very good job once they learned the skilful ins-and-outs of their craft; none of them, certainly, had ever been involved in a protest of this sort, or had seemed to be taking an active, vocal line in politics.

Perhaps he should have been turning his crusading eye on things nearer home, things just down the corridor. . . . When he heard the approaching footsteps he sat down at his desk, and only looked up when, out of the corner of his eye, he saw that three figures had entered his office.

One of them was indeed Sandy Jackson, his foreman, a ten-year veteran on the *Times* staff who had come to Pharamaul by way of Glasgow, where he had learned his trade, and South Africa, whither he had emigrated after the war and which, he had once said briefly, "didn't suit." He was a small spare Scotsman, about forty-five, of that homeward-looking kind which, normally as staid and somber as Edinburgh Castle, came to festive life three times a year—on Burns Night, Saint Andrew's Night, and Hogmanay.

On these occasions he assumed the kilt, and with it an accent as thick as burnt porridge, a high-stepping lust for the eightsome reel, and a thirst so prodigious that it was a byword even among his fellow exiles.

Jackson was standing nearest to his desk, looking as if he would rather be back in Glasgow, or even Johannesburg. Ranged on either side of him were the other two delegates. They were both young men, whom Stillwell knew only as good workers, good people at staff parties, and, for all he knew to the contrary, good citizens all round. They were Joshua Malabar from the composing room, and Koffie Sanka (he had not believed the name until he saw it on an electoral roll) from printing.

Each of them was the slim, energetic, alive kind of Maula, whom he always thought of as the future hope of the country: a country which could certainly use such qualities, to counterweigh its lazy, pastoral, and custom-ridden past.

Tom Stillwell wished them all the best of luck; but Goddamn it! he had a newspaper to get out. . . . He said, as gruffly as he could:

"Now, what's all this?"

It was Jackson who answered him. "It's nothing to do with me, Mr. Stillwell. I'm here because it's my department that's been held up. But believe me, I've no mind for this nonsense."

"Well, get back to work, then! And as quick as you can. You've wasted nearly an hour already."

Jackson shook his head. "I can't run the presses by myself, can I? And that's what it would amount to. They won't do a hand's turn to get the paper out."

Tom Stillwell thrust out his chin. "Who won't?" he demanded, and waited in formidable silence for the answer.

The two Maulas looked at each other for a brief moment. Then Joshua Malabar, who sported a little tuft of black beard, and a pair of modishly tight blue jeans, answered him. His tone was soft, almost deferential, but his words were entirely to the point.

"Sir," he said, "we did not like the editorial piece, and we do not wish to print it."

"Well, that's just too bad," said Stillwell, heavily sarcastic. "But it just so happens that we already have an editor here—me—so you don't have to worry your head about what goes into the paper. All you have to do is help run the presses, and I want those presses running just as soon as you can get back to them."

It was a tough line—much tougher than he had ever taken, inside the office—and he hoped that the shock tactics would work, if only as a time-saver. But Joshua Malabar had other ideas, and it became clear, immediately, that they were not just this evening's ideas; they were part of Joshua Malabar himself, and they had been waiting there all the time.

"Sir," he said, with the same soft formality, yet the same decision. "I do worry my head about what is written in the paper. It is my paper." He glanced sideways towards Koffie Sanka. "It is *our* paper. It is the paper of Pharamaul. That is why we cannot agree to print such a piece as you have written. It is insulting to the President, the head of the state, and to the National Party."

Tom Stillwell, in any other circumstances, would have been touched, and indeed honoured, by this evidence of involvement on the part of this staff. By God, there were people in Pharamaul who really *cared* about the *Times*. . . . But he had given a lot of thought to the leading article he had written, and a lot of anxious weighing of the pros and cons. If Joshua Malabar was involved in this, so was he.

"What I wrote was not insulting," he insisted. "And even if it was, that is my responsibility."

"But it is not true."

"That's for me to judge."

Jackson came to life suddenly. "I told you, laddie. Mr. Stillwell's got a job to do, and we've got a job to do. If we get them mixed up, where's it going to end?"

Now it was Koffie Sanka's turn to come to life, and he took it as if he had been waiting for just such a cue. He was a smaller edition of Joshua Malabar, minus the beard and the tight jeans, minus everything except a certain bright determination. But this, and his twin loyalty, came into full projection as he said:

"Mr. Stillwell, we are both your employees. We are both very happy in our work. But we are also members of the National Party, and we cannot agree to print such insults. They are calculated to undermine the state."

Now where, Stillwell thought, where in the name of God did you pick up that particular phrase? . . . He looked from Sanka to Malabar, and back again, and noticed something extraordinary. These men were not made nervous, nor even especially keyed up, by this confrontation; both of them were perfectly composed, in a situation which most other people would have found distinctly harassing. He saw that he would have to argue his case, however briefly; the voice of authority telling them what to do was not going to be enough.

"They are not insults," he answered. "That leader is simply a warning that if things go on as they are in Pharamaul, the whole country will be ruined. If you've got any sense at all, you'll see that I'm right. There isn't a word there that isn't the gospel truth, and you must know that too, unless you go round with your eyes shut and your ears full of wax!"

Koffie Sanka made his second contribution. "The President has given us great things. It is very wrong to attack him like that."

"The President has given you a hell of a lot more than this country can afford, and some of his friends have been lining their pockets in a way this country can't afford, either, and that's the plain truth." Tom Stillwell sat back in his chair, and wagged his forefinger at each of them in turn. "Now you two just listen to me, and then tell the other men what I've said. What you're doing is going on strike, and that's fair enough in some cases—the right to strike is something I was fighting for, before either of you was off your mother's back. You can strike for more money, you can strike because of working conditions, you can strike for free Coca-Cola, if you like the stuff. But you *cannot* strike because of what goes into the paper, and that's flat."

"But we think it is wrong to write such things," said Joshua Malabar, not quite so decisively.

"Then don't buy the paper! That's your privilege too. Boycott it. Tell your friends to boycott it. Try to make us bankrupt. But don't refuse to print it, unless you want to lose your jobs." He saw from their expressions that he was at last getting somewhere, and he shoved it home as hard as he could. "I'm telling you, I mean that! You mind your business, I'll mind mine, and that way we'll get along all right. But if you don't go back to the printing shop *now*, and start those presses running, you're all sacked! The whole lot of you."

"This is intimidation," said Joshua Malabar.

"Call it what you like," Stillwell snapped. "It's an order, anyway. You just get back to work. Otherwise you can leave *now*, and I'll get the damned paper out myself, and I'll sign on new printing staff, first thing in the morning. Got it?"

There was silence, a long silence, and then without a word they turned and walked out of the room. Jackson made as if to speak, and then he followed them out in the same silence. Presently the lights dimmed for a second or so, as they always did, and Tom Stillwell heard the sound of the presses starting up.

He expelled a long breath, as if he had just run a hard race. The relief was very great. Yet at the same time he felt, for a moment, almost ashamed of himself, because there was no doubt that he had scared them into giving up. Was that the proper line for a radical editor to take with his staff? Worse still, would he have spoken to a delegation of Yorkshiremen in the same way? . . . He had been fired up, because this tussle had involved so many important things—even freedom of speech—and because the editorial itself had set in train a surge of indignation, which was still with him when the deputation arrived. But had it made him much too tough in his handling of it?

He decided, after long reflection and several pints of beer, that he couldn't have done anything less. The price of winning might be high, in human terms, but the loss of this skirmish would have been infinitely worse.

It turned out, however, that it was not exactly a win. In fact, it was scarcely a draw. Of the three lorries which made that night's delivery of the *Times of Pharamaul*, two met with curious accidents, which in turn meant that Tom Stillwell's clarion call for action was muted to a semi-private whisper.

Lorry No. 1, with a small load of papers for Gamate, missed the night train. It had a puncture, the driver said, on its way to the station; and he produced all sorts of evidence in support of this, including a tire so neatly pierced that no suicide could have matched it, for either accuracy or dispatch.

While the man was getting help, much of his cargo was pilfered.

Lorry No. 2, bound for the main news agency which handled deliveries over the southern half of Port Victoria, had even worse luck. It was flagged down at a street corner, by men who looked like policemen, or ambulance men, or street-cleaners—the evidence was very sketchy. The driver was then pulled out of his cab, without too much violence, and the lorry driven down to the harbour.

There, the jettisoned bundles of papers floated slowly out with the tide. They travelled quite a long way, observers said, before they became waterlogged, and sank from sight.

Only Lorry No. 3, the one with the smallest load, got through to its destination, the minor news agency which covered Port Victoria's northern suburbs. It met with no trouble, though there was a strange, mixed-up story, never properly established, of a man lying in the road, seeming to be hurt, and a slowing down, and other men suddenly appearing out of the shadows, shaking their fists, and the scared driver—a white man, down on his luck and glad of any employment—accelerating away from the scene which could have been innocent, might well have been nothing of the sort.

The net result was really all that mattered. The *Times of Pharamaul* issue for that particular day became a real collector's item, for two good reasons. Because of its leading article, it had considerable scandal value; and because of those various mishaps, its circulation had been cut by more than two-thirds.

These strange events were never explained: not by the police, who were baffled; nor by the drivers themselves, whose evidence was a maze of ill-starred recollection; nor by anyone else. The subject, though freely debated, was certainly never resolved within the *Times* office, where the innocent faces outnumbered the surprised by a very wide margin.

Tom Stillwell presently came to think of the whole episode as a short story he had once dreamed up: a story he would one day write, if only, like a million other newspapermen, he could find the time.

So far, he had only scribbled down a title: The Day of the Last Laugh.

President Dinamaula had driven to the opening of the new session of the Legislature in splendid state. The Government had recently presented him with a second official Cadillac—a vast, pure white, open model in which he sat on a miniature throne, flanked by a bodyguard of men in the new Government House uniform of scarlet and gold, clinging to the platform which ran all round the car.

This magnificent chariot, with a police escort, outriders on motorcycles, and a long train of ministerial cars behind it, wound slowly through the streets of Port Victoria, decorated for the occasion with flags, banners, and giant placards with the presidential portrait on them. The police sirens wailed, the people ran alongside, cheering and waving their arms. The procession took more than an hour on its journey, and attracted huge crowds wherever it went. The day was, naturally, a public holiday.

Nicole Bracken, sitting with Molly Crump in one corner of the House of Assembly gallery which accommodated the diplomatic corps, the official wives, and any distinguished strangers who might wander that way, looked about her with a melancholy feeling which she could scarcely disguise. It was not because she and Molly were grass widows for the day, their husbands being involved in the ceremonial of this occasion; it was because she thought, as David did, that the Legislature had become one of the most depressing places on earth.

It had settled down into a 15–9 majority steamroller, and the poor official opposition might have been beating the air with ostrich feathers, for all the good they could do. Everything that Dinamaula wanted went through like—well, David had once said, like a dose of salts, and though, since the children had been present when he said it, she had felt obliged to object, she was not objecting to its truth.

Of course, there was a new Prime Minister who had succeeded the President; but he was only Chief Murumba of Gamate—a silly old stooge who did nothing but nod to the sound of his master's voice.

In debate, the Port Victoria vote totalled a solid, vociferous eight; and the Gamate contingent, though split by the President's marriage troubles, still added another seven. Fifteen votes out of twenty-four, used like a fist after perfunctory discussion, meant that the National Party could follow its own sweet will, in anything it chose.

It had turned the Legislature into something like a joke: a

terribly expensive club limited to twenty-four members, of whom fifteen sat back and enjoyed their privilege, while the other nine, camping out in the forlorn cold, made futile gestures of revolt.

The coming election was not going to change any of this. In fact, Dina might well find a way of making it worse.

At that thought, Nicole sighed so deeply that it could be heard above the buzz of voices round them, and Molly Crump, a perceptive friend, turned to look at her, and then whispered:

"Cheer up!"

"My feet are killing me," said Nicole.

They had known each other for nearly fifteen years, and during that time certain shortcuts in understanding had been established.

"Is that quite true?" Molly Crump asked.

Nicole smiled. "No, of course not. I meant, all this is so *awful!*"

"What's awful about it?"

"Everybody knows it's so phoney!"

Now it was Molly Crump's turn to sigh. "I suppose so. . . . But here we sit, just pretending, like everyone else. . . . It's funny to think how involved we all are, still."

"If you want to know, I feel less involved every day," Nicole said.

"But darling, you can't be! Though I know it's stupid, if you start to think about it. *My* husband once had to arrest Dinamaula, and yours had to cart him off to England. Now yours is marching in a procession in his honour, and mine is worrying all the time about security, just to make sure that he has a smooth ride. Honestly, if you think of all the work they've both done——"

"Just so that the old swine can show off." Nicole's voice was savage. "It's not fair. David's having an awful time these days, and he says it's the same for Keith."

"Yes. Keith's not very happy, I must say." Then there was an excited stir below them, and the sound of opening doors and traffic moving. All round them, people were craning their necks, trying to see over the edge of the balcony. "That must be them now."

There was the slapping sound of rifle butts coming to the Present Arms, and the screech of a bugle corps playing the first bars of the national anthem. Below them, a thunderous voice, like that of some demented toastmaster, called out:

"Rise for his Excellency the President of Pharamaul!"

"About time, too," Nicole Bracken muttered, and came very slowly to her feet.

President Dinamaula's speaking style had altered. The deep voice and the measured delivery were still there; but to these had been added a kind of smouldering authority, a massive assurance of power, as if there could be no possible argument against anything he said. Today, as he delivered the formal, stylized address which opened the new session, the occasion was made even more Mosaic by the fact that the President read his speech while remaining seated, with his aide-de-camp, Paul Jordan, standing on one side of him and the Speaker of the House on the other.

The elegant gilded mace, so kindly presented to the Legislature of Pharamaul by the parent body at Westminster, lay on its tapestried table in front of him. Whether it should have been there or not, it seemed all the time to be *his* mace, *his* badge of office, just as this was *his* House of Assembly. Everything combined, in fact, to make this nothing less than a Speech from the Throne.

The President read it without any expression save a total, armoured confidence.

"During the coming session of this house, my Government will introduce the following legislation:

"A bill to establish control of the movement of currency both in and out of my country;

"A bill to set up a national bank which shall be the sole authorized financial agent of my Government;

"A bill to nationalize the timber industry;

"A bill to nationalize the Port Victoria Power Company;

"A bill to improve the salaries and working conditions of certain sections of the civil service and the police force;

"A bill to establish permanent headquarters for the Russian Technical Mission;

"A bill to extend the borrowing powers of my Government, as may be necessary from time to time, without reference to the Legislature;

"A bill to establish a permanent commission which will supervise the press and radio industries of my country;

"A bill to define more exactly the powers of the Judiciary;

"A bill to authorize the issue of arms to the police force in certain circumstances;

"A bill to authorize the setting up of a Nuclear Power Authority;

"And such other bills as my Government may from time to time find it necessary to introduce.

"I pray to God that He will prosper your deliberations."

The heavy voice ceased, to be followed by utter silence. One could almost hear a last, unspoken sentence: "Never mind about God."

That was all for that day, save for the triumphant procession back to the Palace, and a reception there which started as a formal affair and later became, some said, the biggest, rowdiest booze-up which those hallowed halls had ever seen. It was on the next day, when the debate on the speech was opened, that the storm broke.

It was brought to its violent breaking-point by Chief Banka of Shebiya, the leader of that battered opposition which, during the past year, had tried to rally its ranks and present some kind of a front against the steady, trampling march of the National Party. It was his task to speak first in the formal debate, and when he rose, the House was expecting him to do his valiant best. But few were prepared for the bitter attack which he launched, not only against the Government but against the person of the President himself.

At times sour, at times angry, often insulting, sometimes venomous, it was the fiercest indictment of the President and his policies which the Legislature had ever listened to.

"Yesterday," old Chief Banka began, after the customary phrases needed to initiate the debate, "many of us in this House, and many distinguished visitors too, were kept waiting while a procession in honour of our great President made its journey through the streets of Port Victoria. It was the kind of procession which would do honour to an ancient king—except that there were no royal elephants to drop dung on the slaves who followed the royal circus. It was the kind of procession which this country cannot afford. It cost much money—and we have no money. It showed us the President's beautiful new car—another kind of elephant, painted white, costing seven thousand pounds—and it showed us also what is wrong with our country. And after the procession we were forced to listen to a speech which showed us what is wrong with our President."

Chief Banka, in the face of angry murmurs, hitched at his robe. "I will speak, if you please, without the little dogs barking. I will speak for the people who have to pay for such shameful waste and such a show of false pride."

Already there were more protests, and the Speaker, an earnest, somewhat nervous young man who spent most of his time with his nose buried in Erskine May's *Proceedings and Usage of Parliament*, trying to sort out seven hundred years of precedent, came to life. He called out: "Order!" in hesitant reproof, and a muttering silence fell again.

The old man took up his tale, on the same scornful note of indictment.

"That great white elephant on which the President sat is part of the sickness of our country. That sickness, which will destroy us unless we turn away from it, is brought on by two evils. One is extravagance, the other is the hunger for power. On extravagance, I have spoken many words in this House. You have all read, or heard of what was printed in the newspaper about the money thrown away on toys. And it is no secret that the Chief Secretary, Mr. Bracken, has warned us many times that——"

A loud, arrogant voice interrupted him. "We do not need white men to tell us our business! Those slave days are over!"

Silence fell as Chief Banka, whose eyesight had grown feeble, peered across at the Government benches, trying to identify the interrupter. But he might have been any one of a dozen men, who now stared back at him—some mocking his known infirmity, some angry with his words, some ready to join in the taunting because, in the Maula proverb, when a lion roared, every hyena felt himself a lion.

Chief Banka could not find his enemy, and he took the best way out, by striking back at the voice itself.

"It would be a brave man who said that we no longer need help and advice from our white friends, and perhaps it was a brave man who spoke. Let me say to that brave man: any child who is not blind or deaf knows that this country is spending more money than it can afford, is throwing money to the winds. We had hoped that the President, in telling us what we must do during the new term of the House, would give us wise guidance. But what did we hear? Did we hear the counsel of a wise man? Did we hear talk of saving money, of hard work, of giving food to those who need it, and prison to those who steal it? No! We were told that the newspaper which dared to speak out will be controlled, that the police will be given guns, that there will be a national bank full of foreign money——"

The angry murmurs, which had been growing on the Government side of the House with each new sentence, now reached a point when Chief Banka could no longer be heard. He looked towards the Speaker, and the Speaker, after a moment of painful indecision, rose to his feet. In the Mother of Parliaments at Westminster, this would have been the signal for instant silence; in Pharamaul, the rules had already grown spongy, like soft coral, and it was some moments before he could make himself heard.

When he spoke, it was only to say: "Let the House come to order."

Chief Banka whipped round at him. "Let those mangy dogs come to order!" he shouted. His voice was cracked with bitter feeling. "It is not I who——"

The rest was lost in a bellow of anger from the Government side. The uproar crested into a great wave, and when it ebbed again, there were now three people standing up: the Speaker, Chief Banka, and the Prime Minister, old Chief Murumba of Gamate.

It was he who, in the first breath of silence, managed to make himself heard. In the quavering voice which some wag had christened "the lion's bleat," he said:

"A point of order, Mr. Speaker. We have been called mangy dogs. This is not an expression of Parliament. I ask for a ruling."

Perhaps because their voices were now exhausted, or perhaps because the two men—one on each side of the House—who were imitating the barking of dogs sounded so foolish as they yapped in counterpoint, another silence fell. The Speaker, who was in the mood to wish himself an ordinary member again, or at least a herd-boy on his father's farm, or even dead, fell back upon honoured precedent.

"I did not hear the words 'mangy dogs,'" he declared, striving to seem both deaf and authoritative at the same time. "If I had heard them, I would have ruled them un-Parliamentary." He was doing his brave best, in a situation for which the only cure —forbearance, and a general shriving of souls—was not obtainable. He said again: "Let the House come to order. The leader of the Opposition has the floor. The debate should continue."

Chief Banka was not the man to miss his chance. "Thank you, Mr. Speaker, for giving me the freedom and protection which certain men on the other side would steal away, not only from me, but from the whole country." The sound of several police car sirens, at first faint and then growing louder, lent point to his words, and held some would-be interrupters at bay. "Let us return to that great speech by the President—that great speech which should have called this country to order, just as the Speaker called this house to order, because of a few men who wish to put themselves above the laws."

The concert of the police sirens, coming through the open windows of the chamber, was now so loud, so close at hand, that Chief Banka was forced to raise his voice. But matching this, there was now an interruption from the same anonymous enemy.

"They are coming for you, old man!" the strident voice proclaimed, and the gibe was followed by a harsh explosion of laughter, and then by sudden, embarrassed silence again. There were few men present who, after a moment's thought, could see this as anything but a shameful joke. Once more, Chief Banka took his advantage.

"I hear nothing," he said, "but dangerous echoes of the President's own words. After newspaper control, and control of money and industries, and control of judges, and guns for the police, and a national bank with a special back door for the Government, and foreign loans we can never repay in a thousand years, what were we promised? I will tell you. More spending! Stupid schemes! A Nuclear Power Authority! Will that breed more cattle, catch more fish, grow more mealies? And land to be given to the Russians!" He raised his hands in a gesture of despairing protest. "I tell you, the foreigners are eating up our country! For the sake of loans which disappear into the sand, we have pledged our country, our life-blood! But not all of it. There are other pigs in this trough. The foreigners can only eat as much as is left for them by greedy men who——"

There was a sudden noise outside, a stamping of feet, and the door behind the Speaker's chair was flung open, as if by violent hands. The sound of the dying sirens was wafted through as a new figure appeared, and moved into the light, and stood before them all. It was the President himself.

Because this was the man who was foremost in everyone's mind, there was a gasp of surprise, and then a stormy reaction. All the National Party members rose to their feet, cheering wildly, thumping on the lids of the desks which, in this assembly, were set before each seat; and from the public gallery, which was always a popular vantage point for those idlers with little to do and all day to spend, a clamour of greeting rose, a roaring of the salutation "*Ahsula!* Rain!" which was the President's traditional acclaim.

The Opposition sat glum, letting the tempest break over their heads, while Chief Banka, halted in mid-sentence, remained on his feet, foolishly robbed of power, looking round him as if his weak eyes could not take in more than a fraction of the scene.

At the beginning, he had only known that the newcomer was Dinamaula because the member sitting next to him had pulled at his sleeve and whispered in his ear. But the rapture of the applause would have told him anyway—it could have been offered to no other man.

President Dinamaula stood for a brief moment beside the Speaker's curtained, Gothic chair, swaying slightly, staring round him as if he were counting heads. Then he strode forward, giving the barest nod to the Speaker on the way, and sat down heavily on the Government front bench. There, he turned his broad back on Chief Banka, and began to speak in a low voice to Prime Minister Murumba. Even those least familiar with him could divine that he was more than a little drunk.

Slowly the noise of welcome faded away, until all were silent, and sitting down again. A brave member on the Opposition side —it was Pele Matale, of Shebiya—called out: "The accused enters the court!" but the remark was not answered by anyone. It did not need to be. It was allowed to die, futile and bloodless. It was clear that the President, whether accused or not, was not entering the court at all. He was taking possession of it.

Chief Banka was in two minds whether to continue, or whether to counter this gross intrusion by breaking off his side of the debate. After some indecision, reflected in his worried, weary face, he made up his mind to stand and fight. He addressed the Speaker:

"Sir, I draw your attention to the presence of the President on the Government front bench."

There was silence. The Speaker, looking unhappily from President Dinamaula to Chief Banka, and back again, was also showing a divided mind, plain to everyone in the House; while the President, ignoring his surroundings, continued his rumbling monologue in the Prime Minister's ear. The *impasse* seemed complete.

Chief Banka tried again, his voice now querulous. "Sir, the President has no right to be here! He has no place in this House except at times of ceremony. Did we not have our fill of that yesterday?" And as the Speaker still remained silent, Banka attacked directly: "I demand that you order him to leave the House!"

Silence fell again. Dinamaula turned slowly in his seat, to direct a sardonic glance first at the Speaker and then at Chief Banka. But it was clear that he was going to stay where he was, whatever the ruling, and the idea of his removal by the Sergeant-at-Arms, using bodily force, was unthinkable. In the circumstances, the Speaker took the only course available to him. He backed away from it.

Without getting to his feet—indeed, trying to make himself as small as possible—he said:

"I cannot give a ruling on a constitutional question without consulting the authorities. This will take time. I think the debate should continue."

There were catcalls of delight from the Government side, and an answering growl from the Opposition—yet only a small growl, since they knew that they were, as usual, powerless to make their will felt. Once again, Chief Banka had to decide whether to accept the situation, or withdraw from the field; and once again, he took up the burden.

"Very well, Mr. Speaker," he said. "We, as the only party in this House which upholds the laws, accept your advice without question. Let the President remain. Let him bring in a sleeping mat, and stay here until you have given your ruling. But the House should take note of what we think of this visit. It is scandalous! It is an attempt to intimidate the House—or those members of the House who are not the President's little running dogs!"

He was angry, and flustered, and nervous, all at the same time, and his voice as he shouted "running dogs" was a cracked falsetto, which made those opposite to him break into laughter. The strong words, on the instant, became a joke, the outburst of a foolish old man who should have been sitting by the fireside with his grandchildren. Already the Opposition was losing ground.

Chief Banka rallied himself. Ignoring everyone else in the House, talking directly to the President's contemptuous back, he said:

"I was speaking of extravagance, and throwing money to the winds, and disgraceful behaviour, and now I can speak to the right man, and not waste my time. . . . In the South, you live in splendour, like princes. In the North, we do not enjoy any of these favours. We have no national bank to fill our hands with money. We are refused help, because we oppose the Government. We all know that the railway to the North is broken down. Why is that? Because no money is spent on it. What do we want with a Nuclear Power Authority? Give us back our railway, so that at least we are part of Pharamaul again, so that we are not cut off!"

The same anonymous, taunting voice, which he had heard twice before, crudely interrupted:

"Go home to the North, old man! We will run a special train for you! We promise it!"

Even President Dinamaula, a figure of withdrawn arrogance, was seen to join in the laughter at this sally. Chief Banka waited for it to die away.

"You laugh," he said, on a note of sadness, "because you have made yourselves strong, and put yourselves above the law. On this side we do not laugh, because we are without power. Sometimes we feel that we have no friends in Pharamaul, and that while the Government spends and spends, and the country is brought to ruin, we can do nothing. It may be that we need help from outside. It may be that we should send a deputation to England——"

There was a roar of disapproval from the other side, and a voice called out: "That is treason!"

"It is not treason!" Chief Banka snapped back. "It is because we need help, and we cannot find it in our own country." He leant forward, staring hard at the President's back. "It is because a king rules us, and we will not bow down and worship him, and so he turns his back on us. He turns his back on everything he cannot answer. The newspaper spoke of corruption in high places—we all know that. The newspaper said that it had evidence. Has the evidence been called for? No! Has the newspaper been challenged, to prove what it said? No! Has it been prosecuted for telling lies? No! There is only silence—"

Prime Minister Murumba called out, in the thin reedy voice which was like the voice they were listening to: "One does not answer liars!"

"You do not answer honest men, either!" Chief Banka, near the end of his patience and his strength, began to attack wildly. "There is corruption and deceit in the very highest place of all. I will not speak of the President's shamed wife, who has been driven back to her people. All the world knows of it, and is disgusted. All the world knows that another white motor-car—a smaller car, but also made in America—is attached to the Palace. All the world knows that the President——"

President Dinamaula suddenly whipped round, his face contorted with fury, his voice a lion's roar of anger. He brought his fist crashing down on the desk in front of him.

"*That is enough!*" he shouted. "Stop speaking! Sit down! Or I will have you arrested for talking filth about the head of your country!"

Poor Chief Banka, utterly unprepared, could not even meet the violent onslaught. His shocked face, turning towards the enemy voice, seemed to crumple away to nothing. He tried to speak, through trembling lips which could not form a single word. After a bitter moment, under attack from the echoes of the President's threat, and from scores of hard-staring eyes, he sat down without another sound.

The Government side of the House, and the packed gallery, expelled its breath and its tension in a great "Ah-h-h!" of triumph. Chief Banka dropped his head in his hands, as if trying to shut out the cruel world. Prime Minister Murumba rose to speak, but before he could begin he was roughly pulled down by the President.

Thus it was Dinamaula who now rose, to hammering applause from his massed supporters. He was going to address the House, and it was useless to try to stop him. The handful of opposition members could only sit in unhappy confusion, as silence fell and the menacing figure took charge of the debate.

"I do not care for strict rules," the President began, and his slurred speech was now obvious. "I do not care for protocol, when I have been attacked. I have come down to the House because I was sent a message that a foolish old man was insulting the head of the State. I came to hear if this was true. Since it is true, I will speak."

Chief Banka had now raised his head, and was looking towards his opponent, a few feet from him across the gangway. But there was little strength or energy in his look; he seemed to have become defenseless, in the face of the harsh, malevolent voice which now bore down on him.

"I have been attacked," Dinamaula went on, "and I will answer. I have been attacked by that man"—he thrust forward a menacing finger—"on personal grounds, and I will answer on personal grounds. Let that man"—again the jabbing finger pierced the air between them—"think twice before he speaks of family matters. One of his own family has brought disgrace on our whole country, by his disgusting behaviour at the United Nations. You all know who I mean—this old man's eldest son—I will not name him because I do not wish to foul my mouth. This eldest son was *expelled!*—expelled from America!—because he was found with drugs. What sort of a family matter is that? A public criminal for the eldest son of a chief! And I need not tell you that there are God knows how many more such sons at home, and one of them in this very house, ready to disgrace the father!"

Dinamaula had paused, both for the laughter and also to let his words have their full effect, and this proved unwise. Chief Banka, who had been sitting slack-bodied under the lash of the attack, suddenly rose to his feet. The knifing insults had been too much. Standing a few feet from the President, speaking in a thin piping voice which was still strong enough to carry its spiteful contempt, he said:

"At least I have sons."

The meaning of his words, unmistakable, thought to be unspeakable, hit everyone in the House like a wave of shock. There was a moment of complete stillness, as in the eye of a hurricane, and then the whole assembly exploded. Roaring voices bellowed their anger; fists were shaken, order papers flung in the air; men came to their feet like tigers, and stood screaming at the faces opposite to them.

From the public gallery, also in pandemonium, an object came hurtling down, and landed with a crash at Chief Banka's feet. It was a jagged stone, and its impact was so violent that it scattered chips from the marble floor. Chief Banka rose bravely, and signalled to his followers. They began to leave the chamber.

On their short and perilous journey, they were hooted, and jostled, and shoved, while almost imprisoned in a vile uproar which held the seeds of murder. Matthew Banka, the Chief's second son, trying to protect his father from the pounding fists which beat upon his back, was thrust to the ground, and trampled on, and then rolled down the front steps like a sack of rubbish. The other Opposition members, their hands wrapped round their flinching heads, presently reached safety, under a hail of curses and insults which followed them far down the broad avenue outside.

In ones and twos, the pursuing Government members returned, grinning in triumph, shouting their pleasure, kicking their way school-boy-fashion through the mess of papers which littered the floor. Quiet gradually settled on the chamber, like the aftermath of a lynching when the strung-up heels had ceased to dance upon the poisoned air, and the Speaker came out of the shadows of his throne.

Then President Dinamaula, who had taken no part in the uproar but had watched it with angry, greedy eyes, stood up once more. He was now in complete command, and every aspect of his bearing showed it.

He only spoke two sentences, both of them full of somber threat:

"If the Opposition does not wish to sit in the Legislature, that can be arranged. . . . Of what use are men who choose to be disloyal to their own country?"

The smaller white motor-car, also made in America, was Lucy Help's Ford Thunderbird. Everyone had recognized the reference to it, because everyone knew about Lucy. They also knew about her car, a birthday present from Dinamaula, a flashing prestige symbol which could be seen swaggering through Port Victoria's main streets, any day of the week.

It was only "smaller" because the new white Cadillac, the Presidential chariot, was so enormous; otherwise, her darling T-bird, as Lucy inevitably called it, was big and powerful and swift, and its scarlet upholstery and silvered wire wheels made a dramatic focus for a gaping public.

In it would be sitting Lucy Help—stretch pants, revealing top, flamboyant head-scarf and all: the most exciting figure anyone in Pharamaul had ever seen, even counting the late Bobo Urle. But Lucy Help was more than exciting, more than alluringly dressed and displayed. In her, everyone recognized, with a delicious sense of shock, the very flesh of public sin.

Her arrival at the Palace had caused great scandal. There had been plenty of rumours among the well-informed that the President had formed some kind of attachment while he was in New York; but this had occasioned no more than a little head-shaking, a little shrugging of the shoulders. Was it not natural for a man, even a very great man like the President of Pharamaul, to stray a trifle when he found himself in a strange city, away from his wife, bored and lonely?

Who could blame him? Such things happened, and were soon forgotten. They were also soon forgiven.

It was all the more sensational, therefore, when, a short week after the President's return, Lucy Help—beautiful, extravagantly sexual, young, *white*—flew in to Port Victoria, and was straight away installed in the Palace, in a room (some said) next to the President's very own. Ow!

Fresh rumours flew; the questions multiplied and mounted. What was going on? Was this new woman to stay there for ever? What was Mayika, the President's lawful wife, going to do now? Had the two women met? What had they said to each other? Was it true that Mayika had ordered Lucy Help out of the Palace, and the bold white girl had laughed in her face?

Was it true that they had fought a battle, and torn each other's clothes and hair? Was it true that the new girl made one of the servants taste all her food, before she would swallow a single bite of it? Was it true that the President had found new powers, new appetites, and roared like a bull whenever he lay with this girl? Was it true that she was with child already?

208

Within the Palace itself, the atmosphere was in fact poisonous, but it was not dramatic in any sense except the scandalous. The President, ignoring a dubious situation, seemed well content. Lucy Help was entirely confident, and could not have cared less, either about the scandal or the atmosphere. Only poor Mayika, waddling about her apartments on painful feet (for she had now grown enormous), really heard the whispers and the giggling, really caught the sidelong glances, really smelled the infected air.

She had stood it for a week—a week of misery and secret mocking and disgraced solitude. Then, a greater scandal still, she had been fetched by one of her uncles, and had been taken home to Gamate, leaving Lucy Help, the vile intruder, in undisputed possession of the President, the Palace, and the whole shameful situation.

Lucy Help was not the sort of young woman to find the situation shameful; but she did, after a space, find it dull. She had nothing to do, all day, except cruise around in her gleaming T-bird, spend lavishly in the two or three shops which were worth a visit, or sun herself, not free from peeping eyes, on the balcony outside her bedroom; she had nothing to do, all night, except to lie in an enormous canopied bed, her legs ready to open and close at the will of a lord and master who might or might not be in the mood for such frolics, and then to drift off into sleep.

Before very long, she was bored even with the most expensive toys; bored with the sun; and especially bored with the yawning emptiness of casual employment. She had no one to turn to, not a living soul to amuse her, except Paul Jordan. Like Sybil Bartholomew before her, she began to haunt him.

Paul had known very well that this would happen; a heightened awareness, the product of his loving hours with Frances Hoy, together with the sad fact of their separation, seemed to have given him warning, long before Lucy Help turned up in his office and claimed him as an old friend who might, when the coast was clear, become a credit customer. In the circumstances which now ruled the Palace, the eerie state in which they all lived, it was a situation which held the prospect of great danger. But there was little he could do about that.

He was still a Palace prisoner, and Lucy Help a newly privileged jailer. However carefully he walked, he was vulnerable. It was

Sybil Bartholomew all over again—Sybil Bartholomew with a 110-pound body, the sole purpose of which was raw temptation.

Lucy had not improved, he found: she was still concentrated on Topic A, and never likely to leave it. Sitting on one corner of his desk, swinging those dazzling legs, presenting a sensational vista of nearly-bare bosom within a few inches of his face, she had hardly exchanged greetings before she was off on the trail.

"Did you hear about that awful Brazilian at UN?" she asked, her innocent eyes alight with the pleasure of lewd gossip. "One of the security guards caught him with a girl, bare-assed! They were doing it in a stationery cupboard! Honestly! Stretched out on one of the shelves, like it was a bunk or something. I hope there was plenty of blotting-paper underneath. But can you beat it?" She leant forward, her eyes aglow, her look lascivious. "What's the funniest place you ever did it in?"

Paul pushed back his chair a little way, striving to disengage. "Nowhere special, I don't think."

"Oh, come on! You're a sailor!"

"Sailors aren't different from anyone else."

"But they get red-hot for it, don't they? They save it all up."

"That depends."

His secretary came in from her room next door, jumped at the sight of them, said: "Excuse *me!*" and bolted from sight again. It seemed essential to lower the temperature, and Paul said the first thing that came into his mind.

"Where did you hear the story about the Brazilian?"

"From Dinamaula." She pulled a face. "Whoever else would tell me a thing like that? No one here ever says any thing to me except good morning. They're all too damned scared. That's what I like about you. You don't mind what ideas people get."

"That's not strictly true."

His tone was so cautious that even Lucy Help noticed it. "Oh, come on!" she said again. "Don't be like that! You're the only person in this whole damned graveyard I can talk to. So you be nice to me, and I'll be nice to you, and we'll see what cooks." She paused, and then suddenly asked: "What's a numbered account?"

Paul found it a great relief to be talking about banking, for whatever reason, though it was not one of his special subjects. "It's a thing people have in Switzerland. It's a bank account, only it has a number on it instead of a name. At least, I think that's it. But why?"

"Dinamaula has a numbered account."

"How do you know?"

"He told me. And I'll bet it has a million dollars in it!"

"But why did he tell you?"

She pulled the same face, disdainful, slightly contemptuous. "People tell you all sorts of things in bed. Sometimes it's the only thing they do, after a bit. Know what I mean? You be nice to me," she said again. "I can give you all sorts of information. Like, he wants to marry me."

"But he's married already."

"So what? He says she's no good. He says she's just a cooking-pot wife. Isn't that an awful thing to say? Anyway, he wants to marry me, but he wants me to have a baby first. Or start a baby, and then he'll make it legal." For the third time she made the unpleasant face. "I think I've heard that record before, even in Sutton Coldfield. But what do you think, honestly?"

"I don't think it's a very good idea."

She stood up suddenly, and came round behind his chair, and leant against him. He could feel her firm breasts pressing against his shoulders, as if she wanted them to stake a claim upon his body. "I'd rather it was you," she said, "and nuts to the baby! Know what I mean?"

He sat up straight, breaking the warm contact. It was a movement which could only seem insulting, but at that moment he could have done nothing else. He waited, for extra emphasis: then he turned to face her.

"That's impossible!" he said angrily. "Good God, you're meant to be *organized*—I mean, he asked you to come out here, and you came."

"That's just what I never do," she interrupted, instantly jumping on the one word which was an authentic part of her language. "I'm telling you, that guy's no good! Half the time, he's just a flop." She made an explicit, totally indecent gesture with a curved, drooping forefinger. "It's like a rubber coat-hook. That's why he's getting so tough with people who stand in his way. He has to prove something. If he can't do it to me, then he'll do it to all the people who annoy him. So your lot had better watch out."

It was, from Lucy Help, an unexpectedly subtle line, and Paul sat in silent surprise for a few moments. Perhaps, he thought, if a girl slept with enough men she picked up more than an itch to continue the exercise; perhaps she took in a trickle of common sense, along with all the rest. . . . On an impulse, he stood up, and put himself face to face with her.

"What do you mean, we'd better watch out?"

"Like I said, because he's got to get his own way somehow. He can't stand arguments and fights. He has to win. So your friend Stillwell isn't going to last too long, for one. Nor that old Crump, either. I tell you, Dinamaula's got more things jumping up and down in his head! Pity they're not jumping somewhere else. . . . You be nice to me," she said again. "You're going to need all the friends you can find. And I can keep you right up to date."

Though it was dangerous ground, he decided there was something he must ask.

"What I don't understand is, what's gone wrong between you and him. I mean . . ." he gestured, and in the limited space between them it was almost as if he were reaching out to cup those forward-looking breasts in his hands. "Well, look at you!"

Her expression grew intensely inviting. "You do like me, don't you?"

"I think you're very attractive. That's what makes it all the harder to understand."

"Oh, he was wild for it, to begin with. Particularly after that poor old cow of a wife. He still is, on a good night. And he did promise about the baby, and marrying me, and everything. But now it's mostly just routine. And he's drunk, a lot of the time. Ever been in bed with a drunk? It's like lining up cold spaghetti." She advanced a step, until she was brushing against his body. Under the thin material of her dress, the little mounds began to grow taut, as if to signal him unmistakably. "I bet it wouldn't be like that with you. I bet you're big, I bet you're good."

He retreated once again, but slowly; at that moment she had the most intense physical allure, whatever one thought about her as a person, and he was conscious of a customary, compelling reaction.

"It's impossible," he said again. He added the weakest objection of all. "It's too dangerous."

"I'll make it worthwhile," she said. "You give me a chance, I'll get them in such an uproar. . . . Ever been milked dry?" she asked, her baby face and offered body seeming to combine into a single open cleft, avid for male invasion. "I can do that for you. Anytime. And look—no hands!"

There were many such meetings, many such chance or contrived encounters which started with gossip, swiftly turned erotic, and finished on a note of prime sexuality. Paul did not want her in any other way, but it would have taken a strong man to resist this particular invitation from this particular expert. He was not strong, at the moment; he was lonely, he was fed up, he had been bereaved of his love for three months, and it seemed that it might last for ever.

Presently they arrived at a tacit agreement that it was only a matter of time, and then of opportunity.

It would not be easy, in any case. Lucy Help was closely watched, for a variety of reasons; she was an object of scandal, she occupied a key position, and she was worth watching anyway. Servants became spies, the curious turned detective. Thus she could not, for instance, be seen anywhere near Paul's bedroom, which was in a different wing of the Palace. Her own room was equally out of bounds. The moment must be snatched when it occurred, like a full volley at tennis, like instant coffee.

They snatched it first in a summerhouse near the kitchen-garden, on a faded, musty garden settee, with sunlight filtering down through tall shrubs, and stupid, half-asleep gardeners bending their backs a few yards away. It was terribly dangerous, they both knew, but the impulse was too strong, the lust too goatish altogether.

They were down, they were up, all in five minutes. Lucy, naked under a brief cotton dress which separated as deftly as a sheet of stamps, was extraordinarily skilful. For him, it was like being sheathed inside a blender which, slowly turning, gathered wild momentum till the whole bowl frothed.

"Leave it to me," she had whispered, when he had first moved. "I'll take you all the way, I'll take you right through the gears." He had never known a sexual union so loveless, so untender, and yet so copious in its effect on his body.

They managed to make love, in this brush-fire, inflammatory way, three more times. Once, with a drunken party going on downstairs, they slid into the Palace library where no guest was likely to penetrate, for a frenzied bout which stirred the very dust of scholarship, among the bound volumes of the *Times' Law Reports* and the stacks of unread *Hansards*.

Once it was standing up, braced against a filing cabinet in his own office. Once it was in the total darkness of a coat cupboard: an action brought to an agonizing pause by some footsteps which shuffled down the corridor, and stopped outside, and then went slowly onwards, giving them both the most heart-thumping scare of all their lives.

It was all exciting, all totally sensual, and effective to the point of explosion, as if she were using a suction pump compounded of honey and pulsing warmth. It continued up to the moment when he received a letter from Frances Hoy.

Frances sent him her dearest love, and the news that she might be able to fly out for a holiday, as they had once planned. After that, he could want no one else, and even his body turned neutral and useless when another chance occurred. Deeply ashamed of himself, for a whole range of reasons, he had to tell Lucy Help that the fling was over.

Nowadays, David Bracken hesitated even to ring up for a timed appointment with the President. Gone were the days when he could say: "I'll be along during the morning," or "Let's meet at the club," or perhaps drive round to Government House for an hour's gossip with the Prime Minister. Now Government House was the Palace, and the Prime Minister the President of Pharamaul; now friendship had turned into cool acquaintance, and a man was becoming a myth.

It was difficult to say how and why it had happened; there was only the plain fact that it had, and that his own disapproval of all that was going on had become notorious, and himself, in the process, an outsider.

But on this bright morning, David Bracken was so furious with what had taken place in his office that he overcame all misgivings, and told Dinamaula that he must see him urgently, in private, within half an hour.

The voice at the other end of the telephone gave nothing away, not even curiosity. It was noncommittal, cold, and entirely unruffled. Dinamaula simply asked him to come at the stated time, which chanced to be convenient. It was almost as if he had been expecting the call—which, in the circumstances, was a disquieting thought.

David found the President, according to his morning custom, sitting under the tall elm tree which turned a hundred square yards of sun-baked lawn into a cool refuge, sipping at his frosted lager beer, enjoying the sweets of office. His face was growing fleshier now, David noted, and today there were signs in it of what, in a less august person, would have been plainly called a hangover. Dinamaula did not smile, nor rise, nor offer to shake hands when David, running the gauntlet of a burning sun, reached him in the shade. He simply motioned towards a vacant chair beside him, and waited in silence.

David would have preferred a meeting indoors, free from inquisitive eyes, and he could have done without the beer-sipping also. But his anger had made him impatient, and he launched straight into his story.

It had to do with Joseph Kalatosi, he told the President, and it could be briefly summed up. He had unmistakable evidence that Kalatosi, Joint Chief Secretary with himself, was taking bribes, in cash, from people who came to see him on Government business.

Dinamaula made no comment on this, nor was there any change of expression in his face. He continued to wait, almost as if he were not particularly interested, but felt that he had a duty to listen.

"I had a visit this morning from a man called Serulo," David told him, embarking on the meat of his story. "He owns a delivery firm, and he's trying to expand it. To do that, he wants to take over the old Government garages on Plantation Street. So far, so good—we certainly don't use them any more." None of the small irony in his voice seemed to reach Dinamaula. "Apparently he has been dealing with Kalatosi on some other matter, but Kalatosi wasn't in when Serulo called, so he asked to see me. We talked a bit about the proposition, and I said that if he left me all the papers I'd have a look at them and steer them into the right department. He agreed, and then he said: 'I would like this matter to go through as quickly as possible.' Then"—David's anger was beginning to reach a climax—"he took out his wallet, peeled off a hundred pounds in ten-pound notes, and put them down on my desk!"

He paused for the comment which he felt must certainly come now, but once again there was complete silence. Dinamaula was staring straight ahead of him, seeming to pay more attention to the gardeners patiently hand-picking crabgrass from the scorched lawn than to anything else. Then, in a gesture which he somehow contrived to make disdainful, he glanced down at his wristwatch, and said:

"Well—go on."

In spite of his outraged feelings, David Bracken found himself hesitating before he continued. The lack of response was beginning to make him uneasy; Dinamaula seemed to be keeping deliberately aloof, discouraging in advance any hopes of a sympathetic hearing. David had come here hot-foot with his appalling story. Was it to run away into the dry sand of indifference? He could only plough on, until he found out.

"Naturally, I asked him what the hell he was playing at," David continued, striving for a little less emotion in his voice. "All he did was look surprised. Then I told him to pick up the money and get out. He did pick it up. Then he said: 'Does that mean that you will not sell me the garage?' and I told him that this was out of the question now. He said: 'But it is only what we all have to do with Mr. Kalatosi. It is only dash.'"

Silence fell. The word "dash," the universal African term for a bribe or a tip, the word which David Bracken found so ugly and others so acceptable, hung in the air between them, a small poisonous cloud which could not be dispersed. Dinamaula was still looking straight ahead of him, his full face expressionless. It became clear that he was not going to say anything, even at this crucial moment; he was not going to be any help at all. All that David Bracken could do, once again, was to press on with his account, and hope that he could somehow make it tell.

"I saw Kalatosi as soon as he came in. I told him that it was disgraceful, that such a thing had never happened before in the Secretariat. He didn't try to deny it. All he said was—just like Serulo: 'But it is only dash. What is all the fuss about?' I said that there was not going to be any dash system in my office, and that it must stop immediately. He said"—and here David's tone recalled his violent feelings at the time—"'This is not your office. It is my office as well. We are equals, and you have no right to discipline me.' So I pushed him out, and telephoned you. . . .

That's the story, and I think it's absolutely disgusting, the whole thing!"

David, when he finished, had been expecting to be met by another of those daunting silences, and this time he was prepared to endure it, even if it lasted half an hour. But to his surprise, President Dinamaula answered him immediately, as soon as he was done. Yet the answering voice could not have been more discouraging. "Very well. You have told me your story. What is it you want me to do?"

David Bracken was ready for that, at least—he had never been more ready in his life. "Relieve Kalatosi of his appointment, of course. And have Serulo prosecuted for attempted bribery."

Dinamaula said, carelessly: "Would you like a drink?"

"What? No—not at the moment."

Dinamaula raised a languid hand, and signalled to the servant who was watching them through one of the front windows. Within seconds the man appeared with a loaded silver tray, and on it an ice-filled wine cooler with two more bottles of lager, and fresh glasses. He set this down, bowed low to them both, and withdrew.

"Change your mind?" Dinamaula asked.

"No, thank you."

Dinamaula poured out his beer carefully, with a look of concentration which, like the glance at his wristwatch, was somehow contemptuous. Then he drank, and put down his glass, and said:

"What you suggest is quite out of the question."

His tone was matter-of-fact to the point of insult, and David reacted sharply.

"On the contrary," he said, "it is the very minimum that this thing calls for. Kalatosi himself ought to be——"

The President raised his hand, cutting him off without ceremony. "It seems to me that you are making far too much of this."

"I don't agree at all! The whole thing is disgraceful. It amounts to stealing. Kalatosi is selling his influence. In effect, he is taking a rake-off on Government contracts. What could be more serious than that?"

Dinamaula allowed himself a slight smile. "I can think of a very long list of more serious things, and so can you. It would not include this. This, as Joseph himself said, is just a matter of dash. My people think nothing of it—it is almost traditional."

"It has never been traditional," David protested sharply. "Certainly not in the Government Secretariat. We did *not* take bribes."

"Perhaps you took other things instead."

"I don't understand."

"You took the whole of Pharamaul. Now it has come back to my people."

"That's a ridiculous way of putting it! In any case, we are not talking about past history. We are talking about now, and a Joint Chief Secretary who apparently allows himself to be bribed."

"Joseph sees nothing wrong in dash," said Dinamaula, and added, for good measure: "Neither do I."

David felt his anger returning. "I suppose this is the Consolidated Fund in action," he said bitterly.

Dinamaula gave him a very cold stare. "What do you know about the Consolidated Fund?"

David was not to be diverted any more. "I know it was the basis of the extravagance of our UN delegation. What else it does, or what other money goes into it, I don't know. It sounds highly irregular. And I do know that that kind of extravagance is getting completely out of hand. All the new buildings, all the overspending. . . . The whole thing is being done on borrowed money."

"Exactly. We have many friends. Our credit is excellent."

"But the money has to be paid back!"

"That is a matter between my Government and its creditors. If they are satisfied, then so are we. In any case, it is a political matter, and does not concern you."

"It is a moral matter, like the dash system."

"I do not think that moral matters concern you, either."

"But good God, Chief——"

Dinamaula froze instantly, and then turned upon David a look of such stony hatred that he was brought up short. He could only suffer the deep embarrassment of the moment as Dinamaula said venomously:

"*Do not call me Chief!*"

He was right, of course; it had been a *gaffe* of the very first order, bringing back with a single loaded word all the strife and discomfort of the past. The way the President had jumped on it was the measure of its continuing power to wound.

"I beg your pardon, Mr. President," David said, very formally. "It was a slip of the tongue."

"I think it was more than that." After the flash of anger came the ice. "It shows an attitude. It is the same attitude as you have towards Joseph Kalatosi, in spite of all the changes. He was quite right to tell you that you should not discipline him. He is not a subordinate. You are Joint Secretaries. You *are* equals."

"Not in this matter."

"In all matters."

"Not in the taking of bribes." It was a dangerous remark to make, but David, recovering from his stupid setback, was not less worked up than he had been before. "I'm sorry, Mr. President, but I have to speak plainly. I don't believe in the dash system, and you know very well that I don't believe in all this wasteful public spending. Yet apparently I have to put up with both. . . . I don't think things can go on like this. I'm signing papers, approving things, that I simply don't believe in. The Chief Secretary's job has never been like that. And it doesn't make any difference if he's only *Joint* Chief Secretary."

"Of course," said Dinamaula, "if you and Joseph cannot work together. . . ."

"We can work together perfectly well. But I draw the line, absolutely, at corruption."

"There was no corruption. Serulo was simply sealing a bargain, in the Maula way. I understand that the Government garage deal had already been agreed on."

David looked up, startled and taken aback. In its context, "I understand" could only mean one thing—that Kalatosi had been in touch with the President already, that he must have telephoned the Palace the moment that David was out of the way. . . . Earlier, David might have found the fact especially infuriating; now it was only sad, like so many other things. It was another pointer towards a bleak and baffling future. But he could not in honesty ignore it.

"Does that mean that Kalatosi has been in touch with you already?"

If the President was conscious that he had made a slip, it did not show in his voice. "He did telephone me, yes. He has that privilege, just as you have."

"But I don't think he had any right to use it, on this occasion."

"On the contrary, it is his duty to warn me of any—crisis which may be on the way. Also, he is entitled to give me his side of the story."

The bars seemed to be firmly in place, the barricade complete. David Bracken realized that he had been wasting his breath all the time; Kalatosi had got his stroke in first, and Dinamaula, forewarned, must have made up his mind on the matter before he himself had even crossed the lawn towards the President's chair. Hence the deadlock, hence the impassive denial of justice. . . . No longer sparked by anger, he felt utterly weary of it all: sick of being made a fool of, sick of this ebb tide which sucked and swirled and bore away everything he believed in, everything he had hoped for, for nearly all his working life.

The phrase "losing his grip" sprang into mind, with a dull, jolting impact.

He made his decision there and then. He was doing no good this morning, nor on many another morning; he was not even holding his own. He must get away from all this for a space, put some sort of a margin between himself and the hated current of events. He must think much more about it, at a distance, and alone.

He stood up, his tall figure as erect as the elm tree. "There seems nothing more to be said, Mr. President. You know what my views are. . . . I propose to go on tour now. I haven't been up north for nearly a year."

There was a certain wariness in Dinamaula's face, and in his voice too. "When are you planning to go?"

"As soon as possible. Perhaps tomorrow."

Dinamaula seemed to be making up his mind about something. "Very well. I think that is a good idea. Perhaps you need a break."

"I do."

A long black car came whirling up the drive, and slowed to a halt under the portico. Two well-recognized figures got out, and began to walk across the lawn, just as David had done on his own futile journey. But this couple was likely to have more luck. . . .

They were Joseph Kalatosi, in a cream tussore suit, and Captain Mboku, resplendent in his khaki uniform with the new scarlet-braided trousers. They both seemed in excellent spirits.

David Bracken said good-bye swiftly, and began to walk towards his own car. He passed about ten yards from the new arrivals, who were looking in his direction. But he gave them no greeting, and smiled no smile. He strode past them resolutely, staring straight ahead.

Behind him he heard a smothered giggle, and then a guttural chuckle from the policeman. Let them laugh, the crooks, the bastards. . . . He found that he could not endure this place, nor these people, for a moment longer.

Even the dust-laden yellow road, pitted and furrowed like a farm track, yet stretching in a dead straight line to the farthest horizon, was a refreshment. It had been ploughed after the spring rains, in accordance with Pharamaul's rough-and-ready repair system, which levelled out the central hump for a few weeks, until the carved-down ruts grew deep again; but it was still a hazard for any normal car, and the four-wheel-drive Land-Rover was the only reliable transport for the journey northward.

David Bracken, bouncing about in the driver's seat, sometimes wincing as his head came up hard against the canvas hood, was feeling on top of the world. Besides his suitcase, he carried a spade, some strips of sacking, a twelve-bore shotgun, a forty-gallon drum of water and another of petrol, three spare wheels, and a two-way radio set. He was ready for anything—even for two hundred miles of the Port Victoria—Gamate scenic highway.

He had made an early start, soon after dawn; as he left the last suburbs behind, and headed northwards into the free air, the dew was still glistening on the slopes on either side of him, and the shadows on the hills ahead just beginning to turn from purple to pale grey. There was scarcely any traffic, except for the village buses and vegetable wagons making their first rackety journey into Port Victoria; occasionally a great creaking oxcart, drawn by a span of eight or ten gaunt beasts, would block the center of the road, and then pull very gradually to one side as the sound of the horn blasted the stillness.

Each time, the teamster would raise his beehive hat as David edged his way past, and the boy prodding the lead oxen would do the same; each time, David would return the salutes. The country courtesies were still the best.

He made slow progress, and was content to do so; the smell of burnt grass, the jolting road surface, the very dust on his sweaty hands, all were the things he had come looking for, the things he had felt he must have. The road, which sometimes crisscrossed the deserted, rusting railway line, was leading him on a heartening journey, past small clusters of mud *rondavels*, each with its private wisp of smoke from the cooking fire which took the place of the front doorstep: past yellow mealie-patches with men and women bending their backs to the hoeing: past a dam half full of cloudy brown water, surrounded by a motionless frieze of staring Afrikander cattle: past bush and scrub and the bare bones of eroded hillsides, dried-up watercourses, herds of goats raising their own dust cloud from the pastures they were stripping: past lonely solitudes, past Africa itself.

He ate his sandwiches and drank his beer, cooled in the forty-gallon drum, a few yards from the roadside, sitting under a half-dead thorn-tree, staring round him in that contented wonderment which this corner of the earth could still bring him, even after a dozen years, a hundred such journeys.

Within his view, there was scarcely anything which would have registered dramatically on film; just space, just red-brown soil and misty blue hills, just another dam shimmering under the fierce midday sun, with another herd standing stock-still at its muddy edge; just a solitary grave covered by a mound of stones, under which the robber hyenas had tunnelled till they found what they sought; just *katlagter* birds fluttering their long tail-streamers, and a few huge anthills, eight or ten feet high, a century in the building, and—far away to the westward—the outline of a bare conical hill which copied the anthill shape exactly.

He loved all that he saw. This was the real Pharamaul, the one in possession of his heart, a whole world away from the one he was coming to despise; it was the real Africa also, hot and heavy-burdened and very old. It was a tiny part of that mysterious continent which, years before, a man who had travelled its length and breadth for all his wandering life had promised that he, David Bracken, would never be able to desert.

All this beloved scene, all that he saw as he sat under his

thorn-tree, was, for David, marvellously summed up in a favorite African book title: *This Was the Old Chief's Country*.

Presently he became aware that all he saw as he sat under his thorn-tree had been enlarged by moving figures.

It was a big straggling herd of goats—too big, David thought, with an eye to the arid, ruined grassland all round him—being driven down the road by two small boys. They were both barefoot, and naked except for their tattered loin-cloths; above the sagging belts, their little swollen bellies thrust out like balloons—balloons which could be the token of near-starvation just as well as of a bulging mealie-porridge breakfast.

They were having the traditional trouble with the goats, which wanted to browse rather than to move on. To guard and chivvy their mutinous flock, the boys used all the weapons of persuasion: prodding with pointed sticks, shouting, running to head off the strays, kicking stragglers, smacking bare rumps, pinching the snow-white kids which, avid for milk, butted and tugged at the nearest udder, and brought its owner to a standstill. But when the two herd-boys came level with the Land-Rover, it was their turn to browse.

First they looked round for the owner, and found him, a watchful white man sitting under a thorn-tree, like a chief or a policeman. They gave David Bracken the openhanded Maula salute, and when he returned it they stared at him for a long time, whispering to each other, while their flock, seizing this respite from the eternal goading and shouting, turned aside as if they had been drilled for the maneuver, and began to crop the meager grass at the edge of the road.

The small boys were now peering into the dusty Land-Rover as if it were newly landed from outer space. They were chattering faster than ever. David had finished his sandwiches, and was drinking the last of his beer; thus he had no more favours to confer, at a moment when he was in love with all the world, even with goats and herd-boys.

On an impulse, he clapped his hands together, with the sharp sound of authority, and when the boys looked towards him, he called out:

"*Urriah los!* Jump in!"

The boys, though astonished, did not need a second invitation. The straying goats were forgotten as they began to clamber all

223

over the Land-Rover. They bounced up and down on the seats, they took turns to wrestle with the steering wheel, they bashed their way through the gears, and switched the lights on and off, and fiddled with the windscreen wiper. Then they chanced on the horn, and blew a great blast which blared out across the country-side—and at that, all the goats took fright and, in frantic disarray, began to race away up the hillside, spreading out like a river which had burst its banks.

The herd-boys, recalled to duty by frenzied bleating, jumped down and ran whooping after them. But they did not forget to turn, and give David Bracken a grinning farewell salute.

He drove all that day, as the sun declined and the slow mileage unreeled behind him. The two hundred miles of tortured highway took him fifteen hours, and the day ended with a gorgeous, purple, dusty sunset which set the westward hills on fire. Dusk came quickly, like a sober curtain; and then, far ahead of him, the twinkling of fifty thousand fires outside the fifty thousand huts of Gamate signalled his journey's end.

Though stiff, and achingly tired, journey's end was a homecoming; and nothing had made him happier, in many a long month.

His headquarters in Gamate was Andrew Macmillan's old house, which used to be the "Residency" and was now the "Government Bungalow." There he spent an uneasy first night, after a brief welcome from the police Lieutenant in charge of the local division, who called to see if everything was in order, and a meal of tinned soup, muscular Pharamaul chicken, and prunes and custard—a real caretaker's dinner, cooked and served by the old woman who looked after the bungalow, and its guests, with slow, plodding ill-humour.

David went to bed early, after his tiring drive; but there was a ghost here, as far as he was concerned, and he was a long time getting to sleep. The ghost was Andrew Macmillan, who had spent years of his life in this house, and had walked out of the front door, so long a time ago, to end it with two shots from a revolver cradled against his stomach.

This was the ghost, not only of a friend, but of another man who had given his working life to Pharamaul, and had been defeated in the process. With Andrew, defeat had come from chaos, from murderous violence, from a country in flames. How it would be with himself was still to be discovered. But he could almost hear Andrew's poor spirit talking to him, warning him of what might lie in the future, advising him out of his long experience. Yet long experience had not saved Andrew; it had destroyed him, with a special brutality.

David tossed and turned through much of that long hot night, with the single sheet on top of him slowly becoming drenched with sweat. The old house creaked and groaned continually; he knew that the noise was only settling timbers, aided here and there by the armies of soldier-ants which had been feeding on the place for years. Yet sometimes the creakings sounded so sharp, so regular, that they might have been footsteps; and there could only have been one visitor, by night, to this house of despair.

The dawn light brought profound relief, turning childish fear into solid confidence; and after that, everything went much better.

As Chief Secretary on tour, his first morning in Gamate was a matter of tradition. First, the school choir came to sing to him; thirty boys and girls standing on the lawn in front of the *stoep*, marshalled and conducted by their music master, a gifted young man with a look of such total concentration that he might have been moving in a trance.

The children, immaculately dressed in their spotless school uniforms of white and green—no Maula mother would have dreamed of sending her child to school except in clothes freshly washed each day, with the child inside scoured and scrubbed and polished down to its last square inch—the children piped away like angels, while David sat in an ancient wicker rocking-chair on the *stoep* and drank it in, note by note. There was music in the Maula soul—even in such small souls as these—and it emerged in its purest, most eye-pricking form at these times of ceremony.

They sang some unlikely songs—"Frère Jacques," and a hummed version of "Sheep May Safely Graze," and "D'Ye Ken John Peel." Peel's "View Halloo!" might not have awakened the dead, but its soft travelling through the morning heat haze in the heart of Pharamaul could never have had a stranger echo. They sang, in the Maula tongue, a sad ballad of some little children lost in a forest, who were found—alas, too late—covered by a blanket of leaves, and mourned by the birds which had tried to save them.

At the beginning and end of each song, the children all bowed low, and the conductor, turning, did the same. The concert finished with a song which had become, over the years, a kind of children's national anthem—"*Ekartha i Maula*," the land of Maula is My Home. They sang it sweetly and happily, with childish belief and pride enough to shame the whole adult world.

When it was finished, and they all bowed, and the music master bent low, and then saluted with open hand, it was as much as David Bracken could do to keep his eyes and his voice free from tears.

Pharamaul was still his country, and these people his very own. How could he bear to be robbed of either?

At ten o'clock came the time for a formal visit from the Town Council of Gamate, whom some still called the Council of Headmen. There were four of them, led by Caspar Muru, grandson of old Chief Murumba the Prime Minister. The others were Voice Tula, the official interpreter, who had risen in the world and was inclined to spurn his past years in the role of tribal mouthpiece; and two older men, brothers who had been headmen for thirty years or more—Joshua and Stephen Agura.

They were uncles of poor Mayika, the President's rejected bride; and thus, David Bracken knew, intimately involved in the tribal split which this disgrace had set in train.

But on this occasion, all was ceremony and good manners; not until near the end of the hour-long meeting did the deep bitterness which had crept into Gamate's affairs come near the surface. The first exchanges were very formal, almost stylized; his visitors would have been as astonished, if David had not inquired about the rain, the crops, and the cattle, as he himself would have been if they had refused to comment, in detail, on all these matters.

Gamate had been fortunate in its rains, he learned from the slow dance of question and answer. The cattle had fared no better and no worse than in former seasons, though the prices offered by the abattoir down in distant Port Victoria were not, alas, such as to encourage a man who took pride in his farming and his stock. The maize crop had been poor, barely enough to support the needs of Gamate itself. Even if they had been able to send some part of it for sale in the capital, the prices, once again. . . .

David received the impression, quite early on, that the good citizens of Gamate were feeling themselves neglected; and it was old Joshua Agura, a firm and self-reliant man, who presently confirmed this.

"It is not our custom to plead for justice," Joshua Agura said, "or to make strong complaints. If the prices are so, and cannot be improved, then we must endure them as best we can, for the sake of peace. But it is sometimes our thought that Government is a long way from us, and forgets that we also are part of Pharamaul."

"I am sure that this is not so," David said pacifically. "Government has many troubles, many matters to think of. But there is no feeling that the south is of more importance than the north."

Voice Tula, looking sceptical, asked: "Then may we expect that the railway line will soon be restored?"

"I hope so," David answered. "It is a question of materials."

"There were plenty of such materials in the old days," said Voice Tula, and added, in an ingratiating manner which was not at all attractive: "I should say, in the days of the Chief Secretary."

"I have not heard that the Chief Secretary is dead," said David, who did not want any of them to pursue this line of thought.

Stephen Agura filled in an awkward pause. "Without the railway," he said, "we cannot help feeling that we are cut off. How can we send our cattle to market, even for the poor prices we receive? They must be driven all the way, through dry country, and when they reach Port Victoria they are lean, often worthless. Sometimes they are sold for the price of their skins!"

"It is dry country—" his brother joined in, "because the dams are not well kept. At the least, we need another big dam in this town, and many more on the way south. If Government can build great buildings, why cannot they build dams for people who need them?"

"It is a matter of money," David answered.

Voice Tula said: "There is plenty of money for motor-cars and rich feasts."

David Bracken could not help noticing that Caspar Muru, who earlier had been foremost in his replies, had now fallen silent, and the reason was not far to seek. It was his own grandfather who headed, if only nominally, this "Government" of whom all the others were complaining; and this must mean, in turn, that Caspar

Muru was already involved, on a personal basis, in tribal discontent.

His position might have become very difficult, his authority sapped. But there was not much comfort that David Bracken, another sorrowful unbeliever, could offer to either side. He could only say, in his role of peacemaker: "Though the money is limited, I think we may look forward to a fair division in the future," and hope that some change of heart might make it come true.

At this point the old woman shuffled out on to the *stoep* with a fresh brew of coffee, and silence fell while she served them. David wished that their discussion might end at this point, with Caspar Muru still silent, and the others content to let the talk tail away into generalities again. But no sooner had the old woman left them than Stephen Agura brought up a fresh subject, one which clearly touched him very closely. He said, without preamble:

"Then there is the question of the President's marriage."

David sighed. Once again, he had hoped that this particular subject—highly charged with emotion, involving most sensitive areas of pride and prestige—would not be brought forward. It was scarcely Government business, scarcely his own concern, and he was about to say that he would prefer not to discuss it. But then he changed his mind.

It might not be Government business, but it was obviously Gamate business, Maula tribal business; why should he, a twelve-year veteran of both, choose to ignore it? Was that the way to show his loving concern for these men, and their happiness, and their self-respect? He put a candid question instead.

"Will you tell me what has been the effect of Mayika's returning home?"

Stephen Agura looked at his brother Joshua, and then at Voice Tula, and lastly at Caspar Muru. He saw that they all wished to leave the matter to him, and he spoke accordingly, without hesitation.

"It has been very heavy. Mayika is our niece, as you know. There are many other relatives and family friends concerned in this disgrace. It has caused many quarrels. Some, like us, are sad, some are shocked, some are angry. I cannot deny that certain other men"—his tone grew grim—"have been made happy by it. They would have preferred the President to marry someone else, and when Mayika was insulted and sent home to her village, they said: 'We told you so. We told you the marriage was not suitable. Why should we pretend surprise?' So they were made glad by misfortune. . . . The scandal has divided us bitterly. But *no one* is made happy when they hear of the woman who has taken Mayika's place. That is a deep disgrace, felt by all in Gamate!"

His voice ceased, on a note of trembling indignation. His brother Joshua was nodding agreement. Voice Tula was looking almost theatrically righteous. Caspar Muru had lowered his head, as if to disengage himself from this talk of wounds and disgrace and insult. Was it here, David wondered, that the tribal division started?

"It is a matter which touches us all," Voice Tula declared primly. "How can a man be the leader of a country, and behave like a dog in the streets?" He glanced sideways at Caspar Muru. "How can other men serve such a man, and give him support, when he behaves so wickedly? How can——"

Caspar Muru interrupted suddenly. "Say what you mean! Do not talk in circles!"

Voice Tula, the moralist, was not to be put down. "I am talking in circles because the matter is disgusting. But if you wish, I will say what I mean, and plainly. We do not understand how your grandfather, Chief Murumba, can continue as Prime Minister, and give his support to this behaviour."

Caspar Muru, a capable young man who had already served in many key posts, including Agricultural Officer for the whole area, was ready to take up the challenge. He was still looking unhappy, and it became clear that he did not like his brief; but the family honour—this must have happened many times—was at stake, and at such a moment no one could stand apart.

"Chief Murumba does not support such behaviour," he said sharply. "I know that he has spoken privately to the President. But the President's personal life is not the concern of the Prime Minister. It is not the concern of anyone else, either."

"But why does he only speak privately?" asked Joshua Agura. "Why does he not speak openly? Why does he not denounce this disgrace to one of his own tribe? Why does he not say: 'I will not be the servant of such a man'? Why does he not resign his office?"

"One does not resign office for such a reason."

"It should be a matter of honour to do so," said Voice Tula.

Caspar Muru snapped back: "My grandfather does not need such men as you to teach him honour!" He was very angry, and he might have said harsher things, and made their division more bitter still. But then he surprised them all by another sentence, uttered in quite a different tone. He said: "In any case, I understand that all is not well between my grandfather and the President. I understand that there is disagreement." He was speaking very carefully. "It is not my grandfather's choosing. He is an old man. He has served Pharamaul well. He has earned honourable treatment. But he is no longer at ease. He is hard pressed."

After a long silence, David Bracken asked: "How do you know this?"

"From the *katlagter*," Caspar Muru answered, using an old Maula phrase. "But I do not wish to say more on such a subject." He stood up, and the others were forced to follow him. Then he gave David a formal salute of farewell. "You find us divided, Mr. Chief Secretary. It is a quarrel not to be healed by a few words, nor many words. But it is, as always, an honour to greet you in Gamate. We know your good will towards us, proved over long years. We know where we have a friend."

He saluted again, and then they all took their leave, using the same sort of words—partly ceremony, partly a moving show of affection. David walked with them to the garden gate, where an ancient Humber saloon—the official car, outclassed many times over by the glittering Cadillacs of Port Victoria—was waiting to take them downtown.

It was old Stephen Agura, about to step in, who asked: "May we know when we will greet you again?"

"That I cannot tell," David answered. "But it will be soon, I hope."

"You are staying long in Gamate?"

"Unfortunately no. I go to Shebiya tomorrow morning. Then I must return to my duties."

Joshua Agura, smiling, said: "But I think I can guess where your feet will lead you now."

"You are right," David answered—and it gave him warm pleasure to be able to close their meeting on such a note. "I go, as usual, to pay my respects to Maula the Great."

. . .

The royal graveyard of the Maulas was still home to the same exclusive tenantry as on David Bracken's first day in Gamate. There were only three headstones on the derelict plot of land, set within the fold of a gaunt hill; the place, as always, was overgrown with weeds, and the wind in the cypress trees which stood guard over it sang a mournful, sighing song. To the north, the purple U-Maula hills could be seen, like the saucer-rim of the world; the rest was ringed by a solid rampart of weathered rock. Goats ran bleating away at David's approach; in a moment he had stepped over the sagging wire fence, and stood on holy, neglected ground.

The largest grave, stained and blotched with lichen, bore the Gothic inscription: *Maula the Great*. Near it was a second smaller one, the resting place of *Simaula, Son of Maula*. A little farther on was the smallest of all, topped by the marble figure of a child-angel and more generously inscribed: *Akamaula, Son of Maula. Aged one year. Whom the Gods love, die young.* All that was left of the royal past lay in dust at David's feet, an anointed clan shrunken and withered away to three.

In some ways, thought David, as he stooped to pick off a strip of moss defacing *Maula the Great*, the graveyard told the story of Pharamaul. There had been many other sons and cousins in this dynasty; as possible claimants to the throne, they had all been killed off, or exiled, or slowly poisoned, or driven north to join the U-Maula outcasts. The violent past had seen more royal blood spilt than honour done to it.

Tribal custom had always ruled that no one who died "strangely" might rest in the royal graveyard. Thus these three graves were all that marked the past, instead of a possible twenty: and this sad domain waited only for one more man— Dinamaula himself, who was likely to be the last of his line.

David Bracken always made this minor pilgrimage, when he was on tour. It was partly habit, partly an exercise in public relations, and partly an act of piety. Maula the Great might be dismissed as a bloody-minded old tyrant, but he had made much of his country, with the help first of invading troops, then of administrators; he had come to terms with British rule, and re-fashioned his own character, and his fellow-countrymen's, in the process. He had acquitted himself well; and here, under the sad cypress trees, he lay at peace, with the grown son who had succeeded him, and the small child who had escaped the terrors and hazards of being one of the royal pretenders.

David had meant what he said when he used the phrase "paying his respects." And once again, standing among the silent gravestones, looking out across miles of bush and scrub and brown earth towards the distant hills, he was reminded, with special emotion, of those other words which had come back to him on the road north: *This Was the Old Chief's Country.*

He stroked the warm marble which was the head of the child-angel, and then walked down the winding pathway to the track where he had left the Land-Rover, and climbed into it. Under the canvas hood the heat was baking, and he let the ventilation fan run for a few minutes. Then he drove slowly back to Gamate, and the Government Bungalow, and one of those lunches which seemed rooted in the colonial nursery past—beef rissoles, boiled cabbage, and rice pudding with strawberry jam.

His after-lunch goal was the Gamate Mission House, and his journey there took him through the teeming heart of the town. First he skirted the *aboura*, the great tribal meeting-ground, on which, years ago, he had been forced to stand alone, girded with white uniform, domed helmet, sword, medals, and all, and declare to an empty space that the meeting to be addressed by His Excellency the Governor had been cancelled.

The total, shameful boycott which greeted him had been a bitter blow to authority, and it had been followed by others, in swift succession, until all Pharamaul was in flames, and the flames could only be quenched by blood. It had led, directly, to Dinamaula's exile. It might still be at the core of the President's present attitude.

David could feel easier, now, about that long-ago defeat, though the experience had been unnerving and its consequences tragic. Today, as he drove round the perimeter of this near-forgotten battleground, seemed a happier day, and the times more contented. Yet there had been a certain ill-omen in what he had heard at this morning's meeting. One could never be sure, either in Pharamaul or in a score of other areas of change, what new twist the future could bring. In a slow country, in a slow continent, the boiling-point could always come quickly.

He drove on, feeling as if he were moving through the dust of history as well as its latter-day, choking reality. Though the heat was steamy and the sun still retained a brutal power to smite, the main street of Gamate was thronged with its privileged citizenry. Often the Land-Rover, crawling in low gear, was forced to a halt as the press of people—men gossiping in the middle of the road, giggling girls with water-pots on their heads, children who leant over to pat the car as it passed—made progress impossible.

He kept a firm hand on the horn, and sometimes revved the engine menacingly; but neither mechanical noise nor the supposed authority of the Government pennant which crowned the offside wing made much impression on the public. This was their town, and their own main street, and one of their many hours for walking and talking; and no white man in a green car, no badged messenger from far-off Government, nor even the Chief Secretary himself—for many, old and young, recognized him, and saluted him with smiles and open hands—were going to change customs, or the time of day, or a man's right to walk abroad at his ease.

Very slowly David made his way past the close-crowded, cheek-by-jowl mud huts, and the smoke of a thousand fires, and the wandering goats, and the plodding ox-wagons; very slowly he navigated open gutters, and noisy, impassable street meetings, and naked children walking on their hands, and official black-and-yellow signs—stolen from God knows where—which proclaimed: LIMITED PARKING.

The heat bore down, the flies crowded into the shade of the canvas top, the hundred smells of cooking, of people, of human excrement, cow dung, festering refuse, ancient privies, loaded the air until it was scarcely worth the breathing. Then gradually the Land-Rover drew clear, and he found himself going uphill and out of the town; and with a final honk on the horn to displace a huge Afrikander bull which was straddling the entire roadway, he had reached the Mission House.

Both this and the small chapel attached to it were buildings of classic, tumbledown humility, suitable to a poor teaching order; they were of brick daubed with clay, and their red corrugated roofs were rusty and battered. The man whom David had come to visit was a comparatively new arrival, and so far only a name—

Father Stubbs; and the visit itself was another act of piety, linked to the atrocious past.

Catholic missions were not at all David Bracken's line of country; but the first priest he had met there, old Father Schwemmer of sad memory, was so much a part of the fabric of Gamate that David never came to the town without also calling on the mission.

His first few minutes with Father Stubbs, however, severed many of these links very smartly.

Father Stubbs was a lean young man with a sharply beaked nose and a lot of hair. When David found him, he was standing at a table on the Mission House *stoep*, plucking a chicken—an occupation so unusual for a man in Pharamaul that David stared at him in disbelief. The sleeves of Father Stubbs's rusty brown cassock were rolled up, to reveal a pair of white stringy arms; and its skirts were looped informally into his leather belt, giving him a pantomime air, as if he were one of the junior staff in Widow Twankey's kitchen.

When he saw David he straightened up, brushed some chicken feathers from his hands, and came forward.

"You must be Bracken," he said. He had a harsh, rather disagreeable voice—a voice seemingly ready to argue about any single thing which might be said to him. "I got your message from the police radio man. . . . So you're the great white chief I'm always hearing about."

It was the sort of greeting—a blend of the hostile and the cheeky—which David did not care for at all, and he reacted sharply.

"I'm David Bracken, yes. We don't normally use the label 'great white chief.'" He looked down at the chicken, bloody and half bald, lying on the table. "Don't let me interrupt you. But what is this?—a cookery lesson?"

"You might call it that," Father Stubbs answered shortly. "It's a lesson, anyway. I'm trying to show my house-girl, who doesn't approve, that all the traditional 'woman's work' nonsense is hopelessly out of date."

"I don't think you'd find *any* Maula women actually approving," David answered. "And as for the men. . . . Tribally speaking, plucking chickens is not considered to be a man's job."

"We've got to change all that."

"You mean, by emancipating the women?"

"Exactly!"

Father Stubbs was looking at David with such an air of zeal, such burning enthusiasm, that it seemed better to leave the subject rather than to argue it out. If this new recruit thought that he could get the Maula man into the kitchen and the Maula woman out of it and into public life, then good luck to him. . . . David leant back against one of the shabby, crumbling wooden posts which supported the roof of the *stoep*, and tried to ease off the conversation.

"Well, I just thought I'd call round to say hello. How are you settling in?"

"Very well indeed," said Father Stubbs, challenging anyone to maintain otherwise. "Of course, it was all a bit strange at first. I was working up in South Shields, mostly with the Committee of One Hundred, and Gamate was quite a switch. The priest who had this job before me was Irish, and the old chap before him was a German. This was originally a German order, as you may or may not know. I'm the first Englishman they've ever sent here. Frankly, I think they were taking a bit of a chance, in view of all the awful things we've done in the past. However——"

"What awful things?" David interrupted. Try as he would, he could not love Father Stubbs, and he did not see why he should let him air his opinions unhindered. "The English have done a great deal for this country."

"Oh, come on!" said Father Stubbs belligerently. "Just look round you. Isn't this still pure colonialism? Colonialism at its very worst? Honestly, I could hardly believe my eyes, when I first came here! I didn't know such places existed. It's like the middle ages."

"But Pharamaul is generally quite happy. They have their independence, and in time it will work out all right. Certainly Gamate is quite happy."

"Because they don't know any better!" Father Stubbs answered passionately. "They're being swindled! You don't believe that, do you? Obviously not. Why should you?—you're part of the *status quo*. But I can assure you, some of us see things that the average official just doesn't realize. For one thing, this is still a *slave* economy! And you can take it from me, the run-of-the-mill Maula is not in the least happy, and there's a great deal of unrest. For instance, did you know that there still isn't a decent agronomy policy for Pharamaul? They're still trying to scratch a living from growing mealies and keeping goats! Did you know . . ."

He burbled on, while David Bracken, leaning back to ease muscles newly tortured by road travel in Pharamaul, stirred an errant chicken feather with the toe of his shoe, and wondered about this rather odd young man, raw with the world's discontent, whose crusading zeal had its own built-in blind eye. There was a perfectly good "agronomy policy" in Pharamaul, only it was called Soil Conservation and Livestock Control, and had been in existence over a hundred years. . . . He wondered also if old Father Schwemmer had been anything like this young successor, when he first took up his cross. Certainly he had been nothing like him when he descended from it.

He came to the surface to hear Father Stubbs proclaim: "It's even worse than it was in the old days! There have to be some enormous changes, and they must come quickly!" and he tried to break in.

"But Father," he began.

"Call me Stubby," said Father Stubbs. "Everyone else does. You see, I'm trying to ease down on the formal religious stuff. It doesn't cut any ice these days. In fact, it's about as much use as the bow and the curtsey! And after all, we *are* a teaching order. Did you know we've been in Gamate since 1782? Sounds like Johnny Walker, doesn't it? Born 1820 and still going strong—all that rubbish. But are we going strong? What have we got to show for it? Bible-readings and confirmation classes! Watch Night services! It's all so ridiculously out of date. What I want to do is to concentrate on social work. Discussion groups. Political seminars. Young people's get-togethers. At the moment I'm working on a scheme for a *discothèque*. All we need is the equipment. You've got to make the younger generation feel that they're *wanted!* Do you know, the idea of night classes, and technical training, and advanced courses in bookkeeping and office procedure, hasn't even been tried yet? They haven't even heard of the computer industry! But they will, if I have anything to do with it!"

David had already had enough of modern religion. "Well, I wish you luck," he said. "But I think it's a mistake to assume that you can change a whole way of life in a place like Gamate, by importing a few gimmicks which really have nothing to do with the way people are living now."

236

"Gimmicks!" said Father Stubbs, disgusted. "Now that really is a medieval reaction! I tell you, people in Gamate are crying out for change!"

"Even if that was true, do you think it's your job to bring it to them?"

"Of course it is! What else? I told you, we're a teaching order."

"But I thought that meant teaching Christianity. Teaching submission and hope. That's what Father Schwemmer used to say."

"You must be joking!" Father Stubbs's eyes gleamed with his own missionary fervour. "All that was years ago! Things have moved on! And did you know that Father Schwemmer was actually killed? Killed by people who had simply lost patience with him?"

"I know he was killed," David answered. "In fact, I was there when they cut him down."

"Cut him down?" asked Father Stubbs.

"Yes. He was crucified. Up in Shebiya. But it wasn't by people who had lost their patience. It was by people who were determined to hang on to the old ways. The very old ways. They wanted a certain number of human sacrifices, to give them strength. So they took Father Schwemmer, and the District Officer—his name was Tom Ronald—and his wife." David saw a kind of stubborn disbelief in the other man's eyes, and his own disbelief exploded. "It's no good looking at me like that! I'm telling you what Pharamaul was really like, then. A lot of it is still true, and it won't be cured by a *discothèque*." He realized that his pronunciation might be faulty, and he hurried on. "They killed Tom Ronald, by pulling out his guts while he was still alive. They raped the girl to death. And they crucified Father Schwemmer, alongside a couple of goats to represent the two thieves on Calvary. That's Pharamaul, old Pharamaul, and it's going to need a hell of a long time—probably longer than all your life—to change it. And you'd better make sure that you're using the right methods."

"Of course, if you're going to take that sort of attitude——"

"I'm not taking any sort of attitude. I'm telling you what happened to Father Schwemmer."

"It's my view that he failed because he was lagging behind the legitimate needs of the people."

"It's more likely that he failed because he was too much like Jesus Christ."

"*Who?*"

He made five more calls that afternoon, at the hospital, the police barracks, the vast new school, Government headquarters, and Gamate's own experimental farm. His progress became easier, as the sun declined, but he would have enjoyed it anyway; these were all the places which he had seen grow with the years; some of them were the result of his own weary paperwork, of a decade of patient file-shuffling; they were part of the very flesh of his life, and if one could speak of a dream come true in this humdrum context, then that was exactly what it was.

He was still rather ashamed of the silly scene at the Mission House, and his own irritability with Father Stubbs. But it was certainly nice to see a community—his own—at work on something better than chicken-plucking.

Wherever he went, people had a tale to tell, and they were delighted to be able to corner the Chief Secretary and tell it to him in passionate detail. At the hospital they complained of a shortage of drugs, and of a long-promised iron lung which had still not materialized; at the Government building the cry was for more filing-clerks; at the school the classes were growing much too large, and the midday meal too difficult to organize; and at the experimental farm the preoccupation was with a new and (to an innocent layman) loathsome strain of blue-tongue disease.

Only at the police station, now fully Maularized, were they completely happy in their work, though they could, come to think of it, do with four new motorcycles. . . . David made full notes wherever he went, as he had done for years past; it might have been a wearisome task, if it had not seemed, as it always did, the most important part of his whole working life, the part which really made sense.

But by six o'clock, he found that he was very ready for a drink, in the unwinding atmosphere of the Gamate Hotel; and it was there that the Land-Rover headed, almost of its own accord.

The single-story, frame-built hotel was not the most inviting place in the world; yet, like the Port Victoria Club, it had been home for generations of exiles, from Government officials to tough young men down from the logging-camp, from commercial travellers to railway surveyors, and whether they called it "the water hole," or "sundowner heaven," or simply "the pub," it had always been a wide-field magnet at the end of every working day.

It was a magnet this evening, David saw, as soon as he entered the bar, with its bare boards and wicker tables and chairs, and began to weave his way towards the long counter. The place was crammed, the air loaded with smoke, and the temperature a sweltering ninety-plus.

Behind the bar was one of his oldest friends in Pharamaul: Ted Fellows, the combined owner, manager, barman, bouncer, and arbiter of off-duty behaviour.

Fellows was a good example of the changeless man; a bald ex-boxer whose barrel chest and bulging arms seemed to have been straining against the same off-white singlet, whose vast hands had been swabbing down the same stretch of bar, for as long as David could remember. There might have been neater barmen, more formal hotel managers, but none more energetic nor more in control of his surroundings.

Long ago, it had been Ted Fellows who had had to refuse Dinamaula a drink at this same counter, when the latter was brought up to it by Tulbach Browne of the *Daily Thresh*, in a shameless scheme to promote a row and cook up a story. Fellows had done his manful best, on that occasion, to preserve the decencies while still upholding the strict letter of the law. Now the laws had been changed. But the man who greeted David Bracken with outstretched hand was still a rocklike center of control.

"Hello, Mr. Bracken!" he said. "Haven't seen you for nearly a year." Even as he spoke, he was doing three other things at once: wiping off the last of a wet beer-ring on the bar, tossing someone else's money into the open till, and pouring out the gin-and-tonic which he knew was David's choice. "What's the matter—don't you like Gamate any more?"

"I like Gamate very much," David answered, taking up the glass which now slid towards him. "In fact, I like it more than ever, these days. But there's been an awful lot to do lately. I just haven't been able to get away."

"So long as you don't forget us."

"I'll never do that."

"That's good to hear." Ted Fellows served another drink, rang up the money, and came back to him. "You probably know, there's a lot of talk about Gamate taking a back seat, and Port Victoria getting all the plums." He laughed suddenly, and his colossal chest made the cotton singlet stretch and heave like a circus tent in a gust of wind. "Victoria plums, eh?—that's not a bad joke!"

"You've made better ones," said David, with the privilege of old friendship. He turned away from the bar, and looked round the room, exchanging a nod here and there, smiling across the swirling smoke at a known face. Then his eye was caught by something which he had never seen in the Gamate Hotel before and he turned back to Ted Fellows. "Well, the rules have certainly changed since I was here last."

"You're damn right!"

Ted Fellows knew what he was talking about, without any further clues. He also glanced towards the opposite corner of the bar, where a group of Maula customers were taking their ease at three or four of the shabby wicker tables. They were not mixing with anyone else—so much was obvious; but, though isolated, they were perfectly at ease, perfectly content with their position, and so was the rest of the room.

This had once been a white man's bar; now, by far-away, astonishing directive, it was open to anyone. In a few years, perhaps, Maula would be drinking here with non-Maula, and would think nothing of it. At the moment, each side was gently nibbling at the novel problem, without striking any attitudes or banging any fists. It was, David thought, a typical Gamate accommodation, a truce to pride and prejudice, and he was glad to witness it.

"They don't bother me any," said Ted Fellows. "Though I must say, it felt damn funny at first, like breaking the licensing laws on purpose. But I had a word with all the lads, and we only had one real row. A couple of porters from the hospital started to pass remarks, and I had to tell them their fortunes. Now"—he jerked his head towards the corner group, patient and solemn as statues— "there they are, quite happy, and a damn sight better behaved than some of the roughies who come bollocking in from the logging-camp. But I wish they'd drink up a bit quicker, all the same. Half a pint of mild-and-bitter per half an hour—that's their speed. I'll never get rich that way."

"You're rich already," David said.

"Let's keep that a secret." Ted Fellows swabbed down the bar again, as rhythmically as if he were working out in a gymnasium, refilled David's glass, piled up some empties with a careful hand, and came back to his favourite customer. "That one is on the house, if you don't mind. . . . Do you remember the row there was, when I had to refuse the Chief a drink? That was the only time I ever got my name in the papers. . . . I suppose these days he'd just put me up against a wall and shoot me!"

"That question doesn't arise," said David diplomatically.

"It certainly arose, then. . . . What was the name of that newspaper sod who made all the trouble?"

"Tulbach Browne."

"That's the chap! What happened to him?"

"He came back for Independence. In fact he wrote something about it. Since then he's left us alone."

"Thank God for that. He was a real prick!"

David, now perceptibly more relaxed, said: "You're probably flattering him."

Ted Fellows laughed. "I'd hate to have to find out for sure." Then his face grew serious again. "As a matter of fact, we've got another one rather like him, right here in Gamate."

"Who's that?"

"Father Stubbs."

David Bracken was surprised. Though he had thought Stubbs a silly and disorganized young man, he had not yet considered him as a center of real discord.

"What makes you say that?" he asked. "Father Stubbs didn't strike me as much more than a bee-in-the-bonnet type."

"You must have met him, then."

"Yes. This afternoon."

"Well, I'm not claiming he goes round stirring up trouble *on purpose*, but that's what's happening, either way. And it's just too easy, these days. It's like I said—everyone up North is more or less fed up, because P.V. seems to be collaring all the loot. And now good old Father Stubbs jumps up and says, 'Come on, let's change everything overnight.' What it's got to do with religion, God only knows! 'Just call me Stubby—everybody else does.'" Ted Fellows made an impolite noise through his pursed lips. "His job is to run the mission, isn't it?—not to teach the Maula kids how to play bingo and dance the frig, or whatever it's called. And he's always on about the freedom of women. I swear to God, he'll end up with a good old-fashioned spear in his kidneys, one of these dark nights!"

"Does he come in here?"

"A damn sight too often," Fellows answered. "Because he's always arguing the toss about something, getting people's backs up. Honestly, if you think back to old Father Schwemmer . . . And he's such a rude bugger, isn't he?"

"I think that's a very fair description."

"Well, I don't mind that particularly," said Fellows, professionally broad-minded. He refilled David's glass, and poured a small tankard of beer for himself. "I'm one myself, now and then. As a matter of fact, Mr. Bracken, *you* can be a rude bugger when you want to."

"Thank you."

"Not at all. But for you and me, it's all in the day's work, isn't it? I have to keep order among a bunch of half-soused customers, and you have to ginger up some of the old diehards in Government, get them to take their fingers out. Isn't that so? But Stubbs has to be difficult all the time. Makes a hobby of it. And if you disagree with him, you're automatically a bloody fool, or worse, and he tells you so in that chicken-shit voice. Excuse me, Mr. Bracken. But he just gets me riled, every time he comes into the bar." Fellows looked across the room towards the door, which had swung open, and his eyes narrowed. "Oh, Christ! Here comes another lot I can do without!"

David, turning on his elbow, asked: "Who's that?"

"The Kremlin commandos. And I don't mind saying, they give me the creeps."

David found it easy to locate the newcomers, for the simple reason that the crowd thronging the bar seemed to draw aside as they advanced, giving them all the room they wanted. They were three men: two very large, square-headed characters in blue overalls, with holstered pistols in their belts, and a third, smaller, neater figure whom David recognized, with a definite sense of shock.

It was the Russian Ambassador, Mr. Spedkhov.

"Well, I'm damned!" he exclaimed. "What's he doing up here?"

"That's the Russian Ambassador, isn't it?"

"Yes."

"Been here three or four days, poking about. The two strong-arm boys are regulars. They're with the agricultural mission. That's what they call it, anyway. About ten miles east of here. Growing hybrid wheat or something. I don't think!"

"Why do you say that?"

"Tell you in a minute."

Spedkhov and one of his armed aides had seated themselves at a corner table, while the third man walked up to the other end of the bar, advancing with that massive arrogance which large men equipped with guns could always command. Ted Fellows moved along to serve him, and could be heard to say: "Yes, sir! Three large vodkas—coming up-ski!" Vodka in Gamate, thought David, wondering; it was like a submarine in the Sea of Galilee. Father Stubbs could hardly complain that things were lagging behind, as far as twentieth-century drinks were concerned. Then, on an impulse, he put his own drink down, and walked across to Ambassador Spedkhov's table.

Spedkhov saw him coming, and stood up. The smile on his face was somewhat wintry, but it was still there, and his handshake was ready enough. The armed man beside him also stood up, towering over David like a blue-grey cliff. His face was really rather awful—a sort of bulging pumpkin encased in yellow, pitted skin— and his eyes like little slotted peepholes. He did not smile. If he had done so, David thought, it must surely have been for the very first time. Ignoring this menacing *décor*, he said:

"Good evening, Mr. Ambassador. What a surprise to find you here."

Spedkhov looked at him with controlled disdain, as a man looks at another man when the other man is obviously two or three drinks ahead of him. His tone when he answered was like his smile—cold, impersonal, but just polite enough to pass for the currency of social intercourse.

"Good evening, Mr. Chief Secretary," he said. "I had been informed that you were on tour."

"You must be on tour as well."

Spedkhov seemed to consider this before answering: "Hardly to be called that. I am visiting our new agricultural station here."

The third man now arrived with the vodka, set out on one of the hotel's best tin trays, and David expected to be asked to sit down, if only for courtesy's sake. But all the Russians remained

243

standing up, silent, watchful, as though commanding him to leave them alone. Slightly nettled by this maneuver, he said:

"I'd like to see that place of yours myself."

"I am afraid that this is not possible," Spedkhov answered, almost before David had finished speaking.

"But surely——" David began.

Three pairs of cold, unwinking eyes were now fixed on him. "We are not yet ready for visitors," said Spedkhov. "In any case, it is to be a simple research station. We plan to experiment with wheat. There is nothing to see that one cannot see in many such places elsewhere."

"I'm still interested in what you're doing."

"I regret, no guests can come yet. It will interrupt our preparation."

With all the stubbornness of authority and gin-and-tonic, David countered: "Mr. Ambassador, I hardly think you can classify me as a guest."

But Spedkhov, well qualified to match such insistence, was not giving an inch. "Please do not misunderstand me. When we have something to show, we would be delighted to welcome the Chief Secretary in his official capacity. But in the meantime"—he shrugged, his only movement since they had first shaken hands— "we must make this rule."

"I am very disappointed," David said. "I shall not be here again for some time."

"So. Then there will be much more for you to see on your next tour." Suddenly, into Spedkhov's tone, there came what sounded like a deliberate, insulting infusion of acid. "I am sure Mr. Kalatosi would be glad to advise you when such a visit would be welcome."

"What's up?" Ted Fellows asked, when David, black-browed and ready to quarrel with anyone, returned to the bar. "Got the brush-off, eh? Was it about the agricultural station?"

"Yes."

"I could have told you. I asked if I could see the place myself, and did I get the soldier's farewell! You'd have thought I wanted to shoot the boss right through the charlies!"

"Bastards!" said David, reaching for a fresh drink. He was really very angry. "Why did he have to behave like that?"

"Don't work yourself into an uproar," said Fellows. "There's nothing to see there, anyway."

244

"How do you know?"

"Because I took a look anyway, just to spite them. I climbed the nearest hill with my binoculars, and did a bit of fancy bird-watching. But I could have saved my breath. There's nothing there, I tell you—*nothing!* Just ten square miles of bugger-all—scrub land, with reels of barbed wire round it, and notices saying 'Keep Out' in English, Afrikaans, and Maula. Can you beat that? Whatever it is, it must be all underground. Funny sort of wheat they're growing," Fellows grumbled on, beginning another attack on the bar counter with an evil-looking, grimy cloth, "if it's all done downstairs in the dark. Sounds more like mushrooms, eh! In fact, it sounds more like girls, if you ask me. How about a refill, just to take the taste away!"

David telephoned Nicole later that night—rather too late, if the long delay, the humming wires, and the sleepy voice at the end of them were anything to go by. But there was something else in Nicole's voice besides sleepiness: a sort of anxiety, a wary caution, as if the caller might not have been her husband at all, but some feared stranger.

Only at the end was he able to sort this out, and track down what lay behind it; to start with, it was the run-of-the-mill, husband-and-wife exchange, with slight marital overtones of "Where is my Wandering Boy Tonight?"

"Are you all right, darling?" Nicole asked, after three or four sentences. "You sound a bit odd."

David, sitting in Andrew Macmillan's old armchair, in Andrew's shabby sitting-room, in Andrew's dimly lit, creaking bungalow, braced himself in a determined effort to improve his diction.

"Sorry, darling," he said, making a bad shot at the ashtray and stubbing out his cigarette on a glass-topped table. "It's been rather a boozy evening."

"You don't have to tell me," Nicole answered. "I can almost hear the bubbles. Where were you?"

"At the hotel." A few of the more compressed bubbles escaped, not too well smothered. "Sorry," he said again. "But it's so marvellous to be up here. And I *have* been working as well."

"I believe you. . . . How was Ted Fellows?"

"Blooming. He sent his best respects."

Nicole, warming up, giggled for a moment. "That doesn't sound too like Ted. What did he actually say?"

"He said: 'Give her a hug from me.'"

"That's more like it." He heard a sigh, even over two hundred miles of wire. "I could do with a hug tonight. . . . What else have you been doing, besides propping up the bar?"

"Well, I called on lots of people. Wandered round a bit. Talked to the Council. And I had an unexpected session with Comrade S."

"Goodness!" said Nicole, after a short pause while this cryptic message sunk in. "What's he doing in Gamate?"

"God knows. I'll tell you more when I see you."

Nicole, well-trained in certain subtleties of communication, switched subjects without delay. "Are you moving on tomorrow?"

"Yes. I'm going up to Shebiya."

"Do give it a hug from me."

"What?"

"Well, we only spent our honeymoon there."

"Fancy you remembering."

"Fancy you forgetting. . . . Oh darling, I wish you were here! There are all sorts of funny things going on."

The edge of anxiety was back in her voice, and David, in spite of a wayward attention, felt himself compelled to notice it.

"What sort of things?"

"Oh, people talking about more big changes. And there are crowds wandering round the streets, as if they're sure something is going to happen. It's all rather sinister, really. Everyone's asking everyone else what's going on—there was something on the wireless about an important announcement—but nobody has any idea what. There are loads of policemen everywhere, and cars rushing about. Actually there is some kind of demonstration tomorrow— a trade union march—but I don't think it's that, exactly."

David wished that he could say something to reassure her, but too many other things—the long tiring drive, the meetings, the careful note-taking, the discussions, clashes, arguments, the recent intake of alcohol—all were against him. She had given him such a long answer. . . . He remained silent, feeling inadequate, aware that he would do no better for at least another twelve hours, while Nicole's voice again came faintly, from a long way away:

"I'm sorry to be so gloomy, darling. But Port Victoria really has been rather a mess today. It's so different when you're here. And then Martha has a cough, and Timmy is worried about his exams. And I've just had another *long* talk with Simon. He says he absolutely *must* go home. I'm afraid he really means it, this time."

His 6 A.M. hangover did not last; hangovers never lasted long in Africa, where a combination of clean air and therapeutic sweat drove them back where they belonged, cowed to nothing like spiritless dogs. David had a moment of sadness as he set out for Shebiya, since he would much rather be driving towards Nicole, when she seemed to need him, than moving further away from her.

But such sadness could not last—not on this hundred-mile northeasterly jaunt along a winding, yellow, bush-compressed road; not on a morning of high endeavour under clear sunlight; not on a journey through this mysterious U-Maula country, the innocent-looking domain where, even now, a twelve-bore shotgun strapped under the dashboard seemed the best guarantee of safe arrival.

Boy-explorer stuff, he thought: big-white-hunter stuff: dauntless-frontier stuff: stuff of daydreams and old colonial terrors and simple showing-off. But he did not mind any of these self-accusations. CHIEF SECRETARY DEFIES TRACKLESS JUNGLE, he thought, in colossal headlines, and set the Land-Rover charging up a modest hill as if he were covering the last desperate half-mile to Khartoum, or Ladysmith, or Calcutta's Blackest Hole.

He even sang as he topped the crest, and saw before him a wide crowded plain, purple and brown and withered yellow, where cactus fought it out with wild orchid, thorn-tree with throttling ivy, and the ants and the goats and the vultures took what spoils were left.

Nicole would have called this his Indian Scout mood, and gently derided it. But that did not matter either, any more than the hangover or the dust or the jolting road. He had been too long in captivity, to the worst of New Africa. Now he was free, in the best of the old. Once again, this was the Old Chief's country, and his very own.

He reached Shebiya, as he had planned, at noon, with no more trouble than a broken shock-absorber which would have to stay broken until he got back to Gamate; and his host met him at the front door of the bungalow with so hearty a greeting—"Good morning, sir! Absolutely on the dot! Do come in!"—that he might have been modelling his style on a whole generation of District Commissioners who had served their time in such lonely outposts as this, perpetually longing for the company which never came.

This was Para Pemboli, who had taken Charles Seaton's place when the commission service was Maularized, and had been installed as the Government's man-on-the-spot in Shebiya. He was a tall, youngish U-Maula, son of a former headman, a local boy of unexpected caliber who had been David's principal prop when they were setting up the canning factory at Fish Village. Now, translated, he had taken to his new job with enormous enthusiasm, bombarding Port Victoria and the Chief Secretariat with a daily stream of letters, dispatches, memoranda, working papers, background briefings, and development schemes of visionary scope and impressive detail.

David always thought of him, and privately spoke of him, as "Mr. Keen." There were people in the Scheduled Territories Office just like this one—operators whose binding slogan was "Notice Me!", eager beavers zealous to the point of embarrassment. Yet Mr. Keen had been an excellent choice for District Commissioner, because he had his way to make, against all the odds of custom and history.

In this pursuit he worked, he wanted to work, he loved his work, he lapped it up and asked for more. The overflow of paper might be tiresome, but the man himself was a matter of bright promise.

Now Para Pemboli said, again: "Come in! The sun's over the yardarm!" and led the way inside.

It was strange to enter, with certain interior qualms which he would never purge, the house which David must always label the "murder bungalow." Though he had spent some enormously happy years here—as a brand-new District Officer, with Nicole as a bride, with Nicole and Timothy their firstborn son—yet the house itself had got off to such a dreadful start that it could never catch up, never shed its loathsome aura. The ghosts were far too sad, and most potent in their sadness.

It was here that another happy couple, Tom and Cynthia Ronald, together with old Father Schwemmer, had been surprised by the invading mob, and dragged away to a death so terrible that no U-Maula, branded member of a guilty tribe, had ever spoken of it again.

Tom Ronald was still here, an ex-rugger-hearty pouring drinks into cracked glasses, and calling his wife "old girl"; Cynthia was still here, the glamorous beauty whose bond with her unlikely husband was so close and so explicit that, it had always seemed, nothing except an earthquake could keep them from making love within the next five minutes, spectators or not. Above all, Father Schwemmer was still here, a gentle guileless priest and servant whose atrocious death had always been, for David, an everlasting stain, a kind of curse on black mankind.

David had striven hard to conquer that feeling, along with many other onsets of fear and anger, in the course of the years; by now, much of the memory was compassionately blurred. But it could still return to plague him, in unguarded moments; and most movingly in this murder bungalow itself, the warm nest from which his friends had been untimely ripped.

As if specially commissioned to dispel the gloom of environment, Para Pemboli had now grown wonderfully cheerful. He fairly skipped about as he dispensed the drinks, and the cocktail biscuits which seemed as foreign to Shebiya as vodka had been to Gamate. He was dressed as District Commissioners had always been dressed, in this part of the world, in white shorts and a bush jacket with prominent epaulettes; the gleaming black flesh thus displayed made him look almost flamboyant, so strong was the contrast in colour.

It was, also, very strange to note how his speech seemed to duplicate an earlier model; this was really not a U-Maula talking at all, but a colonial expatriate who happened, astonishingly, to be black.

"Of course, I'm just playing myself in," he told David, when they were discussing certain details of office procedure. "As soon as I get really on top of the job, I won't have so many questions. At the moment, I'm still feeling like Tail End Charlie."

"I think you're doing very well," David answered. Para Pemboli was so likeable, as well as so eager, that it would have been almost wicked to discourage him; and in fact David did not want anything changed except the multiple output of paper work, which could be halved by a few constructive second thoughts. "Between ourselves, it's not too early to tell you that your name is being put forward for a gong. The C.M.G., in fact."

This must be catching, David thought, in the moment before Para Pemboli replied. He would never have dreamed of using such dated, bewhiskered slang as the word "gong" for a decoration, particularly the august Companion of the Order of St. Michael and St. George, if Pemboli were not modelling himself so closely on some generic character from the imperial past. Within the next few minutes, they would both be talking about chota pegs and pukka sahibs, unless the line were drawn. . . . Yet he was glad to see that Para Pemboli, newest product off a very old assembly line, was clearly astonished by the news.

"The C.M.G.!" he repeated, and whistled as people used to whistle when they were told some transparent lie in public. "Gosh! Like Mr. Seaton once said to me, you could knock me down with a grand piano! I thought a C.M.G. would take years!"

"It depends on the circumstances." The circumstances, in this case, were that Whitehall wanted to keep Pharamaul as sweet, united, and industrious as was possible in the prevailing ill-humour, but David did not think he need elaborate. "Of course, this really is between ourselves."

"Mum's the word, Mr. Bracken," said Para Pemboli, who seemed to have access to a very deep vein of old-style cliché. "You bet I won't let on to anyone. But I suppose I have you to thank for this."

"Well, it's part of the Prime Minister's list, actually."

"Ah! But we all know the drill!"

"Let's keep it anonymous, shall we?"

"Jolly good show!"

Later, at lunch, which was itself another caricature of colonial usage—tomato soup, stringy mutton cutlets, tinned peaches, and wedges of processed Swiss cheese in their original silver wrapping —Pemboli left his dreams of august patronage to deal with country matters, matters which both of them had nearest to their hearts.

"How are things in Port Victoria?" he asked. "We've been hearing such a lot of rumours."

"I was just going to ask you that myself," David answered. "Has there been anything on the wireless?"

"Not yet."

David came to the alert. "Why 'not yet'?"

Pemboli looked faintly embarrassed. "Only because of the rumours. I did not mean anything special. But it seems to me that Government must have some new plans in the pipeline."

"Very likely," said David, as he tried to make a blunt knife slice through some authentic Pharamaul gristle. "I was talking to my wife on the telephone last night, and she seemed to think that there was something in the wind."

"How is the beautiful Mrs. Bracken?"

"Very well. She sent her regards to you."

"That's really awfully good of her! You rang her up from Gamate, then?"

"Yes. I had an interesting day there. Met all the usual people. And one unusual one. Do you know Spedkhov, the Russian Ambassador?"

"Oh yes! He made an official call here, on his first tour. So he was in Gamate?"

"Yes. He was looking over their new wheat station, or whatever it is. As a matter of fact, I asked if I could pay them a visit, and got a very short answer. I don't suppose you've seen the place, have you?"

"Well, yes." Once again, Pemboli was looking rather embarrassed, as if it worried him to know a little more than the Chief Secretary himself. "But only at the beginning, when they were laying the foundations."

"Foundations?" David queried the odd word. "What sort of foundations does an experimental farm need? You mean, for the barns and suchlike?"

"Oh no. This is all much more complicated. Too complicated for me, I don't mind saying. But there are going to be lots of different buildings, spread all over the place. There were huge bulldozers scooping away the earth."

"Because everything's underground?"

"Oh, rather! That's for storage, they said. Apparently it's much cooler like that."

It all sounded just a bit too smooth. David gave Pemboli a long look. "Is it really a farm?"

"Why, of course, Mr. Bracken. What else could it be?"

"God knows. But I'd like you to keep your eye on it, even though it's not really in your territory."

"I'll do my best, Mr. Bracken. But as you know, they don't allow any visitors at the moment. They say there's too much work going on. And in any case——"

"What?"

"They specially asked me not to talk about it."

"But it's part of Pharamaul! It's your own country!"

"Technically speaking," Pemboli answered, once again sounding so cautious that David wondered if the other man were not making a fool of him, "that is no longer true. It is land granted to a foreign power—like an embassy, eh?—and so it belongs to them, not to us. One's got to stick to protocol, don't you think?"

In the circumstances it was a silly subject to pursue, David decided; whatever side of whatever fence Para Pemboli was on, he himself would do a damned sight better chasing up the facts for himself. He switched subjects abruptly, and talked about the Shebiya traditionals—crops, water, cattle, health, overcrowding—until the end of the meal, when his host said: "Well, so much for tiffin!" and led the way outdoors. Then, over coffee on the *stoep*, Pemboli announced:

"I'm afraid I'm wearing my other hat this afternoon. Magistrate's Court. We convene in about half an hour. Would you like to sit in? There's one quite interesting case."

David would have much preferred to lie down, in a cool bedroom in comfortable twilight, but duty, from which he had strayed the night before, now called, with the same nagging insistence as had ruled most of his working life.

"All right," he agreed. "Let's go down together. But don't put me up on the bench. I must have spent years of my life there. I'll be quite happy in the police box."

"Whatever you say. After that, we can relax a bit. I've asked the two young Bankas over this evening. They've got one or two things they want to discuss."

David smiled. "I can imagine."

"It's all so complicated," said Para Pemboli, and sighed the sigh of a man for whom even the award of the C.M.G. could scarcely assuage his heavy burdens. He raised his glass of brandy—South African, and very good. "Well, no peace for the wicked, eh? I'll say chin-chin!"

In Magistrate's Court, after some customary, quite straightforward prosecutions for theft, brawling, public drunkenness, and carnal knowledge of a female minor, there was what might indeed have been quite an interesting case, except that it turned out to be no more than another chapter in a contest to which David Bracken had himself given a preliminary hearing, about eight years earlier.

On the surface, it had begun as a simple matter of stock theft, when one man asked: "Where are my cattle?" and the other answered: "What cattle?" But such were the complications of doubtful ownership and disputed rental of land, and the counter-charges of illegal grazing, loans unpaid, dowries held up, damage to property, suborning of witnesses, and the mysterious increase of one man's herd by contrast with another's, that it was still a matter of urgent appeal, after eight long years.

David had heard a great deal of it before, and, calling on his memory, could detect certain subtle shifts of evidence, certain massive lies which had now been added to the general body of witness. Yet it gave him pleasure to know that a tribal tradition of dispute, a tendency to carry on endless argument from one generation to another, was still strong; and that the judiciary, in the person of District Commissioner Para Pemboli, could still summon the enormous patience which suited an enormous continent.

But in a room full of droning voices, and circling flies, and heavy afternoon heat, it also made for sleep; and there were moments when, sitting in his chair in the police box, surrounded by old friends and new, gleamingly accoutred recruits, he found himself nodding off.

At one point of wakefulness he heard an old man in the witness-box declare, with magnificent, Biblical righteousness: "Since I saw with my own eyes these three men setting fire to the hut with torches, you should pay no heed to disgraceful lies!"

Something tugged at David's memory, and after a moment he scribbled a note: "At one of the earlier hearings he said he was asleep." A policeman took it across to the magistrate's bench, while the court waited; and Para Pemboli, with admirable promptness, addressed the witness:

"Did you not once tell the court that you were asleep when the fire began?"

The old man, about to answer back vehemently, suddenly checked his tongue. His look grew puzzled and confused. Then he turned reproachful eyes towards David, who inclined his head. Finally the old man, discountenanced, but trying to sound as if the point were neither here nor there, answered:

"That is so, now that it comes back to me. I intended rather to say that I saw these men watching the fire, and smiling among themselves."

But now there were other people round him also smiling, especially among the police who had been enjoying this byplay, and very soon the old man's evidence came to a lame finish, and he was dismissed. A blow for British justice, David thought, winking indecorously towards the bench. Who could now deny that the law never slept?

Back at Pemboli's bungalow, only one man was waiting for him, instead of the two he had been expecting. Only Matthew Banka, second son of the leader of the Opposition, rose from the cane chair on the *stoep* as David and Pemboli climbed the steps. Immediately they had shaken hands, the young man made his brother's apology.

"I am sorry that Benjamin cannot be here to meet you," he told David. "But he is not very well today, and thought it best to stay at home."

This was quite possibly true, David thought, as he expressed his formal regrets. Benjamin Banka was often "not very well," sometimes in privacy, sometimes not; he had become a casualty of easily-won poisons—too much drink and "soft" drugs, too many women, too much adulation from boozy inferiors, too much insolence which earned him quick reprisal and a history of bloodied noses.

It was equally possible that, having lately achieved a degree of public disgrace unusual even for one of the "Banka boys," he preferred not to come face to face with that upright man, the Chief Secretary. It was no loss, in any case; his younger brother Matthew was by far the best of Chief Banka's twenty-strong litter.

Matthew Banka had improved out of all knowledge. *I would never have voted for him*, David sometimes said to himself, thinking back to the fat, cocky, spoilt child who had been the Matthew Banka of a year or so ago. Then, if he had not been the Chief's son, he would hardly have been fit for the crows. . . . But that stern judgement had been proved wrong.

Matthew Banka, like his father, was one of the handful of men in Pharamaul to whom increased power—even the modest power of an Opposition M.P.—had brought an increase in stature. He had shed most of the nonsense of the past, including the self-delusion that because he was his father's son he was important, and worth listening to, and worthy of deference. He had grown sensible, where his elder brother had turned even more stupid; he had put himself to work, just as brother Benjamin had taken to his bed, in sloth and squalor equally disgusting.

If it ever came to a really big row in Pharamaul, David thought, and Dinamaula lost the fight, and Matthew Banka managed to stay alive, then this young man. . . . But this young man, after the first greetings, was already speaking again, and what he said was very much to the point.

To David's surprise, there were no opening formalities, no stately to-and-fro of question and answer, as had been the case in Gamate. Here in Shebiya, it seemed, they were really fed up, and Matthew Banka hammered home the message from the moment he started to speak.

"When I said that you were welcome, Mr. Bracken," he began, "that was really true, not just the polite greeting. Sometimes we think that you are the only friend we have in Pharamaul. But what are we to do?" Already his voice was urgent, as if the suppressed feelings were so strong that they could break surface within a few seconds. "Here in Shebiya we are ignored! We are treated like outcasts, like the lepers in the old days! We have no railway to the south, we have no money for our needs, we have no power to make Government listen. What can we do, to escape being cut off completely?"

"Pharamaul is still one country," David answered mildly. "I know that there are certain difficulties——"

"With great respect, Mr. Bracken," Matthew Banka broke in, "it is *not* one country! Not any more. I speak freely, because I know His Honour"—he gestured towards Para Pemboli—"agrees with me. We no longer have our just rights. The Government in Port Victoria takes everything, and if you are outside Government, you can starve, for all they care! My father has toiled without ceasing to make this one country. It is all he wants to do, in his old age. But now he is called leader of the Opposition, and so what happens to him? He is beaten! He is insulted! He was driven out of the Assembly, and so were we all. All the world knows that we were treated shamefully!"

"Yes," David answered. There was nothing he could do to stem the flow of protest, the tale of outrage, and he did not particularly want to. "I know it, and I thought it was disgraceful. But may I ask, is your father well?"

Matthew Banka answered harshly, from an angry heart:

"He is as well as an old man can be, who has been forced out with blows, like a criminal. He is still in Port Victoria, though I begged him to come home with me."

Para Pemboli joined in. "I sent him a message myself, advising him to return. After all, he is our Chief, as well as a member of Parliament. How can we let him be treated as if he were a traitor? They've simply sent him to Coventry!"

"I know nothing of Coventry," said Matthew Banka irritably, "unless it is a place where honourable men, trying to work for their country, are kicked and thrashed like dogs. Some of us nearly lost our lives, while the police turned their backs, and Dinamaula watched it all, and laughed!" His voice changed suddenly, as if he had reached a prepared point, and must now establish it beyond doubt. "Mr. Bracken, there is something I cannot help asking, because our people ask it every day. What has happened to the Chief?"

"You mean, the President?" David asked.

"I mean God Almighty, if he chooses to call himself so! Perhaps that is for next week! But what has changed him from the man he was?"

It was a question which David Bracken had asked himself, over and over again, during the past months, but this was the first time that anyone in Pharamaul had spoken it out loud, and waited for his answer. He felt that there was need for great care here, as far as he himself was concerned; he still had a position to be proud of, a position worth defending, and outspoken words had a habit of filtering back to their target—in this case, the man to whom he owed all his loyalty, the President himself.

Yet he was alone in a room with two men, friends of himself, friends of their country, to whom he also owed a great deal; and there were involved in that owing certain decencies, like straight answers to troubled questions. He summoned his wits, and did the best he could, in a key deliberately low.

"I will answer you as a friend," he told them. "You both know my own position—we need not speak of that. It is true that there have been great changes in Pharamaul. It is also true that I can hardly understand what has become of the man who . . ." he hesitated, ". . . who I believed would be a fine ruler of this country. Perhaps I don't understand Africa any more, and that's about the saddest thing I could ever say. All I can tell you is that the proverb about power, and the way it can corrupt men, seems to be true. The President has great power——"

"And so he is greatly corrupted!" Matthew Banka joined in. "I knew that you would think as we do!"

It was rather more than David had been prepared to say, and he did not want these exact words put into his mouth. The ground here was very delicate, the ice as thin as it could be. Matthew Banka, in desperate mood, might well look for public support, for official backing, wherever it could be found; but David could not possibly be the man to supply it, and it would be wrong to raise his hopes. Seeking to disengage, he shook his head vigorously.

"No, I do not think as you do, altogether. You have your troubles, I have my own. I am sad because the country is not well run, you are sad because you seem to be standing still, because you feel cut off from the prosperity in the south. But it is not real prosperity, is it?"

"It is real enough for those who pick up the dibs," said Para Pemboli. "All we want to do is make sure that we get our fair whack."

"I think that's a simplification." David was glad to be on safer, more impersonal grounds. "What this country can and cannot afford is a very complicated subject. At the moment there is great extravagance, as you both know." He nodded towards Matthew Banka. "I am sure your father was right in many of the charges he made, and he was certainly a brave man to make them. But——"

"But look what happened to him!" said Matthew Banka passionately. "It could have cost him his life! Mr. Bracken, you said that you are our friend. It is known that you disapprove of what is being done. It is known that you are ashamed of this Government. Then *be* our friend! Help us! Tell us what to do. *Lead us!*"

There could only be one answer, even to such a cry from the heart.

"I cannot lead you," David said. "You know that, very well. The Chief Secretary is not such a man. . . . I have my own particular job, which is to supervise the civil service, and that means that I can play no part in politics. This is for you, and your father, and all the others who wish to see this country strong, and prosperous, and honest."

"First we want our own rights," Banka insisted. "We are part of Pharamaul, whatever Government may say. How can we make them see that?"

"By patience, and persuasion, and hard work." David might have been writing his own epitaph, and Andrew Macmillan's, and a thousand other epitaphs scratched in the blowing sand. "There is no other way."

"Patience! Are we to wait until we starve to death?"

"It need not be like that. Things move on, people change their minds, or come to their senses. But it is really true what I say—there is no other way."

"There *is* another way," said Matthew Banka. He exchanged looks with the District Commissioner, looks which seemed to indicate that David had arrived some days late on the scene of discussion. "If we cannot be heard from far away, then we must move closer. We must gather all the people, and march to Port Victoria, and tell Government that we insist on our just rights."

"That's a ridiculous idea!" said David sharply. "You know perfectly well what would happen. There would be violence, perhaps bloodshed. In any case, you would be turned back by the police, and Government would close its ears, and you would be worse off than ever."

"We cannot be worse off. Government no longer has *any* ears for us. I say that we should gather together, and march. And there is someone else who says so, who tells us so all the time. Someone you would respect."

"Who is that?"

"He is in Gamate, but he has been here many times, speaking to all who will listen."

"No one with any sense would listen to such a man."

"Not if he were a priest? Not if he were Father Stubbs?"

Later, when he was alone with Para Pemboli, David spoke his mind.

"That idea of marching on Port Victoria," he said, "is one of the worst I've ever heard. Whoever joined a thing like that would be charging headfirst into trouble. I've met Father Stubbs, and whatever his merits as a priest, he's just a bloody fool, as far as Pharamaul politics are concerned." He looked closely at the other man. "I hope you're not encouraging the idea."

Para Pemboli, at ease in his armchair at the end of the day, seemed to have shed some of the disciplines of office. "I'm neither for it nor against it. So I must be sitting on the fence, eh? But that fence has a spike or two in it, I can tell you! Perhaps if you understood what we're up against in Shebiya——"

"I know perfectly well what you're up against," David retorted. "God damn it, I *know* this country! But I also know what can happen, if things start getting out of hand. We've had quite enough of that, even in my time."

"We want to take them *in* hand," Pemboli answered, now rather less than neutral. "Living up here has been like starving in a *rondavel*, while the rich blokes up at the big house throw a lot of parties. You can hear the noise, you can shove your nose up against the window and watch the fun, but you can't get inside. Honestly, you can't blame people for wanting to grab their slice of the cake."

"This isn't the way to get it."

"Maybe not, Mr. Bracken. In fact I'm inclined to agree with you. But it hasn't been easy, telling people to wait and see. You say, 'Patience is a virtue, the meek shall inherit the earth,' and all that guff, and *they* say, 'But what about the lion and the lamb, eh?'"

"What about the lion and the lamb, for Heaven's sake?"

Para Pemboli was almost winking in conspiracy. "It was something Mr. Seaton used to say. I've always remembered it—a jolly good giggle! 'The lion shall lie down with the lamb. But only one shall get up!'"

The last leg of David's journey, thirty miles down to the coast at Fish Village, was the one he had been especially looking forward to. He had always had a soft corner in his heart for this small harbour town, where the fishing had grown, under his own hand, from an indolent local activity to a fully-fledged curing and canning industry.

It was always good to see something actually working in Phara-maul, something which these once despised U-Maulas now ran by themselves; and it would be good also to renew his friendship with Chief Justin, the youngest local ruler in the whole island, and a man who, like Para Pemboli and Matthew Banka, promised to transform and enlighten the future by his own gifts.

The road had been much improved since the old days, when it was not much more than a rough-cut jungle track. Then, it had to be cleared, once a year, by the *klembuki*, the so-called "way-makers," who made a hard-working, hard-drinking festival of their hacked-out, hatchet-axe-and-knife progress through the forest.

Now the greedy jungle, the slimy entrails of encroaching vines, the dank embracing tendrils which had once reached out to join hands above the track, had all been driven back for good. Now it was a solid, secure, much-travelled road, which linked Fish Village with the languishing railhead at Shebiya.

This was another part of the north which, like Andrew Mac-millan's house and the Ronalds' bungalow, was full of old ghosts and wicked memories. It was along this road that the small armed rescue convoy, landing at Fish Village, had snaked its way up to Shebiya, to take by surprise the revolted tribe, the madmen who had already led their hostages to atrocious slaughter.

That had been a night and a day best forgotten; but the brutal journey was always there, ready to be recalled, and it was there now, as David set out on his last lap. But before he had gone ten miles, his reliving of the cruel past came to a dead stop.

The previous night, just before they went to bed, Para Pemboli had suggested that David and he should keep in touch on the police radio, until David reached Fish Village. It had been a curious exchange; when he had questioned whether the link was really worthwhile, since he would only spend a couple of hours on the road, Pemboli had argued, with more than late-night persistence, that he would feel much happier if David maintained a listening watch.

He gave the impression, not that he knew something, but that he did not know enough, and had grown uneasy on that account. In the end David had agreed, without too much enthusiasm; it seemed a sheer waste of electricity. Thus it was a sharp surprise suddenly to hear, above the crackling of the radio, a voice saying loudly: "Shebiya calling Mr. Bracken, Shebiya calling Mr. Bracken. Over!"

He pulled the Land-Rover to the side of the road, turned off the engine, and took up the phone. So far he had only heard an unknown voice, a hard policeman's voice; but as soon as he had answered, and clicked the switch again, Para Pemboli came on the air.

Pemboli did not waste time. "Mr. Bracken, your wife rang up from Port Victoria a few minutes ago. She said it was important to telephone her immediately. Over!"

David was conscious of a pang of alarm. "Did she say what was wrong? Over!"

"No, sir. Just that you should telephone. I said I would pass on the message."

Their slow exchange, with its continual switch-flicking and formal pattern, continued, on an increasing note of urgency. The dictated pauses of the radio link were not designed for crisp conversation, but the words themselves lost none of their impact on their complicated journey.

"All right," David said. "I'll ring her up as soon as I get to Fish Village."

"She said immediately, Mr. Bracken. She was very particular about that."

"But I'll be in Fish Village in under two hours."

"Sir, your wife seemed to think that you should not go on to Fish Village, but come straight back here."

"Didn't she give any reason?"

"No, sir. But we were cut off at the end."

That was more than enough for David. "Message received," he said curtly. "I'm turning round now. Over and out."

There seemed to be tremendous difficulty in getting through to Port Victoria; the girl at the Shebiya telephone exchange grew progressively more harassed as calls went unanswered, ringing started and then stopped abruptly, and communication was cut off as soon as it was made. Twice David heard Nicole answer the phone, and then, after the single word "Hello?", disappear into limbo again.

While he waited, impatient and full of futile irritation (God damn it! he thought at one point; there wouldn't *be* a telephone system up here if it wasn't for me!) he had time to feel the impact of regret, and of foreboding also.

If only he had been a little more helpful the other night, when Nicole had obviously been worried and nervous. If only he had turned round then, and driven straight back instead of continuing his journey away from her. If only he had listened, instead of burbling and hiccupping. . . . When finally he got through, he was as contrite as any errant husband could ever be. But that, it seemed, was not what was needed.

Nicole sounded keyed up, and very cagey, as if both of them were being monitored by unfriendly ears, as if there were a man standing behind each of them, ready to break in and pronounce them enemies of the State. He caught the atmosphere very quickly, and reacted to it, and found himself copying her wary phrasing, her careful neutrality.

"Darling, I'm sorry to make you change your plans," she said, "but I didn't think you ought to go up to Fish Village. It's not wise at all."

"Why not?"

"Well, Government isn't likely to be very popular up there, just at the moment."

He was mystified, yet immediately conscious of people who might be listening on the wire—conscious even of Para Pemboli sitting in the next room with the door open—and all he could do was answer:

"All right. I'm back in Shebiya now. Do you want me to come down to Port Victoria?"

"I think you should." The wires between them hummed and crackled; somewhere in the background—whose background? Nicole's? the telephone exchange? some nameless eavesdropper?— there was faint thudding music, the kind they both disliked. Then her voice came through again, carrying far more than the words themselves. "Darling, I'm sorry to sound so mysterious. But I think you ought to be here. All sorts of odd things are happening."

"I understand," he answered. "I'll start back now. . . . Are you all right?"

"So far. . . . We've got a man on the door."

"*What?*"

"Just what I said."

"But good God! Darling, have you been in touch with Keith Crump?"

"Keith's gone."

"How do you mean, *gone?*"

"I'll be waiting for you, darling. Come back soon."

Then her voice, and the telephone itself, and the precious tie between them, were all gone as well.

7: LET OUR WATCHWORD BE "ONE PEOPLE! ONE LEADER!"

MAJOR KEITH CRUMP of the Pharamaul Police was indeed gone. It had happened to him so quickly, it had crested to such a neatly timed crisis at the end, that he was left for ever after with the belief that it had all been carefully contrived, even rehearsed, and that he had been the victim of a well-thought-out professional hoax.

But that was not much comfort, when he contemplated the wreckage of a career to which, like David Bracken, he had given a solid, single-tracked twenty years.

It had begun and ended with a tremendous row with his second-in-command, Captain Mboku. Crump had had rows with Mboku before; rows about suspected police brutality, rows about the non-reporting of incidents which bore the unmistakable smell of tyranny, rows about the use of informers, and evidence suppressed or distorted in order to secure convictions, and strong rumours of a protection racket initiated and run by the police themselves.

This time, the row was about a series of false arrests, followed by "fines" levied on the spot, within the prison compound: and this time, the evidence was altogether too strong for Keith Crump's stomach.

The enormous, bull-headed police-captain stood silent, and expressionless, and seemingly uninterested, as Crump stated the facts and then ripped into the culprit.

"I've been looking at the charge sheets for last week," Crump began, as soon as Captain Mboku was in his office. "I've been comparing them with some independent information I've received about the number of people brought into the main police station, and actually put into cells, and then released. It doesn't add up right, not by a mile."

Captain Mboku said nothing. He continued to stare down at

Crump, seated behind the desk, as if he were not involved at all, and did not intend to be. Crump, whose tactics had never included losing his temper, tapped on a pile of papers in front of him.

"Here are the figures," he said, "and I want an explanation. In those seven days, from Monday morning to Sunday night, eighty-three charges were recorded, and the chaps were brought into court later on, and disposed of. Eighty-three is about normal, for this time of the year. *But*"—he gave Mboku a straight glance as he emphasized the word—"during those seven days, another *one hundred and four* people were brought into that station, under arrest, and put into the cells, and then released after a couple of hours. It doesn't make sense. What's it all about?"

Captain Mboku continued to look down at him, with an arrogant lack of concern. The big fleshy face and the smoky eyes were still without expression. After a pause which was itself an insult, he asked:

"What can I say? I don't understand this at all. What is this *independent information* that says a hundred and four people were brought in? Where does it come from?"

"From men I can trust."

"Are they policemen? Or are they some criminals?"

"I'll ask the questions," Crump snapped back, "and you answer them."

"Whatever you like," said Mboku, with a disdain which was surely meant to be infuriating.

"*Sir!*" said Crump, using a much harsher inflection.

"Sir."

"That's better. Now let's go back to what I was talking about. Last week there were a hundred and four extra people rounded up and brought in. You needn't query my figures, because they're guaranteed. What I want to know is, why were they brought in?"

"If they were brought in, it was for interrogation."

"Then why were they put in the cells?"

"Perhaps it was easier to deal with them there."

"I don't doubt it. . . . But before people are put in cells, they have to be booked on the charge sheet. You know that—it's one of our strictest rules. So why weren't they booked?"

Mboku shrugged his colossal shoulders, bulging under the khaki tunic. "I suppose because it seemed they had done nothing wrong, and were let go. It was to save paper work."

"You can save paper work by interrogating them in the charge room, or one of the offices. You know perfectly well that they are *not* to be interrogated in cells, because it scares them, because it looks like undue pressure. And that's the next thing I want to deal with. What happened to these people when they were in the cells? When they were alone for a couple of hours with two or three of your policemen?"

Mboku, now deliberately unhelpful, said: "No good to ask me— *sir*. I leave all that to the station sergeants. I suppose they were asked the usual questions. When it was found that they were innocent, or they could not help the police, they were let go. But I'm only guessing."

"Balls!" The crude word marked the end of Crump's patience, the beginning of an absolute split between them. "I happen to know what went on, in eight different cases, and I'm absolutely certain that it's true of the rest, and that you know all about it. These eight men were brought in under arrest, not just as suspects, or to help the police. Mostly it was for disorderly conduct. As soon as they arrived they were chucked into a cell. They were threatened. At least four of them were beaten up. One of them had his toes stamped flat. One of them had cigarette burns all round his mouth. In the end they *all* paid five pounds, and they were allowed to go." Crump sat back, his eyes hard. "Multiply those eight cases until they come to a hundred and four, and it comes out at five hundred and twenty pounds a week. In fact, it's a simple racket. It's called extortion. But the idea that the Pharamaul Police should go in for it is disgusting! I want to know who gets the money."

"There is no money," Mboku answered carelessly. "I deny all these charges. They are ridiculous."

"Don't lie to me! I know what you're doing, and I have plenty of proof. And you won't get your hands on my witnesses until I'm ready to bring them forward. What I want now is to hear your explanation."

"There is nothing to explain. This is all foolish stuff." Mboku's gross face, at last, betrayed some of his hatred for the man in front of him. "As foolish as to try to spy on me."

Crump stood up. Captain Mboku was still half a head taller,

266

but he did not mind. The true size was not in the height. He said curtly:

"Very well. If you won't talk now, you'll talk later. In any case, you're suspended from duty. Keep away from this office, keep away from the station. Tomorrow there'll be an official inquiry, and I'll run it. If I find that you're involved—and I know damned well that you are—you're out—out for good!"

"You cannot dismiss me," Mboku countered. "Not on your own decision. My job is protected by Government contract."

"I'm perfectly aware of that. But I *can* suspend you, and then make my report. I think you'll find that the President will do the rest."

"What will you bet?" asked Mboku, suddenly insolent.

"My next year's salary. Now get out and stay out!"

The well-carpentered play turned out to have three acts; the next one was shorter, and the one after that shorter still, before the falling curtain brought down the appointed doom. Act Two started with a bang and a quick puff of smoke, as if designed to wake the audience up after their sojourn in the bar. Before Crump had done anything about setting up an inquiry, before the matter was an hour old, and was still, as he had supposed, highly confidential, a dispatch rider delivered a letter from Joseph Kalatosi.

Joseph Kalatosi (identifying himself, Crump noted, as "Chief Secretary," without any dilution of title) was brief to the point of crudeness:

> "I am commanded by His Excellency the President" [his letter said], "to inform you that the suspension placed on Captain Mboku, Pharamaul Police, is hereby lifted, and is not to be reimposed. There will be no further proceedings in this matter."

Major Crump, completely astounded and very angry, jumped swiftly into action. He had scarcely finished reading the message before he reached out for the telephone and dialled the Government Secretariat. He had expected Joseph Kalatosi to be difficult to get hold of, perhaps "not available now," perhaps "away for some time," and he had been ready to battle it out until he made contact; but to his surprise, and later suspicion, the other man came on the line as soon as the call was put through. Everyone was very sharp on cue today. . . . However, if Kalatosi had been waiting for the call, he was not waiting with anything in his hand except a knuckle-duster.

He was adamant, and not prepared to argue. The letter explained itself, he answered, in response to Crump's furious query. The affair of Captain Mboku was closed. It had been disposed of.

"What the hell do you mean, *disposed of?*" Crump demanded in a voice near to shouting already. "It's Mboku who's going to be disposed of, if I have anything to do with it. I'm his commanding officer, and I've suspended him from duty, and he's going to stay suspended, somewhere near the roof, until I've cleared all this mess up."

"There is no mess to be cleared up." Kalatosi was completely smooth and confident, as if his invincible hand of cards was already displayed on the table, and he had only to reach out and scoop up his winnings. "The letter said that the matter is closed. It is a direct order from the President."

"Do you mean that Mboku went running straight to the President, and told him a lot of lies?"

"Captain Mboku had an interview, certainly. There were no lies. The result of the interview was the letter I sent you."

"Well, I'll have an interview myself!" Crump said savagely. "I'm not going to stand for this sort of thing. Mboku is as guilty as hell, and he's going to get what's coming to him, right where the chicken got the axe. I'll see the President myself."

"You can always try," said Kalatosi, and the smooth voice was now mocking. "But I wouldn't advise you to. His Excellency is extremely busy."

"Not too busy to see a crooked bastard like Mboku!"

"His Excellency does not receive crooked bastards. It was fortunate that he had a moment to spare, and could prevent an injustice being done."

"Injustice!" Crump knew that it was no good losing his temper, but the blank denial was goading him to fury. "He'll know all about injustice, when I've told him the facts. I've got enough on Mboku to hang him twice over! He was simply running a racket—rounding people up, throwing them into jug, and then selling them their releases!"

"Clearly that was not the President's view."

"Then it damn soon will be!"

There was a sigh from the other end of the telephone. "He really is very busy," said Kalatosi. Then there was a click, and that was all for Act Two, Scene One.

It was indeed true that the President was very busy, and he seemed to have impressed the fact on his staff.

"I'm awfully sorry, sir," Paul Jordan said, when he answered the phone. "But he did say, no more appointments for two or three days."

"But this is urgent, damn it! I've turned up something that— well, anyway, ask him to make an exception."

"Sir, I know it won't be any good. In fact, he said I wasn't even to bring any names in."

"*Is* he busy?"

The hazard of an open switchboard at the Palace dictated the answer: "He won't make any more appointments. That's all I know."

"Then I'll write. Will you get a letter to him?"

"I'll try, sir."

Keith Crump wrote a brief outline of the facts, and asked for an interview to explain them and to put his side of the case. He said, quite politely, that he had been surprised that his orders had been countermanded without any opportunity for discussion. He added, equally politely, that as far as he was concerned, Captain Mboku must remain under suspension until the matter had been clarified.

Less than an hour after he had fired this modest broadside, Mboku himself walked in, with a perfunctory bang on the door which did not wait for an answer. He must have been moving fast, if the spreading sweat-stains on his tunic were anything to go by. In fact, he must have been moving fast, in every way.

Crump, taken by surprise, glared up at him. "I thought I told you to keep away from this office."

Mboku's only reaction was an enormous grin, which split his moonface like a slice of a melon. He stood in front of Crump's desk, a bulky giant in a jovial mood, and thus mocked him, in silence, in insolent disregard of all jurisdiction. Crump stared back at him, on the edge of explosion and of sick foreboding also. This must be Act Three already; and in it, something had gone wrong —wrong for himself, gloriously right for the man opposite.

For some reason, ex-Sergeant Mboku, under suspension for gross misconduct, likely to be dismissed, was certain that he was now sitting in the five-pound seats. It could only make sense, in one awful way.

Crump did not have to wait long for the answer. Suddenly Mboku stopped grinning, and, aping Crump's expression in crude mockery, glared back at him. Then he said:

"This office is now my office," and slapped a piece of paper down on the desk.

It lay between them, like a declaration of war, a short-fused bomb, a blatant threat of disaster. Whatever it was—and Crump refused to pick it up, refused even to look at it—it had given Mboku an arrogance which could never now be cancelled out, which destroyed for ever the structure of command, as the two of them had known it in the past. In the disciplined balance of rank, they had now reached the end of the road.

"What are you talking about?" Crump asked.

"It's all in the paper."

"Never mind about the paper. What did you mean, this is your office?"

The wide, cavernous grin was returning to Mboku's face. "It is in the paper," he repeated. "It is an order from the President. You said you would not obey him, so he has dismissed you. I am in command here. This is my office, and you are in my chair."

Sacked, Crump thought, while his heart, which had leapt suddenly, seemed to fall slack again, leaving only the hollow and the pain. Sacked at second hand. Sacked by one of his own men, a man whom once, long ago, he had chosen as right-hand marker from a job lot of recruits. Sacked out of the blue, by a man with a big triumphant grin and sweaty-brown armpits.

Mboku was still talking, even as the intolerable blow began to make its weight felt.

"It is all written down. The President orders you to take to-night's plane. The arrangements have been made already. You are to hand over your keys to me. The President said that no man who disobeys his direct order can remain here. If there is any money needed to finish your contract, it will be sent on to England."

"Just shut up a minute," Crump said, low-voiced, without heat.

Now he was taking it in, inch by cold inch. He could almost feel the claw-marks of despair climbing up his back. He was out of a job, at forty-nine, with a few hours' notice and no known prospects. The past, to which he had given all loyalty, had come tumbling down, in half a dozen sentences; the shattered present made him feel sick. The future would deny him the only real job he knew, in the only country he loved.

Policeman's honour, which had always shone like a jewel in Pharamaul, which he had striven with all his might to preserve intact, had passed at a stroke into ready-infected hands.

He remembered betting his next year's salary that he would come out on top in this contest. It had turned out to be a true wager, with a horrible twist to it. Mboku wouldn't win the money, because it wasn't there any more. But he had certainly won everything else.

David Bracken drove south at a furious pace, the Land-Rover with its broken shock-absorber taking and giving fearful punishment. He stopped once, in Gamate, to pick up some petrol and to have a quick word with Caspar Muru of the Town Council. But Muru had heard nothing definite, only vague rumours of "trouble down south," and now the telephone link seemed to be out altogether. He knew nothing at all about Crump.

David said good-bye and set off again, pushing the car to its limit. Nicole's quiet summons had set many thoughts rolling and jostling round his head, and none of them could be happy ones.

When he was halfway between Gamate and Port Victoria, he began to notice the people. He found that he was passing successive groups of men and women, some trudging on foot, some on horseback, riding pillion; he was meeting ancient cars, and carts laden with furniture and family, and bicycles with a passenger balanced on the cross-bar. They were all moving north, in a stream which gradually grew to something like a flood.

Presently, round a corner of the road, he saw one such group resting under a tree, and he stopped his car. He *must* find out what this was all about. . . . There was an old man, and a young man and woman, and several children; there was a dog with a lolling tongue, and a donkey burdened down with a mountain of bundles, and two chickens in a wicker cage. David got out, and walked over to them.

They had been talking, but now they fell silent, and watched him carefully. When he was near, the old man raised his open hand in salute, and David returned it. No one else moved. The young man, who had been looking at the Land-Rover with its Government markings, was watching David with something like hatred.

"What is your journey, old man?" David asked politely.

The old man mumbled something—it sounded like the name of one of the villages near Gamate. But he did not say it as though he wanted David to know; if it had been lost in the mumble, he would have been just as happy.

One of the children, a little ragged girl with braided hair, edged near him, and the young woman called her back sharply. Then they all stood or sat in silence, under the dusty tree with the sun scorching the earth a few feet away. Each side seemed to be waiting: the weary Maulas for him to go away, David for words of truth.

He tried again. "There are many people on the road," he said. "All travelling to the north. What is the cause?"

The old man shrugged, but did not answer.

"Have you heard any news?"

Now it was the young man who answered harshly: "We know nothing."

"Have you come from Port Victoria?"

"Near Port Victoria."

"Is there some wrong there?"

"I cannot tell."

There was nothing to be gained here, however much he pressed them. They did not like him, they did not trust him; he was a white man in a Government car, asking questions; a stranger-enemy threatening trouble. David hesitated; then he saluted again, said: "A peaceful journey. *Ahsula!*" and walked back to the Land-Rover.

When he glanced towards them before starting, they were still staring at him, wordless, waiting for him to go away.

He took up his hot, jolting, onward-pressing journey. Throughout that long day, he had kept the car radio switched on, hoping for a news bulletin from Port Victoria. But the radio station in the capital seemed to have fallen into the same sort of twilight as many of the people he had met that day; there were none of the normal programs, only an endless chain, now blaring, now fading, of martial music, unbroken by any human voice.

Then, towards nightfall, when he was only fifty miles short of his goal, the pattern altered. The music ceased abruptly, and there was a long humming silence, and then a jumbled assortment of items from one of the BBC's overseas services, which sounded as though it had been taped at odd moments of the day.

Someone read the news (dock strike in Liverpool, Health Service uproar, pop-star in paternity suit). Someone played the sad guitar. Someone (Mr. X, the novelist) gave an angry account of his reaction to Mr. Y's review in the *New Statesman* of Mr. Z's definitive biography of Mr. A, who was believed to be the actual character depicted in Mr. B's notorious *exposé, Satanism and Society.*

Then there was another silence, which was not too hard to endure. Then more martial music. Then a voice, slightly breathless, announcing: "Please listen for an important declaration by a Government spokesman." Then a different kind of voice, rough, authoritative, charged with full power, came on the air; and David recognized it before half a dozen words had been spoken. It was Captain Mboku.

Only this was no longer Captain Mboku; it was now Colonel Mboku, speaking (in his own words) as "Chief of the Security Forces."

"Citizens of Pharamaul!" the big voice boomed out. "Listen to me, and tell your friends what I have said. This is Colonel Mboku, chief of the security forces of your country. I bring to you greetings from our great President, who has asked me to speak to you on his behalf, since he has heavy work to do, seeking out those who would destroy him and bringing them to justice.

"These are his words to you. Remain calm. There has been a vile plot against the state, but it has been defeated. Since the danger of treachery remains, it has been decided to put an end, once and for all, to the scheming traitors. All opposition parties are hereby declared illegal. Those who support them are enemies of the state. They will be crushed, and all the guilty ones will be punished without mercy."

The short tirade finished with a string of barking commands, "I say to you again, remain calm! Go about your usual work tomorrow! Do not listen to enemy voices! Report any tricks to the authorities! Trust your leaders! Trust our great President Dina-maula! Denounce all who oppose him! Let our watchword be: One people! One leader!"

Then the band played the national anthem, and following it there was complete silence as power faded and Port Victoria went off the air.

After that, David drove on with a kind of bemused ferocity, wildly eager to reach the end of his journey even though he could not imagine what lay in wait at the finish. The idea of a "vile plot" was something he could not possibly believe in; Chief Banka and his shrunken band of followers were as likely to try to overthrow the Government by illegal means as were Liberal peers to storm their way into Buckingham Palace.

If the Opposition were indeed "enemies of the state," then so were the water-buck in the zoo.

None of it made any sense, except in a nightmare world where men in power, intolerant of all opponents, went straight for the throat of anyone who dared to raise the voice of protest. And as for *Colonel* Mboku—one would as soon have promoted a jackal and called him a lion.

There must be something terribly wrong in the town he was trying desperately to reach; the town where his wife was waiting (with "a man on the door"), the town where he had lived and worked for so long, confident that the rules would always be kept, and the fabric of the law would only grow stronger.

Now it seemed to have been taken over by a man shouting "They will be crushed!" and, in the same threatening breath, "Remain calm!"

Far ahead of him, usurping the horizon, there was an ominous blood-red glow in the night sky. It was only the loom of Port Victoria, with its wide spread of street lamps and lighted shops; but fancifully one could imagine the city below to be in flames, burning up in a wholesale eruption of violence and hatred. The truth was less dramatic. When at last he reached the outskirts, he found Port Victoria to be, not in flames, but in the grip of a new officialdom.

Astride the road leading through the northern suburbs was a roughly made roadblock which, in his eagerness to reach home, he nearly ran into: a barricade of trestles, of the sort normally used to seal off road works and excavations. There was a line of flicker-

274

ing kerosene flares to mark it, and a policeman swinging an oil lamp to warn all travellers to slow down. When David stopped, his car was instantly surrounded by other policemen who came out of the shadows.

They were all armed, and their revolvers, directly pointed at the car, had the immediate menace of all careless weapons.

One of the advancing men, a tall young police corporal with a lined sweaty face, thrust his head inside the hood of the Land-Rover, and demanded:

"Where you from?"

David Bracken decided to play it very carefully indeed. Men with guns tended to use them; fingers, trembling on the trigger, sometimes squeezed a little too hard. There would always be an apology afterwards, and a funeral well attended by authority, but Nicole and the children could not live on that for the rest of their lives. He said:

"I am the Chief Secretary. This is an official car. Who is in charge here?"

The corporal, proud of his small empire, did not like this at all. "Answer the question! Where you from?"

"I live here, in Port Victoria. Burnside Avenue."

"Where you *from?* Where you come from now?"

"Gamate."

There was a concerted intake of breath from the men pressing round the car. Gamate seemed to have been the wrong word to use. The corporal, who had a torch in his hand, first shone it directly into David's eyes, and then let it roam round the interior of the Land-Rover. It fell unluckily on the twin barrels of the shotgun, protruding under the dashboard, and the policeman exploded into words:

"You come Gamate? You hide a gun? You better get out damn quick!"

"I will not get out," David answered, deciding to chance a little toughness on his own account. "I have been to Gamate on an official visit. I told you, I am the Chief Secretary, Mr. Bracken. This is a Government car. Look at the flag, look at the markings. If you are in charge here, you must have heard of me. You'd better let me through. Otherwise you'll be in trouble."

There was a pause, and some muttering from the surrounding darkness. But the firm voice had done much to take the heat off the moment; and when another man, shining the oil lamp on the drooping pennant, said: "It is true. See the colours," the crisis suddenly passed.

"But you have a gun," said the corporal, with less insistence.

"With two barrels," David answered, repeating in Maula a hallowed local joke. "One for my wife, one for her mother."

The laughter exploded all round him, and the crisis was past. The corporal, deprived of his flashing vision of glory, did the best he could to cover up.

"We are on guard here," he said. "All cars must be examined before they pass."

"I understand that."

"You are for the Government?"

"Certainly. I work for the Government."

"Then you may pass." The corporal suddenly became a mainspring of official activity. "Move those barriers!" he shouted, withdrawing his head and waving his arms with great energy. "Hurry up! This car is on Government business!"

The trestles were trundled aside, leaving a narrow gap for the Land-Rover to pass. Putting the car into gear, David leant out of the side window. There was no point in claiming a victory, but no harm in a random taking of the temperature.

"Thank you!" he called out. "I will tell Colonel Mboku how you do your duty."

In the half light of the flaring barrier lamps, the police-corporal's face split into a wide grin. "Thank you, sir! Colonel Mboku great man! He take care no damn traitors try to kill the President. He take damn good care!"

It had been swift, ruthless, and effective, with just the right balance of persuasion for any waverers. Only at the beginning, when there sprang up in a dozen different quarters of the town a dozen identical rumours—of a plot to overthrow the Government, an attempt to kill the President, a march on Parliament by "armed terrorists"—was there confusion, and delay, and silence from authority. But as soon as the pot really began to boil, and the streets were thronged, and one man looked at his neighbour in suspicion and fear, authority pressed the button and swung into action.

In a single night, Port Victoria seemed to lose its innocence, and accept the embrace of the fiercest of guardians, who would not be denied, who seemed to have thought of everything.

On that night, police cars with loudspeakers toured the streets, repeating over and over again: "The trouble is over! The plot has been crushed! No one who obeys the law is in danger! Keep calm! Return to your homes!" When some men, curious or afraid, refused to return to their homes, but loitered in groups on the street corners, many were bundled into police wagons and taken away. The warning word spread swiftly, and by midnight all the main streets of Port Victoria were deserted.

On that night, armed police hammered on the door of Chief Banka, and the seven members of the Opposition who were in the city, and perhaps two hundred others who were known to support the Opposition party. Some of these doors were locked, and the men behind them asleep; some were peacefully open, with family and friends taking their ease. But whether locked or left open, the policemen passed through the doors, and bore away the men inside.

When the men protested, and the women behind them wept, the answer was always the same: "It is an order from the Government. Do not argue. Get into the car!"

On that night, a certain man resisted street arrest and shouted: "Leave me alone! I will walk where I choose! I do not believe all these lies!" He was clubbed senseless by a policeman, and thrown like a sack of bloody maize into the police wagon waiting at the curb.

On that night, men and women within earshot of the prison heard screams coming from behind the walls, a rise and fall of panic cries which were repeated many times over as the hours wore on. Many times, also, there was the rattle of a disciplined volley of rifle shots, which echoed like blows across the silent town.

The screams were genuine enough; but, it was said later, the noise of shots was made by men shooting into sandbags. Yet who could have known that, at such a dreadful hour?

On that night, fresh and fearful rumours began to spread from house to house, sometimes by telephone, sometimes by whisperers who crept furtively up to back doors. The rumours, whether detailed or vague, were all to the same effect; that any man who did not support Government without question, or had been heard to speak against it, or was from the discontented north, was being thrown headlong into jail. Many such had been shot already.

On that night, the great *trek* northwards began, by people who had come to fear for their lives. Behind locked doors and drawn curtains, with children crying and women whispering, the swift, heartbreaking preparations were made; and by dawn the first members of a wretched, laden cavalcade were on their way. When they passed the roadblocks, the police mocked them.

"Better walk fast!" they shouted. "Better ride like the wind! Better keep beating that old donkey, that three-legged horse! Remember, we can always catch you if we wish! It is hard to let traitors and plotters escape! You are lucky today—but keep hurrying!"

On that night, an armed sentry was posted at the gate of the Chief Secretary's house, to be relieved by another at the stroke of every hour. Nicole Bracken did not learn of this until next morning, when she saw Gloria the nurse-girl taking out a mug of tea, and staying to gossip with the policeman on duty, and presently to laugh. When she returned, Nicole asked her:

"What on earth is the policeman doing there? What did he say?"

"He said he was on guard, mam."

"But why, Gloria?"

"To see that the master was safe."

"But the master is away."

"Safe when he comes back, mam."

It didn't make much sense. It made even less when Gloria, full of hot secrets, went on:

"He said the U-Maulas tried to kill the President yesterday."

"I'm sure that's not true, Gloria."

But Gloria was now the expert, and her face showed it. "He said they had caught some of the men, and shot them in the prison. He said all the U-Maulas had better run away before they are killed. Will I tell Simon, mam?"

"No," said Nicole. "You will do nothing of the sort."

But later, loud words and cruel laughter from the kitchen showed that Gloria had not been able to resist passing on her news. It was then that Nicole, on the edge of desperation, had telephoned Keith Crump's house, to hear a stupefied, weeping voice—it was Jonathan, the Crump's houseboy—answer: "Major

Crump, Mrs. Crump, all children go away to England yesterday. Oh missis, please tell me what to do!"

After that, she had got through to Shebiya, and just managed to catch David on his way to Fish Village, where news of such a turmoil as this, multiplied by a thousand angry voices, could easily spark a mindless, murderous reprisal.

On that night, the lights burned brightly and endlessly within the great façade of the Palace, where the guard had been trebled, and the front portico, the courtyard which flanked one side, and the long, strangely shadowed perimeter of the garden resounded to stamping feet, the slap of rifle-butts, and constant challenges, all conducted under the glare of floodlights urgently brought in from the dock area.

The President had many visitors during these hours which should have been dark; foremost among them was Colonel Mboku, whose long black car—specially marked with a triangle of lights, so that it was never challenged—slid in and out of the Palace gates as if the man inside were a fisherman faithfully tending his net.

There were some who said that he was making sure of the President's safety; some who said that he always bore fresh, important news; others who could only testify to loud voices, angry disputes; others still maintained that the President, playing host at the wildest party the Palace had ever seen, constantly summoned Colonel Mboku by mysterious means, and that even so great a man as the new Chief of Police must jump up and come running when the illustrious Leader, happily preserved from his enemies, snapped his fingers.

On that night, it was, as always, a short watch for the sleepy, the drunk, the contented lovers, and the blameless. It was a very long night for the fearful and the guilty, and for the strong men who mounted guard on all of them. But by morning, all was over.

Though many rules had been broken, many hopes proved wrong, yet many plans had come to exact flower; and Port Victoria awoke to find itself sewn up tight, in fresh-pledged, loving loyalty to its ordained ruler, whose new title—the Lord Protector —had best be remembered.

Not till two days later did President Dinamaula break his silence, and he referred to this delay in his first broadcast address, which was announced four times every hour during the preceding afternoon. Every home that had a receiving set was thus alerted, and the warning signals were relayed by loudspeakers strung on hundreds of lamp posts and trees throughout the city.

When finally the national anthem was played, and a solemn voice proclaimed: "The President and Lord Protector will now speak to the people," Dinamaula had the largest audience of his life.

It was a short speech, delivered in a slow, throaty monotone which did not disguise the force and fierce determination behind it.

"I have waited a long time to speak to you, for two reasons," the Lord Protector began. "First, because I have had very difficult work to do, dealing with the nest of traitors and bandits of whom you all know. Secondly, I wished to wait until Colonel Mboku, the Chief of the Security Forces, was able to assure me that he had brought these disgraceful matters under control. He has informed me that at last all is quiet. So it is now my heavy duty to tell you what has been taking place, both in secret and in public.

"Four days ago, it was reported to me that there was a criminal plot to usurp the Government, and that the traitors involved were led by those ambitious men who call themselves the Opposition. It was necessary to act instantly, without leave of Parliament, in order to safeguard the state. I therefore signed an order-in-council suspending the constitution, and instructed Colonel Mboku to take all necessary measures to put down this revolt.

"The so-called Chief Banka, leader of this opposition to the lawful government, was immediately put under arrest, together with as many of his supporters as we could find. Many others, with bad consciences, have run away like rats from Port Victoria, and I need not tell you where they have gone. Such men are no loss to Pharamaul!"

For the first and only time, Dinamaula's tone changed, as if he were coming to a crucial part of his speech, where he must above all carry his supporters with him.

"To my sorrow, it was also necessary to take into custody former Prime Minister Murumba and certain others who opposed my will and the will of my people. I took this heavy step as a matter of urgency, in the best interests of the country, and the reasons will be made clear, as soon as the forces of law and order publish their evidence. Finally I found it necessary to dismiss the former head of the police, Major Crump, who saw fit to disobey my orders and was involved in certain provocative acts which were likely to injure the Government.

"Major Crump has already left the country. All other enemies will be brought to trial in due course, and if found guilty they will be punished. Let no man forget that the penalty of treason is death! You may be sure that the new Chief of Police, Colonel Mboku, will be vigilant at all times. But remember he is acting for *you!*

"Let us turn away from these criminal and disgraceful plots, and look to the future. We are now one united country, under one leader. There will be no more nonsense about opposition. Anyone who acts against the Government will be crushed without mercy! You who support me have nothing to fear; I have given orders to Colonel Mboku to deal harshly only with your enemies.

"But I will not tolerate carpers and critics; I will not tolerate people who act against me, or write against me, or whisper against me. If you hear the smallest whisper, run to the nearest police station. You will be rewarded with as much as a hundred pounds! In return, I demand your full loyalty and support, in order to make our beloved country strong and free.

"I have declared a national emergency, and assumed full powers, and I have also accepted the title of Lord Protector, because that is now my life's work on your behalf. Give me your love! Give me your help! Give me your obedience, without question! Long live the new, free Pharamaul!"

2

"More new stamps!" said Timothy Bracken, delighted, as he spread the contents of the packet out on the table. "Oh, Daddy, thank you! Aren't they lovely?"

Martha, leaning over his shoulder, said: "There's one of the new hotel."

"But it's not finished yet!"

"It's finished on the stamp, isn't it?"

Timothy was busy counting. "There are eight new ones, Daddy. That makes twenty-six altogether. We're almost as good as Ghana."

"That's something to think about," said David.

"Did you choose the patterns, Daddy?" Martha asked.

"No, I don't do that any more."

"Well, they're still jolly good. I *love* the triangle one. It's got a picture of the whole island."

"And Dinamaula."

"Well, of course!"

Nicole came in from the kitchen, where she had been reassuring a scatterbrained Simon that soup *and* chicken *and* a cheese soufflé would not be beyond him, if he just took things slowly and carefully, in the right order.

"Look at all the new stamps, Mummy," said Martha. "Daddy brought them."

"Good gracious! More stamps? But we've only just had the new Christmas ones."

"This is *pictorial*," Timothy explained. "Christmas was *commemorative*."

"Oh, I see."

"Those are nice long words," said David, leaning back in his armchair to soothe an aching frame. He was intolerably tired after the day's work; with each week that passed, it seemed to grow more and more difficult for him to unwind, to recover from the Secretariat and enjoy the family. It seemed, also, to need one or two extra drinks each night, which was something he had never taken into consideration before. "What else did you learn at school?"

"Not much," Timothy answered. His last school report had announced, curtly: "Seems to lack interest," and he had become defensive about the whole subject. "We're doing Henry the Eighth."

"It's time somebody did."

"What do you mean, Daddy?"

"Nothing. Silly old father's joke."

"We're all learning a new prayer," said Martha. "We're going to recite it every morning."

"Well, that's nice," Nicole said.

"It's about Dinamaula," said Timothy.

Their parents exchanged a glance. With hardly any mention of the fact, "Dinamaula" was becoming a word of cold foreboding between them, as it was for many other people in Port Victoria;

when linked with a "new prayer," it did not lose any of its power to trouble. After a moment, David asked:

"What new prayer? What does it say?"

Now it was the children's turn to look at each other, but the reason was different. "You start, Timmy," said Martha. "You're better than I am."

"No, you."

"Ladies first," Nicole commanded. "It doesn't matter if you can't remember all of it."

"It's quite short," Martha announced. "It's exactly forty words. The headmaster said: 'Forty words for each of the forty great deeds of our President.' Did you know he did forty great deeds, Daddy?"

"Well, it's possible. . . . Let's hear the prayer."

Martha assumed a prim reciting face, and a voice to match it. "Lord Protector——" she began.

"It's 'Oh, Lord Protector,'" Timothy corrected her. "Don't you remember? 'Oh' is for the first great deed."

"What was the first great deed?" David asked.

They both replied simultaneously: "He freed his country from the oppressor!"

"Of course—silly of me. Go on with the prayer."

"Oh, Lord Protector, look down on us, the children of your country, and take us into your special care, so that . . ." Martha faltered to a stop. "That's all I can remember," she said. "We've only had three lessons."

"I know the rest," said Timothy. "So that we may grow up to be loyal, steadfast, and obedient, and worthy of your great love and leadership. Amen."

"*Amen?*" Nicole asked, horrified.

"Yes. That's for the last great deed."

"Whatever was that?"

Once again the children were able to chorus: "He made the desert fruitful."

In the ensuing silence, Martha said: "It's *rather* like in church, isn't it?"

"Very like," her mother answered. "But I don't think——"

The doorbell rang, interrupting her, and the children rushed out into the hall. This was an Uncle Alex night, and there could be no system of priorities which did not put him at the top.

"Good God!" said David, almost to himself.

"Darling, that's absolutely *awful!*"

"Isn't it?"

Excited voices in the hall, and a squeal of delight from Martha, indicated that Uncle Alex was getting, and returning, his usual bountiful welcome. Then the troupe appeared, led by their guest, bearing a small wicker basket.

"Oh, Mummy, it's *kittens!*" exclaimed Martha. "Two of them. A black and a white one."

Nicole, who had been forewarned, said: "Well, don't forget that they're yours, and you must look after them yourselves. Have you thanked Uncle Alex?"

"Thank you, thank you!" But only the basket could claim any real attention. "Can we take them out?"

"Just for a minute. Then it's their bedtime. And it's your bedtime, too."

While the kittens were being cherished and made much of, Alexanian settled down with his drink. Not for the first time, Nicole noticed how lined and grey he was becoming, how the tracings of lively humour were deepening into a creased mask of frustration and bitterness. The tall Jew seemed to be passing into the same category as her own tall husband—careworn, perpetually worried, losing the spring of a hopeful future, settling for less and less every day.

It was sad and enraging at the same time; why should men like these become blunted and despairing, while the people they had served so faithfully, for so long, flourished like high-grade thieves? It wasn't fair—and at that point Nicole checked herself. About six months ago, she and David had taken a solemn oath never to use the phrase "It isn't fair" again, however fierce the temptation.

"Otherwise," David had said ruefully, "we'll wind up by never saying anything else." It had been a mildly funny idea then. Now it was so utterly depressing that she could have cried to remember it.

From the other side of the room, Martha let out a small shriek. "Ooh! It scratched me!"

"Don't tease them, darling," said Nicole. "They're only babies."

"And as babies, they ought to be christened," said Alexanian, "if a Jew may suggest such a thing. What are you going to call them?"

The children looked down at the kittens they were holding. Timothy had the black one, Martha the white. They were about six weeks old—small bundles of fluff and fur, their eyes still inclined to stay half-closed against the world.

"Blackie and Whitie," Martha suggested.

"I know," said Timothy, suddenly inspired. "Dina and Lucy!"

"That's silly," said Martha. "We don't know if they're going to be boys or girls. They haven't decided yet."

"It's a jolly good idea, all the same."

"All right, children," Nicole called out, in one of her firmer voices. "Now it really *is* bedtime."

"Where on earth did they pick that up?" David demanded, when the two had gone unwillingly to bed, cherishing the kittens to the last, planning saucers of warm milk. "Dina and Lucy— really, I'm quite shocked!"

"At school, I suppose," Nicole answered. "But honestly, I'm past being shocked at anything. And it wouldn't be the worst thing they've picked up at school, would it? Did you hear about the new prayer, Alex?" She told the story, quoting as much as she could from memory. "I think that's absolutely blasphemous! Shouldn't the bishop take it up with Dinamaula?"

"I don't think he'd get very far," said David. "The Lord Protector has obviously set up a rival firm."

"But it's so bad for the children."

"Don't you want them to be loyal, steadfast, and obedient?"

"Not to—" She stopped, as a footstep slurred in the passageway outside. "That sounds like dinner. Do bring your drinks in."

Dinner, as a meal, was not a success. The soup, villainously burnt at an early stage in its career, arrived at the table scarcely warm; the chicken had been scorched to a cindery nothing; and the cheese soufflé, which was Alexanian's favourite, had subsided with a soggy thud long before it reached the dining-room. "I'm so sorry," Nicole kept saying. "I thought Simon was going to be all right tonight."

"You'll have to speak to him again," said David at one point, surrendering before a chicken-leg which would not have yielded to a chisel. "I know he has his troubles, but this is ridiculous!"

"I think *you'll* have to speak to Gloria," Nicole answered. They had been too long married, and Alexanian was too old a friend, for this to be more than a minor tragedy, comparable with a blown fuse or a laddered stocking. No tears need flow, no marriage vows be cast aside, no burning social *gaffe* committed to a tear-stained diary. "It's Gloria who keeps putting him off his stroke."

"How does she do that?" asked Alexanian, who had decided, without too much regret, that he was not hungry after all, and was concentrating on some white Burgundy which was beyond the reach of careless hands.

"She bullies him all the time. She's rather awful, really. It's because he's a U-Maula. She keeps on saying—I've heard her, often: 'Go home, old man. Go home while you can.'"

"She could be right about that."

"I know." Nicole looked across at her husband. "Darling, would it be such a terrible thing if Simon did go home?"

"Just a defeat, that's all."

Sadly, the bad dinner was perfectly suited to the bad mood. None of them seemed to have anything in the way of resources to call on, at this state of the tide which they all knew to be running against them.

"It's not as if it were just that disgusting prayer," Alexanian said, when they were talking about the cult of the Lord Protector. "We now have"—he ticked the items off on his long fingers—"two Dinamaula statues, a Dinamaula Square, the Lord Protector's arch of triumph in the middle of the park, a Dinamaula dock— made of very inferior concrete, by the way—and a Dinamaula High School. I suppose they'll rename Port Victoria itself, before very long."

"Actually that *is* in the wind," said David. "My colleague Mr. K. was kind enough to mention it to me."

"Not Dinamaulaville, for Heaven's sake!" said Nicole.

"No. But something with the name Maula in it. To honour the dynasty, which makes more sense. Punta Maula—something like that."

"Why not Punta Bracken? You've done just as much for it."

"That's not quite true."

"I much prefer New Alexania," said Alex. "I have paid for a great deal of it."

But it was difficult to maintain any level of good humour, when the reality troubled them all so much.

"You-know-who isn't the only one who's been getting big

ideas," Nicole said. The oblique reference was becoming common-place in white Pharamaul, where a real or fancied Big-Brother-is-watching-you belief was steadily gaining ground. Lucy Help had become Mrs. Mayday, and Colonel Mboku a softer version al-together, Merci Beaucoup. "Did I tell you about the Crosth-waites' gardener?"

"They sacked him for letting all their flowers die while they were away on holiday," David answered. "Or so I heard at the club."

"But they didn't sack him! They couldn't!" Nicole's voice was positively outraged. "He didn't water the garden, or the lawn, or do a single thing, for nearly three weeks, and of course when the Crosthwaites came back from Lourenço Marques the whole place was a shambles, and they told him to pack up and leave. But the very same day two men came round to the house, and said they were from the union. Don't ask me what union," she said, in answer to David's raised eyebrows. "Just the union, that's all they said. They told Mrs. Crosthwaite that if she didn't take the gardener back, no one else would be allowed to work there, ever. They said the Crosthwaites could be *deported* for discriminating against Maulas! So they had to take him back, and now he sits under a tree all day and never does a stroke of work." She smiled suddenly, at David's look and at her own vehemence. "Darling, I know I sound like one of those revolting Afrikaner housewives, always screaming about the *kaffirs*. But this really is true. If they had a *white* gardener who behaved like that, he wouldn't last five minutes. But as it's a Maula, he can stay on forever, and get paid for doing nothing."

Gloria came in, to clear away the ruins of the chicken and the half-empty plates, and conversation languished while she was in the room—another precaution which, even a year ago, they would all have thought ridiculous. When she had gone, David took up the tale.

"Last month there was another prime bit of nonsense. You remember Ted Fellows, up at the Gamate Hotel? Well, they cancelled his drink license, just like that. Not for anything he did—he ran that pub like a battleship. They just said that they wouldn't renew it. There was no appeal, and he had to sell up and retire."

"That must be because——" Nicole began.

"Exactly!" said David. "He refused Dinamaula a drink nearly fourteen years ago, because that was the law then. So now he's out."

"That's the meanest thing I ever heard!"

"It was also a calculated swindle. Without the drink license, the hotel was nothing. So it was a forced sale, and Ted actually lost a lot of money on the deal. But a couple of Maulas bought the hotel, and *they* got their license next morning. Even though the nearest they'd ever come to running a pub was running their own home industry—which was boiling down bits of old kidney to make tallow candles."

"Darling, why didn't you tell me?"

"It was just too depressing."

The doomed soufflé was brought in, also as depressing as anything which had been said that evening. Nicole made her last apology on its behalf, and as they wrestled with its minority, eatable sections, Alexanian took up what seemed to him, on a personal basis, the most important part of David's story.

"No one can object to Maularization," he said. "It's perfectly natural, it's a normal development in any of the new countries of Africa. If we have a Maula president, we should certainly have Maulas in every position of authority, right down to the head Customs officer at the airport. But not just with a wave of the wand! Responsibility takes time. It needs to grow. Will your two Maula lads do as well as Ted Fellows, up at Gamate? Maybe in ten years, yes, they will. But *now?*—they should be learning the bar trade from the beginning, starting with polishing the glasses and sweeping up the sawdust, like my father!"

They had never heard of Alexanian's father before. "Tell us *that* story, Alex," David said.

"It is very short—and for him, very long." Alexanian's harassed face softened, at a memory which must have remained dear to him, for as long as he could recall. "My honoured father came to East Africa as a little boy, nearly a hundred years ago, from Poland, where there had been a pogrom—a polite way of saying that all the Jews were rounded up, kicked, beaten, spat upon, imprisoned, accused of ritual murder, their beards pulled out hair by hair, their teeth drawn one by one until they said where their money was hidden, stripped of their possessions, and told to keep moving until they no longer defiled the sacred soil of the fatherland. My honoured father started as a café dishwasher in Zanzibar, he became a waiter, he became a hotel manager, and he died as the owner of the Excelsior Hotel in Nairobi."

"But Alex," Nicole said, "that's wonderful!"

"Certainly it is wonderful. One can only be privileged to be the son of such a man. But if he were alive today?—a Polish Jew, a hotel operator in Kenya? I would not give him much chance of holding on to his job—or his hotel either. He would be told: 'There are a hundred native Kenyans who need your work, who can do your job. Do not exploit our people any longer. Go away —and leave the keys of your hotel.' In six months, the Excelsior Hotel would be a slum, run by lazy relatives of the Minister of Tourist Attractions. I assure you, David, it is going to be the same thing here."

"You needn't assure me," David answered. "I can tell a cold draught when I feel it."

But Alexanian had one more personal point to make. "Kenya has expelled—or is going to expel—all its Asian and Indian traders. So will Uganda and Tanzania, probably. Behind all the smokescreen and the lies, there is only one reason, and it is purely racial. The Asians and the Indians are ten times smarter than the Negroes. They have too much power, too much money, and the Negroes want to move in and take it away from them. Well, I am not Asian, nor Indian. But I am Alexanian the Jew, the foreign trader who also has too much money and power. When our Government has finished with people like Ted Fellows, and Keith Crump, and the civil service, and the *Times of Pharamaul*, and Barclays Bank, they will turn on me. 'Go home, Alexanian the Jew!' they will say. 'You have exploited us long enough. Dina-maula's nephew—the one with the honours degree in herbal medicine—is taking over as chairman and managing director. But leave your keys, and leave your money as well. It is only stolen!'" Alexanian drained his glass, with a defiant, despairing, bitter flourish. "Shall I see you in Bournemouth, Mr. Chief Secretary?" he asked. "Let us run a little boarding house together. Strictly kosher! And *no* coloureds!"

When Alexanian had gone, long after midnight—because it had been a night for late drinking, and lengthy sad silences, and paying no heed to the time, Nicole, curled up on the sofa, said:

"Darling, you must always tell me the bad news."

David, who was pouring himself the last of many whiskies-and-soda at the sideboard, asked over his shoulder:

"How do you mean?"

"Well, I was thinking about poor old Ted Fellows, actually. He was so good at that job, and now you say he's just been pushed out. He's one of our friends, but you kept it all to yourself."

"There's not much point in making two people depressed."

"It's not *two people*. It's you and me. And when something like that comes out, it makes me worry about a lot of other things as well. I mean, is your office worse than you've told me?"

David came back with a brimming glass, and sat down opposite her. "It's pretty bad. But you know that already. I hardly count at all, these days. Joe Kal is the man of the moment. He's set up as the King of Dash—he actually uses the phrase. When he has a caller, he pulls open a drawer full of banknotes, and says: 'That's the kitty. Rather small today, isn't it?' Then, if you want something from him, you're expected to contribute."

"But that's disgraceful! Can't you stop it?"

"I can't stop anything."

"Does London know about this?"

"Some of it. But there's not much they can do, either."

"What do you mean, some of it?"

David, gulping at his drink, and then nursing it close to his chest, took on a lecturing tone, as sometimes happened when alcohol had overtaken most of his normal reactions.

"Because my communications with the Scheduled Territories Office—which has a right to know what's going on, since they put up a great deal of our money every year—are not quite as informative as they might be. I can't very well send telegrams or dispatches *en clair*, saying that the other Joint Chief Secretary is a crook, can I? I can't get private telegrams or dispatches coded up, either, because Joe Kal has access to the cipher section. I *can* write personal letters from the office, and seal them up, and put them in the 'Out' tray, but I happen to know that they have a habit of coming unstuck again, before they reach the mailing office. I can write letters from this house, but I'm damned sure the same thing happens. So, for their three million a year, London aren't getting a very clear picture of life in dear old Pharamaul."

"Perhaps you ought to go over."

"I've thought of that."

"But what could you do when you got there?"

"God knows!"

He sounded so hopeless and helpless, so forlorn and defeated, that Nicole was instantly fired up, moving to the rescue as if this were a child in danger rather than a man in hazy despair.

"But you've given your whole life to this *bloody* country! Darling, it's not fair!"

"Now then. We said we wouldn't use——"

"But it's true!"

"And it's not a bloody country, anyway. It's *our* country."

"For how long? What's the good of pretending? You know they're kicking out all the people who've done the building-up, all the people who still want to help. Alex happened to meet Keith Crump and Molly at the airport, just before they left. They were both nearly crying. A man like Keith. . . . And Alex will be just the same when his turn comes, and he knows it already. So will we. . . . Are we going to wait till *we're* dropped off at the airport, with the children and a couple of suitcases? With the police saying, 'It is forbidden to export more than one hundred pounds in currency,' and a line of immigration people grinning their heads off?"

Spiritless, David answered: "There's so much work I still want to do. And it needn't be like that, anyway."

"What's going to stop it? *Who's* going to stop it?" She looked across at him, sitting slack and grey-faced, with a half-empty glass of whisky held against his chest like a tattered piece of armour. "Oh, darling, I love you so much—but if you could only see yourself, if you could only see what the last few months have done to you. You look"—she was nearly in tears, tears of rage, tears of mourning—"you look so *old!* You've been crucified! And when you think what it's done to us . . ."

"What's it done to us?"

"Very nearly the same thing." She swallowed, fighting off the tears which would defeat her determination to make her case. "David, do you know how long it is since we made love? *Four months!* And the awful thing is, we haven't wanted to. Even at the worst times in the old days, it was still a comfort. Now the idea is just a nuisance. Not even that. It's more like an embarrassment. Because you're almost always dog-tired, and you have to cope with that stinking office next morning, and I have to cope with the house and the meals, and we don't want any more children anyway. . . . So it's 'Goodnight, darling, sleep well,' and it's 'Goodnight, darling, sleep well,' and the next thing we know, it's daylight again and everyone's queuing up for the lavatory."

"But have you wanted to make love?"

"In theory, every single night for the last four months. In practice, the sad answer is no."

"So it doesn't really matter."

"Oh, *David!*"

Later, he came up to the edge of her bed, swaying slightly, and said: "Move over."

"Darling, you don't have to."

"I want to."

"All right." She sat up, and looked round for her bedroom slippers. "I'll just go to the bathroom."

"Do that," he said, and lay down, his hands clasped behind his head, like any privileged member of this club. Yet he could not help thinking: *Christ, why does she have to go to the bathroom? . . . I'm as old as God, anyway. . . . She said so herself. . . . I couldn't give her a child if we went on all night. . . . All week. . . .*

When Nicole came back, she found that David had turned his face away from the light, and buried it under a fold of the blanket, and seemed to be fast asleep already. Quietly she climbed in beside him. He grunted, but did not move at all. Presently he was snoring, and it was—she could not help it—the ugliest sound she had ever heard.

When she had stared at the shadowy ceiling long enough, she edged her unwanted body away from him, and withdrew into single solitude again. If he had woken now, and come to life, she would have screamed her disgust, her raging anger. . . . Soon her tears became real and uncontrollable, and her mourning bitter indeed.

In all their long and loving marriage, it was the first time— the very first time—that she had offered, and he had agreed, and she had doubted, and he had confirmed. Yet even after such a naked parade, such plain advertisement, a shaming, desolate nothing was the night's answer.

3

For the third and then the fourth time, Tom Stillwell of the *Times of Pharamaul* read the handout from the Information Division of the Government Secretariat. The Information Division had recently redesigned its note-paper, and the emblem at the top, under a sculptured profile of the President, carried the motto: *Strength Through Truth*.

Summoning all his strength, Tom Stillwell re-read the truth:

"It is officially announced that former Prime Minister Murumba, who was arrested on suspicion of plotting against the State, has died of heart failure while in police custody. He was aged 72, and had been under doctor's care for some months. It is understood that before his death he made a full confession of all his crimes."

Alone in his modest sweat-box of an office, with the telephone silent and only distant noises coming from the newsroom down the corridor, Tom Stillwell thought for a full hour before he did anything. Then, having weighed all the chances he could foresee, and dismissed all the alternatives save one, he put a piece of foolscap, and two carbons, into his typewriter, and flexed his stubby fingers over the keys.

He typed—experimentally, because it was not quite what he wanted to say—"A TRUTHFUL GOOD MORNING TO ALL LYING MURDERERS!" Then he continued typing, with long pauses, for nearly two pages—seven hundred words.

When he had finished, and re-read, and altered, and approved, he put the original of what he had written into his desk drawer, the second copy in his inside pocket, and the top copy, with a few words added in longhand, into an envelope. He addressed this to an old friend, a drinking pal of many years' standing, George Maginnis. Underneath he typed the address: "*Rand Daily Mail*, 174 Main Street, Johannesburg."

He looked at his watch, and found it was eleven-fifteen. Forty-five minutes—just right. . . . He called out to Maria, his secretary next door: "I'm going out. I'll be back after lunch." Then he got his car from the parking place at the rear of the press room, and drove out to the airport.

He was looking for another old friend, and he found him; an airline pilot taking his ease with a cup of coffee in a corner of the restaurant. The pilot had a flight-bag and a thick folder of papers on the table in front of him. He looked ready to go.

"Hello, Jock," said Stillwell.

"Hello, Tom! Long time no see!" The pilot, who was big and burly and sun-tanned, waved a gold-ringed arm. "Take a pew. Have a coffee."

Stillwell shook his head. "I can't stop, I'm afraid. Are you off at twelve?"

"As per usual."

Stillwell pulled out his envelope, and laid it on the table. "I've missed the post with this," he said, "and it's important. Do me a big favour, and drop it off in Johannesburg."

"Now then, now then!" the pilot answered, in mock alarm. "You know the regs, Mr. Stillwell, as well as I do. Private carriage of mails—defrauding the Post Office—penalty of fifty pounds for the first offense."

"I'll buy you a drink when you get back."

"A drink, he says!" The pilot picked up the envelope and read the address. "*Rand Daily Mail*, eh? Are you writing for them now?"

"Now and then."

"I wish I had time to write," said the pilot. "Money for old rope, if you ask me." He slipped the letter into his breast pocket. "O.K., me boy! Will do."

"Thanks a lot, Jock. You won't forget it, will you? It *is* important."

"You sound just like my wife," said the pilot, "but she's prettier, thank God. Don't you fret yourself. I'll deliver it in person, on the way into Jo'burg."

"Thanks again."

"I'll be taking that drink as well!"

Tom Stillwell lunched very well at the Port Victoria Club, though he kept his solitude at a side table, since the only people he seemed to know nowadays were the shrunken Splinter Woodcock gang, whom he could not stomach, and the staunch supporters of the National Party, who—whether they were politicians or civil servants—seemed to move and talk and react under a parallel, blinkered hypnosis. Everyone else was in jail—or, now, dead.

Over coffee, a man who was something in the Public Works Department asked him, with a kind of gleeful curiosity: "Did you hear about Murumba?" and he answered: "Yes, I'm afraid I did. Prime Minister Murumba was a friend of mine," and the man said, with the same sort of interior satisfaction: "That's what happens when you go against Government."

Not in Yorkshire, my friend, Stillwell thought; not in Canada, not in Barbados, not in Norway. . . . Then, after one more brandy than he had ever drunk at lunchtime on a working day, he went back to his office.

Once there, he took the original of his leading article from the desk drawer, and sent it along to the composing room. Then he waited; and while he did so, he placed—against himself, the only taker—a very large bet that the next man to come in would be poor old Henshaw, still the chief sub-editor and still the spongy buffer-zone between editor and print shop.

After a long delay, poor old Henshaw did indeed shuffle in; as glum as ever, a walking example of the Man Least Likely to Succeed, and bearing in his hand the two foolscap sheets which Tom Stillwell, half an hour earlier, had sent down to that sensitive area, the compositors' lair itself.

"It's more trouble," said Henshaw, and sniffed. "This time, I must say, you can't really blame 'em. It's this here leader, Mr. Stillwell."

"What about it?"

"They won't set it up, that's what. Joshua Malabar says——"

"All right," Stillwell cut him off curtly. "If they won't, they won't. Just forget about it."

It was the most surprising thing that Henshaw had ever heard his editor say. He searched for a clue. "You mean, you're going to rewrite it?"

"Not on your life! I'll spike it."

"*Spike it!* But, Mr. Stillwell! You wrote it, didn't you? Don't you mind at all?"

"Yes, I mind."

"Then don't you want to see the lads?"

"Not this time. I know damn well it wouldn't do any good."

"What about the leader, then?"

"Leave the column blank." By the look on his crumpled-walnut face, Henshaw was becoming sadly confused, and Tom Stillwell spelled it out for him, gently and firmly. "Print the official hand-out about Murumba as it came in. Give it a box on the front page. But no other comment, and no follow-up. Then leave my first leader blank."

"But what's it all mean, Mr. Stillwell?"

"It means I've had enough, lad." Tom Stillwell, rising to his feet, smiled at the old, forlorn ruin opposite him. "I'll tell you something I worked out this morning. I'm not claiming it's original." He drew a deep breath: a long sigh for Pharamaul, for lunchtime brandy, for the crash of many public and private hopes. "It's never too late to wake up—that's what I worked out. It's never too late to realize when they're making a right tit out of you. Once you swallow that, everything else is easy."

It was one of those marvellous, pearly African mornings, when the assured and confident sun chose to rise slowly and gently, setting the eastern ocean well aglow before it went to work on the dewy cobwebs of the island itself. The small house which had been Tom Stillwell's home for more than ten years also came to life slowly and gently, with a wisp of blue smoke from the stoked-up kitchen stove, and a muffled alarm bell from a bed-side clock, and the sound of running water, and then a whining creak as the front door opened.

Tom Stillwell, in his rumpled pyjamas, came out on to the polished red *stoep* just as the expected paper-boy trotted up the garden path.

The boy, a small sharp capitalist who ran his paper-round as tautly as if he were studying to be a cost-accountant, grinned up at him as he reached the steps.

"Papers, *barena*."

"Thank you."

"Tuppence extra for last week. Colour supplement."

"I'll leave it out for you."

"Thank you, *barena*."

He ran off again towards his laden bicycle, while Tom Stillwell sat down on the swing-seat and unfolded the newspapers. There were two of them, as usual—his own *Times of Pharamaul*, and the

Rand Daily Mail, which came in every day on the plane from Windhoek.

He took up the *Times* first. This was an important hour—perhaps the most important hour of his life—and he wanted to relish it before it fled for ever. He saw within a moment that Henshaw had done his job properly. There on the front page, neatly boxed in, was the bald announcement of Prime Minister Murumba's death; and there, inside, was the accusing blank space, two whole columns long and wide, which should have held his own leader, which should have said something important about this undoubted crime.

In his own newspaper, he had been silenced, and the crime was passed off as innocent truth. But the other paper had spoken up for him. Friend George Maginnis of the *Rand Daily Mail* had really done him proud.

The *Mail* gave prominence to the official death announcement, as a news item, and underneath had added: "See Editorial Comment, p. 12." On page 12, there was a short italicized lead: "*We are glad to reprint, from the* Times *of Pharamaul, Editor Thomas Stillwell's comments on the circumstances surrounding Prime Minister Murumba's death.*"

Then there was a nicely-spread headline:

"CRIMINAL LIARS!"

Then came his own leader.

"On another page, readers will have seen the official announcement of the death in prison of Prime Minister Murumba. We cannot guess what our readers' reaction will be, but we are strongly aware of our own.

"It is the duty of this newspaper to rake over the disgusting rubbish contained in this bulletin, and place it under the microscope.

"It contains four separate and distinct lies.

"*First*, that Prime Minister Murumba was arrested 'on suspicion of plotting against State.' THIS IS NOT TRUE! He was arrested because he would not condone the wasteful display, the corruption, and the tyranny of President Dinamaula's rule, and he dared to stand up and say that he could not continue in office unless a halt was called to such misconduct. The private defiance earned the public disgrace.

"*Second*, that Prime Minister Murumba 'died of heart failure while in police custody.' THIS IS NOT TRUE! Certainly this brave man was in police custody, but he did not die of heart failure. For many months he had been beaten, and tortured, and starved, in an effort to make him confess to nonexistent crimes. At the end, still in solitary confinement, he died a broken and abused old man—and it must not be forgotten that, even as these words are read, many of the hundreds of political prisoners who lie rotting in Port Victoria jail are also being beaten and tortured.

"*Third*, that Prime Minister Murumba 'had been under doctor's care for some months.' THIS IS NOT TRUE! We have sworn evidence from another prisoner, released four days ago, that Chief Murumba was being refused all medical aid.

"*Fourth*, that Prime Minister Murumba 'made a full confession of all his crimes.' THIS IS NOT TRUE! Chief Murumba was a man of deep conscience. He would never plot against the State, nor would he confess to crimes which did not exist. For his own stubborn honour he died; and much of the honour of Pharamaul died with him.

"There is an old proverb in the north of England which runs: '*Clogs to clogs in three generations.*' Clogs are the shoes of poor people; and the proverb means that unless he behaves honourably and prudently, the grandson of a poor but successful man will throw away all the efforts of his father and his grandfather, will waste the precious past, and will sink back into poverty again.

"There is a danger, in Pharamaul, that our own proverb, our own epitaph, will be: '*Tribe to tribe in three generations*,' that the ancient, bloodthirsty tribal rule, which was relaxed by Maula the Great, rejected by his son Simaula, but now revived by his grandson Dinamaula, will lead this country back to the evil times of a hundred years ago, when

Pharamaul was an iron-fisted tyranny, when no man could raise his voice against his ruler without spilling his own blood.

"Many times in the past, this newspaper has spoken out against the creeping dictatorship of the present government of Pharamaul. Now we have been brought face-to-face with our last crossroads.

"Unless we wish to become, for ever, a nation of what we crudely call *rau bachas*—tail-waggers, bottom-wavers, wretched slaves fawning upon men whom we have elevated to the status of gods—then it is time to call a halt.

"We can best do honour to our first political martyr, the late Prime Minister Murumba, by denouncing, bringing to judgement, and punishing the wicked régime which has murdered him!"

He read it with slow satisfaction, and at the end—for all its grim subject-matter—he was smiling. He had dealt his best blow, and it had not missed. . . . Presently he walked back into the house, and woke his wife; and when they had drunk their coffee in the early sunshine, they went on with their packing.

The police had a wild and woolly time rounding up copies of the *Rand Daily Mail*, which was read by a fair-sized *élite* who wanted to know a little more about the outside world than the *Times of Pharamaul* had space for. The *Mail* had disappeared from the newsstands by mid-morning; street sellers were ordered to surrender all their stocks to the nearest police station; and then there began a series of swift raids on private houses, to impound as many copies of this disgusting libel as could be tracked down.

At the Port Victoria Club it was found that some unknown opportunist had already absconded with it. Up at the Palace, it was ceremonially burnt on a garden bonfire. Tom Stillwell himself left his own copy in a prominent position on the front *stoep*. But by the time the police discovered it, he and his wife were already seated in their Johannesburg plane, waiting for the doors to be closed and the taxiing to begin.

There was, at the very end, a moment of exquisite farce. The passenger door of the plane was slammed shut, and then almost immediately opened again. There was some shouting, and a panting policeman appeared inside the aircraft. He walked along the aisle till he came to Tom Stillwell's seat; then, with a very stern look, he thrust a piece of paper towards him.

"What's this?" Stillwell asked.

"Deportation order," answered the policeman. And as Stillwell made no move to accept it, he shouted: "Take it! Take it!"

"I don't need a deportation order," said Stillwell. "I'm leaving of my own accord."

"You must take it!"

"No, thank you."

"If you do not take deportation order, you will not be allowed to leave!"

After that, it seemed proper to round off the joke by complying. In flight, sipping an early drink and holding his wife's hand, he read that his offense was "endangering the safety of the Republic by spreading false rumours," and that if he ever returned to Pharamaul he would face imprisonment, for up to five years.

While policemen poked through a baffling jungle of files, and secret talks went on, and orders filtered down from the highest in the land, there was no issue of the *Times of Pharamaul.* Then, after two blank days, it reappeared on the streets and in the shops, as suddenly as it had dropped from sight.

There was a slightly new look to it, principally on the front page, where the masthead now included a head-and-shoulders drawing of President Dinamaula, and underneath a banner with a rather long motto: "Total Loyalty! Total Respect! Total Vigilance!"

Its lead story, on the day of its reappearance, was the promulgation of special regulations for newspaper and other conduct, with penalties attached. These new laws were four in number, and quite explicit.

"There will be no mention of political parties which are now disbanded—

"There will be no defamation of members of Government—

"There will be no printing of false statements, rumours, or reports calculated to bring officials into disrepute—

"Penalty: A fine of £250, or two years' imprisonment, or both.

"There will be no statements which cause alarm or hostility—"Penalty: Five years' imprisonment."

On the center page, Koffie Sanka, the new editor, had tried his hand at a leading article.

"Our readers, who are our dearest possessions," he began buoyantly, "will in future notice many changes in their very own newspaper. The harsh tyranny and ambitious maneuvers of the former editor have been ended. There will be no more vile rumours, no more stupid criticism of Government. From now onwards the *Times of Pharamaul* will be written BY loyal Maulas FOR loyal Maulas!

"This is a very fine moment to pay our respectful tribute to the greatest Maula of all, our own President. Few may realize that his fame is known far beyond this country. It is not an exaggeration to say that the earth trembles as the Lord Protector speaks!

"But it must be noted that his greatest love and care is for his own country, and so it is time to sound a warning. So far the Lord Protector has been very patient, in the face of little men who insult him, and bigger men who would like to take his place. So far, the Leopard has rested motionless upon the throne, his haunches not yet flexed, his claws still sheathed!

"But in face of shameless provocation, this will not always be so! We have printed elsewhere the new laws, based on the laws of our great good neighbour, Sierra Leone, which have been passed so that our rulers may be protected from insults and scandalous attacks.

"But there can be more than insults! There can be treason! So let all the opposition take warning! If there is treason anywhere, whether in our capital city where the jail is full of miserable dogs of traitors, or in the north where certain hyenas have taken refuge, it will be hunted down and it will be crushed without mercy!

"In this our first message, we demand for our Lord Protector all the tributes which you will find on our front page: 'Total loyalty! Total respect! Total vigilance!' "

4

She was coming to him at last! Paul Jordan, sitting in his Palace office with the doors firmly shut, read and re-read the magic cable from New York. It was easy, and delicious, to conjure up Frances Hoy's blessed voice as he read:

"All fixed. Arriving via Windhoek 9 p.m. Saturday 28th. Book me in at the Jordan-Hilton. All love. Frances.

She was coming to him at last, and there were only three short days to go.

Paul put the telegram down on his desk, and began to consider a traditional problem, the how and the where. There was no Jordan-Hilton available, in his own confined world; he lived in a small set of rooms at the Palace, and he could no more have introduced Frances Hoy there than he could have reserved her a room at the club. It must be the hotel or nothing—"the hotel" being an old-fashioned, crumbling, delightful relic of nineteenth-century colonial living, the Prince Albert.

He began to think about the Prince Albert, in a little more detail. If he booked her into a single room, it would hardly be possible for him to go up to it. If he booked single rooms for both of them, it would alert the management, who knew who he was, and what he was, and were quite capable of ringing up the Palace and asking why the President's A.D.C. wanted a hotel bedroom in Port Victoria when he had some very superior accommodation of his own.

The only answer was a suite. There, he could join Frances in her sitting-room, with a reasonable degree of propriety. After that, who was to know what was going on? Who would dare to try to find out? Who would bother them, when they emigrated, as swiftly as possible, from the sitting-room to the bedroom?

Encouraged by such marvellous daydreams, he presently rang up the Prince Albert and booked a suite for Miss Hoy. Then he settled down to wait. It was wonderful to have daydreams of any kind, to counteract the poisonous atmosphere up at the Palace, to counteract Lucy Help.

Lucy Help had never given up. She had found no substitute for what she called "being laid by the aide," and when Paul grew tired of it, and then disgusted, and had finally contracted out, she never came to terms with the astonishing withdrawal. There had been some terrible scenes, during which she seemed entirely careless of the fact that, in a listening, alert Palace, avid for scandal, full of servants, full of privileged and envious spies, every word could have been overheard.

Lucy was in a strong position, and she knew it, and she pressed it for all it was worth. There was one final, awful confrontation, on the very day that Frances Hoy was due to arrive. Though it started with reasonable good humour on both sides, the steep nose dive into conflict which followed was the crudest she had ever made him endure.

She came into his office towards noon, in a pair of flower-patterned shorts which clung to all significant areas like a loving leech, and a halter designed more for urgent containment than for coverage. She took up her usual perch, on one corner of his desk, and exclaimed:

"Christ, it's so bloody hot in this dump! How do you manage to stay cool?"

"Will power," he answered, reacting to the friendly approach. "I just pretend it isn't so awful after all."

"That's all right for you. Will power is what you've got. I never had any." She leant forward, bringing all her equipment within striking distance. "How about a call for Help, one of these days?"

Quickly he was on guard again. He should have had more sense. . . . "You know how it is, Lucy. There are too many people watching."

"They were *watching*, as you call it, when you first brought that nice subject up. But we still managed to make out, didn't we?"

"God knows how. Honestly, I don't think it's possible now."

"Why not? What's changed?"

"Just that every time it happened, we were taking more and more chances."

Her eyes, her mouth, her whole face grew sullen and discontented. "Well, it hasn't happened for a hell of a long time, has it? Christ, I'm growing cobwebs, just where it matters most! What am I meant to do?—sit around like a dummy, eating chocolate creams, getting fat like that poor old cow of a wife of his?"

"You're not getting fat."

"How would you know? You haven't had a test run for months." She made another forward movement, so that her taut bosom came within a few inches of his mouth. "How about finding out what sort of shape I'm in?"

"Really, we'd better not, Lucy."

"Don't give me that!" She was suddenly furious. "Give me something else instead! Give me something to work on! I want a white one, damn you! A big white one, not a little bit of burnt wick! I'm telling you straight—you follow me upstairs, and get plugged in, pronto! Or it'll be the worse for you."

He stood up, and backed away from her. He had never known such lustful fury in any human being. "That's ridiculous. It's much too dangerous."

"It'll be too dangerous if you don't!"

"What do you mean?"

She was staring at him with glowering eyes. "Work it out, you dope! What's happened to all your pals? Crump—kicked out! Stillwell—kicked out! Bracken—due for the skids, any moment. I told you, I warned you it was going to happen, didn't I? Well, now it could be my turn to pull some strings. Do *you* want to be kicked out?"

Paul had had enough. "As a matter of fact, there's nothing that would please me more. I'm sick of this place, and sick of this job, and I want to get back to doing something worth while. They can kick me out, as soon as they like."

"You mean, in disgrace? What about the good little sailor boy? What about the record?" Suddenly Lucy changed her tune. She got up from the desk, and came towards him. "Paul, just do what I want, lay me good a couple of times, and I swear to God I'll see you're sent home. With everything O.K. With a medal if you want one, for Christ's sake! For distinguished service. But I've got to have the service first. Know what I mean?"

"Not from me." His disgust made him speak very roughly indeed. "The answer, once and for all, is no."

Lucy turned away, as if defeated. Then she whipped round again, still fighting. "And I know why the answer is no! You lousy liar. It's not because it's dangerous at all. It's that girl! Isn't it?"

He was struck by a dreadful guilt and fear. Could she have found out about Frances Hoy? Did she know that the plane was due that very evening? Did she know about the suite at the Prince Albert? There was a sudden, terrible possibility that the Palace, that colossal whispering gallery of rumour and gossip, had somehow got hold of the details, and that Lucy Help was in on his secret. After a pause, he asked, very warily:

"What girl?"

"You know bloody well what girl! That Chinese cracker you touched off in New York. You've still got a yen for her, haven't you?" And as Paul did not answer: "Well, it's too late for hot pants now! You should have got rid of it while you were there. You'll just have to settle for me. How about it?"

She did not know. Thank God, she did not know. . . . While Lucy, still fuming, was waiting for an answer, Paul walked out of his office, and, before long, out of the Palace altogether. He need not come back that night—and he thanked God, with special fervour, for that as well.

Frances was thinner than he remembered, and paler also; the faint, delicate shadows under her eyes made her look like a tired child. When they moved into each other's arms behind the closed door of the suite, he could almost feel the weariness in her slim body. But her shining eyes and clinging mouth were the very same. She was not less lovely, not less adored, not less wanted, from their very first touching.

"Yes, I'm thinner," she murmured, when she felt his hands moving over her shoulders. "I've been pining away, that's all. But now I'm going to put it all back again. Very quickly. Starting now."

"You're beautiful," he said, and kissed her again. "Was it a bad journey?"

"Not really. Accra was like an oven. And we had rather a long wait at Windhoek. I don't recommend the Non-European lounge there."

"Oh God! What an awful idea!"

"Never mind. It's all over now." Her arms tightened round him. "Oh love, I love you so much! It's wonderful to be with you again!"

"Have you had dinner?"

"Sort of. Enough, anyway." Her soft body was moving against his, in a well-remembered, most precious way. "Shall I unpack first? Or not?"

"Not."

"Instant Pinkerton."

"Yes, please."

But they had scarcely lain down on the wide bed, with his

hands touching her beautiful breasts, and hers stroking him to-wards an assured ecstasy, and she had only just whispered: "It doesn't matter if it's quick, like the first time," when there was a loud knocking on the outer door of the suite.

Its crude violence made them draw apart, and they lay motion-less in the darkness, shocked to silence, as the knocking was re-peated, seeming even more insistent.

"It must be a mistake," Paul said softly, after a moment of confusion. "Or some stupid mix-up with the room numbers. Don't worry, darling. They'll go away."

"Oh love," she said. "It would be *now!*"

She reached out her gentle hands to him again, and as she did so they heard a key snapped into the distant lock, and the lock turned, and the suite door open. There were voices, and then footsteps crossing the sitting-room. Then the knocking fell heavily on the bedroom door itself.

Paul switched on the bedside light and spoke in a whisper. "I'll have to get dressed, and see what it is. They must have used a pass key. But it can't be anything."

"All right," she answered, in the same confederate tone which, sadly, seemed to debase the moment altogether. "I think I'll dress too."

A voice on the other side of the door called out: "This is the manager. Open the door, please."

Paul was drawing his clothes on swiftly, while Frances, at a sign from him, went through into the bathroom. The voice came again, louder: "Open your door, please." He saw the handle turning to and fro, and it seemed an appalling intrusion, even though the door was secured with an old-fashioned draw-bolt, and could not be opened from the other side.

He tried to decide whether to answer, how to act in such a wretched situation. But while he drew on his coat, and still hesi-tated, his mind was made up for him by a second voice, a different voice, a voice he recognized. It said, loudly and harshly:

"Lieutenant Jordan! Open this door. Or it will be broken down."

An unreasoning, guilty panic took hold of him. This was im-possible, this was *awful!* . . . He stood irresolute before the door, and saw its handle twisting again; and then Frances came out of the bathroom, dressed as she had been when she arrived, her face painfully tense, and he made a signal with his hands, meaning *Lock the door after me,* and when she nodded, he drew back the bolt and stepped into the sitting-room.

Instantly he pulled the door shut after him, and heard the bolt pushed home with a solid click. Then he turned to face the intruders. He recognized the manager, a fussy be-spectacled Maula who had hitherto been a friend. He was already prepared, though incredulously, for the second figure. It was the towering form of Colonel Mboku.

Something slotted swiftly into place, like the door-bolt behind him. This could only be Lucy's doing. She must have found out somehow, or been told; and so she, and the Palace grapevine, and now this big brute of a policeman, had combined to ruin everything.

The crude trick made him very angry, and thus defiant. He stood in front of the door, and looked from one to another of his visitors. For some reason he wished that he were in uniform, like Colonel Mboku. The situation, unpleasant and degrading, needed all the backing he could muster. But there was only one line to take, anyway.

"Good evening, Colonel," he said coldly. He had always loathed the policeman—just a big bastard of a sergeant, a born drill-pig, and now a man of crushing authority. He turned his fire instantly on the manager. "What is the meaning of this? Why have you come in?"

The manager, perhaps unused to counterattack in such delicate circumstances, blinked his eyes several times. But then he rallied quickly. "It was reported that the hotel rules were being broken," he said. "This is not your suite. It is the lady's suite. We cannot have this sort of behaviour at the Prince Albert."

"What sort of behaviour?" Paul was more aware of Colonel Mboku's sardonic attention than of anything else, and resolutely he ignored it. "We were not causing a disturbance. We were not giving any trouble. What's this all about?"

"It is forbidden to have men in the bedroom," the manager insisted. "The lady must come out. She must leave the hotel immediately."

"But that's ridiculous!" Already a cold despair was beginning to take hold of him. This was really serious: the trap had sprung, and it gripped them both cruelly. "You know you had no business to open the door of this suite without permission."

Colonel Mboku spoke at last, with insolent authority. "It was done under my orders."

Paul faced his enemy, and did not bother about politeness. "What's it got to do with you? How does it concern the police?"

Mboku nodded towards the bedroom door, his expression contemptuous. "That sort of thing? It does not concern me at all. It is not a police matter. It is a matter of morals. If we had to take action every time a girl lay on her back, we would not get much sleep. Less than the girl! But there is something else which does concern me. I was told that you were in the hotel, and I am delivering a message from the President. You are to return to the Palace at once."

"But I'm not on duty tonight."

"It is an order."

The manager chimed in. "And the lady must come out! It is disgraceful!" He was beginning to shout, wanting to reclaim the center of the stage, the only important part of this invasion. "It is a scandal! She must leave at once! Both of you must leave! We cannot allow——"

Behind him, Paul heard the bolt being withdrawn. As he turned, the door opened, and Frances Hoy came out of the bedroom.

He could only love and admire her composure, which was brave and absolute. He could only rage inwardly at the horrible, shameful moment, as the two men stared at her—the manager with shocked distaste, Mboku with lascivious and insulting eyes. Paul could almost hear the coarse, disgusting speculation—had they done it yet, had they been interrupted in the middle, had they finished already when the door was unlocked? . . . Frances, who must inevitably have been aware of this, remained calm and expressionless, and this seemed to provoke the manager, who said in a voice grotesquely excited:

"This is disgraceful behaviour! The Prince Albert is not like this. It is forbidden to have men in the bedroom. This is not China! You must leave at once."

She said, quietly: "Very well," and walked back into the other room.

Colonel Mboku, robbed of his pleasurable moment, turned to Paul again. "And you are to report to the President."

"I will do nothing of the sort!" Paul answered furiously. "I will look after Miss Hoy! I will not have her bullied and harassed like this!"

Mboku shrugged his gross shoulders. "Please yourself. The President did not place you under arrest. Not at this time. But I have given you his order. You must take the consequences of disobeying it."

"Out!" said the manager. "I give you ten minutes!"

When they had gone, Paul helped her to collect her things, unable to speak for shame and sorrow, and then they went down to his car, pursued by stares and whispers as they passed through the lobby. It was after eleven o'clock, and there was no other hotel he could take her to. He drove her to their only known refuge, the Brackens.

They were followed all the way by a police car, clinging stealthily, using its sidelights only. But as they drew up at the house the trailing car peeled off and moved away, with the driver talking busily into a hand microphone.

The Brackens were marvellous, as Paul had known they would be. There was a warm welcome from Nicole, and the minimum number of questions, just enough to establish the gruesome facts; and after that it was the spare room for Frances, and a campbed in the sitting-room for himself, and, very soon, brief and understanding goodnights for them both.

Paul allowed her time to get into bed, and then he went up to make sure she was all right. Frances was sitting up against her pillow, in a nightdress which she had once "bought for him" in New York; under its pale transparency her brown body glowed with soft, sensual appeal. But she looked so unutterably weary that he knew they would only say goodnight, and that he would leave her to sleep alone.

She was too exhausted, and they were both too shocked, for love-making. The scene in the hotel had been so ugly, so brutal, that it must still cast a shadow between them, forbidding all love until time itself had done some cleansing.

She held out her arms, and he went into them as if into a safe harbour, and kissed her, and held her close. But he said, immediately:

"Shall we just sleep tonight?"

"I think so, love. If you don't mind."

"You know I don't."

He could feel her body still tense, still outraged. "Darling, who was that awful man?"

Within his arms, she had shivered as she asked the question, and he tried for lightness when he answered: "Some call him Merci Beaucoup. Others call him Field-Marshal McLuhan. I call him the biggest bastard on God's earth. Actually he's Colonel Mboku, the head of the police."

"What a horrible brute! He was enjoying it!"

"Try to forget about him, darling."

"That'll take some doing."

"I know. . . . Bedtime now?"

"Yes." She held up her face, like a dutiful, tired child. But she was still brave, and loving, and thinking of him. "I'm glad I came, Paul, all the same. I'll show you soon, I promise."

In the morning, the ordained end came swiftly. Just after 7 a.m., a dispatch rider on a monstrous khaki motorcycle came roaring up to the Brackens' front gate, and delivered two letters from a brass-bound pouch. One was on embossed Palace note-paper, the other stamped "Immigration Control." They both had to be signed for.

The first told Lieutenant Paul Jordan, R.N., that he was dismissed from his post as aide-de-camp to His Excellency the President, and that the disgraceful circumstances of his removal would be reported to the appropriate authorities in the United Kingdom.

The second informed Miss Frances Hoy that since the new regulations regarding entry visas for people of Asian origin had not been complied with, she was thereby declared a prohibited person and was to leave Pharamaul forthwith.

"Asian origin!" Frances exclaimed, when she had read the letter which Paul had brought up to her. "What the hell? I'm an American citizen, aren't I?"

She had bounced so swiftly from sleep into indignant wakefulness that Paul could not help laughing.

"Oh, darling! Does this mean war?"

"I wish it did. And what's all this about new regulations?"

"That means, new since last night."

"What a racket!" But she was now reading, with a frown, the letter which Paul himself had received. "Darling, this isn't very good, is it? I mean, sending in a report about you?"

"It's not going to help much." Yet he was already weighing his freedom, shared with Frances, against a career which seemed to have come to a dreary halt anyway, and he could not feel too downcast. "Don't forget, I'll have my own story to tell. And we both want to leave, don't we?"

"I want to go anywhere with you."

"Then we ought to be drinking champagne."

Downstairs, he found David and Nicole already up, and waiting for him in the sitting-room. Champagne was not on the breakfast menu, but an early cup of coffee enlivened them all. Paul gave them both the letters to read, and Nicole was the first to react.

"But Paul, how awful for her! To be pushed out like that."

"I don't think she minds very much. Though as an American citizen she takes a pretty dim view of being called an Asian." He thought for a moment. "As a matter of fact, that's not really true. She's very proud of her Chinese ancestry. You ought to hear her some time. She's Chinese-American, and that means the best of both worlds!"

"She really is a gorgeous girl," said Nicole. "And sweet, too. Is this serious, though?"

"Very serious."

"But Paul, that's marvellous!" Nicole, still an ardent member of the trade union, could be enthusiastic about other people's marriages even at half-past seven in the morning. "I thought we'd never get you off!"

"Well, thanks."

"You know what I mean."

David, like Frances Hoy earlier, had been frowning over the letter from the Palace. "This could be pretty rough on you, Paul," he said. "I don't like the sound of it at all."

"It's wonderful, actually. It means we can both leave together."

"But that stuff about being dismissed in disgraceful circumstances."

"I'll just have to sweat it out."

There was a sound of skimming feet in the corridor, and

Martha, her pigtail flying, her dressing-gown streaming out behind her, rushed into the room.

"Mummy, Mummy!" she exclaimed. "A Chinese lady just came out of the bathroom!"

"I know, dear."

"But *Mummy!*"

"It's just someone staying here. Now run along and get dressed."

When Martha, still thunderstruck, had gone, David said: "I suppose you'll have to leave today. *She* will, anyway. And if you want to go with her——"

"There's the noon plane to Johannesburg," said Paul. "I'm going to catch that if it kills me. After that, we can take the South African Airways flight to London. There's one every night."

"You know, I think I'll come with you," David said—and his own astonishment almost matched Nicole's. "I'd like to tell your admiral what a good job you've done here, and try to spike all this nonsense. And I *must* talk to London myself."

8: RETURNING TO LONDON FOR ROUTINE CONSULTATIONS

DAVID BRACKEN could not decide whether he liked London because the spring weather was so gorgeous, or because Pharamaul had lately become so dreadful. Walking along the path bordering St. James's Park lake, with the view divided between the serried ranks of ducks conning the children out of their bread crusts, the pre-lunch lovers writhing on the grass, the staid citizens, bowler-hatted like himself, averting their eyes from nature, and the sunlight warming the hallowed spread of the Horse Guards Parade, he decided that, just for once, he was perfectly happy in this tidy paradise.

How safe it all was, how calm and secure. How settled was the pattern, how wonderful the policemen. . . . Now, just at this moment of April and tranquil ease, he preferred it above everything else. Just for once, he did not feel he was in exile, and he did not, for a moment, want to be back in Port Victoria.

He had been in London for nearly two weeks, working moderately, relaxing gently, enjoying the change of pace and air. He had decided, from the very first day he arrived, to take his time over the visit; and if, unflatteringly, some other people seemed to have this same idea of non-urgency, that had not altered his intention. The visit, which in Pharamaul had seemed a matter of emergency, was proving quietly useful; and now at last he was on his way to the promised interview with Sir Goronwy Griffith, head of the Scheduled Territories Office section—an interview which he hoped would prove to be the most useful of all.

It was true that the London visit had started unpromisingly, and that his first welcome had not been encouraging. He found that the man he had to deal with, initially, at the S.T.O. was Charles Seaton, the former District Commissioner at Shebiya, and Charles Seaton, now on his way up in the world, had altered notably.

In shorts and a bush jacket, working hard and patiently to make something out of his modest empire, he had been rather an attractive character. Now, installed in a comfortable corner at head office, he was on his way to becoming a comfortable cat.

"I wish you'd given us more warning, old boy," was his first greeting, when David, after a long tour of the Commonwealth Office's lofty, echoing corridors, had finally tracked him down. "We're up to our eyes in work here!" He pushed to one side the copy of the *Financial Times* which had been lying in front of him. "I'd have thought you would have written, or sent a telegram."

"I only decided on the spur of the moment," David answered. He had been taken aback both by the words and the manner; Charles Seaton had already assumed the mantle of the man at the center of things, and David, a lifelong man-on-the-outer-edge, had never quite lost his juvenile awe of the contrast. Here in the S.T.O. they pulled the strings; out there one had to jump whenever the tug was felt. It had come to seem as natural as the solar system. But damn it all, Charles Seaton. . . . "There are a lot of problems I want to discuss urgently."

"Urgently" was evidently not a popular word hereabouts, and Seaton's first reaction was a slight frown. His other reaction was to ignore it for the time being. He asked, in the superior tone of a superior person:

"How's my old stamping ground, up at Shebiya?"

"That's one of the things I want to talk about. There's a definite——"

"And young what's-his-name?—Pemboli? How's he getting on? Shaping up all right?"

"He's doing very well. I put him up for C.M.G., as you know."

"Oh, yes." Seaton affected to be coming to terms with a stiff problem. "I knew there was something. . . . We decided not to go ahead with that, for the moment. A little too early, don't you think?"

"I wouldn't have put his name forward if I'd thought it was too early," David answered, nettled. "I thought you wanted the new local people to get that sort of recognition as quickly as possible."

"Oh, quite! But dash it all, Pemboli! He's only just taken over my old job. He's *learning*."

"You mean, he's got to join the usual queue?"

"Well, that's one way of putting it."

"I imagine you'll get yours first."

Charles Seaton, slightly pink, reacted with lofty detachment. "I don't think we need go into that."

"All right. Let's get back to Pemboli. A few honours and awards spread about in Pharamaul might do a lot of good. They might make my job easier, for a start. We're having a great deal of trouble, and there's plenty more to come."

"Trouble? There's been nothing much in your dispatches about that, surely? In fact"—Seaton put his fingertips together, like a judicious schoolmaster—"we don't seem to be getting much from you, of any sort."

"That's because I can't get any confidential stuff through to you."

"Isn't that a matter of organization?"

"It's a matter of a Secretariat which isn't under my sole control. The people I would be complaining about have access to all the files. They wouldn't scruple to open my letters."

"You're exaggerating, I imagine?"

"*No I am not!*" David was finding it difficult to keep his patience, in the face of this bland, well-tailored non-acceptance of faraway problems. "You've got to realize that things in Pharamaul are in a very bad state. That's the only reason I'm here."

"Poor old Pharamaul," said Seaton. "Our eternal problem child. . . . It really has been a nuisance, hasn't it? All it does is cost us money—and of course a great deal of complicated work. And the people are so *stupid!* My God, when I think of the fantastic amount of trouble I had, organizing that ridiculous election——"

"There's been a steady deterioration since then, as you must know already." David, finding that Seaton really was getting on his nerves, tried to cut this affected nonsense short. "But I think things are coming to a serious crisis, and very soon. That's why I have to see Griffith. It really is important."

"The P.U.S. is extremely busy at the moment, I happen to know." If I were the Permanent Under-Secretary, David thought, I would object rather strongly to that particular contraction. "Our master," Seaton went on, "is very zealous, very zealous indeed."

"Our master," the office jargon for the cabinet minister who was Secretary of State, was another odious affectation, in this context. Pitched somewhere between the sarcastic and the insolent, it was meant to imply that all politicians, nominally in control of their departments, were a bunch of nuisances, simple boobs-in-office, only fit to be handled and manipulated by the people who actually made the decisions and did all the work.

Seaton had really picked up the folk-culture of Whitehall very quickly. Even his tone of voice when he said "our master" and "zealous"—insincere, derisory, full of controlled impertinence—was authentic.

"Well, I want to see Griffith, busy or not," David said stubbornly.

Charles Seaton sighed. "I doubt if that's on, at this stage. Perhaps I should tell you something, which you may not know. The P.U.S. likes reading things, then talking about them. He likes people to do their homework properly, and put it all down on paper. As a factual basis for discussion, if there *has* to be a discussion. Then he knows exactly what the form is. My advice to you would be to go away, put up a full-scale brief, and let me have it. Then I'll see if I can fix up a meeting."

Suddenly David had had enough of the interview. He had come all this way, he was doing all the worthwhile work, he was taking all the load, while this lazy pompous idiot, as smooth as clotted cream, was apparently in a position to make his life even more difficult, and to patronize him at the same time. He stood up, the poor country cousin asserting his pride at last.

"There'll be a meeting, whether you fix it up or not!" he snapped. "That's what I've come for. If I say something's important, then it's important. I'll write it all out, if that's what the Under-Secretary prefers. Then I want to talk to him about it."

Seaton, whose hard-gloss finish must have been thin as well as new, backed away instantly. "All right," he said, appeasingly. "Let's do it that way. I'll push it all I can, you may be sure of that."

"And I can't work properly in my hotel. I'll want an office here, or part of one, and a girl to take dictation."

"All right."

"And I'll start tomorrow morning."

Something quite different had made him feel a little better. At least the lovers were happy.

He met Paul and Frances in the downstairs bar of Scotts in Piccadilly Circus, traditional haunt of wandering colonials and other exiles who preferred the well-trodden water-hole. There, drinking equally traditional whisky sours in one of the oak-panelled alcoves, they gave him their news.

"We're going to be married!" they told him, and waited with shining eyes, as breathless as every other pair of confessed lovers in the world, for the amazement, the delight, the sheer wonder of it all to be expressed in suitable terms.

David did his best. "Well, that's marvellous!" he said. "I *am* glad! I hope you'll be very happy!" Nicole would have done this better, he decided; like most women, she could still coo over the news of young love as if it were the very first time it had ever blossomed. "When's it going to be?"

"Not for ages, I'm afraid." It was Frances Hoy who gave the sad part of the news, while a hand-holding Paul Jordan gazed at her with public and private rapture. "I have to work out my contract at the UN—that's three months, at least—and then I'll be going to San Francisco to get the family blessing."

"Well, at least we have one half of the family on our side," Paul said. "Mother adored you!"

"Do you really think so?"

"I'm certain! Who wouldn't?"

David Bracken, beginning to wonder why he was there at all, essayed a modest cue-line. "You've been down to see your mother already?"

"First thing we did," Paul answered. "And it was a terrific success. I doubt if Little Petherick will ever recover."

"Your mother was a bit mixed up at first," Frances said. "You know, with me suddenly arriving from Africa and everything. She said, 'I've read all about you having to leave Kenya. I think it's disgraceful! But at least you'll have lots of friends here.'"

The idea of Frances Hoy hobnobbing with turbaned, bearded bazaar-keepers deported in their thousands from Nairobi struck them all as funny enough for another round of whisky sours.

"What about the career?" David asked, after they had drunk once again to the romantic aspects of the future. "Any developments?"

"Couldn't be better," Paul answered. "Just marvellous! You talked to someone about me, didn't you?"

"Director of Officer Appointments," David answered. "An admiral, no less—I thought I'd aim high. Actually he once put me ashore in a ghastly landing-craft at Salerno, when he was a lowly lieutenant, just like you, but that's another story. Anyway, he seemed to know all about you already. He said, 'Jordan?—that's the chap who blotted his copybook in Pharamaul, isn't it?'"

"Oh God!" said Paul.

"Oh, you're famous, all right. . . . I said: 'Yes. That's the one! They used to call him the Demon Lover of Port Victoria.'" David felt that he might occupy at least part of this stage. "Actually I don't think your admiral was taking the Pharamaul story very seriously. I told him what had really happened, and the sort of job you've been doing, and at the end he said: "Sounds as though he needs a bit of sea time. And I wish to God it was me!'"

"But that's exactly what happened!" said Paul, delighted. "I'm really terribly grateful to you. When I made my call on their Lordships—I still think of them as that, only now they have some dreary title like Ministry of Defense, brackets Marine Category— the man pulled out a file the size of a helicopter pad with a horrible chunk of paper labelled Medical Reports. Then we got talking, and I said I was going to get married, and he said, 'Then it's about time you went back to sea.' So—First Lieutenant of *Ceres!* Honestly, you could have knocked me down with a bucket of suds. She's one of the new——"

"But who was Ceres?" Frances asked.

"Goddess of Agriculture. *So* appropriate."

"I want to impress them down at Pompey," she said, and they both burst into such delighted, private laughter that David felt he could safely leave them. At least something had turned out absolutely right.

Now he made his way out of St. James's Park, and, having a few minutes to spare, took the long way round to the Commonwealth Office, instead of climbing the steps into Downing Street. He skirted one edge of Parliament Square, looked up at Big Ben to check the time, and turned into Whitehall, slowing his pace to a gentle stroll.

The memory of that cheerful meeting in Scotts had to compete with something else which had happened during his stay, something so uncheerful that the contrast was depressing beyond words. He had rung up Keith Crump at his Bayswater hotel, and, after several false starts—Major Crump was out, Major Crump was in Liverpool, Major Crump would call back as soon as he was free, *Mrs.* Crump was not at the hotel—he had made contact at last. But when the brief phone call was over, he wished that he had never tried.

"I'm afraid I've got to rush, David," Crump told him straight away, in a colourless voice which sounded as far from rushing as it could possibly be. "I wish we could meet, but just at the moment my time's not my own. You know how it is."

"Is Molly with you?"

"No. She's back with her mother, for the time being."

"But you have got a job?" David asked. Crump, even in those few words, had sounded so subdued, so different, so awful—as if he had broken his mainspring, and did not expect a replacement —that David was already sorry to have made his intrusive call.

"Yes, I've got a job."

"What sort?"

"It's in security, actually."

"Well, good for you! That sounds right up your street. But can't we meet, Keith? I've still got a few more days. As many as I like, in fact."

"I'm afraid not," Crump answered, and David knew already that, if he had weeks to spare instead of days, the other man would still not want the two of them to meet. "I have to be on call pretty well all the time."

"But what's the job, exactly?"

There was a long wait on the wire. Then Crump said, in a voice ashamed and hopeless: "Nothing much. It's in security. I told you."

"But what? Government security?"

"Financial security." There was another long pause, and then: "You might as well know, old boy—it's driving an armoured van. Picking up wages from the banks, and delivering them. I had to have something, and it was all I could get. But we're really very smart—we have a uniform!"

Then he rung off.

David, nearing the entrance to Downing Street, found that his slow pace must now be checked to nothing. Unexpectedly, there was a huge crowd milling about at the street corner, and a solid line of blue police uniforms trying to seal off the approach. A television camera-unit stood sentinel near the curb, and half a dozen photographers were darting to and fro, avid for action.

The police, with arms linked, were doing their best to hold firm against a determined column of marchers, with flailing banners and screaming voices, who were trying to break through the cordon.

David, too long absent from this hub of civilization, had never seen such people before. There were men with great bushy beards, and men with matted hair hanging far below their collars; men with placards, and men with rolls of khaki bedding slung across their shoulders. There were girls in mini-skirts with the same shoulder-length hair, and girls in thigh-length boots and military capes; girls with faces of mottled lard, girls with drugged eyes who could well have been dead before they started.

They were all roaring and screaming and howling—howling for justice, howling for blood, howling for fun. There was not one of them who did not look absolutely filthy—but there was far more filth here, far more crazed indifference to the outcome of violence, than was to be seen on the atrocious surface.

It could only be called the ugliest of mob scenes. A big man in a greasy duffle-coat seemed to be conducting a private and appalling orchestra, urging on the attack with continued, strident shouts of "Wilson OUT! Wilson OUT!"; and the staccato barking sound, full of the purest hatred, was taken up by the marchers as they wrestled with the police, and butted into them, and kneed them in the groin, and tore at their helmets and their clothes.

When two police cars tried to force a passage between the attackers and their own men, they were brought to a halt as the man in the duffle-coat instantly changed his bellowing command to "Fall down! Fall down!" and men and girls all dropped like sacks in front of the car wheels.

One by one they were patiently dragged away, and dumped in the gutter, and there they began to sing. It was a dreary chant, which David had never heard before; but presently he picked out the words, and recognized them. So this was, "*We shall overcome.*" . . . As the singers came to the end of their sad, malevolent dirge, the harsh battle cry rang out again: "Wilson OUT! Wilson

OUT!" and there was another vicious surge towards the police line.

David, astounded and shocked, turned to the man nearest to him. He was a small tubby young man in rumpled blue overalls and a flat green cap like a flying saucer which had crashed for the last time; and he was grinning with simple enjoyment as he watched these fascinating goings-on in the heart of London—a crisp stone's-throw from the House of Commons, a rotten tomato-toss from No. 10 Downing Street. But when David asked him: "What on earth's happening? What's this all about?" the entranced spectator quickly turned serious and disapproving.

"It's Vietnam, mate," he answered. "Or else it's Rhodesia. Might be university grants. You never know, these days. If you ask me, I'd shoot the lot of them."

"Shoot who?"

"This lot." He jerked his thumb towards the Downing Street corner. "Students!" His face took on something like the loutish hatred of the rabble they were watching. "Going to college on my money, and then carrying on like this! Why aren't they studying, that's what I want to know? I'd like to see the police really take the piss out of them." There was a sudden howl from the crowd, still trying to break through, and the solid blue line wavered. One of the police cars started rocking from side to side, and the sound of pounding fists matched the voices for violence. "Just look at that. Students! Don't tell me!"

"I want to get through," said David. But it was obvious that he could not. "I didn't think this sort of thing was allowed in Downing Street."

"Why not?" the man asked belligerently. "Why shouldn't they create a bit in Downing Street? It's a free country, isn't it? It all comes out of taxes. I'd like to shoot Wilson myself, come to that."

"Why?"

"Letting in the nignogs, that's why! This used to be a white man's country, mate. Look at it now. They come in here by the million, turbans and all, twenty of them living like pigs in one room, poncing on the women, taking all the best jobs, taking our money——"

"What's your job?" David asked.

"Redundant," said the man. "National assistance. Nine pound a week, that's my lot. I was stigmatized." He suddenly raised his voice, like a cock which must crow or crack, and joined the idiot chorus: "Wilson OUT! Wilson OUT!" Then he turned back to David again. "Students! Don't you tell me! I'd like to sack the lot of them. If *I'd* gone to college, there wouldn't have been any of this lark!"

He would not even try to get through, David decided, and as quickly as he could he left the stomach-turning scene and doubled back, round Charles Street and into the Foreign Office entrance. Now he was late instead of early, and he cursed all scruffy demonstrators who barred the way of honest citizens.

With the remembrance of the hateful riot fresh in his memory, he was beginning to like London a little less. But when, in the foyer of the Commonwealth Office, he was given the message, he began to like it not at all.

The porter knew who he was, and had the words ready.

"There's a message for you, Mr. Bracken. Will you see Mr. Seaton as soon as you arrive."

"But I have an appointment with the Permanent Under-Secretary," David objected. "And I'm late already. I'd better see Mr. Seaton afterwards."

The porter glanced down at a sheet of paper in front of him, though it was obvious that, as a man of universal competence, he hardly needed to do so.

"Sagronwee went out half an hour ago," he answered, and David wished he could have whipped off the difficult name so neatly. "He won't be back till after lunch. That's why Mr. Seaton left a message."

There wasn't any comeback to that. "All right. I'll see what it's all about."

It was ten days since David had last seen Charles Seaton, and four days since the long-awaited appointment with Sir Goronwy Griffith had been confirmed. Though David had been hoping never to waste any more time with Seaton, the interview with Griffith was something on which his mind had been set, from the moment he had climbed into the plane at Port Victoria airport.

He had a little more time, as he plodded down those resounding marble corridors, to hope that this was only a short-term setback. But after that, he began to hate the day he had ever entered this dead-handed, hope-killing, corpse-lined mausoleum for his first interview, fifteen years earlier.

Charles Seaton greeted him with the kind of disarming friendliness which was itself a parody of civil service public relations, like the tax-inspector who, having ordered a delinquent to report to him without fail, opens with "Thank you so much for coming" before administering the chop.

"So good of you to drop in," Charles Seaton began, and the words, even at their face value, were so inappropriate and so phoney that David felt the cold breath of misgiving already creeping in his direction. "The P.U.S. *does* apologize for not being able to keep the appointment. But he had to go to the House to talk to our master. It's those wretched immigrants again. There's a whole *chapter* of P.Q.s coming up."

Well, that was reasonable, David thought; parliamentary questions had to be answered, and the Permanent Under-Secretary was the man who had to feed the facts into the machine. Perhaps this wasn't going to be as bad as he had suspected.

"It can't be helped," he said. "Of course I understand. I'd better come back when he can see me. Will you fix another appointment?"

"Well, actually, old boy," Seaton said, taking the first careful step across the boundary from social fantasy to hard fact, "he rather wants me to deal with it."

There was no reason why David should pretend to be pleased about this, and he did not even try.

"Well, I don't want you to deal with it. I want to talk to Griffith. I want to discuss my report."

"Oh yes, your report." The report, David now saw, was lying on the desk between them, and Seaton made an airy gesture towards it. "Jolly good, if I may say so. Situation in the proverbial nutshell, and all that. But the P.U.S. seems to think it doesn't take us much further. In fact, he doesn't *really* understand why you're here."

David was beginning to sniff the poison, and, with this odious man, he need make no secret of it. "That was your idea, wasn't it?"

"What do you mean?"

"Christ, don't fool around with me! I mean, you gave him the report, with some bloody little memorandum suggesting that it was a lot of rubbish, and he left it to you to get rid of me."

Seaton was now looking so injured, and at the same time so remote from this vulgar conflict of opinion, that David was sure he was right. After a moment, the other man said, with the correct amount of detachment:

"I can assure you that *here*"—he might have been speaking of some hallowed inner courtyard of the Vatican—"we don't do things like that. Everything is dealt with strictly on its merits. In the case of Pharamaul——"

David made an enormous effort at self-control. "I don't need a lecture on the case of Pharamaul. The case of Pharamaul is set out on those eight pages." He pointed to the report. "I sweated blood to get it exactly right, and it *is* exactly right. It shows the sort of mess the country is in. What I want to know is, what's to be done about it? What did Griffith actually *say*?"

Charles Seaton had his answer ready for this, at least.

"As a matter of fact, old boy, he's rather inclined to blame you."

David, though astonished, tried to concentrate on the small surface of fact showing above this great iceberg of nonsense. "Go on."

Charles Seaton flipped over the top few pages of the report. "A lot of this we knew already, of course, though naturally it's helpful to have it spelled out in detail. The imbalance of the economy, and so on and so forth. Clearly, there's been gross extravagance, and also—what was the phrase you used?—systematic plundering of the treasury. I rather liked that. . . . But the point is, you should have stamped on it, from the very beginning. I mean, let's face it, old boy. That's what you were there for."

"That is not true," David answered. "I stayed on because I was asked to, by the S.T.O., and by Dinamaula himself. I wasn't there as a watchdog, or as a detective either. I had no political power at all. I was there to run the civil service, to keep the machine going properly until the Maulas could take over."

"I think it's fair to say," said Seaton, "that the Maulas have done just that." He smiled a very cheerful smile, as if a point scored in the heart of Whitehall was a point scored against the whole world of darkness. "At least, they *think* they have. I might mention that, as well as giving us a local headache, Pharamaul is beginning to put the Intelligence laddies into an awful flap. You know what they're like, of course—there's a communist under every bed. Now they seem to think that the Rooshians are moving in on Pharamaul in a big way. Something about a rocket base, or some such rubbish—good heavens, as if we didn't have enough to worry about already!"

"I mentioned that as a possibility in my report," David reminded him. "All I know for a fact is that they made an outright grant of four million pounds for ten square miles, freehold. Officially it's an experimental wheat station. Judging by the security arrangements, and the amount of concrete being poured, it's nothing of the sort."

"Oh quite, quite! As a matter of fact I side-lined the bit about the concrete, and the P.U.S. said: 'Isn't there something called *hard* wheat?' which I thought not bad in the circumstances!" Charles Seaton was warming himself agreeably at the fires of recollection. "But of course, if one takes a slightly wider view, it's part of a general pattern, isn't it? I mean, there's pretty well a Russian naval base at Alexandria, this very moment. Next stop Aden, next stop Zanzibar—no, that's Tanzania now, isn't it?—and of course Zambia and Kenya seem to have sold out already. In fact, you might say"—he put his fingertips together, in the same schoolmasterish gesture he had used at an earlier meeting—"that most of the continent, which used to be coloured red on the map, really *is!* Where that's going to put South Africa, heaven knows!"

But David, in spite of wretched setbacks, was still clinging to his one little country.

"I'd like to get back to Pharamaul," he said. "You've seen my report. Presumably Griffith has read it as well. It shows pretty clearly that the country is bankrupt twice over, as well as being deeply divided internally. If things go on like this, it really could tear itself to pieces. The question is, what do we do about it? What do *I* do about it?"

"Well, I've no doubt you're right on the facts," Seaton said, as if he were initialling a hotel bill after a cursory glance at the items. "But another question is, do we have to get so worked up about them? I mean, it's only Pharamaul. . . . After all, they *are* independent, aren't they? Has it ever occurred to you that you might just be wasting your time?"

David's last call, before he beat a sad retreat, was on Sir Hubert Godbold, the honoured predecessor of Goronwy Griffith, the man who had first recruited him and last inspired his admiration; and that was desperately sad also.

Godbold, retired for nearly five years, now lived alone, in a small cottage near Winchester; and there David joined him for lunch, after hiring a car and enjoying a gentle drive through the prosperous farming country of the Hampshire Downs. It was a bright sunny day, and the countryside was beautiful, with that special sleepy warmth which England's southern countries could still display, even as they were eaten alive by progress. On any other day, in any other mood, David would have surrendered to it wholeheartedly.

But he was still in a fragile mood of mourning, twenty-four hours after his crushing defeat at the Scheduled Territories Office; and what he saw, and what he felt, and what the two of them talked about, during their long session together, seemed to do nothing but dot the i's and cross the t's of David's stupid, mistaken zeal. Signed, sealed, and delivered with polite disdain, the message had at last reached him.

With the very best motives in the world, he had backed the wrong horse; and the crowd, and the jockeys, and the trainers, and the bookmakers, and the stewards themselves were all beginning to turn their backs as they forgot about the Pharamaul Stakes, and made ready for another race, or for no race at all.

David had been looking forward to this long-promised lunch, with a man who had had as much to do with the mainspring of his life as any other human being. But before long it became, by gradual descent, part of the same dreary scene of defeat.

Sir Hubert, who was sandpapering a rickety front gate before giving it a spring coat of paint, straightened up cautiously as David's car came to a stop outside. He was dressed in a deplorable old pepper-and-salt suit, of the kind which David had not seen since he had sorted out his father's old clothes on the morrow of the funeral; he was still wearing his bedroom slippers; and he had forgotten to comb his hair.

Seeing him then, watching him as he did many times during the next four hours, David could not help feeling, with fear and compassion mixed: *Is this what I shall come to?*

Here was a man, much admired by David himself, reasonably rewarded by the great world, who had given his life to the faithful performance of duty, who had done the state some service. In his time, Godbold had had the disposal of many millions of human beings on his conscience and under his command.

Now he had come to a halt—a halt vainly masked by pretended animation; pottering about in shabby disarray, patching up a front gate which should have been thrown away, or chopped for firewood, or repaired, or replaced, years before.

The name on the front gate, the name of this singular man's last retreat, was "End Cottage." For David, as he renewed an old acquaintance, all the chronicles of vanished empire seemed to shrivel down to this mortuary label, and to a discarded man in musty, outdated clothes still fussing over an odd job of maintenance, because he had nothing better to do.

Sir Hubert Godbold, it seemed, was full of the problems of spring.

"I'm delighted you could come down," he said, as they shook hands. "Of course, I've invited you under false pretences. You're really here to help me with the weeds! A little hoeing? A little spraying? How would that suit you? Last year the nettles very nearly got ahead of me! But I'm determined to win, this year."

"It's a very nice place," said David, looking round the half-acre of bedraggled garden. "You must be enjoying yourself here."

"I'm still trying to get it shipshape," Sir Hubert answered. He led the way up the gravelled pathway, towards a one-story stone cottage with a drooping thatched roof. "Summer will be here before we know where we are! See that?" He pointed towards a lopsided birdhouse clamped precariously on to a dead tree stump. "I put that in last year. This is a wonderful place for birds. Though of course they're like children. You have to tempt them."

"How do you tempt them?" David asked, not sure whether Godbold was being serious or not.

"You must go to a lot of trouble over their food," Godbold answered promptly. "Breadcrumbs?—well, breadcrumbs are all right, particularly toasted breadcrumbs with a little butter still there. But they're rather dull as a staple diet, don't you think? Birds like something a bit more exciting. Bacon rind—yes, certainly. Beef or mutton fat, excellent! But ham fat, chopped ham

327

fat—that's the stuff to give the troops! I can assure you, David, I've come out of this front door with a cupful of chopped ham fat, and within *minutes* about thirty or forty birds are absolutely queuing up for it! Everything from magpies to wrens. And of course my own personal favourite, *parus major*. Rudely called the Great Tit. Mind you, once there's a magpie about, you don't see many of the other birds. Magpies are the real bullies——"

They enjoyed two most acceptable drinks, and then came lunch, which was slapped down in front of them by a mutinous old woman who looked at Sir Hubert as if he were the outgoing skipper of a slave ship, and at David as if one more mouth to feed must surely take her past the breaking-point. Lunch consisted of soup like warmed-up gravy, liver and bacon seemingly brought to a standstill by the fires of hell, and a broad wedge of delicious Wensleydale cheese, which not even the most malevolent of housekeepers could spoil.

"Mrs. Magnus does her best," said Sir Hubert, as he observed David's liberal helping of the last course. "One misses the Travellers' Club, of course. I get up to town about twice a month —for board meetings, and so on. Otherwise it's a very quiet life."

"But you are enjoying it?" David asked.

"*Carpe diem.*" Godbold brushed some crumbs of cheese from an untidy moustache. "Were you a classical scholar? No— it was law, wasn't it? *Carpe diem, quam minimum credula postero.* Which means, roughly: Make the most of today—you cannot trust tomorrow." Then suddenly, amazingly, his face and manner seemed to change; on the instant he came to the surface, and it was like a man waking from a drugged sleep—but waking to a full and forceful parade of his wits. "Thank you for sending me your report, David. . . . I thought it very well done—and very depressing also. Tell me, did you get anywhere with Griffith?"

Over the last of the cheese, and then coffee on a shaded porch, David poured out his full and miserable story. It was a great relief to share his burdens, and he realized how much he must have been missing people like Godbold in the last few months, the sympathetic and knowledgeable friend who would not betray him. Yet even as he gave the other man all the details, all the stages of defeat, he knew that he himself, and his report, and, probably, his whole career must be very nearly doomed.

Godbold, in decline, could never change anything in his

favour. He would sympathize, he would comment, he might even try to pull some strings. But the strings, like spiders' webs, would not draw anything after them. They would only catch the light briefly, and stretch thin, and snap, and blow away forgotten on the next wind.

When David finished his recital with the words: "So I might just as well not have come," he knew that this, the saddest of all epitaphs, was exactly true.

Sir Hubert, who had been smoking a small Dutch cigar the colour of a parched lawn ("Can't afford proper cigars, these days"), did not answer him directly. Instead, he bore down on the problem from a different angle.

"I'm afraid the S.T.O. section is going through a bad phase, at the moment," he said. "They're in retreat, naturally—as they lose their responsibilities they're being cannibalized by the Commonwealth Office. Now they're not much more than a rump administration. My successor will probably be the last Permanent Under-Secretary with these special duties."

"That means, in effect, that we've written off places like Pharamaul."

"Written off?" Sir Hubert examined the less-than-official phrase with his accustomed care. "I think that verdict is a little harsh, because of course we still give them quite substantial sums of money. But in the case of Pharamaul, I should say the feeling there is that we have done our best, and that it's time for us to be thinking about fading away. Obviously, they have rejected the past completely. But then, that's their privilege."

"But it's such a waste," said David. "Think of all the work we've done there, for over a hundred years. Think of all the money, with absolutely no return at all. Now it's all going to go down the drain."

Godbold nodded. "That is true, and sad, and one can be excused for feeling bitter about it. But if that's the way the people of Pharamaul want it . . ." his voice tailed off.

"I sometimes think you were right to oppose independence," David told him, after a pause. "You know, in the old days, when there was so much discussion about it. I wish I hadn't argued quite so hard."

"No, you must never believe that! You were on the side of the angels, though it may not look like it today. Of course, what they are doing now is a great waste, as you said—a waste of us in the past, and of Pharamaul today. But I think we must stand by what we said at the beginning. Independence can only mean exactly what it says. It's *their* country, and they're free to set it on any course they choose."

"But that doesn't mean that they have to start *stealing* as soon as the controls are off! It shouldn't be a signal for corruption, for utter stupidity! I never thought Dinamaula would go that way, or allow his people to go that way. He was so good at the beginning. We had exactly the same ideas about everything."

"You may have thought so," said Godbold. "And he may have thought so too, quite genuinely. But deep inside him, I don't think he ever got over the period of exile. So when the chance arrived, when power was put into his hands, all the resentment came to the surface, and the tendency to corruption followed."

There was a drowsy peace all over the garden. Sir Hubert's well-fed birds were singing contentedly. Bees were beginning to make their rounds, plundering in the hot sunshine. If this humble backwater was sad, by comparison with the old days, it must at least be comforting, for a man scarcely concerned with the world beyond the hedge. At this tranquil moment of time, David could almost feel himself, fatally, drifting into the same mould.

"So there's nothing more to be done? Nothing more for me to do?"

"You should work out your time faithfully." Sir Hubert smiled. "I'm sure you're going to do that anyway, because you are that kind of man—you, and thousands like you in the past. But no—basically we can do nothing more for Pharamaul. We can't put the clock back. We can't send in troops, as we did the last two times they were in chaos. 'A company of Her Majesty's Foot Guards having been brought in to quell an insurrection'—you remember the quotation. 1842, wasn't it? The result of that was years of peace, and modest prosperity. But they don't want it to be done like that any more, and now they have the final say. In fact, we *promised* them the final say."

"Then they'll just go back to the tribe again."

"Very likely. Africa seems to have rejected the black-and-white partnership idea—the idea I believed in, above everything else; the idea which was tried out in the Rhodesian Federation. That came down in ruins within a few years—and the Africans did not mind at all. In fact they were glad. They wanted to run their own show, even if they went bankrupt in the process, even if their grandchildren lived to curse them. The result is what you see—a tormented part of the world, and due for many years of the same ordeal. Pharamaul—your Pharamaul—will have to go through the same torment."

"But all we wanted to do was help them! We *were* there as partners."

"Ah, yes. That is how we see it. But there is an African memory, and it is longer and more bitter than ours, and it runs counter to our own, in every last detail. Never forget, we have done some terrible things in Africa. We may think they are forgiven and forgotten, but of course they are not. The rule of the Belgians in the Congo, of the Germans in Tanganyika, the South Africans hunting Bushmen on horseback, as if they were pig-sticking, in South-West, the British double-dealing and bloodshed with Chaka and Cetewayo, the slave trade—there is no end to the indictment. Africans remember these things, because they still tell stories about them, they still sing about them. They remember them as the Moslems still remember the crusades. That was a noble slaughter for Christ, seven centuries ago—but the Middle East has never forgotten it, the hatred is still there. And Africa still remembers—it almost relives—its own centuries of cruelty, and deceit, and theft, and bad faith, and atrocious treachery. Now they hear us say, 'We'll share your country with you!' Can you wonder that, now they have the power, the rejection is so violent, so complete?"

His voice was strong to the very end, and then, when the silence lengthened—because David could think of nothing more to say— Sir Hubert seemed to fade gently out again. He dozed for four or five minutes, while David stared round him at the garden which could not after all bring him peace; and then the old man woke with an old man's start, and smiled vaguely, and said:

"Well now—what about an attack on those weeds? And oh yes—if you would just give me a hand with the washing-up. Mrs. Magnus can never stay after twenty past one, and of course, these days one doesn't like to insist."

David drove back as dusk was falling, tired and dispirited as he had never been before. Godbold, near the end of his road, had only served to demonstrate that he himself had reached the same point of stagnation with twenty years to spare. Perhaps Crump would give him a job, hanging on to the back of his armoured van. . . . He turned in his car at the hire garage, and took a taxi to his Kensington hotel.

The Royal Belvedere, Cromwell Road, S.W.7, was not very smart. It was not very anything. It catered for overseas visitors, trapped by package tours, who had to watch their pennies, and north-country trippers for whom the word "Kensington" still conveyed a certain metropolitan *chic*. Walking up the crumbling front steps, David now felt that he could match Sir Hubert Godbold's "End Cottage" with his own End Hotel, any day of the week.

In the lobby, which was rather like the Port Victoria Club on a small, grubby scale, the snuffling porter with the wet ginger moustache intercepted him, as he was making for the lift.

"There's a gent to see you, Mr. Bracken. Says he's one of your oldest friends." The porter pointed towards the frosted glass doors of the lounge. "I put him in there."

"Thank you." David turned, and made his way down the short passage. Though it was unlikely, he hoped that it would turn out to be Keith Crump after all. At least they could go out on the town together, and whoop it up for dear old Pharamaul. But his visitor was not Crump, nor one of his oldest friends, nor even a friend of any kind. In fact it was the very last man in the world he wanted to see: Tulbach Browne of the *Daily Thresh*.

His natural reaction, given full freedom, would have been to turn right round and walk out again. But civil servants could not behave like that, however compelling the wish; and Tulbach Browne had jumped up with such alacrity as soon as he caught sight of him that David knew he was truly cornered. The other man, he observed, had not changed; the rumpled suit, the ferrety look, the air of having to deal with naught but fools and liars— all were still authentic.

Tulbach Browne took charge straight away. "You're a hard man to find," he said, as if David had been lying low for purely disreputable reasons. "I asked at all the *usual* hotels. Finally one of those clots in the Commonwealth Office came up with the right answer. For a change."

David knew that he would have to dispose of this tidily, exhausted though he was after the grim day and the traffic-choked drive back. "How did you know I was in London?"

"I tried to ring you up in Pharamaul," Tulbach Browne answered. "The secretary bird had flown. . . . I must say, you chose a damned good moment to clear out."

"What do you mean?"

Tulbach Browne smiled his unpleasant smile. "Don't tell me you haven't heard the news." And as David still looked puzzled: "You haven't a clue what I'm talking about, have you? By God, no wonder we lost the Empah! Just the north marching on the south, that's all. With all the earmarks of a civil war."

"I don't believe it."

"I didn't think you would. You chaps certainly run true to form, don't you? What do you suppose your continent is *really* like? *Song of Africa?* Moonshine on the Kalahari? Mboya meets Mgirla? Well, I've got news for you. We had a flash from Johannesburg this morning. They like to keep an eye on these things, and I can't say I blame them. There's a huge protest march coming down from Gamate, and Port Victoria is bracing up for it. In a big way. Including arming the police." Tulbach Browne's eyes suddenly narrowed, giving him a truly unpleasant look of mistrust. "Are you sure that's not why you're here?"

"No."

"Why, then?"

"Nothing special. It's just that I haven't been back for a long time."

"Mr. Bracken in London for routine consultations, eh? *Belated* consultations, one might say. May I have your reaction to this strange turn of events?"

"No."

"You express surprise? Astonishment? Stupefaction?"

"No." David was not going to be needled into anything, until he had found out the truth.

"Then you knew this was going to happen?"

"Of course not."

"Then you must be surprised, astonished, stupefied, etcetera."

David was tempted after all, by the wish to end this silly intrusion, into giving an opinion. "I should be surprised if this was anything more than an ordinary political demonstration. They're always having marches and rallies in Pharamaul. They enjoy them.

But the average northerner isn't interested in a march on Port Victoria. At this moment, he just wants to stay home."

"Well, he's not staying home. *At this moment*, he's more than halfway to Port Victoria to argue the toss about his rights, and if I know anything it'll end up in bloodshed, like all the rest of these stinking little African zoos. . . . Are you going back there?"

"Of course I'm going back."

Tulbach Browne shrugged. "No accounting for tastes. My guess is that you'd be a damned sight better off here." He looked round the shabby room, with its tarnished mirrors, its fake-leather armchairs, its marble chiming clock stopped at some forgotten half-past four. "Even here. . . . Maybe I'll be seeing you later, then?"

"Are you going out?"

"Try and stop me!" Tulbach Browne answered, with grisly relish. "I wouldn't miss this little punch-up for all the tea and toast in Whitehall!"

9: FIRM MEASURES ARE NOW BEING TAKEN

▪▪

1

LIKE A VAST ARMY of soldier-ants, intent on one target, the great tide of straggling columns pushed slowly southwards. There was not room for them all on the main road, and so some moved painfully on a pathway parallel to it, trudging in a straight Roman line which led them over hills, and across valleys, and along dried-out water-courses, and past small hut-circles which had not seen so many men since the circle had first been marked out on the parched earth, by some hopeful head-of-family dead these hundred years.

Other men followed the red-rusted railway track, now so overgrown with weeds that goats could be seen grazing on its iron pasture. These men limped and plodded along the sleepers, for mile after mile; towards sunset they moved as if they were sleepers themselves. But they, and their brothers taking the hill tracks, and their comrades treading the main highway, were united in one purpose.

In anger, in despair, in hunger, in jealousy, hatred, and humility, in simple faith and cunning calculation, they were leaving their homes, and marching upon Port Victoria, to claim what the great President had promised when he had greeted them, calling them "My people!" on that long-ago, first day of freedom—that Pharamaul, now a lion among countries, belonged to them all.

They were for the most part a ragged army, though the small contingent from Fish Village, marching in their white boiler suits with the stencilled Government markings, was smart enough to flatter any procession. They carried many banners, ragged also, and they stirred a towering cloud of yellow dust as they picked up both speed and people on their steady advance.

Father Stubbs was in the van, his brown cassock looped up to give his striding legs full freedom. His banner proclaimed: "Give us this day our daily bread!" and he waved it and twirled it from time to time as he exhorted his followers: "Close up! Close up! Keep moving, lads!" Some sophisticates in the ranks just behind him, borrowing from another culture, had made up a chant: "All the way with Stubbay!" and whenever he heard this he turned, and grinned, and tossed his banner upwards in delighted salute.

There were other banners—"Colonialism OUT!" "We Demand Our Just Rights!" "Down With The Greedy Men!"—just as there were other leaders marshalling their people and encouraging them onwards. Though there was a certain number of idlers and trouble-makers and persuadable fools, there were men here with a better purpose than most.

There was Chief Justin from Fish Village, with his overalled followers—followers now out of work, since the canning factory was closed for lack of certain vital spares. There was Caspar Muru, with a face set in proud grief, mourning before all the world his dead grandfather, dishonoured in death as a criminal. There was young Matthew Banka, also mourning a father who was still held in prison, still branded as a traitor. There were the two old Agura brothers, uncles of the disgraced Mayika, fiercely resolved on justice and public decency. There was Pele Matale, member of the Opposition, now outlawed and branded in the same way.

Each day they pressed on at their best speed; each night they camped in the best shelter they could find, and lit fires which glowed hopefully in the darkness, covering a whole hillside. Many fell exhausted and parched and footsore as soon as they came to a halt, and were looked after and meagerly fed by other, stronger men; and the two lorries which were travelling with them brought up the stragglers, in a kindly whipping-in which bound them all together again as one determined band of brothers.

They were a band of brothers four thousand strong by the time they were forty miles from Port Victoria.

Two days short of their goal, they came under steady observation. Men with cameras came and took their photographs; the wandering British Council team which had been recording the folk songs of Pharamaul made a record of this enterprise also, under the title "March Like a Lion, Leap Like a Lamb"; other men from the newspapers came to watch and to report, and, since Father Stubbs proved talkative at any hour of the day, they took all his words down—words such as "Protest of Desperation" and

"Freedom Rally" and "Battle for Justice" and "Better Dead than Duped"—and gave them, or thought they gave them, to a waiting world.

The newsmen were not to know that for many days their world waited in vain. Under a special decree of national emergency, all outgoing cables were destroyed as soon as they were handed in. They did know that the telephone service with the mainland had been suspended, but they put this down to a normal African inefficiency.

There were other people, more potent, more purposeful, keeping a watchful eye on the marchers. Twice a day policemen in cars drove out from the capital, and took notes, and counted heads, and talked on their radios as they sped away again. It happened for the last time when the procession was one night away from Port Victoria. But there was no opposition, no attempt at preventing the advance, no barked command; simply a silent, guardian vigilance which made the nervous afraid, and the rebellious angry.

Then, at noon next day, when they had reached the outskirts of the northern suburbs, they found their way totally barred by a steel-grey, half-tracked armoured car, also labelled "Police," straddled across the road.

At the sight of it there were angry shouts, and cries of "Police spies!" and a great waving and shaking of banners as the procession was forced to a halt. But it seemed that their way was not barred after all. Within a few moments, the hatch of the armoured car was flung back with an iron clang, and the huge head and shoulders of a man emerged.

His face was gleaming with sweat, and he drew a deep breath of the fresh air—air still hot enough, but far better than the baking furnace which had lately imprisoned him. In his hand he held a powered megaphone—a "bull-horn"—and through this he greeted them.

Not twenty of them recognized Colonel Mboku, not two hundred had ever heard of him. But they recognized the voice of authority—and of friendly authority also.

"You are welcome!" Colonel Mboku shouted through the bull-horn, and the astonishing words echoed down the ragged lines until they had astonished the last weary straggler. "I bring you a message of peace and help. Follow this car. It will lead you to the cricket ground, where we all met on the day of independence. Government has set up tents there, and cooking pots, and fires for you. There you can rest. There is food for all! There is *bariaana* for all!"

At the mention of *bariaana*, the fiery home-brewed beer which all Pharamaul knew, there was another astonished murmur among the marchers. But it was Father Stubbs who reacted most forcibly.

"You cannot bribe us!" he shouted out. He shook his fist towards the armoured car, and Colonel Mboku, and the watching policemen. "We have come to demand our rights! We must speak to the President!"

"You will speak to him tomorrow," Mboku answered, looking down at the angry, gesticulating priest as if he were the most law-abiding citizen to be found within a hundred miles. "That is a solemn promise. But follow me now to the cricket ground. There you can rest after your hard journey, and sleep in peace. Then tomorrow at noon there will be a great *aboura*."

As he finished speaking, Colonel Mboku dropped from view; the circular hatch slammed shut again; and the armoured car started its engine with a roar, and maneuvered slowly round in a circle, the steel claws of the half-track leaving great scars on the surface of the ground. Then it rumbled and clanked down the road towards the city center. Uncertainly, suspiciously, hopefully, sometimes jauntily, the marchers limbered up their aching limbs, and hoisted their banners, and picked up step, and followed it.

When they came to the next crossroads, there was, of all things, the famous Pharamaul Police Band, in dazzling white helmets and spotless uniforms, with here and there a leopardskin, here and there a gleaming tuba or trombone, waiting to welcome them.

On command, the band wheeled neatly into place, just ahead of the armoured car, and then, with clashing cymbals, booming bass drums, and brass-throated trumpets, it led the marchers onwards, to the tune of *Entry of the Gladiators*, putting them in great heart for the last mile of their journey.

All that evening on the cricket ground, where the scoreboard, unaltered from a match played four months previously, recorded: "Port Victoria, 296 for 6 declared: Visitors, 202 all out," the marchers from the north enjoyed rest, and good eating and drinking, and the best of fellowship. For many, it was the first meat they had tasted since they left home; for all of them, the oil-drums full of *bariaana* supplied the most generous offering, the most splendid hospitality of their lives, and there were few who held back from the temptation.

Even Father Stubbs, for whom the home-brewed beer was foul-tasting muck, fit only for pig-swill, did his share of roistering, passing from one group to another with a full dipper and cheerful words of encouragement. Later he gathered his own group round him, and led them in brief prayer, and in a singing of *Onward, Christian Soldiers!* and then in political discussion, when the plans for the morrow were carefully drawn up, and the watchword was declared to be: "No Surrender! No Victimization! No Nonsense!"

All next morning, police cars with well-tuned loudspeakers toured the streets of Port Victoria, announcing a single short message: "All supporters of the National Party must wear their colours at the *aboura!* Show your loyalty to the President!" They did not come anywhere near the cricket ground, where the marchers woke late after their weary pilgrimage, and long talking, and deep drinking, and their exhausted sleep.

No one bothered them, or counselled them, or held out the hand of friendship. The police guard on the gate turned away all visitors, with the order: "The *aboura* will open at noon." The marchers were left in isolation, to wake, and yawn, and scratch, and stretch their stiff limbs, and consider what the new day might bring them.

At the stroke of noon by the pavilion clock, the main gate was opened, and all those who wished to join the great *aboura* began to assemble.

The police, who seemed in a strangely jovial mood, were in full control from the start. About half of them were armed, and the rest carried the skull-cracking, ebony knobkerries which in Pharamaul took the place of truncheons. But they did not seem even to be thinking of using them; the weapons appeared ceremonial, no more than part of their uniforms, as the policemen directed the marchers from the center of the cricket field towards the covered stand.

"You are honoured guests!" some of them said, ushering the marchers forward. "You have pride of place at this *aboura.*" In a few minutes the stand had become full of the visitors, just as the field itself began to fill up with the citizens of Port Victoria, almost all of them wearing the National Party colours of red and black.

Presently a convoy of trucks made its appearance at the main gate, and drove slowly up to the stand. As their doors were opened, and the first few men appeared, climbing down awkwardly as if they were unused to movement, a murmur of surprise, and then a steady howl of rage, rose from the center of the ground. These were the long-hidden political prisoners, specially released to attend the *aboura!* But had they not been branded, for weeks and months, as criminals and traitors? The catcalls multiplied as man after man in prison clothes made his appearance.

Many of them were thin and broken, and there were affecting scenes among the marchers as, sometimes, those nearest to the prisoners found their friends and greeted them. When Chief Banka of Shebiya climbed down, assisted by two policemen, a great shout rose from the stand as soon as he was recognized, drowning the cries of "Traitor!" and "Criminal!"; and men came forward to salute him and press his hand.

He looked painfully frail, and very old; the prison dungarees hung in folds from his wasted body, and he found it difficult to hold himself upright, even to greet a man from his own tribe.

He was given the place of honour on the front bench of the stand, next to Father Stubbs.

Then a much louder noise was heard outside the grounds, and people looked towards the main gate again. This time it was the steel-grey armoured car, which lumbered in, its engine roaring in low gear, its tracks rattling and clanking like an iron foundry. Once again, its claws bit and tore the earth as it advanced.

In front of the stand it wheeled round, and came to a halt. The thundering engine was stilled. It now had a loudspeaker mounted on the roof; but no human beings could be seen inside. Even the driver had only a narrow slit in place of a windscreen, and the sides of the car were featureless save for smaller slits, and the black-painted letters "POLICE." It stood in front of the stand, a squat castle of steel which could never be stormed.

Then some more police arrived in two trucks, and took up their station behind the armoured car. These men were all armed with revolvers, and a number of them seemed to be drunk.

But the armoured car, faceless, non-human, impregnable, was

undoubtedly in charge. As soon as the police had restored order, and the prisoners had been seated, and their friends had returned to the higher benches, and the shouts from the National Party supporters on the center field had died away, the loudspeaker on the car roof opened up—first with a blast of heavy breath, and then with words, blaring and echoing as if expelled from iron lungs.

The citizens of Port Victoria had by now come to know this voice well. It was Colonel Mboku.

"The *aboura* is now begun," he told them, and the phrase, though formal, sounded full of weighty meaning. "We greet the marchers from the north. They should tell us first why they are here."

There was silence from the benches in the stand, as men looked at one another uncertainly. Then Father Stubbs stood up, and came forward to the central microphone. His beaky nose was upthrust, his long hair unkempt after his rough night; but the brown cassock and heavy leather belt gave him a certain authority, and there was no reaction from the crowd except silence.

Father Stubbs began on a sharp note of belligerence.

"You should tell us first why we have been met with guns, with an armoured car, with rows of policemen!" he shouted. "We have come in peace, to demand our rights! We will not be intimidated!"

The armoured car answered him: "There is no intimidation. The police are for your protection. It may happen that you have enemies here. But I do not wish to talk about policemen. Tell us why you have come."

Father Stubbs, still mutinous, still using his most querulous tone, began to speak again. He spoke briefly, and it was mostly in slogans which had a certain ring of falsehood, since they only aped and mimicked the marchers' banners: "We will not be victimized!" "The north is starving while the south is fat!" "We are not a colony of Port Victoria!" "We fight for justice!" "Give us freedom, not slavery!"

It was strange, outlandish stuff for most of his audience, but he was still heard in silence, as a priest should be. It was only when he shouted at the end of his speech: "Where is the President? Why is he hiding from us?" that there was a long growl from the

341

center of the field, a growl which swelled into angry shouting. In face of it, Father Stubbs stepped back, and sat down.

He had made no headway—a fact which became clearer still as Colonel Mboku, from his iron shell, answered him roughly:

"Do not attack the President! That is treason! The President does not hide from anyone. He will come when he chooses to come. Let us hear some more of these fancied wrongs of the northerners. So far I have heard nothing but insults and lies."

After a moment, Chief Banka made as if to rise, but his wasted muscles could not support the move, and he fell back in pitiful weakness. He was helped to his feet, and brought forward slowly; and as he came into full view, the whole temper of the crowd changed.

Chief Banka had been so vilified during the last months, so scorned as a traitor, so threatened as a criminal: so many words had been written to his dishonour, so many voices had been heard naming him as the most shameful of all creatures, that the very name "Chief Banka" had come to seem an odious term, beyond the regard of any honest man. The opposing crowd could only think of him as an animal to be hunted down without mercy, and cursed if he escaped.

It was many minutes before he could be heard, so loud were the shouts and angry screams and violent roaring which met him; and when at last he spoke, his voice was so feeble, his bearing so miserable, that he could make no impression, even if there had been men and minds prepared to accept him as a human being with human rights.

He did his best, in faltering tones. A few of his words could be heard—"Our country has become a prison"—"Liberty has been stolen away"—"We are ruled by a king with power of life and death." But then, at the end of certain insulting phrases: "The President has become a tyrant! He is also a coward! Where is Dinamaula, the tyrant, the liar, the murderer, the coward?" the microphone went dead. As Chief Banka continued to mouth into it, the armoured car began to bark back at him, harshly, imperiously, with hateful menace, with a threat of doom.

"We have heard enough of this!" Mboku shouted. "Your words are treason, and treason is death! No one can attack the President like this, and live!"

Chief Banka, in a moment's pause, cried out towards the armoured car: "I will be heard before I die."

Few even of those close to him could hear the defiant words, but the armoured car was listening with sharp steel ears. *"You have been heard!"* the answer came back, sinister, all-powerful, sounding like the last words of a hanging judge. Then the voice on the loudspeaker changed, to a tone and to phrases which seemed to have been rehearsed or committed to memory. "Now all of you present—hear this! The President has ordered me to deal with this plot, and to punish the plotters, once and for all. If one part of the country rises to attack the Government, the Government must act without mercy. The President has therefore signed an order condemning all such traitors to death. I, Colonel Mboku, have been commanded to carry it out." There was a pause, and then a final sentence, smooth, contemptuous, legal: "The signed order may be seen at any police station tomorrow."

Then, in the ominous silence which had now fallen on the whole vast concourse, three wide flaps in the turret of the armoured car fell forward, with sharp ringing cracks like three iron pot-covers dropped upon a stone floor, and on the instant three machine-guns began to fire on the people massed in the stand.

Just as the silence had been shattered, beyond bearing, beyond belief, so men were shattered with it, and began to fall. Chief Banka, target of a thousand hate-filled eyes and a hundred bullets, was the first to die, his head nearly severed from his body by this iron hail; and Father Stubbs met at least an honourable death as he bent over the old man to succour him.

The two old Agura brothers were mown down, cut to pieces, as they rose in horror at the sight of Chief Banka falling; and Matthew Banka, shaking his fist on high as he looked down at the body of his father, might have been signalling for his own death, so swiftly did it follow. Caspar Muru, grandson of a man already miserably slain in captivity, had only time to clutch at his torn chest before he joined this honoured ghost in the same agony.

Now the machine-guns, manned by skilful executioners, began to aim higher; men on the upper benches were starting to fall, or to scream in rage or terror, or to make futile efforts to hide behind the rampart of the dead. Blood was already dripping down the steps towards the lower ranks; wherever it reached the hot stonework, it steamed before it became caked into dark-brown filth.

Driven to frenzy by the murderous noise, the sight of falling friends, and the savage venom of the armoured car which had become a fearful mowing-machine, the very scythe and sickle of death, men began to run away, to fight and wrestle and flail at each other as they sought to escape.

At this, the jovial armed policemen, drunk or sober, broke ranks and began to hunt them down.

It was guns and clubs against walking sticks, against raised arms, against nothing. It was a matter of killing all who did not wear the National Party colours, and the hundreds of luckless men who had not this passport, or were marked for death by their prison clothes, were easy targets as they ran this way and that, and found their way blocked by other men who would not let them escape, and who pounced on them as soon as they were sighted, naked to their enemies.

Presently, taking their example from the rampaging policemen, everyone on the *aboura* ground who was protected by a red-and-black armband, or a scarf, or a ribbon, or a child's flag, started to join in the sport.

Many of them, it turned out, had come prepared. They carried pangas, the heavy curved knife like a *machete*, like a butcher's chopper—and indeed, during the past week of rumour and threatening report a certain sound had become familiar all over downtown Port Victoria, the sound of pangas being ground and sharpened and honed to a razor's edge on the curbstones, as men sat in the cool of the evening, and prepared their weapons, and talked of an armed invasion which must be halted, and laughed at the thought of the slaughter which was to come.

With savage, barbarous cruelty, with pure delight, with pride—for were they not protecting their great President against his treacherous enemies?—they now went to work on the scores of desperate men who sought to elude them, the hated marchers who threatened the safety of the state, and must not escape their doom.

Having fled the machine-guns which still crackled and roared through iron throats and spat pouring lead into the stand behind them, the marchers now had to run the deadly gauntlet of their fellow men. They sprang this way and that, twisting and turning like hares in a cornfield as they found their way barred, and turned in terror as the hunt closed in on them. Like coursing dogs, the jovial policemen, and the citizens now in triumphant holiday mood, ran them down one by one, and shot them, or clubbed them, or sliced them to gory ribbons, or tore at them until the pulpy flesh gave way. One by one, the last screaming hares, which had been men, fell, and endured their final agony, and died.

There was, at one corner of the cricket ground, a high barbed-wire fence designed to prevent children climbing in to watch the matches without paying for the privilege. A few of the terrorized marchers tried to scale this, and were laughed at as their jerking bodies were torn by the barbs, and they were brought to a halt, tethered by their own flesh, and were killed by flung stones or flying baulks of wood, or a whirling thrown panga or a quick police bullet.

One of the men who had escaped from the stand was Chief Justin of Fish Village, at the head of a band of other young men in their white boiler suits. They were the easiest of targets, but they gave great sport, since they were all young and agile and desperate to live. Some of them, in their white suits, cornered at last, took to the trees which bordered the cricket field; these they climbed up with maddened strength, and perched high in the branches like nesting birds, and tried to shelter among the green leaves.

Presently a policeman would run up, summoned by good citizens; and he would raise his revolver, and take aim, and fire, and perhaps miss; but one by one these white nesting birds were picked off, and their bodies plummeted downwards, thudding and splintering on the baked earth, while bloodstained leaves fluttered down after them, as if the tree itself wished to shed its guilt.

Later these young men from Fish Village passed into Maula folklore as the Big White Birds in the Trees, and it was said that as their bodies dropped to earth their white spirits flew upwards on wildly-beating wings.

When all was done, and the last screaming had died away, and the last rivulet of blood had congealed on stone or run into the thirsty earth, the tents of the marchers were uprooted and thrown together into a huge pile, and set alight, making a vast stinking bonfire which burned far into the night.

345

By its flaring light there could be seen, high up on the score-board under the sign which recorded "VISITORS," the naked body of old Chief Banka, triced up and strung by the heels as a monument to justice, a fearful warning to traitors. It happened that his wizened genitals, falling downwards, pointing earthwards, had taken on the look of an ancient erection, as his racked body began to stiffen.

"The first time for forty years!" said the mockers, as they paraded beneath this poor shrunken shell of manhood. "You see what it is to have twenty sons!" In their coming and going, they laughed all traitors to scorn, and called loyal blessings on the President, and drank the last of the brew of *bariaana*, which not this old man hanging high in shame above them, nor the men strung on the barbed wire, nor the big bird corpses crumpled at the foot of the trees, nor the piles of dead meat in the grandstand, would ever need again.

2

Simon the houseboy had watched from afar as his beloved Chief was slaughtered. It was Simon's half-day off, and he had wandered down to the *aboura* ground to see what he could see. But since he could not bring himself to wear the colours of men who had become the sworn enemies of himself and of all U-Maulas, he had acted with great care. He did not venture more than a few yards past the main gate, and onto the verge of the cricket field.

From there, through the strung loudspeakers, he had heard Chief Banka's faltering speech and the roar of hatred which greeted it; and when the microphone went dead, he had seen the machine-guns open up, spitting death, and the Chief of his despised tribe falling from view. He saw other men in the front of the stand begin to fall also, and at this fearful sight he had turned swiftly, and sped away.

Now he was safe home again, sitting in a wicker chair at the scrubbed kitchen table; and on the table, for no reason at all except that the sight of death had made him miserably afraid, was his own panga with the carved and polished hilt which his father had given him long ago, which he always kept sharpened, just as (so rumour ran) other men all over the city had lately been sharpening their own, in what was always called "the music of the curbstones."

He was still plunged in deep shock at what he had seen, and he brooded in helpless misery on this, and on his future, and his life. If such things could be done to an honoured Chief, what would they not do to a houseboy—even the houseboy of the Chief Secretary?

Presently his enemy, the hated Gloria, came into the kitchen from her room. For many months, as the northerners sank deeper and deeper into public disgrace, she had only spoken to him in taunts and insults, and this afternoon, he thought dully, was to be no exception.

"Well now!" she said, standing above him with her hands planted on her hips. "You are back early from your day off! What is the matter with you, old man?" She always called him old man, though he was no more than fifty-three. "Did you spend all your money in the beer shop? Or will no one talk to your tribe any more?"

Simon said nothing, and gave no sign of hearing. He continued to stare straight ahead of him, with an ache of hopelessness in his breast, and the pain of what he had seen at the *aboura* still in his eyes. Gloria, finding him so low in spirit, warmed to her work.

"I do not know why I should talk to one of your tribe. I do not know why I should have to work in the same house. My friend asked me yesterday, 'Why do you work in a house which holds a traitor? Why do they not give him up to the police?' Tell me, is your old Chief, the great traitor who is always in the newspaper, still in prison?"

"No," Simon answered, in a faraway voice. "They have set him free."

"Do not believe it!" Gloria said scornfully. "He will never be free. They do not free traitors. They will keep him in prison until he dies."

"He is freed," Simon repeated.

"You have lost your wits, old man!" Her glance shifted, from the hunched figure of Simon to the table in front of him. "Tell me, what is the panga for? Do you put it on the table and worship it? Or is it to slice up the meat to send to the prison, to keep your old Chief alive?"

Simon straightened up suddenly, and for the first time he

347

looked straight at her mocking face. "*Woman!*" he roared out, in desperate anger. "Be silent!"

Gloria, though astonished at this show of spirit, recovered swiftly. "Do not speak to me like that," she snapped. "I will tell the missus about the Hoover."

Simon came to his feet. Once he had faced his tormentor he found that her long-held power was ebbing swiftly away. "You will tell the missus nothing."

"I will! I will! It will take more than an old man to stop my mouth!"

Simon picked up the panga, and swung it deftly. His muscles were still supple, and the lessons his father had taught him long ago—how to strip a tree of its vines, how to harvest a patch of mealies, how to cut thatch, how to skin a buck, behead a chicken, let the blood run from a pig's throat, using in each case this same dextrous weapon—all these were still part of the skill of his race, and thus within his own knowledge.

All the small and large tricks of cutting were still in his fingers, his wrist, his forearm, and his memory. Recalling such skills, proud of them, he swung the panga up to within a few inches of this hated neck.

"Be silent," he warned her, now quiet. "Or I will stop your mouth with this. I tell you, I will do it now, unless you are silent."

Gloria backed away from the threatening blade and the determined man, until she was standing in the doorway which led into the back-kitchen. There, feeling safe, feeling sure of herself, she grew spiteful and taunting again.

"I will tell the missus of this, too! She will sack you, she will send you back where you belong, up in the jungle with your tribe!"

"I have warned you once," said Simon, and advanced. "It was the last time."

"Old fool!" Gloria called out. "Put away your little knife. You are not in the jungle now. But you will be tomorrow, when the missus sends you back to your tribe!"

The gleaming panga came up again, and Gloria, falling back, did not move quickly enough. She could never have done so. With the same deft movement of his forearm, Simon swung, in a neat half circle, and the knife-edge sliced into Gloria's throat, while her tongue still clacked. The stroke, well calculated, bit only an inch deep, but, like a chef's first thin carving, it was enough. The scarlet blood spurted violently, and Gloria's mouth slopped and gurgled, and thus drowning she toppled backwards into the outer room, and twitched once, and lay in fearful death.

Simon said: "Woman, I told you!" and then, with no triumph in his soul, with no more than the same hopeless misery in his heart, he walked back into the kitchen, sluiced the stained panga under the tap, and dried it on a tea towel. Then he sat down at the scrubbed table again, with the panga set like a workaday kitchen knife in front of him, and wondered—as he had been wondering for months and even years—what he should do.

The only thing which had cheered Nicole, on that depressing day, was to overhear an important colloquy below her bedroom window.

"Timmy, you mustn't *gaze* at Mummy so!" Martha had commanded her brother.

"But she's getting so *huge!*"

"She's only great with child."

Now, waking from the afternoon nap which her indulgent doctor had ordered, Nicole was back with depression again. A third of the way through her pregnancy ("And we ought to be thoroughly ashamed of ourselves," David had said, though he did not really mind at all), she felt at a very low ebb of spirit, which nothing now going on in Pharamaul—all the rumours, all the hints of trouble to come—could allay. It had been a completely awful week, with an absurd and appalling start.

Someone—some true enemy or careless friend—had broadcast the story that the children were calling their black and white kittens "Dina" and "Lucy"; and the foolish item must have travelled through some very strange channels. The outcome was an official visit from two policemen, expressing great shock and outrage; a royal ticking-off which she had to endure as best she could; and the departure of the kittens in the police car—"They must be destroyed!" said the senior policeman sternly: "They must be publicly executed!" Undoubtedly he meant it.

She herself had been merely disgusted at a barbarous abuse of authority. But the children had been horror-struck, and then heartbroken. With David away, it had been one of those wretched

349

incidents which should only belong to nightmare, which could catch a family unawares and wound it deeply.

She missed David all the time—David, who had now been marooned in Johannesburg for four days, unable to complete the last leg of his journey owing to the total ban on flights in and out of Pharamaul. He had managed to ring up once, with his depressing, his really awful news about London; and all she could give him in return was her own sad tale—the kittens, the reports of a "march on Port Victoria," the general wretchedness of public and private affairs.

Alex had been a great comfort during this time, but he was not David; and Alex had troubles enough of his own. It seemed that the State Trading Corporation had been authorized to take over the total movement of goods to and from Pharamaul; and all export-import firms, starting with Alexanian's, had been given six months' notice either to wind up their business or "be absorbed." Compensation would be in the hands of a Government arbitrator.

"Simple theft!" Alexanian had said, when he reported the news. "Thank God I have stopped being surprised at anything."

"But will you be all right, Alex?" Nicole had asked him.

He had smiled. "Oh yes. I shall be a comparatively rich but very sad old man."

Now Nicole shifted her position on the bed, trying for more comfort and less awkwardness. She felt at a sad state of the tide of life. Why did her babies get so colossal so quickly? Why did she have to feel like a balloon full of water, and look so awful in anything except a potato-sack almost from the beginning? She sighed. Really, the only thing to be was a man. All the fun and none of the trouble. Well, not *all* the fun, thank God. But that was what it felt like, sometimes.

She became aware that for quite a long while she had been hearing raised voices from the direction of the kitchen. It was nothing new, unfortunately—just one more thing to put up with. Gloria and Simon would never get on, in this life or the next. . . . Presently, after the voices, she thought she heard a sort of thud.

It might have been the kitchen door slamming, or Gloria dropping something, or Simon putting out the rubbish bin. But since it was followed by silence, blessed silence, she soon forgot about it. She closed her eyes again. Just ten more minutes. Then she must take her balloon full of water out to tea.

Timothy was at a loose end, and cross with all the world, and in a mood to take it out on anyone he met. Martha had settled down with some silly old picture-puzzle, and would not play with him, or talk with him, or even look at him. His mother was upstairs, resting, because she was full of the baby and had to take it easy. Gloria was nowhere to be seen—and he did not want Gloria anyway. He was too old for a nurse-girl, especially one who could still ask rude questions about whether he'd been to the lavatory.

As he usually did when no alternative was offered, he walked through to the kitchen. Simon, silly old Simon who wanted to go home, was better than nothing.

Simon was still sitting at the kitchen table. He looked up when Timothy came in, but immediately his head swung round again, centering on space, and he retreated into his private world of doubt and terror. Timothy, unjustly ignored, made haste to claim his attention.

"Can I have some cake, Simon?"

There was no answer. It became clear to Timothy that this was a day when no member of the human race had any time for him, and he resented it strongly.

"Simon!" he said, using something like his father's voice when he was irritated. "I told you—I want some cake."

Simon, recalled from vacancy, said: "Not till tea time."

"But I'm *hungry!*"

"You must wait."

Timothy liked this less and less. Faced with straight denial, he tried coaxing. "Please, Simon. Cut me a piece. Just a little piece till tea time. I'll get it from the bread bin."

Simon stirred himself. "Do not go in there. Do not trouble me. Run away."

"Then give me some cake. Just a little piece."

"No. Do not be a nuisance."

Timothy, scandalized, said: "You're not allowed to call me a nuisance!" He advanced towards the table, and Simon, turning, found the small indignant face and the corn-yellow head within a few inches of his own. "I want some cake," Timothy repeated.

"It's not *your* cake, it's *our* cake. So cut me some." His eyes fell on the table. "Cut me some with your panga."

"No."

"Why not?"

"There is no cake till tea time."

"But I'm *hungry!*"

"You must wait."

The wheedling voice and the blank answers might have gone on for ever, but Timothy had now grown impatient. "Then I'll cut it for myself," he said, and reached out his hand for the knife.

"*Leave that alone!*" Simon suddenly screamed. "It is mine! It is not for you! Go away. Do not bother me. You drive me mad!"

Timothy, startled and therefore put out of countenance, turned cheeky. "I don't want your silly old panga. Gloria says pangas are for savages. Why should I want it?" But he reached out his hand for it again, none the less.

Simon was quicker. His own hand slid across the table, and grasped the carved handle. For the second time that afternoon, in one neat flowing movement, the slicing blade was hefted, and raised, and balanced, and poised for its next appointed use.

The terrible cry which rang through the house brought Nicole up through the surface of sleep with a brutal start. She lay still for a moment, with a thudding heart, wondering if it could have been the end of a dream. But then she knew that the cry must be real, because her ear had recognized it, and now her mind. The voice had been the voice of her son.

She rose heavily from the bed, put on her shoes, and went out onto the landing. There she stood and listened. But there was not a sound in the house save a ticking clock down in the hall, and then a distant click which might have been a door closing. She found with dismay that the waiting silence was even worse than the cry. She hurried downstairs.

The kitchen door was not only closed; it was locked on the inside, something she had never known. In a frightful panic she turned, and went across the *stoep* and round the front of the house, running, thinking: "I shouldn't really run like this, even now." Breathless, sick-hearted, she pushed open the door of the back-kitchen, and came upon Gloria without warning, so that she nearly stepped on her body.

The gaping throat-wound was uppermost, still spilling its blood —blood already being lapped by flies, and wasps, and a battalion of ants, and even a gaudy butterfly. There were two red-rimmed footprints leading away from it and out into the garden.

Nicole said: "Oh God!" and edged in terror past the obscene corpse. She ran into the kitchen, and then to the sink, where she vomited in a scalding, uncontrollable spasm of sickness. Her heart seemed to be thundering and pounding in every part of her body —in her eardrums, up against her throat, down against the baby. She rinsed her mouth, and wiped it with a shaking hand, and turned from the sink.

It was then that she saw her son lying on the floor behind the kitchen table, seemingly bleeding to death from a truncated forearm; and on the table, that convenient chopping block, something which she thought at first was a wax-grey claw but which, coming nearer, pierced by deadly terror, she was then able to recognize.

As soon as he was clear of the northern suburbs, and the trim well-kept lawns, and the white women who might order him to stop and tell what he was doing, and the occasional policeman who might do the same, swinging a knobkerry the meanwhile, Simon started to run. He was a heavy man, a soft man, a man in his fifty-fourth year. But fear drove him onwards, in panting desperation; and even when he had reached the extreme of exhaustion, he still ran on, in a clumsy parody of the long loping stride which his father had taught him, as he had once taught him to use a panga.

If he could only run far enough from Port Victoria, Simon thought, in his terrible guilt and despair, and come near enough to his homeland, he might still be safe. With this spur, and sick for home, he kept running on northwards for Shebiya, which after so many years of exile, so much pain and heartache, he must somehow reach, and there find peace and safety.

There were certain words which kept running round in his head, just as he kept running himself, with a heavy-laden, pounding rhythm. "You have lost your wits, old man!" the hated Gloria had shouted at him, so little time ago. In his heart, Simon knew that this was true. Indeed, it had to be true. He had done such fearful things, mixing innocent and guilty blood in one bowl, that if it was not true then he was damned for ever. But if he could once reach Shebiya, and be among his own people, and bury his head in shame, and never look back, and never have to face his master, he might still find refuge.

So he ran on northwards, the yellow dust choking him, the sweat pouring from his body, his heart ready to burst. After five miles, he shed his flapping kitchen apron, tossing it into a hedge as if he were tossing away the forfeited part of his life. He ran past small hut-circles, and herds of goats, and anthills, and dry thorn; he ran up hill, and then down, and then along great barren stretches of the baked and burning earth.

He ran past a plodding ox-wagon, and the astonished driver, who had never seen a man running in this fashion, in thirty years on the road, turned to watch him for a full mile before he shook his head, and turned away again, and laid a resentful whip across the patient backs of his span of oxen.

Simon ran on and on. Though he was in his fifty-fourth year, and soft from eating the Europeans' food, he ran northwards for eighteen miles, on tormented feet, with gasping lungs. Then, towards sunset, deadly exhausted, panting for the breath which could not reach him fast enough, parched beyond endurance, he came to his last stop.

He reached this last stop at a certain crossroads, marked by a crumbling signpost. The flaked black paint on the sign said: "Gamate, 180 miles. Shebiya, 275 miles." Even as he spelled out the letters, Simon saw that he would never reach either of these places. He knew that he must now stop running, for fear of death. But even as he realized this, and clasped his arms round the rough upright of the signpost, he found that this fear of death had reached him too late.

A huge wave of pain struck him on the breast-bone, and at the same moment a boiling gout of blood surged upwards into his throat. Clutching the signpost, which said "Shebiya, 275 miles," he slipped slowly earthwards. Great splinters of sun-warped oak pierced his inner arms, but, with his hammering ribs ready to burst, the pain was nothing. There was a greater pain in store, and suddenly he knew it.

At its crest, his tortured muscles gave way, and he slid to earth: slumping to the foot of the signpost, the precious signpost to home, which still held out this promise of "Shebiya, 275 miles." He had only to run 275 miles more. . . . Then he gave up, at this first and last sign; at its foot he bowed, he fell, he lay down; and where he bowed, there he fell down dead.

3

Tulbach Browne was engaged in some ferocious bargaining, which he always enjoyed. But this time there was a difference. He *had* to get what he wanted; and that was liable to come a bit expensive.

What he wanted was to get out of Port Victoria, and reach somewhere, anywhere, on the mainland of Africa. He had had a lot of luck getting in to Pharamaul, in the first place; starting one day ahead of David Bracken, he had just caught the last plane from Windhoek to Port Victoria—a plane which was promptly taken out of service and grounded "for the duration of the national emergency."

That might mean a delay of weeks; and in the meantime, he was sitting on his marvellous story, which no one else could possibly match. It began: "Colonel Mboku, one of the few African military murderers not educated at Sandhurst," and it told the whole story of the massacre, which Tulbach Browne had viewed from the cab of a police van bringing prisoners to the *aboura*. But now he was fatally stuck. The new emergency laws forbade all cables, and all overseas telephone calls; and there seemed to be no possible method of getting away from the island, and putting his story on the wire.

He was stuck, like a stork with a juicy toad in its beak, but with both legs trapped in the mud. No planes were allowed in or out; the airport was under heavy police guard; the one small ship which plied to and fro between Pharamaul and Cape Town was not due till the following week. A fishing boat would take days, perhaps weeks, to make the five hundred miles to the opposite coast, even if the weather held.

In fact, the only man who could help him was the man he was now talking to, in a very secluded corner of the Prince Albert Hotel: Jeff Gibson, the secretary, flying instructor, principal shareholder, and general big noise of the Port Victoria Flying Club.

"It simply can't be done, old boy," had been the first reaction from Gibson, a fifty-ish ex-R.A.F. pilot who seemed to be authentic to the very last degree, from handlebar moustache to wartime slang, from boozy red face to flamboyant yellow scarf.

"Our club license could go for a burton, in the first place. Not to speak of grounding *me*, maybe confiscating the kite. I tell you, these lads get really cheesed off if someone breaks their ruddy rules!"

"But *are* you breaking the rules? Has all flying been banned?"

"All commercial flying, yes."

"So what? That doesn't cover a private flying club, does it? You could just be taking a practice spin."

"I could just be taking a practice jump in the oggie, but I'm not!" Gibson twirled his huge moustache, and then his empty glass. "How about another noggin?"

"No—this is on me," Tulbach Browne chipped in. He signalled to a waiter, and gave him the international finger-wave which meant "same again." Then he turned back to Jeff Gibson. "I don't see why you can't fly anywhere you like. It's not breaking the law."

"It's certainly bending it a bit, old boy. The inference of the new regs is that all flights to and from the mainland are banned. Right? So that includes Pharamaul Airways, the daily plane from Windhoek, you, me, and old Uncle Tom Cobbleigh. If in doubt, bail out! I don't want to be the first flying type they make an example of." He brooded, though briefly. "I've heard that song before. . . . I tell you, in a country like this they've got you by the short and curlies."

"But even if that's true, who's to know about it?"

"They'll know damn soon when they see me coming back!"

Tulbach Browne was ready for that, too. "Not if you landed up north somewhere, and then flew in here on a short hop." He raised his glass: "Cheers! Don't forget, I'll make it worth your while."

"Bung ho!" the pilot answered. "You'll certainly have to."

It was the first breakthrough. But Jeff Gibson had not finished with the list of obstacles standing in the way.

"The trouble is, old boy, I've only got three kites. One was pranged by some clot last week, and we can't get the spares for it. This country's run like a closing-down sale—'Positively your last chance.' The second one is locked up at the airport, with a great big brute of a fuzzy-wuzzy standing guard over it. He'd rather shoot than shit, any old day! The third is out at the club airfield." Gibson gulped at his drink again. "Fair enough—no

356

pain. But it's only a string-bag job. It's a Gipsy-Moth trainer, older than God—we call it the BC10." He guffawed so loudly that heads were turned from all over the Prince Albert lounge. "We only use it for teaching bumps and turns. If some stupid erk prangs it, we'd be better off with the insurance, anyway. But I wouldn't try to fly it across five hundred miles of the cruel sea, for a thousand quid."

Tulbach Browne decided to move in. "We can't pay you a thousand," he said. The "We" stood for the *Daily Thresh*, which he had early established as the party most concerned. "But if you're interested in two hundred. . . ."

The pilot, a poor man beginning to smell blood, batted this one back forcibly.

"You must be joking!"

"Two hundred pounds is a lot of money."

"Who to? Pull your finger out! I told you, we could lose our ruddy license, *and* the kite. We could come down in the drink. Quite apart from me being shot at dawn for breaking the law. I wouldn't even give it a prayer—not under five hundred quid."

"Two fifty," Tulbach Browne countered. "We're not made of money."

"And I'm not made of Pilot-Officer Prune-juice! I told you—de-digitate!"

Tulbach Browne, searching his memory, came up with some matching slang. "*Dieu et mon doigt*, eh?"

"Bang on!"

They bargained briskly for some time, over successive drinks; the trip was already on, Tulbach Browne knew, but there was a limit to what the *Daily Thresh* would stand for, even for a story like this, and Jeff Gibson already had more than a suspicion of how important it was. Finally they struck a bargain, at £350—Port Victoria to Windhoek, starting at dawn next morning, with no guarantee, and absolutely no reference, in print or otherwise, as to how Tulbach Browne had made his escape.

"Righty-ho!" Gibson said at last. "They laughed when I sat down to play. . . ." Their eighth drink had just been served, and strict concentration had ebbed. "I'll be up half the night as it is, buttoning on a spare tank. You're getting one hell of a bargain!"

"After you with the handkerchief." But Tulbach Browne still had something else to tell him, and he broached it very carefully. "Let's get down to the nuts and bolts. What time do you want us to be there?"

"Cock-screech, old boy!" Gibson answered cheerfully, with an appetite which must have been rooted, and constantly renewed, in the stirring past. "Sparrow-fart, in fact—call it what you like. Let's say four ack emma. Then I can——" he broke off, alerted at last. "What do you mean, *we*? Is there going to be someone else?"

"I promised to give someone a lift, as a matter of fact. A girl."

"But hell, be your age! BC10 is a two-seater! There won't be any room for a spare bod."

"She can sit on my knee." The third passenger was an important part of Tulbach Browne's total story, and he was determined to clinch the expensive deal on his own terms. "What difference does it make, anyway?"

"Just the difference between getting to Windhoek, and running out of air halfway. All same Berlin to Biggin Hill. Dicing with death, like the man said." But Gibson was not really opposed. "For a start, you won't be able to bring any luggage with you."

"That doesn't matter."

"Christ, you must really want her on your knee! What girl is this?"

"She's called Lucy Help."

Jeff Gibson, with a drink poised between his lips, jumped so violently that most of it splashed over his knotted silk scarf. He did not even bother to wipe it off. "Absolutely no dice!" he declared, with the utmost determination. "Lucy Help! Christ, you'll get us *all* shot!"

"She only wants to get to Johannesburg."

"And I only want to live! Have you gone stark staring bonkers, old man? She's the President's prime bit of crumpet! If he even *heard* about this, he'd chop us up for rissoles!"

"I'll make it five hundred," said Tulbach Browne. "That's all the money I've got, and it's a damn sight more than the trip's worth." He produced his last idea. "You can always say I pulled a gun on you."

"You might as well do that, right now! Jesus H. Christ! Why did I ever volunteer?"

. . .

As BC10, groaning and creaking like a wicker laundry-basket, began to taxi across the bumpy field, and Lucy Help snuggled her delicious bottom well down into Tulbach Browne's lap, she shouted in his ear:

"Have you ever done it like this?"

Tulbach Browne, who had had several sessions with Lucy already, was not at all surprised. "As a matter of fact," he shouted back, "yes, I have."

"What, in the *air*?"

"No—I meant, in a car."

"Oh, that. . . . Getting kind of bumpy, isn't it?"

"That's the plane." Browne had Lucy Help's bulging flight-bag, bearing the proud crest of Pharamaul World Airways, between his feet, and he asked, against the rising windstream: "What's in the bag?"

"Money."

Tulbach Browne laughed. "That should keep you warm. Just like this, eh?"

"Better."

"Well"—the single engine was now revving up to a veritable scream—"don't forget, we're giving you a lot more for your story."

Her reply was lost as BC10 began its take-off.

The heavy-laden Gipsy-Moth, with its extra fuel tank, needed a long run, and the long run took them across a field which, though dignified by the label of the Port Victoria Flying Club's landing-strip, was corrugated like some exotic shirt-front. In the half-light of dawn, they might have been careering across an endless nightmare desert, with a pack of spectral wolves snapping at their heels, striving to bring them down.

It seemed ages before the bone-shaking take-off run came to an end, and the plane rose in peaceful flight. But when they were airborne at last, and climbing steadily, Jeff Gibson turned and gave them the thumbs-up sign, grinning cheerfully.

"Piece of cake!" he shouted above the engine noise and the tearing wind. "Windhoek, here we come!" He directed a practised leer at Lucy Help. "Don't mind me," he said. "But try not to rock the kite."

Then he settled himself in the pilot's seat, and started a slow banking turn eastwards, to take them over the coast.

359

They had hardly crossed the sharp creamy line, just visible in first light, which was the division between sea and land, before the engine began to splutter.

They all listened to it as it laboured—the rise and fall of revolutions, the hacking internal cough, the sudden surge of power as it picked up again—with an acute alarm which could not be put into words. I'm too old for this sort of thing, Tulbach Browne thought, as Lucy Help's shapely body suddenly lost its charm and fear took over. I ought to have waited for a proper flight, I ought to be home in bed, I ought to have retired last year.

Fancy putting one's trust in this string-and-glue contraption which should have been sold for fire-lighters twenty years ago. . . . Soon, far too soon, there was a final splutter, and the engine died; and BC10 began a peaceful glide back to earth.

Jeff Gibson had turned their nose westwards again, as soon as he became aware of real danger; and before long he saw the line of surf coming up, and the black shadowy mass which was the eastern coast of Pharamaul. In the strange silence, broken only by the sighing wind of their passage, he called over his shoulder: "Sorry, chaps! Slight technical hitch! I'll have to put her down somewhere." Then he forgot his passengers, and concentrated on a private quest for life.

They had not gained sufficient height for a glide back to the airfield; there was nothing ahead except bare rock country, with here and there the tiny glimmering of village fires. Gibson peered this way and that, weighing the odds, searching for their best chance, with the beginning of desperation taking hold of him; the pale light from the east was not strong enough to show him anything except shadow piled on shadow, and dark patches which might have been fields but which, when he dropped lower, turned out to be outcrops of rock, or trees lurking under the lee of barren hills.

They were still orphans in this wilderness, and their time was about to run out.

Then, just within their grasp, he saw a small black rectangle on a hillside; and he brushed the streaming sweat from his forehead, and said aloud: "That's got to be it, Jeff me lad," and he put the plane's nose down—at the last second before they stalled—and made straight for it.

It still looked like a ploughed field, or a big mealie-patch, as he came within two hundred feet of it; and he called out over his shoulder: "Hang on! We're going in!" and levelled out for the slowest descent which heaven would allow.

The band of net-men held their breath as the bird approached, hardly able to believe that the longed-for capture was to be theirs at last. They could see that this was not the big bird, which had not flown for many days; but it was a bird of the same breed, a smaller silent bird with one gleaming eye, and it was falling straight into their trap.

They spoke to each other in fierce, triumphant whispers: "It comes! It comes!" and then their leader called out: "All lie down!" and each man dropped where he had been standing, and lay in faithful guard at the edge of the net.

The bird plunged earthwards; they could hear the wind whistling and sighing in its exhausted wings. Then suddenly it was upon them. It hit the corner of their net, and was trapped by its claws, just as they had planned. The net tore asunder with a rending sound; and then, with a screech, the bird plunged its gleaming beak into a shoulder of jagged rock, and crumpled, and arched over on its broken back, the sparks flying wildly as it fluttered to a stop.

Fantastic silence fell; all was forest-still. They had caught their bird! Presently, without speaking to each other, they crept forward, pushing aside the strands of the ruined net, and looked at their prey, and touched it. Their knives were ready, but there was no need for any finishing strokes. The bird was clearly dead, and strange torn things were spilling out of it: soft entrails, unexpected shapes.

The leader touched the mangled ribs of the bird, and smoothed his hand over the hard surfaces, and made his judgement. It was a moment of such triumph that the next step was vital to all their lives. All power could be theirs, if they kept faith with their oath, if they reached out their hands and fastened on the bird's magic with all their might, with all their appetite, and made it their own.

"You remember what we swore to do," he told the net-men. He raised his knife, and they all followed him. "We cannot eat the body of this bird. But for strength we can taste its eggs."

10: CERTAIN DIFFERENCES OF APPROACH HAVE BECOME APPARENT

DAVID, forewarned of terrible news, had been expecting to meet many things when he let himself into his house; but he had not expected to meet Alexanian, who strode out of the kitchen wearing an apron and swinging a dishcloth, as soon as the front door shut. Alex, coming close, embraced him in a way strangely natural, though it was still most affecting to feel the clasp of his arms, and to hear him say:

"My friend, my friend!"

David, in sudden fear, asked: "What is it, Alex? Has anything—"

"No, no!" Alex, deeply moved, reassured him as quickly as he could. "Nicole is resting upstairs. But all is well."

"And Timmy?"

"In hospital, of course. I saw him this morning. The verdict is satisfactory progress."

"Well, thank God for that!" David put down his suitcase, and passed his hand across his eyes. The return home, which he had been dreading, was at least accomplished without further terrors. "But Alex—what on earth are you doing like that?"

Alexanian looked down at his plastic apron, which bore emblems of kitchenware above the motto "COME AND GET IT!" and could only have been imported from America, and smiled at last. "I am housekeeping, naturally. What else? Ah, you should have tasted my kosher corned beef hash at lunchtime!"

"You mean, you're doing everything?"

"With the help of Martha, yes. I thought it better. I would have brought some servants with me, but—well, suddenly Nicole cannot bear the sight of a black face. You can understand that?"

362

"Yes, of course," David answered, though it was in fact the most wretched epitaph which could ever have been devised for their long and faithful sojourn in Pharamaul. "I'm terribly grateful to you, Alex."

"*Bitte sehr.*" Alexanian pointed towards the hall table. "There is one important letter for you. At least, it looks important. From the Palace."

"Then it's not important." But David slit open the ornate, embossed envelope nonetheless. It was, as he had been expecting, a summons to see the President. The wording was curt, and specified that he was to report immediately on his arrival.

For the first time in his official life, David did nothing at all about it. He was not going to be hurried, or bullied, or pressured, on an evening such as this. Upstairs, he talked for a long time with Nicole, a wan shadow of the wife he had left behind him, so short a while ago, and then with Alex again. He visited his son in hospital, and the sight of the pale, pinched face, and the forearm which was now brought to an obscene halt by a bulging, square-cut bandage, swept him near to tears again.

He comforted Martha, still terrified by a world which had been so cruelly turned upside down. He drank as much as he felt like drinking, which was a good deal. Then he drove out to the Palace—the center, the mainspring of all this filth and misery.

He was stopped by armed policemen, and his identity checked, three times before he entered the Palace: once at the main gates, once again when he was halfway up the drive, and then on the front doorstep itself. But when at last he was admitted, he found that, inside the great house, all was utterly still, as if the whole Palace were brooding on fate—its own, and that of the hundreds of thousands of people for whom it was the symbol and the sword of power.

Presently the butler returned, treading the marble hallway as if proud of his echoing footfalls; and when David was ushered into the presence, he found that he was to meet President Dinamaula, not in his small private study, but in the huge colonnaded salon where formal meetings and official parties were held.

Though this was an obvious piece of stage-management, David was not in the mood to be daunted, and he made the long approach to the President's desk at his own easy pace. No dictator's tricks were going to get him down, ever again. . . . Dinamaula was staring at him as he approached, his face set in the same brooding watchfulness as seemed to infect the Palace itself. But close to, his glance was baleful, and it was reflected in his voice as he spoke:

"You are late. You arrived in Punta Maula more than five hours ago. Why did you not report, as I ordered?"

David stood in front of the desk. He knew that he was not going to be asked to sit down, and the discourtesy confirmed him in his mood. There was nothing more to be lost, on this enemy ground; all was gone already.

"I had a lot of things to see to."

"Then you disobeyed my order deliberately?"

"I was in no hurry to meet a man who could sanction what was done on the *aboura*."

It astonished David to hear his own voice saying such a thing, and clearly it astonished Dinamaula even more. There was quite a long interval before he retorted: "I will not allow you to be insolent, whatever mood you are in! You are blaming me, because of your personal troubles." His voice, for a moment, held some genuine regret. "Do not blame me for your son's hand. It was done by one of those murderers."

David, afraid of losing his self-control at this direct reference, answered harshly: "I do blame you! You have poisoned this country, so that a good man like my houseboy can go mad, and commit a terrible crime like that. My son is maimed for life. My wife . . ." he swallowed the rest of the sentence; he could not allow this stranger to come so near. "But don't call that man a murderer. It's you who are the murderer, hundreds of times over!"

Yet even as he said it, he was conscious more of sadness than of anger. Was this how it was all to end, with a slanging-match and a final burst of temper? Were nearly fifteen years of hope and hard work, real achievement and real heartbreak, now to be distilled down to contempt and disillusion, on both sides?

In his mood of black despair, David might, even then, have tried for something different, some revival of hope, if Dinamaula had not taken up his challenge, with ferocious ill-humour.

"You forget yourself!" the President snarled at him. "It is not for the first time. . . . What you call murder was no more than

364

justice, and if you had been there, instead of fooling about in London—without my permission—you would have known it! Colonel Mboku is in full charge of security, and if he tells me there is a plot against me, beginning with a march on the capital, I don't question his judgement and I don't sit back and wait for it to happen. I strike first! I tell him to crush it!"

"Very convenient," David answered. "Nothing like a man who can carry out orders. But there will come a time when Mboku will tell *himself* to crush you."

"What does that mean?"

"Haven't you heard about African colonels? They take over from presidents. I could give you quite a list, but why should I bother? You'll have to watch Mboku for the rest of your life. It could be a short watch."

Dinamaula, clearly enraged, stood up. The idea of keeping the Chief Secretary on his feet, like a schoolboy in front of a headmaster, was not working out; the other man stood too tall for that kind of discipline and, in his present mood, was far too unruly for discipline of any kind to have much effect.

"If that's the way you feel," Dinamaula said, on the same snarling note, "why the hell did you come back here? Why didn't you stay with your precious friends in London, working out how to get Pharamaul back into the Scheduled Territories Office? I'm sure that silly little Welshman would be glad to pay your salary!"

Shorn of its foolish and insulting aspects, this was a question to which David, and Nicole with him, had given hours of thought, and it turned out to be an easy one to answer, even as late as this.

"Because I still want to stay on here, and help clear up the mess."

"Very noble of you, *old boy!*" It occurred to David that Dinamaula might well have drunk just as much as himself, with the same sort of effect. "Unfortunately for you, fortunately for us, there isn't any *mess*, as you call it. The country is back to normal, Colonel Mboku has imposed law and order——"

"He can't rule Pharamaul just with guns."

"*I* rule Pharamaul. Colonel Mboku takes care of security on my behalf. And Joseph Kalatosi is entirely competent——"

"Kalatosi is a thief." It was the second time that David had interrupted, and now he pressed home the advantage. "You know it, and I know it, and when the time comes to balance the books, everyone else will know it. And that's really what I'm talking about, not about a bloody-minded policeman shooting up a grandstand full of people because he doesn't like them. Balancing the books. . . . You took over this country as a going concern, and we were glad to hand it over like that—law and order taken for granted, without bullets, money in the bank, an honest civil service, a police force with a fine man in charge—in charge of fine men. That was the whole idea of our being here. Now it's all gone, every single thing I've mentioned; all the building-up, all the hard work, all running away into the ground with the blood, with the money. . . . Don't you see, you've thrown away a whole century! You're back where you started, where your grandfather started. He set himself up as a king, he killed off all the opposition, and ruled as a tyrant——"

"Do not speak of Maula the Great so insultingly!"

"You know it's true. And even he didn't go as far as you have done. He would never have spent or stolen all the money, and then borrowed some more, and kept on spending or stealing that."

"I've told you before, finance is our own affair. We do not belong to you any longer. Pharamaul is not a *farela*, a little dog, any more."

"It never was."

"It was, it was!" Dinamaula shouted. "I was a *farela* myself. Remember what they used to call me?—the Resident Commissioner's little dog. And when I tried to do something about it, I was thrown out, exiled. *You* got me exiled. Well, now it's my turn."

David, surprised at last, stared at him. "You can't be serious." But he knew that he was. This was what Godbold—the wise, defeated, superannuated man—had told him: that the exile had never been forgiven. He asked the most important question of his life. "Is that what went wrong between you and me?"

"It was the start of it, yes."

"But honestly, I don't understand."

"What white man can ever understand Africa?" Dinamaula answered contemptuously. "I will tell you exactly what went wrong, if you like. Certainly the exile was the start of it. Do you expect me to *forget* that I was kicked out of my homeland, and had to spend five years in a place like Acton?"

"But you did seem to have forgotten it. Don't you remember how we talked on Independence Day? At the garden party here? You said"—the day and the words now seemed so far away that David could hardly recall them without embarrassment—"you said to me, 'It means a great deal to me that you are staying on. Let us make this a real country.'"

Dinamaula himself was far from embarrassment; the recollection only angered him. "At that moment, I probably meant it. The trouble was, you never left the Governor-General's garden party."

"What?"

"You still saw yourself as the colonial boss in a white helmet. You still tried to keep this country a little offshoot of England. You still tried to tell me what to do. You still tried to stop every new idea I had." He mimicked: "'It'll cost too much. You can't afford it. You're not ready for it.'" He went on with his recital of grievance, building up to a pitch of bitter anger. "You even tried to stop us joining UN! That was just a bluff, and I called it. We did join UN, and I found out what African independence can really mean, and I did make a real country out of Pharamaul, in spite of you, in spite of idiots like the Urles. . . . Perhaps it really started with something that stupid American senator said, ages ago. He was giving me the new-boy lecture—in this very room! He said: 'As long as you have people like the Urles and Mr. Bracken in your corner, you won't go far wrong.' Bloody insolence! As if you people were still my managers, my handlers!"

"It was nothing like that at all. All I wanted was to work out some kind of partnership."

"With your lot as the senior partners, for ever! Well, thank God you didn't fool me for long!"

In the ebb and flow of this strange nighttime charade, conducted without witnesses, without an audience, on the enormous shadowy stage of what had now come to be called, David remembered, the "Throne Room," there could be no decision, no sort of shape to the scene, no clear view of either the beginning or the end. All they were doing, he realized, was to stand face to face and fire off the last of the ammunition, the dross of discontented minds, with Dinamaula still proudly enthroned and himself still walking his lonely tightrope.

The bitterness of his impotence suddenly overwhelmed Da-

367

vid; sorrow and despair, rage and alcohol, all swept him onwards, on a great wave of denunciation.

"Well, you certainly got your wish. . . . You're in the driver's seat, and no one else dares say a word to you. . . . You're having your good time now. They all did, didn't they—Nkrumah, Sukarno, the Nigerians—they all had a wonderful time, till the bills came in and the whole thing blew up. Kaunda will be next! But God damn it! those were just joke countries! Ours was going to be different!"

"It is not 'ours'!" Dinamaula shouted, catching fire from David's own tone. "It is mine!"

David laughed, and he felt—he knew—that it was to be his last laugh in Pharamaul. "For how long? Till the bills come in? Till the Russians take up their mortgage? Till Mboku gets drunk and puts a bullet through your skull? Either way, the country will be ruined, *because* it is yours, because you are like all the others— vain and greedy and corrupt. Africa has been half crucified by you people, and now you're doing the same thing to Pharamaul. You're the last of a rotten first crop——"

The furious bellow echoed and re-echoed throughout the vast reaches of the room, setting the vaulted ceiling ringing:

"Silence! I could order you to be killed for that!" And then three final, violent words: *"You are dismissed!"*

11: THE FUTURE LIES BEFORE US, CLEAR AND FULL OF

AS SOON AS David Bracken had gone, President Dinamaula put him instantly out of mind. It was not difficult; he had many larger problems to consider, besides those of Government personnel. There could be something about "at the conclusion of his contract" in the newspaper. Joseph Kalatosi would take care of the necessary deletions from the official list. . . . Dismissing the matter as he had dismissed the man, the President left the gloomy shadows of the Throne Room, and, treading easily, went through into his private study.

There, he rang for a servant to pour him a drink, and for another to make up the fire. A mid-winter night, even in fortunate Pharamaul, could turn chilly and treacherous. Then, on an impulse, he pressed a certain switch on his desk, and spoke into a microphone:

"Turn out the guard! Turn out the guard!"

Secure in his room, with an armed sentry on the door, the President could hear his own voice echoing and re-echoing round the Palace grounds, as a string of loudspeakers relayed the message, from the floodlit portico to the farthest gatehouse. He heard the sound of running feet, and barked commands, and the crash of rifle-butts on stone and gravel and concrete. He glanced down at his watch. Twenty seconds. Thirty seconds. Thirty-five seconds. . . . Then there was a knock on his door.

"Who is there?" he called out.

"A friend, Lord Protector."

"Give the password."

"Freedom!"

"Come in."

The guard-commander entered. He was a young police-lieutenant, eager and dedicated; though he panted slightly, his back was ramrod stiff as he gave a tremendous semicircular salute, and reported:

"Guard all present and correct, Lord Protector!"

"Very good." Dinamaula had also studied the drill-manual. "Tell me, what are your orders?"

The guard-commander looked puzzled. "To keep the Palace secure, Lord Protector."

"How do you keep it secure?"

Now the policeman was definitely flustered. "We—we stop visitors."

"How do you stop them?"

"We challenge them, Lord Protector."

"And what if they are strangers who cannot account for themselves?"

"We—stop them."

"You shoot them!" Dinamaula roared at him. "Is that understood? That is what your guns are for! Anyone who cannot explain his presence in the Palace grounds—shoot him on sight!"

"Yes, Lord Protector."

"That's better. Now, who is your Commander-in-Chief?"

The lieutenant was quite certain about this one. "The Colonel, Lord Protector."

"What colonel?"

"Colonel Mboku."

"He is *not* the Commander-in-Chief! I am! You owe your loyalty to me! Do you understand?"

"Yes, Lord."

"Do not forget it." Dinamaula, who had been standing by the fireplace, pointed to his desk, which had always been placed with its back to the french windows. "I want this moved. Send in two of your men."

"Yes, Lord. Permission to retire, Lord Protector."

"Carry on."

When the men came, Dinamaula gave his directions. The heavy desk, fashioned of teak carved by cunning hands long dead, was turned round, so that it now sat securely in an angle with the back of the chair to the wall, and the long windows directly in front of it. Halfway through the awkward operation, a small chirping lizard, of the kind called a *gecko* ran up the wall in alarm at all these sounds and movements, and stayed high up near the ceiling, fearful to see what might come next.

With the guard dismissed at last, Dinamaula sat down. He reached for his drink, and swallowed thirstily, and banged the glass down again. Then he put his elbows squarely on the solid desk-top, and began to think.

He did not—he would not—think of David Bracken. He turned his mind away from all such stupid nonsense, and thought of his kingdom.

Pharamaul was now quiet. Indeed, it had never been so quiet. Down south, not a mouse stirred; all the mice had been trodden on, once and for ever, and the Punta Maula jails which were the mousetraps were empty except for common criminals. Up north, they had taken their crude revenge as best they could, but it was no more than the bite of a flea, compared with his own fierce stroke.

Up in Fish Village, that fouled nest of the U-Maulas, they had rounded up all the foreign Maulas, about fifty in number, who for one reason or another chose to work in the fish factory. These had been killed out of hand, and their bodies mutilated. Then certain men with a rustic sense of humour had taken over, and proposed a joke.

In a small consignment of tinned, tender-fleshed crayfish tails, due for export, the meat had been replaced, unspeakably, by particular trophies from the corpses.

A twelve-tin case of this choice delicacy had been delivered, by a messenger who unfortunately escaped, to the Palace kitchens, and then—by some luckless jester who had since died—to the President himself. Crudely stencilled "THE LONGEST CRAY-FISH TAILS IN AFRICA," it had served as a joke for a few hours, until all laughing mouths had been cursed into silence, and then shut.

The U-Maulas, always so uncivilized, could have their little by-play, if they chose. When it got out of hand, he, the Lord Protector, would act again.

The President drank deeply once more. Then he bent to a secret drawer which was part of a built-in safe, and drew out a fat scarlet file labelled: "TOP SECRET: Project PICAM."

It had long been his favourite file, to be studied and enjoyed for hours on end, and he had only to turn a few pages to find the particular diagram he sought.

It showed his island of Pharamaul as a dot off the coast of Africa, with a fan of lines radiating outwards from it leading towards the heartland of the continent. It was like a colossal spider's web, though the pointing fingers were aimed outwards, not inwards. They were each labelled in compass degrees, and then in mileages; and the great arc was itemized below, like a recital of battle-honours soon to come:

Luanda, Portuguese West:	027°,	1,100 miles.
Salisbury, Rhodesia:	078°,	1,800 miles.
Lourenço Marques, Portuguese East:	098°,	1,800 miles.
Pretoria, S.A.:	100°,	1,500 miles.
Johannesburg, S.A.:	103°,	1,500 miles.
Durban, S.A.:	109°,	1,750 miles.
Cape Town, S.A.:	134°,	1,150 miles.

As a matter of additional insurance, which he had not communicated to anyone else, he had added in his own hand:

Lusaka, Zambia:	1,600 miles.
Nairobi, Kenya:	2,600 miles.
Tanzania:	2,590 miles.
Uganda:	2,500 miles.
Congo:	1,500 miles.

As that well-remembered U.S. senator had once said, one had to bring this thing down to dollars and cents. . . . The President was still working on the cents—the compass courses to these secondary targets, in case there was some challenge to his plans.

But on this single sheet of paper was set out the pattern, the master-plan, for the cleansing of Africa. At the moment, secretive strangers still held the key to the door. But one day, when it was all going to come true, *he* would be the man who turned that key, and pressed that giant's trigger. It would be his right, as a true giant! Was it not all set down in the titles he had been born to:

"Urn of the Royal Seed, Ruler and Kingbreaker, Lord of the Known World"?

With such weapons, with such close computation, he could hardly be less than Lord of Africa. Given the same sort of chance, Castro of Cuba, and the same stranger-ally, had both turned chicken-hearted. But not he, not he!

The President closed the file, and looked again at its title: PICAM. It stood for "Pharamaul Inter-Continental Atomic Missile," but he was still not quite satisfied with it. It still lacked total authority. It sounded vague. He had thought of POMP— "Pharamaul Overseas Missile Project." Then there was OBA— "Operation Black Africa." There was his so-far favourite, his double-edged FFTW—"Freedom from the West."

It would come, it would come. . . . The Lord Protector of Pharamaul put the file back in the safe, and secured it, and reached out for his drink again. Now, for reasons which he did not even choose to think about, he was himself free, and before long his great country, under great leadership, would give a great continent its liberation.

High up on the wall, the little bright-eyed *gecko* lizard, always wary, not daring the smallest chirrup, watched this master carefully. Why did he make such great upheavals? At any moment, it seemed, there could be surprises, huge upsets, even the end of small lizard worlds.